CW00381125

1

A
FISTFUL
OF
COLLARS

MARK FARRER

ISBN: 1539845753
ISBN-13: 978-1539845751

To Claire
For her tolerance and understanding,
without which my tenacity would count for nothing.

PROLOG

Guy waggled a finger in one ear, unsure and confused in equal measure as to what he was hearing. "What do you mean, *keep her?*"

"Jack's exact words." Conrad was staring into space, an eyeless statue with the phone still in his hand.

"His exact words?"

"Well, no." Conrad looked up at the ceiling and then across at Guy. "*Fuck her, mate. She's all yours*' were his actual exact words."

"You're shitting me, right?"

"Do I look like someone who's shitting you?"

"No." Guy had to admit, Conrad did not. He looked like someone bereft, perhaps going through the first of the stages of grief. At a loss, rudderless in his canoe of ambition as he helplessly watched his only paddle drift down the creek. "So, what - we just let her go then?"

"What? No!" Conrad wheeled and confronted Guy, pointing his index finger and glaring at him. "Winners never quit, and quitters never win."

Guy digested this for a moment. He wanted to skip the five stages of grief and get to acceptance. Conrad was having none of it, insisting they visit all stages, in quick succession. He was already on denial.

"Yeah…" argued Guy. "But if you never win… and you never quit… then you're just… stupid."

Conrad grabbed the front of Guy's sweater, taking some skin and chest hair with it. "You're stupid, you fucking…" Conrad scrabbled for an insult and settled on

"… dick holster."

Ah, ok, now anger. Guy tried to push on to bargaining. "Look. We let her go. She hasn't seen us, right? She doesn't know who we are. So, we let her go. Take her somewhere out of the way and release her, drive off. Then we come up with a Plan B for the money."

"You like Plan B's don't you? No. No time for a Plan B. We are committed. Committed to Plan A. We find a way to make this work."

"But Jack said he didn't want her back."

"Maybe he'll change his mind. Maybe he's bluffing."

Oh, thought Guy, now back to denial. "So…?"

"So, we wait." Conrad released Guy from his grasp and thrust his hands deep into his pockets. "We wait and I have time to think. This could be a blessing in the skies."

"You mean *in disguise?*"

"Whatever."

Guy watched as his friend scuffed his shoes, kicking at invisible fluff on the floor. Shoulders hunched, he paced up and down and finally out of the room leaving Guy to tick the last box on the list: depression.

Seconds later, Conrad flew back into the room and slammed the door.

"Quick. Move that table over here!"

"What?"

"Table. Here. Now. Against the door."

"What are we doing?"

"It's a badger!"

"What?"

"There is." Conrad panted. "A fucking badger. In the hall."

A series of loud thuds and scuffling sounds came through the door, followed by a noise like a startled rhino and the dark fetid smell of a wet angry mammal. Guy stood disoriented watching Conrad pile furniture up against the door to the hallway. "Where did it come from?"

"The Glentress Forest Scary Wild Animal Nature Reserve. How the fuck should I know? Am I English?"

"What's that got to do with anything?"

"Badgers are wild animals aren't they? Native to England."

"This is Scotland."

"Scotland. England. Same thing. You're English, you should know about them."

"I'm not a badger expert. I'm from Cobham. You don't get badgers in Cobham."

"I'm from Hong Kong. You don't get badgers in Hong Kong."

"Bet you do. They probably use badger penis as some kind of aphrodisiac."

Conrad ignored him. The badger continued to scrape and push at the door, the sound of its grunts echoing through the empty hallway.

"What does it want?" Guy, for some reason, was now whispering.

"I don't know." Conrad shook his head in disbelief. "You'll have to get rid of it."

Guy did a double-take. "What do you mean *I'll* have to get rid of it?"

"You are much bigger than me. We Chinese, very small. Very delicate bones."

"Ah, yeah. Now, hang on a minute. I might be wrong… but isn't that complete bollocks?"

Conrad's hackles rose and he did his best to loom over Guy, threateningly. "Listen, -"

"No, you listen."

"What?"

"Shhh. Listen." Guy nodded his head towards the door. "I think it's gone."

They both sat, ears pricked, holding their breath, straining to pick up any sounds from the badger. When they heard a high-pitched metallic screech from the bedroom opposite, Guy almost hit the ceiling.

"What the fuck was that?"

"Don't know." Conrad nodded to the closed door. "Go check. Maybe the badger's got into her room."

Guy got to his feet obediently and ventured towards the bedroom door. He turned the handle and let the door swing slowly open.

The room was unoccupied, severed cable ties lying discarded on the bed.

"Er, Con?" Guy grimaced at his friend and shook his head.

Conrad remained motionless on the floor, still sitting with his back to the table barricade. He closed his eyes, took a long, slow breath and looked up at the stained ceiling, exclaiming loudly. "Would anything else like to go wrong?"

The silence was broken by his phone going off, followed by the sound of an angry badger going newly berserk.

Both on the other side of the door.

"Aw, shit." Conrad put his head in his hands

PART ONE

FOUR WEEKS EARLIER...

ONE

Liv and Conrad were lying in bed, the sun weakly glinting into their bedroom through the dirty windows. The room was artless and artful at the same time, strewn with fabrics, canvases, boxes, week-old takeaway cartons and empty wine bottles. Liv was sucking on a cigarette, watching the smoke drift up towards the ceiling, an ashtray lying on her chest. Conrad was flicking through images on his iPad, biting the inside of his cheek. His left leg was outside the sheet and he bobbed his foot up and down as he flicked and mumbled to himself.

"What are you looking for?" she asked, barely interested.

"Inspiration."

"As usual." She bit her tongue as she realised she'd said this out loud.

"What you mean by that?"

"Nothing."

"That tone."

"What tone?"

"That exasperated: *as usual.* A criticism. A judgement."

"Sorry, I didn't mean it like that. I'm really tired. Working too hard."

Liv huffed the last drag of her cigarette into the air and smeared the butt messily into the ashtray. She was frustrated. Frustrated with him. Frustrated with life. This was not how things were supposed to go for Liv Nightingale.

Olivia Florence Nightingale - the names were her mother's idea - was born in Simpson's maternity ward in Edinburgh as the city rang in Hogmanay 1985. She cried with a lusty bawl which would never leave her and as she grew, her hair reddened and thickened, until she became almost a parody of a brazen, forthright, bundle of Scottish fizz and energy. Her smile could light up a room and her party-girl persona played well with everyone she came into contact with. She had twinkling emerald eyes that shone with boldness and intelligence and, as she made her way through the thicket of social networking which passes for private school privilege and education in Scotland's capital, she gained a reputation as star pupil, sportswoman, and larger-than-life personality. She took to wearing increasingly outlandish outfits, not to seek attention but to stamp herself on her environment and make people look to her as a leader and example to follow. Her hairstyles and makeup increasingly came up against the straitjacketing school rules and her hemlines and footwear constantly trod the line between acceptability and the downright slatternly.

Her name was commonly shortened to Liv, although many called her Lightning, and she took to sporting a shocking green lightning bolt of colour in her Pixar Brave locks. She was academically gifted, and a keen student able to party, gossip and neglect her studies only to find that all the unremarked input that had wafted around her during term-time had effortlessly penetrated her skull and quick bouts of cramming allowed her to synthesise it all into A grades, apparently at will.

As her teenage years advanced, she became a veteran of Edinburgh's nightclubs and party scene, associating with other like-minded youngsters who reckoned themselves style icons and pushed the envelope of acceptability and imminent celebrity. It was inevitable that she would find her metier in Art & Design and no-one was surprised when she aced the admissions process and attended Glasgow School of Art. Her four years at the Renfrew Street outpost of iconoclasm and eccentricity suited her down to the ground, with one exception: they did not provide a course in fashion and Liv desperately wanted to be the next Stella McCartney. While she lacked the famous family background and conventional good looks of her idol, she was long on attitude, ambition and commitment - and was not at all shy about letting people know what she wanted to achieve, and what she felt she was capable of.

She tried every trick she could to work fabrics and clothing into her artwork and her degree portfolio largely consisted of outlandish designs made from found-materials and incorporating smart fabrics to sport messages and e-ink images which shifted with their surroundings and flaunted and taunted onlookers. She wanted to provoke and promote her image and her name and took every chance she got to do this - in and out of college. When she graduated with a First, great things were expected of her.

She became her own creation - LIV, all upper case - and worked at it night and day, with constant attention to detail and a burning need to see her name in lights and on labels. It was only in those lonely, wee small hours, usually when coming down from some prolonged high after all-night partying that she sat quiet and empty in the dark and wondered whether the Liv she had created was actually her or some artificial construct. One which grew around her like a carapace, limiting her oxygen and light, so that she had to live even larger and force-grow the outer Liv into being ever more outrageous in order to allow that thin whisper of breath through the outer shell and into her soul.

Her curves, and her willingness to expose or exaggerate them in her clothes, drew many admirers but she assiduously vetted any men to make sure they possessed some ability, connection or talent which could assist her in her plotted course to stardom. If not, they were jettisoned like toilet waste from an express train. Those she welcomed were embraced and devoured until she had consumed the content she required and moved her attention on elsewhere. She had no truck with time-wasters, and they, knowing they were being dumped even while she did it to them, seemed content to have been there and done that, grateful for their moment in the spotlight and their time with a meteor.

The end of her degree year was the first time she ever tasted failure and disappointment and she didn't like it one bit. In applying to fashion houses and couture establishments in London and Paris she discovered that her Art degree didn't count for as much as she thought the GSoA reputation would. As she watched the vacancies fill without her, she realised that she needed to further her qualifications and have them embedded in textiles and fabrics, so she decided to pursue a Masters in Textiles.

The School of Textile and Design was one of the eight faculties of Heriot-Watt University but, unlike the others, was set down away from Edinburgh at a separate campus on the outskirts of Galashiels in the Scottish Borders. Bedded in a steep natural valley, forming part of the floodplain of the River Tweed, this area could be beautiful and serene, or damp and depressing - sometimes both on the same day - but Liv immediately loved the place. That first sunny September morning, standing outside the School she felt like a bird of paradise newly landed in a field of chaffinches, all busy pecking away while she stood apart and surveyed the unfamiliar horizon looking for fame and fortune. Within days she was the school's star attraction and an echelon of disciples, wannabees and hangers-on started to form effortlessly around her - like iron filings to an electric field, drawn by her magnetism and charm, her natural warmth and attraction. She fed off their energy and adoration and shone like a beacon, lighting up the place and starting no end of trends and styles which outlasted her.

And that was how she had met Conrad. One Sunday evening, standing at the crowded bar in the Union Building waiting to be served, she had turned to whoever had just barged her elbow in the crush and found herself staring at the liquid black eyes of a handsome young man who was looking deep into her very bosom.

That had been over a year ago.

Since completing her Masters (with another First, obv) Liv had applied herself energetically to trying to break into the fashion establishment. Her days were spent furiously sketching and gathering swatches of fabric which Conrad had sourced for her, and conjuring them into individualised designs. Her prototyped garments and fragments of outfits she illustrated in elegant, stretched watercolours and ink.

In the evenings she worked a shift at the 24-hour ASDA superstore in Galashiels. This was her contribution to their joint finances - Conrad covered the majority of their living costs via a generous, albeit shrinking, allowance from his father. His other contribution was in the kitchen where, nightly, he would attempt advanced alchemy by wrangling ingredients into something edible - usually without success. Last night's meal, she winced to even use the word, was his take on mac'n'cheese. It had looked and tasted like burn victim's arsehole.

With cheese.

Conrad's other contribution to their relationship, in the bedroom, also left something to be desired. What he lacked in expertise and (ahem) girth, he at least made up for in enthusiasm and stamina; she increasingly found herself dissatisfied at being treated as his own personal bouncy castle. However, since he was currently the closest thing she had to a meal ticket, here they both were until... something turned up.

When she got home each night she would wrote letters of enquiry, enclosing her CV and samples, then work through the early hours scouring the internet for fashion news and gossip, wrangling all she could into a blog and reaching out to anyone she could find in social media to increase links to her site, make new contacts, find that person who could offer her a way in to the world she so badly craved.

Once every couple of months she would pack up all her pieces and sketches into a wallpaper catalogue of works, ideas, trends, and illustrations and head off down to London for a few days. If she had made any new contacts she would try and arrange meetings with them, even if only introductory chats in Pret or Starbucks. Staying in the cheapest hotels or hostels she could find, she would spend as much time as she could wandering the West End, hoping to bump into fashion designers or rag trade bosses on the lookout for talent. She would hoik her unwieldy portfolio around Wardour Street and Soho, Bond Street and beyond, establishments small and large, leaving her business card and some samples and in the hope that someone would show an interest, someone would bite.

The whole thing was taking an interminably long time and she didn't feel as if she was getting anywhere. She was twenty-four years old, had left the college at Galashiels a vastly different place than the one she found, and had bagsful of energy, invention and drive. But the only thing that seemed to be progressing well at the moment was her cirrhosis.

And in the meantime, Conrad seemed to think he could swan around and follow his muse as the inclination took him. He would skip lectures and only sporadically attend tutorials, spending more time on the phone to garment manufacturers in Hong Kong than he did on his portfolio. He preferred the structural, practical and managerial aspects of materials rather than the hands-on creation, design, wizardry, and artistry that she felt was central to the whole endeavour. Sure, he would occasionally idly sketch some ideas and then languidly hand them to Guy and ask him to "make it so." His idea of a joke: a pun on "Make it. Sew." The rest of his time he would be by her side, pawing and clawing at her in a paltry attempt at foreplay. Many times she yielded when she should have resisted.

She looked across at Conrad now, still skimming

through his iPad. "What do you need inspiration for?"

"Project."

She recognised the lack of prepositions and short sentences signified he was sulking. "I thought you'd just finished one?"

"Did. Extra one. Optional."

"Well, why not give it a miss? Just this one?"

"In Hong Kong, if you leave a gap, someone else fills it." He volunteered.

"Yes. But we're not in Hong Kong. We're in Scotland."

"Scotland. Hong Kong. Same thing. It's a doggy dog world."

"You mean *dog eat dog*."

"Whatever."

He continued flipping through images, distracted. She tried to leaven her earlier sharpness, soothe her tone. "I could help you with ideas."

"Yes. You could." He replied, meaning the exact opposite.

"Why not?"

"In Hong Kong-"

"Will you stop with the *in Hong Kong* cobblers? It gets on my nerves. What's wrong with my ideas?"

"Nothing."

"They're a damn sight better than yours!"

"What do you mean?"

"What I say. Do they not understand English in Hong Kong?"

"I not stand in your shadow." Sometimes Conrad's English betrayed him. He had tried hard throughout his boarding school years to adopt the tones and accent which marked out the entitled and the noble. But under stress or when he got angry, he dropped prepositions, or confused conjugations, emphasising his Chinese accent.

"No? Well, I'm certainly not standing in yours." Liv bridled.

"In Hong-." He stopped himself. "I don't have a shadow."

"No? Well, that must be because you're not standing in the light."

"What does that mean?"

"Work it out for yourself." She flung the bedclothes off and rolled out of bed. Grabbing a thin gown off the back of a chair, she wrapped it around herself and strode from the room, bare feet slapping on the parquet floor.

Conrad closed the iPad cover and put it to one side, staring up at the ceiling in exasperation, wondering how a quiet Saturday morning had turned so quickly into another row. Being generally oblivious to all his inadequacies, he was similarly blind to any concerns Liv had about his sexual prowess. To him she was a beautiful, fiery and vibrant sexual goddess. Slightly older, and more experienced, but with a rich and slightly husky voice, that had always turned him on. Her pre-Raphaelite hair an almost impossible shade of red, her strong nose and cheekbones delicately flecked with freckles, those green eyes sparkling beneath arched, manicured brows. With her long tresses and heavenly curves, she was Boadicea and Botticelli's Venus all rolled into one and he was infatuated.

Her walk was an exaggerated sway, made more daring by the high heels she always chose to wear, and the wide curve of her hips and bust. The term hourglass could never have had a more perfect illustration made for it and her statuesque bearing was usually further enhanced by her choice of outfit. On the day he met her she'd been wearing a tight-fitting tartan dress with scarlet edging which swooped and fell over her movements like a silk sheet in a gentle breeze. He had fought a desperate urge to just walk up and inhale the very scent of her.

But boy, could she press his buttons. She was so driven and talented but all too aware of what she wanted and what she was capable of. Conrad, no shrinking violet himself, found that he felt in constant competition with her to achieve. Quite what exactly, he wasn't sure. But her very presence was intoxicating and exhilarating, which made him all the more ambitious and expectant of himself. Together, he believed, they could conquer the world.

But to do that, first he would need to mustard up all his strength.

Conrad Ho was born and raised in Hong Kong before the handover to the Chinese in 1997. His father, Clive, was a wealthy businessman with tailoring establishments in Kowloon - the sort of places often frequented by stopover tourists looking for a bespoke silk suit to be made in 48 hours before their flight to Australia or the Middle East. Clive was a baby-boomer, born after the fallout from the Second World War and into a territory with which he would grow and burgeon, watching himself and the colony go from hand-pulled rickshaws and dilapidated trams to towering citadels of glass, a shrinking reclaimed harbour, and homes on Victoria Peak worth a king's ransom.

He had inherited the Chinese work ethic and ploughed every ounce of his time and effort into his business, to the disappointment of his wife, and to the bemusement of his son who he sent off to boarding school in England as soon as he could, aged eight. With a poor grasp of English and a slight frame topped with a feminine face and a healthy shock of jet black hair, Conrad found himself bullied and abused, pilloried and macerated by the English public school system, so beloved of ex-pats and imperial throwbacks.

During the day he would try and play the class clown and joke his way out of beatings and wedgies; during the long dark nights he would lie beneath his blankets conjuring up fantasy worlds where he was all-powerful and all-conquering, waiting for the cold hands on him that sometimes never came. The masters rated him highly in terms of his potential, and often complimented him on his skills. However, the shy and dreamy boy took this the wrong way and used it as an excuse to sit on his laurels and expect success and rewards to fall his way. When, inevitably, they didn't, he soured and grew resentful. Where was his wealth, fame and success? Everything was always someone else's fault and he never received what he felt he was entitled to. He became ever more bitter, snapping at those around him and alienating himself further from others. And so, this self-fulfilling downward cycle grew and his wakeful persona became ever more sarcastic, biting and cruel.

He had few friends - in truth, only one, a sickly boy called Guy who grew with him. Together in the shade of the other intellects and bullies in their school, they survived by sheltering together. Conrad would lord it over Guy, treating him like a slave and a lesser mortal, using him as the only vessel he could project his resentment onto as he was himself treated badly in turn.

Guy, for his part, looked up to Conrad as the only boy who treated him less badly than the others. Over the years, the pair retreated into a friendship only they understood; a pairing that whilst extremely odd from the outside, inside gave both of them sufficient heat and warmth to keep them going against what they saw, in their different ways, as an unjust and untrustworthy world. If nothing else, they could at least depend on each other.

Leaving school with some (though hardly world-shattering) qualifications, Conrad prevailed upon his father to use what connections he had to secure him a place at the University of the Arts in London. His father also provided him with a substantial monthly allowance and a lease on a palatial flat in Bayswater. But it was these which were to prove the undoing of Conrad's, and ultimately his father's, dreams. Being capable of throwing lavish parties, which secured him a coterie of fawning hangers-on and leeches, went straight to Conrad's head. Presuming himself talented and popular, and able to afford to indulge himself and his many new friends, he found himself spending more and more time on planning and organising parties and less and less on his studies. This self-indulgence grew to dominate and he would occupy his time with creative musings on upcoming party themes and extravagant set-pieces or outlandish costumes, telling himself this all contributed to his enhancing the contents of any "personal statement" which might be required to get on in the fashion business.

But the place at UAL had required his father to heavily milk some substantial contacts and call upon significant favours. He had agreed to it solely on the basis that if Conrad showed no aptitude at the end of the first year he would lose his place. Although Conrad was never apprised of this condition, it never actually became an issue - he was ejected before the end of his first year anyway due to frequent nonattendance and, as far as his tutors were concerned, an almost total absence of talent or artistic flair.

Initially under a cloud, disillusioned by what he saw as partial blindness to his intrinsic qualities as an artist and visionary on the part of his tutors, he was now despairing as his father had rowed back heavily on his financial support. Unable and unwilling to cut back on his expenditure, his debts started to mount and his attempts at robbing Peter to pay Paul put an increasing strain on his ability to keep up appearances. Conrad found himself, for perhaps the first time in his life, somewhat at sea and wondering if bolting from London (and his many creditors) might not actually be such a bad idea. Inevitably he turned to the only other contact he could think of that might provide him some assistance in a tight spot.

His old school friend, Guy.

And so it was that Conrad found himself enrolling at Heriot-Watt School of Textiles & Design in Galashiels where Guy had just completed the first year of his four-year degree course. The pair had picked up pretty much where they left off a year ago and Conrad soon found himself buckling down, with few distractions in the Borders compared to the frenzy of opportunity that London had afforded him. He even started developing an actual interest in the mechanics and manufacture of materials. Inspired by his limited success at woodwork and metalwork and car repairs from his school days, he focussed on the structure and makeup of fabrics, their tensile strength and physical properties. He even prevailed upon his father - on each of his subsequent visits home - to let him tour workshops and factories, sweatshops and manufacturers in Hong Kong and Shenzhen. Gradually, over the course of his studies, he came to regard himself as an expert in manufacturing design and an idea began to grow in his mind as to how he could put his skills and interests to good use.

And it was in his third year on the course when he became aware of a new star in the Design school firmament: a Masters student who was, by all accounts, vibrant, brilliant and beautiful. Conrad was immediately determined to meet her and it was in this frame of mind, that he squeezed himself alongside her one evening in the student bar, elbowed her sharply as they stood crushed up alongside each other and then felt the breath leave his body as he found himself looking into the sparkling green eyes of a stunning redhead, her pale breasts almost bursting out of a low-cut bodice making the room close in on him.

She was the living embodiment of a Titian statue of liberty. Or the prow of a ship.

It was lust at first sight.

The next morning Conrad brought her in a cup of tea and some toast and marmalade while Liv shucked herself in bed and prodded the pillows into supporting her.

"Post." He dropped a slew of letters onto her lap and padded back out to the kitchen while she slurped at the hot tea.

"Mmm. What do we have here?" She leaved through

the envelopes. "Bill, spam, spam, statement probably… or something boring from the bank. We've changed the terms and conditions on your account from something essentially irrelevant to something slightly more irrelevant but more punitive. Full details contained in the enclosed little booklet you can use to fill up your swing-bin. Hmm, what's this?"

This envelope was thicker, paper of sturdier stock with a watermark even. And there was lovely delicate aroma lifting from it. She turned it over, saw the Chanel logo stamped on it in black and immediately dropped it back onto the duvet and placed her cup and saucer deliberately back on the bedside table.

Calm, she thought. Calm.

She brushed her hair back from her face with both hands and then picked up the envelope again, breathing deeply and slowly. She could feel her pulse beating in her temple as she ran a finger down the edge of the letter to tear it open. At some point, as she read the clear type, she realised she had been holding her breath and she had to force herself to breathe, in and out. When she got to the end of the letter, having checked there was nothing written on the back of the paper, she turned back and read it through again. When she'd finished the second time she placed the letter and envelope back on her lap and stared blankly out of the window. After a few minutes she focussed down onto her hands and realised she was shaking. She called for Conrad who came hurriedly in, uncertain of her tone.

"You ok?"

"I-. I-." She looked up at him, concern frowning his face. "I really don't know."

"What's the matter?"

"Chanel have offered me the job."

"Chanel? I don't get it." He scrunched his face up further. "What job?"

That was when she remembered she hadn't told him about it. She had meant to, but hadn't. When she had asked herself whether she should tell him she had answered most definitely in the negative, so she had left it at that and just not told him.

Until now.

Fuck.

She took a deep breath and told him. And that was when she realised why she hadn't told him in the first place. Conrad didn't just hit the roof, he rendered it obsolete and sailed through the wreckage into the ionosphere, incandescently thrusting onward and upwards. She tried to bring him back.

"Calm down a little, won't you?"

"Calm down? Calm down? Calm down?" He was pacing the bedroom as agitated as she'd ever seen him.

"Yes, calm down. Try and put this new information I've given you into perspective. Actually, no, first congratulate me and be happy for me. *Then* try and put it into perspective."

Conrad stared at her, hard, and put his hands on his hips. "I can't."

"Can't what? Which of those things can't you do?"

"Any of them." He looked at the floor and scuffed one foot across the carpet.

"And why not?"

Conrad pointed a finger at her. "You know that's exactly the sort of job I've always wanted."

"Did you apply for it?"

"No."

"Are you qualified to do it?"

"Not yet, no."

"Well, that's probably why you didn't get it. I, on the other hand, did apply for it and am qualified."

"You didn't tell me, though, did you?"

"Well, no. I didn't. That is… a fair point."

"And why didn't you?"

"Because… er, this?"

"Not because you didn't want to compete against me?"

"Pah!"

Conrad glared at her. "Are you ridiculing me?"

"No."

"What's with the *Pah!* then? What does that mean?"

Liv bit her lip and Conrad took to pacing again. "I'm just as good as you, you know."

"I'm not saying you're not."

"If not better."

"Steady on."

"You put yourself on a pedal stool. I'll be a Head Designer one day!"

"Good for you. And it's pedestal."

"Whatever. You'll see."

"I'm sure I will." Liv scratched her neck and idly brandished the letter. "I, however, am one now."

"Look, can we put this behind us? It's not worth fighting over. Not really." Here they were, some hours after she had opened the envelope, and Conrad was still angrily picking at this scab. Try as she might though, Liv couldn't bring herself to apologise for something she had achieved, even if it had put his nose out of joint. Her strategy, now, was to change the subject and try to make peace.

She hadn't timed it but, at a rough guess, her attempt lasted 27 seconds.

"I know. I know." Conrad sighed and looked at her, his face all crumpled. "It's just that seeing you "win", and knowing this means you're going to leave. It's... difficult." He looked at her, puppy-ishly. "It feels like I'm losing to you. I mean, losing to anyone is difficult for me. I have an inferiority complex."

"Well, it's not a very good one." She raised her eyebrows at him to show it was a joke, but realised that now was not the time. "Sorry."

"And you'll be hundreds of miles away in London."

Liv let this, somewhat obvious fact, sink in for a moment and realised that (a) she was ecstatic about it (b) she really shouldn't let him know that. "Yes, but I can come up some weekends. You could come down. It's not that far. Other people make long distance relationships work."

"Can't you stay up here?"

"I can't do the job up here. It's London-centric. All fashion is, you know that. Look at the joke that was Glasgow Fashion Week - or Edinburgh Fashion Week. Christ, they've been cancelled and shrunk so many times it's not true. London's where it's at. And Chanel? I mean, come on."

"But we'll be apart. I'll be alone." His whining was starting to get on her nerves now.

"I know, baby." She put her arm around his shoulder. "But can't you just be happy for me? Why does this have to be about you? Why can't it, just this once, be about me? Hmm?"

"Don't say that."

"Say what?"

"Hmm. Like that. That's how *he* says it." She knew Conrad meant his father. "And we both know I'm never going to be good enough for him. But I thought I might be good enough for you!"

"You are good enough for me." She kissed his forehead, slick with perspiration, and tried to mollify him despite herself. "But just because something good has happened to me - it doesn't mean something bad has happened to you. It's not a zero-sum game. You shouldn't think of this as winning or losing. This is good for me *and* it's good for us."

"Well, right now, that's now how it feels. I want to feel good about myself too."

His whiny, neediness was just one of the reasons she'd be happy to wave goodbye to this place, this life and him with it. Before she could stop herself, the words had left her mouth: "Yes, well I suppose if you were the sort of person who wanted their friends to do well for themselves, you'd - well - have friends."

"I have friends!"

She knew that had hurt. But on she went, unable to sugarcoat her words. "Friend. Singular."

"I have friends other than Guy."

"Close ones? Really?"

"Yes!" She was hitting a nerve but still she couldn't let go. Conrad was now close to tears.

"Who?"

"Fine. Well, at least Guy is my friend. And he is a true friend. Not some hanger-on. People like that are a diamond dozen."

"Dime a dozen." She couldn't resist correcting him.

33

"And if something good happened to him?"

"I'd... support him."

Yes, she thought as she leapt in to put the icing on this downward-spiralling cake. "Like a rope supports a hanging man."

"Oh, fuck you Liv!" He pulled away sharply and there was real venom in his face, spittle in the corners of his mouth, wild flashing eyes. "Fuck you very much!" He grabbed his jacket off the back of the sofa and stood up. "I hope you'll be very fucking happy with your Chanel contract. And all *your* friends that wish you well."

"Where are you going?"

"You know what?" He looked around for his phone, saw it on the hall table and grabbed it as he strode to the door. "I don't know. I really don't." He opened it and gave her a parting, tearful, look. "But I do know I'm not coming back."

Liv hung her head as the door slammed. She saw what she'd done, heard herself as she'd done it, tried to stop herself from doing it. And failed.

Ah well. Storm. Teacup. Next!

She went and put the kettle on.

TWO

The sound of gunfire chattered and spat across the valley ahead as Dougie hunkered behind a tree, frantically trying to pull together some kind of plan. This was most definitely not how a hitman should behave, he thought.

Of course, Dougie wasn't a hitman. Yet.

What he was, was a junior IT administrator, dressed in combat gear with his face smeared in camo-paint, sheltering from real bullets being fired in his general direction by so-called mates who he would - he fervently hoped - be able to laugh about it all with later in the mess tent. Such was his life on weekends away as an Army Reservist.

But hitman was his ultimate target. Life in IT was humdrum and safe, nothing at risk except one's and zero's and the CEO's browser history - Dougie had tactfully explained to him what NSFW meant. He longed for the excitement and adrenalin of the kill, but his current status was Ammunition Technician, Private.

The Army Reserves had tried hard to persuade him down the route of Communication Systems Engineer as his IT expertise made this a much better fit and they were frequently lacking skills in this vital area. However, Ammunition Technician also had an IT element to it and they didn't like to turn away volunteers - not those who showed the enthusiasm and theoretical knowledge Dougie had displayed at his recruitment interview.

This, though, had acted to counterbalance their first impression, which had been of a pale, stick-thin Herbert with a pierced nose and a shock of bleached blonde hair with a streak of bright blue shot through it across the top of his head. That, they told him, would have to go.

The hair? No big deal. He changed the colour of this regularly so could just as easily dye it black or brown for a weekend and back to scarlet, pink or whatever-this-weeks-colour was on his return.

The piercing, they asked? No problem, he'd just take it out and put it back in again after each weekend.

The wan skin colouring? He worked in IT, he said. They nodded understandingly.

The gauntness? He'd bulk out from the basic training, he assured them.

Fine. Sign here.

Since leaving school, Dougie had tinkered with computers, electronics and gadgets of all kinds. Academically he had never amounted to much but he had read a shit ton of books, mostly manuals, and learnt. He had surfed and googled his way around tech topics that interested him, broken his computer one time and had to resort to fixing it. Then mending his brother's. Then buying bits and pieces off eBay and making his own. Then repairing other peoples' before eventually buying "sold as seen" PCs, getting them working and selling them on as refurbished. Then he'd got a part-time job at PC World as one of the Geek Squad and, from there, he had ended up applying for a permanent role as a Sysadmin assistant for an insurance company just off Sauchiehall Street.

Glamorous it wasn't, but he found himself with plenty of spare time to surf the web at work, in between fixing people's problems by turning things off and on again or uninstalling the various bits of crap they had inadvertently installed by blindly clicking OK when a pop-up unexpectedly appeared and frightened them. He also now had plenty of spare income which he could use to follow his dream. Each month, he converted a chunk of his payslip into Bitcoins and bought assorted weaponry, firearms and ammunition off the Deep Web.

Most - ok, all - of it was illegal. Certainly for him, as he had no permits or training of any kind, unless you counted taking his guns down to the nature reserve at Cathkin Braes and seeing what he could hit. Foxes, squirrels, voles, birds - even once a buzzard - but they had proved a bit trickier and he was concerned that firing bullets up into the air and missing a bird meant the bullet would come down who-knew-where and possibly hit one of the walkers or pleasure-seekers who frequented the area. He'd even considered using the swans as targets but decided against it as they seemed too big and easy to hit, plus he was sure he'd read that all swans belonged to the Queen so if you were caught killing one you could be done for treason or something.

But then - aha! - he'd had a brainwave and realised that this was where the Army Reserve came in. Application successful, months later here he was being trained by professional soldiers and being paid for it. Building up his strength, stamina, knowledge and skills so that, when he felt the time was right, he would offer his own services on the Deep Web.

Killer for hire. Free estimates. No job too small.

One of the pre-requisites, though, for being a hitman he guessed, was the ability to keep a cool, calm head and, at this very minute, this was where Dougie was struggling. The scenario their unit sergeant had talked them through this morning was a recovery operation.

Two of their number had been "kidnapped" and were being held hostage at an unknown location somewhere in the grid-reference squares outlined in red on his map. The rest of the unit had to locate them and bring them back safely. Dougie was one of the recovery team.

What he didn't know was that the bullets they were all using were, in fact, blanks. None of them knew. They had all been told they were real but cost-cutting measures by the MoD meant that belts had to be tightened. You couldn't have fifty raw reservists spraying expensive bullets around every other weekend, that would be lunacy. Plus, health and safety, you understand. Think of the possible legal implications. No, much better to spend the money on unwieldy, unsuitable and ultimately unfinished IT systems. They may cost millions but they had never injured a single civilian.

Not that any of this mattered - the weapons they issued the reservists were unaffectionately known by all as Civil Servants: they often didn't work and, when they did, were difficult to fire.

Dougie's ears pricked up as he heard movement behind him. He spun around and held his rifle out in as threatening a manner as he could muster, only to have it knocked out of his hands by someone to his immediate left who hadn't been there a moment ago. Before he could look to identify them he felt a sack pulled over his head and a number of large military boots begin to kick him across all parts of the body. He struggled and fought but appeared to be heavily outnumbered. One super-sized weight bore down on him, another was throttling him through the sacking and making him cough and choke; innumerable others were inputting random kicks and smacks from what he assumed were the butts of wooden rifles.

All this was done without anyone, apart from himself, making a sound.

Eventually, he decided that resistance was not only useless but was increasing the extent of his injuries so he went floppy and lay still hoping that the beatings would stop and whoever it was would commence stage two of their plan for him, whatever that was. Sure enough, after a brief period, the assault on him stopped and he felt himself being lifted bodily up and slung across someone's shoulders. Then they started to march.

The journey lasted perhaps ten minutes, during which all he could make out were whispered or muffled voices. The sound of gunfire diminished and the air began to turn damp and heavy with the smell of pine needles and wet undergrowth. They were descending, he felt, and on uneven terrain judging by the way his carrier would suddenly lurch from side to side and swear under his breath; breath which was now becoming more ragged and laboured as Dougie's weight took its toll.

When they stopped, it was sudden and eventful. He was thrown forcefully to the ground and smacked his forearm and elbow against sharp stones. He lay, winded, for a few moments and realised that there was no movement, or sound, from any of his attackers anymore. Warily, he tried to pull himself up into a sitting position, only to have his hand find a cold, sludgy substance which immediately gave off a recognisable odour.

He pulled off the sacking from his head and discovered three things:

(i) he was now, indeed, all alone;

(ii) he had been thrown over a dry stone wall and landed close to a colourful array of substantial cowpats, one of which he had just put his hand into

(iii) directly ahead of him, a rather large herd of cows was gently lowing and hustling, somewhat intently, in his immediate direction.

Dougie quickly got his bearings. The field sloped downwards, perhaps a hundred yards or so and beyond that he could make out nothing. The animals moved menacingly closer so he looked to both sides of him. The wall, to which he had his back, stretched out left and right without a break. Perhaps two hundred yards away to his right he could see a gate; apart from that, nothing. He plunged into his brain for facts he knew about cows and surfaced with only one: they can't walk downstairs.

Struggling to stand he felt the impact of the kicks and beatings he had received. His right leg wouldn't bear any weight without spearing him with a pain which ran from his knee to his groin and made him briefly bite his tongue as he tried to hobble. He had a dead left leg which would at least bear his weight if he locked it at the knee, but the pain was considerable and as he hunched there half-leaning against the wall, like some modern day Richard III, he realised he wouldn't be able to climb over it or reach the gate in time. The cows were now less than thirty yards away and had gained speed, cantering almost. He didn't know whether cows had good eyesight or not but if they had originally been working their way toward him more in hope than intent, now they could see him - their prey. They now had a purpose and redoubled their efforts to reach him. This wall of beef looked menacing and dangerous and he knew there had been instances - this second fact now swimming confidently into view - of walkers being trampled to death by a herd.

With no other idea occurring to him, he hurriedly

opened his backpack and rustled in the bottom for a canvas bag he knew was there. Inside it was a highly illegal pistol, a Smith & Wesson Bodyguard 380. He had brought it to help him feel like a killer on this weekend, even if the army wasn't going to equip him like one themselves. He knew it was extremely risky to carry it and, if found, not only was it an arrestable offence but one likely to get him discharged from the Reserves immediately. He'd had no intention of using it. But knowing it was there, as he had patrolled alone without his unit, had given him something of a hard-on; a semi for a semi-automatic.

He pulled the gun from his pack, released the safety and aimed into the air with both hands. The lead animal was now barely ten feet away so, hesitating no further, Dougie fired three rapid shots over the heads of the cows, accompanying this with a lung-emptying yell. The animals reacted as if in a cartoon. The lead cow slammed on the brakes, almost skidding as it did so, huge eyes bulging and stupid pink tongue lolling to one side of its mouth. The cows immediately behind and at the leader's shoulders did the same, careering into each other, creating a bovine pile-up. The more cowardly ones near the rear had already started turning tail and now the cows nearest Dougie started a loud moo-ing and all tried to turn around simultaneously - some clockwise and some anti-clockwise.

Dougie started windmilling his arms accompanied with more yelling and watched, no longer dispirited, as the mass of muscle ahead of him wheeled and crunched into each other; all trying desperately to be first to get away, now that the front of the herd had become the rear. He sank back against the wall as the shit-covered behinds of the retreating cows swayed hurriedly downhill and out of sight. Like the Zulus at Rorke's Drift, one moment they had been in his face threatening his very life, the next moment they were lost in the grass with only the murmurs and susurrations of their song to remind him it had not been a dream.

He let his weight relax against the jagged stones in the wall, then yelped as his right leg gave way again and he started to slump to earth. As he crumpled, his right elbow banged on a sharp edge. In an unwanted reflex, he released his grip on the Smith & Wesson, only to watch it somersault in slow motion into a cold, green patty of poo.

On entering the large mess tent in the camp clearing, his unit greeted him in their usual infantile way: singing *Boogie Nights* but substituting his name, Dougie Knight, into the lyrics. On the plus side, it was always a good team effort. On the down side, he was sick of it. But the more he showed his dislike, the more frequent and enthusiastic their renditions became. His strategy was to try and ignore it, pretend it didn't affect him and hope they eventually stopped.

So far, it wasn't working.

Some would say it was his own fault. On his first encounter with Toenail (Acting Corporal Nail, Anthony), the unit's *de facto* alpha male and all-round champion arsehole, he had foolishly corrected the Neanderthal's pronunciation of his name: "It's not Duggie as in buggy, it's Doogie as in boogie." That first weekend everyone had then substituted the long *oooh* sound into every word they could while still making themselves understood. The second weekend they had all talked like the French policeman from *'Allo 'Allo*, using the wrong vowels sounds to make sentences sound rude. By the third weekend, maintaining this charade had proved too mentally strenuous and some bright spark had had a wet dream and come up with the *Boogie Nights* idea. Winner.

The singing died out quickly, though, as his unit took stock of his appearance. He was limping badly and plastered with cow dung, an effect which actually enhanced the camouflage qualities of his uniform - albeit not in his current surroundings. His Bergen backpack was dragging at his left side unevenly, exaggerating his limp still further and making him look like a stroke victim playing Quasimodo. He lurched, in silence, over to where his unit were seated and flung his shit-stained ammo belt on the table, sending cutlery and mess tins flying, and pinging some of his teammates with flecks of manure.

"You know, you could have killed me out there."

"Hang on, I might be giving a fuck." Toenail grimaced as if trying to shift a stubborn fart. "No, never mind."

"I'm serious!"

"So am I, jamrag." Toenail stood and pushed his face into Dougie's. "If any one of us had been trying to kill you, you'd be dead."

When Toenail spoke, people tended to take him seriously. He was astonishingly tall - perhaps 6'5 or 6'6 - with a shaven head, a mouthful of widely-spaced yellowing teeth and a terrible case of acne. He looked like his face had caught fire and someone had tried to put it out with a hot fork. He walked with a lumbering swing, like a lonely bear on its hind legs, and had huge paw-like hands with fat, stubby fingers and well-bitten nails. Now he was pressing his forehead into Dougie's own, pushing him down with his height and mass.

Dougie didn't want to be seen to back down - part of his training to become a hitman, he felt, was to never yield but resist as silently and phlegmatically as possible when confronted with any obstacle; take a zen-like approach to adversity and improvise a solution. But there was no shame in yielding to Toenail in this company, and no point (at this stage of his hitman-development) in trying to rock the applecart and upend the normal way of things. Only when he had mastered his temper, honed his skills and become comfortable with the ways of killing would he attempt to use his abilities in situations such as this. That time, Dougie was confident, would come. And so, too, would Toenail's.

"I know it was you."

"Yeah?" Toenail's breath seared Dougie's nasal passages. "Go on then, Sherlock."

"None of you -" Dougie pulled back and scanned the group, eyeballing each of them for dramatic effect. "Not a single one of my attackers made a sound. Don't you think that's odd? The whole time I was being bagged and beaten up there was this weird silence where I could hear the birds singing and the wind blowing and the boots landing and the laboured breathing. But no voices. Not a single one. Why would a group of attackers be so strangely quiet, do you think?"

"You got me." Toenail spat the words but a look in his eye made Dougie think that he had, perhaps for the first time, caught the giant off-guard and on the back foot with his intelligence and reasoning.

"Because they knew I would be able to identify them

by their voices if they spoke. That's why."

Dougie withdrew his face, leaving Toenail in no doubt that he believed himself to be the winner in this particular tussle, and calmly sat down at the table. He scanned the faces of his unit to gauge their reaction, but they all looked away, down at their meal, or started jabbering to their neighbour to avoid eye contact with him. He watched as the group hungrily finished their meal, one by one, leaving him alone at the table - Toenail giving him a threatening scowl as he himself stood up and left.

Yeah, scowl all you like, fuckwit, Dougie thought. But I'll get you. Just you wait.

THREE

"She wuvs you, wikkle wikkle Paw. She wuvs you, wikkle wikkle Paw. And wiv a wuv wike that oo know oo should be GLAD! Yeah Yeah Yeah! Yeah Yeah Yeah! Yeah Yeah Yeah, Y-e-a-h."

Tuppence was stroking what passed for fur on Paw's tummy while the cat luxuriated on her lap, it's huge round eyes like smooth sapphire saucers blinking slowly with delight.

Paw was a Sphynx cat, a hairless breed much prized for their looks and intelligent personalities. No fur, just hairless skin which felt like the supplest chamois to the touch. He was thin, his skin a pale grey with golden sleeves on his forelegs, but you could clearly see from his musculature that he was healthy and in good shape. Tuppence thought he was in excellent shape, and so he should be given the quality of food, love and attention she lavished on him.

She loved this gorgeous, strange creature, even more than she loved the Beatles (well, at least their early stuff; she wasn't too fond of them post-Pepper when the drugs and weirdness took them away from their initial pop perfection). Oh, but Paw was her personal pet gollum. His head, immensely large for such a scrawny body, was wrinkled and puckered like an old man. His enormous ears were constantly pricked to attention, listening, searching. And those eyes - huge blue pools with a central almond sliver of black at their heart - made you think they were looking inside you, straight into you and what you were thinking. Then, with the insouciance of all cats, he would slowly turn his head away as if your thoughts were of no value or importance at all.

She had always wanted a cat, she realised now, without knowing it. Growing up as a small girl, her father had been allergic to almost all animals his entire life - even a budgie could bring him out in hives or give him an asthma attack, when he was there, that is - so their home had been petless and airless. She had grown used to it and never thought about it since, until Jack had given her the cat as a birthday present one year and she had spontaneously squealed with delight, and christened it Sir Paw McCatney.

Now an elegant feline, long-used to caresses and acclaim, Paw lay still, a diamond-encrusted collar winking and gleaming expensively in the downlights.

Tuppence looked across the open plan living space to her husband now, sitting hunched over the polished granite breakfast bar, alternately spooning the last of her lasagne into his hungry mouth and chugging on a cold beer.

"How is it?" She asked.

"Hmm?"

"The lasagne. Is it ok?"

Jack burped loudly and mantra'd his usual "Better out than in." Thinking on his feet for a way to respond to her question diplomatically he settled on: "You know me, babe. When I'm hungry I'll eat anything."

Wounded, she went back to her Paw devotion duties. "Can't buy me Paw, No. Paw, no. Can't buy me Paw, No, No." Over at the breakfast bar she watched as Jack took a coin from his pocket, flipped it and then, satisfied with the outcome, reached for his phone.

Jack's real name wasn't Jack, it was Jacek Imbiorkiewicz but since no-one apart from his mother could pronounce this correctly, everyone just called him Jack. His team mates had taken to calling him Jack-Jack recently, partly because of the pronunciation difficulty but also because of his current hairstyle which was essentially bald apart from a single spike of bright orange hair, coaxed by product into staying erect some three inches proud of his skull.

This, though, would be a temporary, fleeting affair lasting no longer than the design of his team's current home strip. As soon as he tired of it, or his photographs were no longer regularly adorning the front pages as well as the back pages, Jack's agent would let him know a refurb was in order and Jack would set to it with abandon. He loved it: the transitory nature of the look, the ability to outdo himself each time a change was needed. Each defining a look for tribes of adoring youngsters, each more extreme and outrageous than the last.

As a good-looking Scottish Premiership footballer married to a fashion model, Jack had taken it upon himself to assume the role of style icon. With his good looks and footballing prowess came endorsements, advertisements, sponsorship. A beautiful model wife on his arm, wearing the latest fashions, and him sporting a new hairstyle, the glamorous couple would get regularly papped outside nightspots, restaurants and celebrity parties.

Jack loved it.

He didn't even mind being called Jack, even though Jacek wasn't actually Polish for Jack at all. And this was one of the many things he didn't mind. In fact, right now, the only things he could think of that he *did* mind were the Beatles, his wife's lousy cooking and that fucking awful cat. What the fuck had he been thinking when he'd bought it? One, it was plug ugly; and two, it had cost a small fortune. But he and Tupp had still been at the extremely horny stage of their relationship and, back then, he literally would have given anything to get into her pants. And sometimes did.

The cat was one stupid permanent testament to that fact; the other was their marriage.

While he waited for a reply to his text, her opened the betting app on his phone and realised he'd laid the favourite only for it to romp home. He was now down £20,000 for the day.

"Bollocks".

"You ok, hun?"

"Huh?" He looked up and over at Tuppence, still stroking the damned cat but now looking at him with a crease of concern across her forehead.

"You ok?"

"Sorry, did I say that out loud? Didn't mean to."

"What's up?"

"Nothin'." He tapped out a new bet and put his phone down. "Text from the physio saying Ollie's injured again."

"Oh. Ok."

"But, Dad, I need the money!"

"Always you need money. Always." Conrad's father spat his disapproval down the phone. "When you not need money?"

"But this is different. This is business." Conrad rolled

his eyes upwards, asking for forgiveness at the white lie he was telling.

"Ha! Which business, hmm? Which business you go all in on and lose this time?"

"Dad, it's Mr Yeo. Nothing to do with gambling, honest."

"Yeo?" Conrad's father hurled a string of Cantonese curses and other non-complimentary epithets at him before reverting to English. "Why you do business with Yeo?"

"He's doing my manufacturing, Dad. A clothes line. *My* clothes line."

"Your clothes?"

"Yes." Conrad felt he might have hooked the old man and tried to upsell himself. "I have a range of clothes that I have designed and Mr Yeo is managing production and logistics in Hong Kong."

"Hmm." The sound was full of disdain but Conrad thought he detected a spark of paternal interest. God forbid, perhaps even pride.

"I just need some money to cover initial costs and secure the contract."

"Secure the contract! Ha!" Conrad could almost hear his father's face turned upwards, appealing to heaven to rescue him from his first-born's stupidity. "Where you are in process?"

"Process?"

"Yes. What have you approved?"

"Erm, I haven't approved anything yet, Dad. It's up to Mr Yeo to sort out-"

"Not for Yeo to sort out. For you to approve. Where lab dips, knit downs, hand looms, strike offs, trim submits, fabric quality submits, prototypes, samples, hmm?"

"But Dad, I don't know what half of those things even are!"

"Ha!" His father exclaimed victoriously "Right there, is your problem."

"Dad!" Conrad tried one last time to appeal to his father's better nature. "Please. Help me this one time. This last time. It's a genuine business opportunity I have identified. Me, not someone else. I am using my initiative and my ideas - my designs - to try and build my own business." There was silence on the other end of the line. Conrad threw in his last hope. "A business I can be proud of. So that you can be proud of me."

The silence seemed to stretch for ever and Conrad felt himself holding his breath, waiting for his father's judgement. Finally, it came.

"Send me your designs. Let me see what Yeo sees."

"But-"

"I'll wait."

Conrad knew better than to argue with that tone he heard. "Hang on." He pulled together the last few emails and attachments he had sent to Mr Yeo and forwarded them to his father. He waited silently for the judgement he hoped wouldn't come.

He didn't have to wait long.

"You know phrase Back to drawing board?"

"Yes, but-"

"Good. That's where you need to go."

"But I - there isn't time!"

"Never time to do it right, always time to do it again, hmm?"

It was one of his father's favourite sayings and Conrad still didn't understand what it meant. "No, Dad.

51

I mean I have a photoshoot arranged and I need -"

"Have you seen your designs?"

"Of course I-"

"Many many colourways! Many many button style! Many many finish type! You know what this mean?"

"Dad!"

"Many many error!" His father was in full flow now, barely letting Conrad interject. ""And Mr Yeo, hmm? He see your designs, hmm? Yeo a fool."

"No, Dad, that's why he wants the money to -"

"Hmm. Yeo want money? Maybe, Yeo no fool. Maybe you fool."

"Dad, I-"

"No money. Drawing board."

Conrad swore he could hear the phone being slammed in the cradle on the other side of the globe.

Jack thumbed through his phone address book. Didn't he know a cute blonde with her own dungeon in the Dundee area? Actually, now he came to think about it, he knew two. Should he, shouldn't he? He pulled a coin from his pocket and flipped it. When it came down tails, he called The Twins, smiling broadly out of the tinted window at the passers-by as the team coach crawled its way through the narrow streets around the stadium.

The coin thing was his version of the dice thing. He hadn't actually read The Diceman - a teammate had described the basic idea to him - but Jack had been immediately attracted to the danger and risk of living your life according to throws of the dice. Select six choices for any given situation and then let the dice roll decide the one to take. No cheating, no second rolls. Just Do It. And to hell with the consequences.

Unfortunately, Jack had quickly found that he had difficulty coming up with six different alternatives every time. He wanted to make no decisions of his own and have the dice responsible for everything but he didn't have the imagination or stamina to keep coming up with so many options. He found himself repeating the same ones over and over, even when they didn't make sense.

Plus one time in the dressing room, the dice had rolled away from him and disappeared down a floor sluice leaving him without an answer to that particular question ('How should I celebrate if I score today?") and no hope of getting a replacement until after the match. Improvising, he'd whittled his options down to two and tossed a coin. In the end it hadn't mattered because he hadn't scored.

When one of The Twins picked up, it sounded like she'd only just woken up. On the seat beside him was a holdall which he unzipped and trawled through its contents as he spoke to her. It was stuffed with assorted BDSM gear: handcuffs, a studded leather collar and chain, a whip, an enormous wand massager, some silver threaded rope, a latex gimp mask.

"Hi, it's Jack."

"Oh, hi Jack."

"I'm in town tonight. You both around?"

"Sure. Why not?"

"Ok, usual time?" He could feel himself harden. "I have my gear with me. Plus... some new toys."

There was the minutest of pauses before she replied. "Cool. Can't wait."

"Maybe we could play the rape game. Are you up for

that?"

Another pause. "No."

Jack smiled. "That's the spirit."

"The nineties called. They want their jacket back." Guy cracked a smile at his own wit but Conrad just stood there at his front door not in the mood to be the butt of his friend's jokes. He was, though, all too aware that he was about to impose on him so had best "play nice."

"Funn-knee." He said, entering without waiting for Guy to invite him in. "You funn-knee guy!" It was times like this when Conrad found it useful to exaggerate his accent and expressions into a stereotypical movie Chinaman, play it for laughs as it were.

"We aim to please." Guy closed the door and followed him into the flat.

Guy lived in a small flat on the ninth floor of an inglorious tower block on a former council estate. An estate agent would call it bijou with a superb easterly outlook. Guy didn't. He rented it from a notorious landlord who should, or should not, have been entitled to rent it out in the first place. Opinions differed on the matter, but rents below market rate were tough to find and when you could also avoid having to pay electricity bills because you somehow used your neighbours electricity without their knowledge - well, what did you know, this quickly became a desirable residence with access to all amenities. It wasn't much, but it was always toasty warm.

"Tea?" Guy dived into the kitchen and put the kettle on in anticipation of a positive response.

"Yes please."

He popped his head around the kitchen door, brandishing a packet of biscuits.

"Rich Tea?"

"Sure. Let's push the boat out, why not?"

"Ok." Guy donned his semi-permanent confused expression. "And we're pushing the boat out because…?"

"Because today, you have the chance to acquire a new flat mate. On the market for one day only, a once-in-a-lifetime opportunity to share-"

Guy interrupted, for once way ahead of him. "You?"

"Ta-da!" Conrad flung his arms out and pirouetted with a beaming smile on his face.

"Ye-e-e-s-s-s." Guy tried not to insert a disappointment into his tone, and failed. "And which charity is this outfit for again?"

"What's wrong with my outfit?"

"There's something about it… I can't quite put my finger on it… that just doesn't… go."

"Go with what?"

"My flat."

Conrad pouted. "Are you saying that you object to sharing your flat with me because of my dress sense?"

"Well, you're half right."

"Hey! I thought we were friends?"

"We are." Guy nipped back into the kitchen and called back into the lounge. "And if you want us to stay that way…" He came back in with two mugs and a plate of biscuits on a tray.

Guy was slightly younger than Conrad, and this was just one more way in which Conrad effortlessly lorded it over him and crow-barred his internal sense of inadequacy until it was a scarred and twisted wreck of a thing. He was a slender and slight young man, with thick blonde hair, pale blue eyes and a narrow chin which never seemed to sprout stubble and made him look permanently hesitant and uncertain. When they'd been at school together, Guy had intuitively flown under Conrad's wing, sensing in him someone who could take decisions which Guy didn't trust himself to take. If sometimes those decisions ended badly it was, Guy thought, better that than no decision taken at all. That was his speciality.

And he had to admit that he had missed his friend when they had gone their separate ways. Originally from Surrey, Guy had found himself somewhat stranded up in Scotland and without a natural home. He tinkered and enjoyed beings hands-on with his own sewing machine, hacking away at second-hand clothes to make new unreconstructed, unconventional items of his own devising. Whilst this had given him plenty to occupy himself with, it hadn't really helped him develop - let alone grow - a social network and his natural tendency to shrink inwards meant that he had greeted Conrad like the long-lost brother he never had when he had turned up at Galashiels. This, however, did not extend to wanting to share every waking hour with him, no matter how much Guy looked up to him. Lines had to be drawn.

"Ok, Guy. Ok" Conrad sat down gingerly on the sofa, taking care not to crease his trousers. "Look, I can see this has come as a bit of a shock."

"I'll say. Usually it's the resident of the flat who invites the guest to stay, not the other way round."

Conrad ignored him. "But there are *very good reasons* why this is a most sensible proposal which I think you should consider - *very carefully* - before dismissing it out of hand."

"Which are?"

"Liv and I are no longer a thing." Conrad swept his open palms towards Guy as if to say *there you have it.*

"That is a reason." Guy said. "Singular. You said reasons, plural."

"I have split up from Liv! Did you not hear me?" Conrad was aghast at his friends callousness.

"I did. And that is still only one reason."

"I have nowhere else to go."

"Ok, we now have reasons plural. Still waiting for the *very good* bit."

"I pay you rent?"

"Now we're talking."

They finished their teas and half of the packet of biscuits. Conrad, already beginning to make himself at home, had his feet up on the tea-chest-cum-coffee-table. Guy was fishing for the remains of soggy biscuit in the bottom of his cup with a spoon.

'So, how long before you make up with her, do you reckon?"

"Oh, we're not going to make up."

"What?"

"No, no, no. Me and Liv? We're over." Conrad dismissed the very idea with an exaggerated wave of his hand.

"Come on, you're just saying that. You've been together ages. Years!"

"May be true. But everything must come to an end."

"Now look. Motorways come to an end. Box sets come to an end. Piers come to an end. But you and Liv? True love never dies, surely?"

Conrad looked at his friend sadly, shaking his head.

"You have never been in love."

"But-"

"No if's, no but's. In fact, far from making up I have revenge to do."

"You don't do revenge."

"What?"

"Revenge." Guy explained. "You don't do it. You wreak it. Or have it. Or take it. You don't have revenge *to do.*"

"Whatever! I must…. take revenge then. On her. She has …" Conrad tailed off, searching for a word. It took Guy a few seconds to realise.

"What? She has what?"

"Belittled me!" Conrad smiled proudly at having secured the right word, then just as quickly dropped the smile when he realised it didn't belong with the sentiment. "She has belittled me one time too many."

"I see."

"No you don't see! You don't see!" Conrad poked his friend in the chest, becoming agitated as the memory stirred fresh emotions within him.

"I see you're going to be staying here more than a day or two."

"Hey! Why so selfish, you? Why do you immediately think about impact of this on you?"

Guy's hackles rose and he put his hand to the side of his face as if making a phonecall. "Hello, kettle. This is pot. You're black."

"Fine. Fine. Have it your way. I thought you were my friend. I came to you for help."

"No you didn't. You came to me for a place to stay."

"And help."

"You want my help taking revenge on Liv?"

"Yes." Conrad prodded him in the chest, in confirmation. "And in helping me get some money."

"Money." Guy frowned again. "You need money?"

"Yep." Conrad nodded, ruefully. "I hate to be the baron of bad news but, yes, I need money. Lots."

"Lots? How much is lots?"

Conrad sighed. "Lots. Lots is… lots."

Now it was Guy's turn to sigh. "Hang on. If you've got no money, how are you going to pay me rent?"

The crowds swiftly dissipated after the game, the streets around Tannadice awash with swinging scarves and singing Dundonians. Honours even, a 2-2 draw.

Jack's team mates were loading themselves back onto the bus for the journey south when he demurred. "Staying in town, tonight fellas." Half of them catcalled him and made rude gestures out of the windows at him; the other half were already plugged into earphones and handsets, calling loved ones or listening to music. His manager held a finger up at him as he was last onto the coach: "Training, Monday morning, Jack-Jack."

"Aye, boss." He watched as the coach pulled slowly away and turned right into the congested traffic. Dressed smartly in suit and tie, holdall by his side, he turned back into the stadium to wait for his taxi.

"Biscuit Tin! Need a lift?"

Jack automatically looked towards the shout, a reflex action based on a long-lapsed nickname he'd acquired on arriving in the UK for the first time. A shiny dark face leaned out of the window of a bottle green Mazerati Quattroporte, white teeth flashing amidst the tinted glass and bright chrome window trim. Jack climbed in, throwing his holdall on the back seat, and DJ pulled away and headed away from the city centre.

"Surprised you're driving yourself, Deej. Must be tired out after sitting down all afternoon."

Diji Yeboah and Jack had played in the same under-21 side together for the first two seasons when they were both new to the Scottish Premiership: Jack arriving from Red Star, DJ from Lille. Both youngsters with promise getting their first taste of the beautiful game as it was played in Scotland. DJ was a fluid right-back with a blistering turn of pace. He was also an excellently connected drug dealer.

As DJ developed into a thrusting wing-back he immediately began to earn notice and garner international caps for his home country, Ivory Coast. Enticed by an interest from Dundee United, he had headed north only to find himself injured on the first game of the season and out of action for eight months. It took him another few months of the following season to regain match fitness, but even when he did, he was never the same player - the shine had been taken off the ball and he was shadow of his former self. Dundee United found themselves stuck with an expensive journeyman they couldn't offload and both parties were now biding their time until his contract expired and he became a free agent. In the meantime, he was able to take advantage of his enforced idleness by expanding his dealing network and "extending his brand" - his words.

"Not my fault the manager won't play me." DJ smiled ruefully. "And you know, it doesn't matter how sunny it gets up here, it's never warm. Sitting on the bench for ninety minutes? Man, it freezes your balls off. Luckily, a toot on this every now and again keeps the cockles warm." He handed Jack a small metal inhaler with a transparent glass nodule at one end. Inside Jack could make out vivid green crytals. He put it to his mouth and snorted. After a few seconds, as his senses started to recover and he felt his headrush subside, he handed it back to DJ.

"Whoa. What's that?"

"New." DJ smiled into his rearview mirror as he signalled and turned. "My own concoction. Good isn't it?"

"Man alive." Jack remained motionless in the passenger seat while he tried to detect exactly what effect the drug was having on his mental and physical state. Giddy, he gave up. "I'll take some."

They chatted about old times for the short ten minutes journey, and when they pulled into the hotel car park, Jack said "Why don't you come to my room, show me your wares?"

DJ parked and Jack checked in. They walked up to his room together - a spectacular suite overlooking the manicured grounds of a luxury Georgian house hotel - Jack with his holdall and DJ with a monogrammed briefcase. DJ flicked the case open and swivelled it to show Jack the contents. The base contained several baggies, glistening with vividly coloured crytals, like something from a sweet shop; the lid contained elastic loops holding chrome and enamel paraphernalia, two cigar tubes, a pack of syringes and a several lengths of rubber tubing.

DJ ran his hand elaborately over the goods on display like a demented game show host. "The doctor will see you now."

After concluding business, Jack stood at the french

doors and looked out over the lawn towards the trees. The various samples he had tried were knifing at the inside of his skull and making his teeth itch. He needed a low buzz to smooth off the edges. "I've got a couple of hours to kill. Drink? Oh, yeah, sorry. You can't. Mind if I do?"

"Go ahead." DJ waved magnanimously and watched Jack examine the contents of the capacious bar along the far wall. "Who is it tonight then?"

"The Twins."

"Uh." DJ nodded appreciatively. "Nice. Well, I better be off. Don't wanna stand around watching you get off your face."

"You could at least wait until I've warmed down!" Jack pleaded. "Common courtesy. Come on! Shoot the breeze. It's been a while. What's happening?"

"Nah, nothing much. I shouldn't have come up here. Mistake. We're mid-table material at best and it's too bloody cold. End of this season, I'm off somewhere warm. I've had it with all this."

"London?"

"Warm, I said. Marseilles. Milan, maybe. Madrid."

"All the M's" Jack noted. "No offence, Deej, but what if the big clubs don't want you?"

"Christ! I don't know. Serie B, then. Or Segunda in Spain. Even Panathanaikos would be better than this arctic hole."

Jack knocked back a large drink, gulping down the rich amber liquid in one and emitting a satisfied sigh. The booze was starting to work, and the daggers in his brain were twisting and turning into brilliant shards, pinching at his cortex and sending delight coursing through his central nervous system. He poured himself another and moved over to one of the sofas, watching hypercolours dance in his peripheral vision as he moved. To his surprise, he seemed to be remaining lucid.

"I like it here."

"Really? You surprise me."

"What's that mean?"

"Well, you're never out of the bloody papers. You and your missus - you're a pap's wet dream."

Jack smiled, poured another drink and then grinned broadly. "Livin' the dream. 'Sides, the labels insist on it. You know, coverage."

"Come again?"

"The labels. My endorsements?" Jack raised his eyebrows and looked over to DJ to see if he understood. He didn't. "My product endorsements? Advertising deals?"

"Ah, gotcha."

"Contracts usually stipulate certain minimum levels of exposure, you know. Part of the deal is to keep the products or brands in the public eye. It's not all fun and games."

"Hmm. And how does Tuppence like it?"

"Ach, don't talk to me about it." Jack took another swig. "She gets on my fucking tits."

"Tuppence?"

"Yes, Tuppence." Jack mimed a mincing walk, glass wavering in his hand. "Miss Fucking Goody Two Shoes. I tell you, I'd divorce her like a shot if it wouldn't cost half my money and brand placement deals."

"But you're the darlings of the tabloids! You could be the next Posh and Becks."

"At least, Posh took it up the arse."

"Did she?"

"Well, so they say. Tuppence. Miss Two Fucking Pence, couldn't unclench to save a drowning lesbian orphan." Jack was starting to look red in the face. "And that stupid fucking cat! Christ."

"Hey, Biscuit Tin. Wives be bitches, man."

"Hmm." Jack considered. "And I bought her the fucking cat. What a fucking idiot."

"But she is a babe, thought, isn't she?"

"'S often the way isn't it?"

"What?"

"Great to look at, hopeless in the sack." He clinked the glass against the half-empty bottle. "Now, if she were more like Joanie, for example..."

"Easy, Tiger."

"But it's fucking ridiculous isn't it? I'm fucking Golden Boot material. And I've got a wife who's so fucking chaste. And demure. And boring! What's the point of having loads of money if I can't get what I want with it. Hmm?" He didn't wait for DJ to answer. "I mean, if only she'd fall under a bus. Or drown swimming. Or take up a dangerous sport."

"You don't mean that, Jack."

"Don't I?"

DJ looked Jack over. His face was flushed, his eyes were rolling in his head and his hands were shaking, but he had an enormous grin on his face. DJ took a business card out of his wallet and snapped it onto the coffee table, tapping it with his finger to make sure he had Jack's attention.

"Listen." He looked steadily and purposefully into Jack's eyes. "I know a man, ok?"

Jack looked at him blankly and didn't respond. "Connections, man? But this is serious shit, you know? I ain't putting you in touch when you're head's not in the right place. But..." He shook his finger in Jack's face. "But, if you still feel this way, a few days time. And you serious. I mean *serious*. You call me, yeah?"

Jack looked into DJ's face and tried to frame a question, but his brain wouldn't let him. DJ watched as his friend struggled to form a sentence and, realising it was not going to happen, he put his hand on Jack's shoulder. "I'll let myself out."

FOUR

Blessed are the meek, thought Dick, and the self-propelled. Behind him, the Mondeo flew around the bend and down the long straight stretch of road that ran from Lyne to Dawyck. It may have been straight but it was also uneven, bumps and dips hidden by the snow glistening brightly in the sunshine on this unseasonably warm afternoon. A mile or so of clear visibility emboldened even cautious drivers to put their foot down and pretend to be Michael Schumacher. To the Mondeo driver, the luminously clad cyclist in the rapidly approaching distance was as much a target as an obstacle. Grand Theft Auto as depicted in the Borders countryside.

Dick's given name was Richard Money but, unavoidably perhaps, everyone who knew him referred to him as Dick Dosh. It had started at St Andrews where he'd been studying philosophy and, although it had offended him deeply at the time, he had been powerless to stop it catching on - and catch on it had - until he was even referring to himself as Dick in emails and other communications. When he had set up a Christian Society newsletter in his final year, he had needed a pseudonym to pen some articles (due to lack of contributors) and Dick Dosh had risen unbidden to his fingertips and found its way into print. The rest was history.

Dick was fair and somewhat freckled, with closely cropped blonde hair and sad puppy dog eyes. He had the facial features of a former rugby player (which he was):

nose slightly crooked, ears slightly cauliflowered, forehead slightly nobbled. Everything about him was sort of *slightly*, apart from his build. Dick was starting to run to fat, 38 and single. He believed these qualities to be not unrelated.

The *age* thing, he couldn't do much about. Nor the *single* thing, he felt. He was intent on becoming a man of God, currently acting as a lay minister and slowly going through the long, drawn-out ordination process of the Church of Scotland. A chubby part-time preacher fast approaching middle-age was not, he knew, considered a good catch and so he had given up hope of becoming a family man and thrown himself headlong into the life of the church. He regularly held services at the various small churches in Upper Tweeddale as well as organising social clubs for teenagers, giving talks at school assemblies, hosting coffee mornings and prayer meetings at old peoples' homes, and leading an ever-increasing round of fund-raising and charity events.

His latest wheeze was a cycle ride from London to Edinburgh to raise money for the ever-needed repairs to the churches he ministered at: Stobo, Dawyck, Broughton and Skirling. They were all old - centuries old - somewhat dilapidated and in need of constant maintenance and attention. And that was just some of his parishioners, Dick mused. Roofing, plasterwork, wiring, underpinning, stained glass windows, architraving, gargoyles, crypts, pulpits, fonts, church bells, graveyard walls. You name it, it needed attention in at least one of the churches and the dwindling congregations brought in nowhere near enough funding to keep them open. And yes, his parishioners were ageing too and, if it hadn't been for the regular donations from wills the Church would have had to close some of these small country kirks long ago.

So now he was deep in training for this latest venture which, by the by, was also helping address the one item in his personal unholy trinity he felt he could do something about: his physique. A 400-mile cycle ride was no walk in the park and given that it was almost ten years since he'd last engaged in any form of sustained exercise he'd sat down and planned a long and detailed training regime, covering diet, jogging, aerobic exercises he could undertake in the privacy of his own home, and of course, cycling. It was the end of November now and he'd allowed himself four months of exercise, steadily increasing in frequency and duration, so as to be ready for his target start date of February 11th, reaching Edinburgh six days later on the 17th.

Starting in London with, he hoped, ten or so local ministers. His intention was, by collaborating and networking with other parishes across Scotland and England, to add more vicars and clergymen as they cycled up country towards Edinburgh, building an ever-larger group of cyclists and garnering more and more media attention with, hopefully, a bigger pot of money raised at the end of the ride. In his mind's eye, he saw this flashing procession of multi-coloured frames, helmets and lycra whizzing down country lanes and high streets with motorbike outriders and camera crews in tow, looking for all the world like the Church's very own Tour De France. God's Own Peloton, he had christened it - and this was the name of the fund-raising pages he'd set up on Facebook and JustGiving.

Dick was only a recent convert to social media, having been put onto it by a particularly savvy grandmother in his parish who used to to keep in touch with her extended family out in Australia. He had quickly seen the potential for fund-raising and publicity, bought himself a new computer and a copy of Social Media For Dummies and, in no short order, had become quite adept.

As the weeks went by and he had become more comfortable in the saddle, he had also found he was more offended by the attitude of many motorists. An increasing number it seemed gave no regard to cyclists on the road and, in some extreme cases, almost went out of their way to make life as difficult for them as possible. Using his now honed social media skills, he had determined to add a new crusade to his already burgeoning list: anti-cycling motorists. Another Facebook page followed and, after the first occasion when he was actually knocked from his bike, he had immediately remounted, returned home and ordered a GoPro from Amazon. One Youtube account later and he was now regularly publicising extended clips from his helmet-cam of road rage, anti-cyclist behaviour and just genuine rudeness by ignorant road users.

Now, as he retrieved himself from a ditch, bruised but otherwise okay, the offending Mondeo was no longer in view. Dick checked that his GoPro was intact and still recording and made a mental note of the time on his watch. Collecting his unharmed bike, he remounted and slowly pedalled home, praying that the footage was good and that, with any luck, it would also have caught the number plate of the offending ignoramus which he could give to the police to assist them with their enquiries.

The bouncer threw Conrad and Guy out onto the wet

pavement and slammed the casino door closed behind him. It was 4.30am.

"Well, that went well." Guy contemplated the empty street from a sitting position. Somewhere a car alarm was whooping.

"Robbers!" Conrad screamed at no-one in particular. "I report you to Serious Crime Squad for.... serious crime!"

"I don't think there is such a thing as the Serious Crime Squad." Guy got to his feet, doing his best to wring out the water from his jacket and brush down his trousers to look partway respectable. "And if there was, I don't think you can report anyone for losing at roulette."

"Table is rigged." Conrad tried to arrange his hair with both hands, sweeping the rain from his elegant haircut and wiping his hands. "They take my money."

"You gave it to them. Not the same thing."

"Who side are you on?" Conrad glared at his friend. "That was the last of my money. I'd scraped together all I had!." He covered his mouth and nose with his hands and breathed noisily into them. "What do I do now, hmm? What I do?"

"Ask your father for more money?"

"He say *No More Money*. He always say *No More Money*."

"Yeah, but he always gives you more."

"Not anymore." Conrad dropped his hands from his face and thrust them into his pockets. "Those days are gone."

"Ok, so we go with Plan B."

"We don't have a plan B."

"Oh." Guy was crestfallen. He assumed his friend was always thinking, always one step ahead. "Well, what about a plan C or D?"

Conrad didn't respond but started walking truculently up the street. Guy tagged along and let his friend think in silence. They came across the car who's alarm was shrieking, filling the street with sound. No-one seemed concerned, no lights were being turned on in the houses either side of the road.

"That's a nice car." Guy could see it was a fancy sports car of some kind. "You'd think someone would care that the alarm's going off."

Conrad glanced at the low-slung coupe, streetlights reflecting off it's turquoise bodywork. "Lamborghini. Hmm, someone with money to burn."

Guy surveyed the street up and down. "Looks like a lot of nice cars along this road. Why don't people who can afford these kind of things buy a garage to keep it in?"

"Because this is Edinburgh. Builders don't build garages when they can build flats and sell them for millions." Conrad shrugged. "Besides, you got something like this you want people to see it. Status symbol."

"Well I wouldn't. I'd want to keep it safe." Guy contemplated the Lambo. "Although, not this one. I'd like a green one. Maybe yellow."

Conrad looked at his friend, astonished. "You know, that's a brilliant idea."

Guy was baffled. "Buying a yellow car?" But Conrad had already turned around, picked up his pace and was striding back up the street with renewed purpose. "Hey, wait for me. Where you going?"

"Going to see a man about Plan B."

"But I need three copies!" Brenda was distraught, looking at her watch. "In the next five minutes!"

Dougie slipped the knife from its sheath and ran it delicately across Brenda's neck. Pinpricks of blood bloomed.

"Hmm. And it's only some of the pages which are printing out half blank?" he said.

"Yes! I've tried it several times now and sometimes page 2 is half-blank and sometimes page 2 is fine but page 8 is half-blank. I don't know what's going on!"

He pushed the tip of the knife into her soft flesh and the trickle became a mighty red damburst soaking her blouse.

"Have you tried it on another printer?"

"No. That's a good idea. Let me go and do that."

The blood poured down her torso and over the printer, pooling in a shining slick.

"And while you're doing that can you email me the file and let me try printing it out? Maybe it'll work for me."

"Will do! Thanks Dougie, don't know what I'd do without you."

"No, neither do I." He said to his keyboard and watched as she disappeared out of his room. "And let's not ask why the hell you need three hard-copies of a Powerpoint presentation which everyone is going to see projected on a big screen. Nor why you wait until the last minute to try printing it out." He looked at the attachment as it came into his inbox. "Fucking hell! Nor why your file is 100Meg for only...." He opened it. "Sixteen slides? What the-"

Brenda came scurrying back into his office. "I've sent 2 copies to the printer downstairs but it's taking an age.

I've just got this little egg-timer thing sitting on my screen."

Dougie looked up at her, seeing the knife now embedded in her chest, red everywhere. "Do you really need three copies of the entire thing right now?"

She bit her lip thoughtfully. "Well, the meeting starts at four but I'm not scheduled to do my bit until 4.45pm."

"Right. Leave it with me. You get to your meeting and find a way to get this printed out before 4.45pm. I'll get Mandy to bring the copies in to you."

"Oh, thanks ever so much Dougie. Thanks really. You are a marvel."

"Yeah yeah." She retreated leaving red footprints on his carpet.

He pulled up a console window on his third monitor and started typing away. "I'm a fucking chump is what I am. A fucking undervalued, underappreciated -"

"Dougie!" This was Mandy, shouting up the stairwell to his room from the floor below. "Printer's jammed!"

Stanley Chu, sat in his office, a bank of monitors behind him showing various images of the Jade Tiger casino floor. On the desk in front of him was a bright pink phone, a desk calculator and a cigar burning in a large crystal ashtray. He was gazing at a small portable TV up on the wall watching a racing telecast from the Happy Valley racetrack when Conrad and Guy were ushered in by the bouncer who had not long ushered them out.

"Fuck sake!" Stanley ripped up the betting slip in front of him as the horses crossed the line. He pulled a thick roll of notes from his suit pocket, peeled off several fifties and handed them to the heavyset man sitting on a sofa off to one side. "Next race, Dark Pacific." The man took the money and disappeared out of the door and Stanley took a long pull on his cigar and watched the smoke drift lazily above his head.

"Mister Chu?"

"Who wants to know."

"Conrad, Mister Chu. Conrad Ho."

"Ho. Ho. Ho." Stanley repeated, trying to place the surname.

"Clive Ho is my father." Conrad prompted.

"Yes! Clive's boy." Stanley looked at him again. "I can see the resemblance."

No-one spoke and Conrad waited to see if Mr Chu would break the silence which was starting to stretch out awkwardly in front of them.

"I'm looking to make some money." Conrad offered.

"Isn't everyone."

"I was hoping that I could make some money for me, and some money for you."

"Go on."

"I understand you steal luxury cars-"

Fuck off!." Stanley spat, picking a piece of tobacco out of his mouth, and pointed a finger at Conrad. "I export luxury marques to discerning customers in Macau, Shanghai and Beijing. I sell them. To order. I do not steal them."

"Sorry. I-." Conrad hesitated, extremely nervous under Mr Chu's hardened glare. "Perhaps I could act as one of your, er, suppliers?"

Mr Chu showed no sign of interest and Conrad wondered how to persuade him he was being genuine. "I have access to a variety of Lamborghini's"

"Gallardo? Huracan?" He leaned forward slowly. "Aventador?"

"Whatever you need, Mr Chu." Conrad replied coolly, spreading his hands. "I can get it for you." Guy tried not to stare at his friend in astonishment.

Stanley gazed in silence at Conrad for a moment, weighing him up. "Leave me your number." He said, at last.

"Sure. Sure." Conrad scribbled his phone number on the back of the business card Stanley was holding out to him. "What is the, er, usual rate?"

Stanley scanned the number and put the card in his pocket. "Ten up front, the rest on delivery. Depends on the model. Extra fifteen for Gallardo, rising to thirty for an Aventador."

"Right. Cool." Conrad nodded and kept nodding wondering how to end the conversation.

"I'll call you." Stanley said, ending it for them both.

Jack sat in the first class carriage, watching the North Sea, the rhythm of the rails and the gentle sway of the carriage relaxing him as they led south. He put his head back and tried to replay the highlights from his session with the twins from the night before. Much of the evening was annoyingly out of reach to him, but he sat up with a start as he recalled his conversation with DJ.

He pulled DJ's card from his wallet and dialled his number. DJ picked up on the third ring.

"Yo. This is DJ."

"Hi, Deej. It's Jack."

"Jack! My man."

"Deej, Do you remember that conversation we had

last night?"

"Which one would that be?" DJ was suddenly rather coy.

"The one where you said you know a man?"

"Sure." DJ audibly relaxed. "Yeah, I know a man. Do I take it you are interested in his services?"

Jack hesitated, listening to his brain to see if this was really what he wanted. Then he had a thought. He took out his coin, murmured under his breath, and tossed it. It came down Heads and he exhaled slowly.

"Yes."

"Okay. Well I'll pass him your number and get him to call."

"Oh. Right. Ok." Jack felt there should be more to it than this. "And how much will it cost and how long will it take?"

"Cost? Sixty big ones. Time? Up to him. You can discuss it with him when he calls."

"Sixty grand?"

"Includes a finder's fee for me." DJ giggled on the line.

"Right. Ok." Jack swallowed. The actual sum wasn't the problem - less than any single one of his many product endorsements - but the clarity the number leant to the proceedings gave this undertaking a new degree of certainty. Finality. "Any idea when he'll call?"

"Nope. But I'll pass him your number now and suggest he calls later. Depends what else he's doing right now, I guess."

Jack looked down at the hairs on the back of his hands and saw them standing to attention. He felt the hairs on his spine go the same way when DJ unexpectedly gave him an out. "You sure you want to do this, Jack?"

Shaking, Jack flipped the coin again. Heads.

"Yep."

"What I'm saying, is that this material is not... our sort of thing." Jonty McKay was Chief Buyer, Head of Sales, and Managing Director of Merry & McKay Ltd. Headquartered at Bankholm Mill in Hawick, the company had been manufacturing wool, cashmere and cotton fabrics and garments since the 19th century. Jonty was a direct descendant of one of the company's founders, a young-looking forty-something with heavy blonde hair, cut short, large thick red glasses and a diamond stud in one ear. He was what passed for bleeding edge fashion cool in the Scottish Borders. He fingered the sample material on the layout board and shook his head sadly at Conrad.

"Why is it not your sort of thing?" Conrad hadn't necessarily expected to be welcomed with open arms - he was an unknown after all - but he had thought any challenges to his proposal would have come from his designs and their quirky nature. Here he was, though, suffering criticism about the material! They hadn't even got onto the subject of his actual designs yet.

"Well, this is a somewhat irregular weave. Erratic, even." He rubbed the cloth between his thumb and forefinger, and pouted a little. "And the quality is... let's say *good*."

"Cool!" Conrad brightened. "So it's good, then."

Jonty smiled condescendingly at Conrad. "*Good* isn't good. Good is actually a quite inferior grade of cloth."

"Huh? This is top quality cashmere. How can you

improve on that?"

"Cashmere yes. Mostly." Jonty rubbed the fabric again, as if trying to bend a spoon. "Something else mixed in with it, I'd say. As part of our design analysis I would get one of the lab boys to do a spectrographic assessment - that would tell us exactly the mix - but my fingers tell me that this is probably 70-80% cashmere. The rest could be anything."

"Anything?"

"Yes. Rat. Yak. Sheep. Even synthetic."

"This is most excellent quality material." Conrad sputtered. "Sourced by myself."

"Yes. Might I ask where from?"

"Hong Kong."

"Ah." That smile again. "Yes, you see Mr Ho. I have been working in the industry a long time - seen it all, you might say. And these fingers-" He waggled the fingers on both hands, like Fagin imagining pound notes. "These fingers can tell the finest cashmere when they feel it. They're not feeling it."

"I paid top quality price for this cashmere."

"Really. May I see?" Conrad handed him a sheaf of papers and invoices and Jonty casually flipped through them. "Yes, Mr Ho. We can't match these prices. I'm not sure anyone could… unless they were mixing their cashmere with other inferior material."

"Then I could source the material from Hong Kong and you make my garments here."

"That's not how we work, Mr Ho. We are very… particular, about the materials we use in our clothing." He handed the papers back to Conrad. "We have our reputation to think of. Most of our customers are luxury brands, high couture clients who demand the very best.

We can't afford to risk losing their business by working with anything but the best yarns and dyes. Look."

He led Conrad over to a table laid with small wooden boxes, unvarnished. Bundles of wool lay in each box. "Feel the difference for yourself. We recognise several quality grades. This is merino wool - for comparison. Soft and hard-wearing, certainly. But when you then feel a cashmere-wool mix you can see the difference. The strands are finer the fibres are softer, sure. Your material is somewhere in this class. Compare it to inferior quality and you can feel the difference, but when you then compare it to 100% cashmere..." He indicated the next box on the table. "Then, I hope, you can feel the difference. And we-" he indicated the final box on the left. "Here, we only use Grade Zero cashmere - not just 100% cashmere but wool taken only from the neck and chest of the goat. The wool here is sparser but more luxurious - which is, of course, reflected in the price."

Conrad was deflated. Even his fingers could tell the difference. Jonty continued his spiel.

"So we use only the finest, rarest cashmere yarns. Then we start to look at the designs." He flipped through Conrad's large portfolio book, pulling a tight face. "We work with our clients to review their designs and ensure they are suitable for manufacture. We will work with engineering and production to refine the designs to make them mass-producible to the highest quality possible at an agreed volume and price. I'm not sure..." He looked up and seemed to soften when he saw Conrad's face. "Come with me. Mr Ho. Let me show you."

Conrad followed Jonty down a corridor, through some battered double swing doors and into a loading bay area littered with large boxes of yarns on spindles. On the wall was a clocking-in station and a series of pigeonholes containing cards and pieces of paper. A whiteboard had various dates and schedules scrawled on it in red marker. They continued around to the far corner where bales wrapped in sackcloth were being manhandled by two men in tan-coloured overalls.

"The wool comes to us in this raw state, packed tightly into these bales, each of which is worth many thousand pounds, and it then has to go through a series of processes to turn it into yarn. I'm sure you're aware of all this, Mr Ho." They stopped by another set of double-doors and Jonty turned to Conrad to make his point clear. "But key to all of this is the blending. And the dyeing. Each of these key steps defines the whole process, you might say. Yes the wool needs to be washed and cleaned and carded and spun but our yarns are blended incredibly carefully, combining different batches or types of raw wool to create precisely the right qualities for each individual product. The perfect mix, if you will, which will create yarns strong enough to survive all the punishing steps of the manufacturing process, whilst remaining delicate and soft to the touch, allowing garments to drape and fold and caress the wearer but, and at the same time, being hard-wearing and long-lasting."

Jonty pushed through the double doors and into a echoing shed where a huge metal hook suspended on ceiling tracks was nursing an elephantine sack of wool across the floor until it hung directly over a circular metal vat some ten or twelve feet in diameter.

"And the dyes we use." Jonty continued. "Here, for example, we're going to dye this batch a beautiful scarlet shade." He passed Conrad a skein of yarn wrapped around a large card that was a beautiful lustrous red that almost shimmered in the glaring strip-lighting overhead. "We create the dyes uniquely - recipes and colours we have used for decades or created specifically for our clients. All recipes jealously guarded, and not just because of the hue." He raised his eyebrows at Conrad. "We make sure we have colours which don't run, don't bleed, don't fade. Our garments will look as beautiful in ten years as they do when they are taken off the shelf."

Conrad watched as the crane's load was lowered into the vat, the sacking container removed and a huge lid swung over, clanging shut on the vat. The workmen screwed the lid down tight and then turned to address one of a number of control panels standing in front of an array of pipes running down the height of the wall in front of them. Conrad could see a blood-coloured liquid make its way down one of these tubes and turned to see Jonty opening what a massive metal door with a large dial on it, like some safe from the Old West.

"The dyed product then gets baked in here to dry. Another key step to make sure the colours fix." The wardrobe contained shelves and racks lined with yards and yards of thread all gorgeously coloured the same glorious ruby red as the card Conrad still held in his hand. When Conrad looked up again from his hand Jonty was already holding open the door out of the dyeing shed and into a smaller holding room.

"We keep the finished yarns here, securely with very - *very* - restricted access, and a clear check-in, check-out policy. Some of these yarns are several hundred pounds per kilo, Mr Ho. From here they will go one of two routes through the factory." He led Conrad along a marked path on the floor. "To create fabrics which will then be cut and made into garments, the yarns are set out onto one of a number of looms. We have different looms for different size cloth and complexity of pattern. But each is intricately programmed by our manufacturing design team, specifying which threads are required where. The corresponding yarns are arranged on these stanchions and threaded onto the warp beam which feeds the loom. You can see here the trail of different coloured threads working their way across this space to be woven into a finished fabric, some will be the warp, some the weft."

The warp beam stood eight feet tall or more and its spindly frame extended out into the floor more than twenty feet. On each arm sat a different coloured cone of yarn and the threads were stretched out along the brackets and over to the loom's mouth, where they converged and disappeared into the innards of the mechanism, like some mammoth multi-coloured spider's lair. Here, in the middle of the large factory floor, looms and machines racketed and hummed busily all around them. Jonty was having to almost shout now to make his voice heard over the hubbub.

"If the yarn is intended for knitwear the threads will be assembled, by hand, onto the needle beds of these old knitting machines. They don't make these anymore you know and we have to scour the world for used and refurbished machines. Our engineering team work round the clock to make sure that all these irreplaceable machines are kept in perfect working order. In the same way as for the fabric, the knitting design is built up stitch by stitch and the programs ensure the relevant coloured yarns are spooled into the design as the garment is built up on the machine." He indicated to a grey-haired woman in a thin pink overall who had paused by an ancient-looking machine and was fiddling rapidly with gossamer threads woven between closely fitting metal teeth. "This lady here is walking the line, checking for imperfections, missed or broken threads, stepping in as quickly as possible to ensure nothing is lost."

"We have separate machines over there for sleeves and socks - basically knitted tubes which are left with finishing edges for closure at a later stage or addition onto a cardigan or sweater."

"Finishing. Washing. Ironing. Inspection. All of these steps performed manually by experienced expert staff who have been working with these materials for many, many years." Jonty looked at his watch and seemed to decide that the factory tour was over. He ushered Conrad out back along the corridor through which they had first passed. As they passed a series of windows set in the corridor wall that looked into a large open plan office containing a handful of desks and shoulder-height screen dividers a young woman popped her head out of the office door.

"Jonty? Can you call Ms Nightingale back asap?"

"Hmm?" Jonty was caught unawares.

"Ms Nightingale! She called about the Chanel collection? Wants a quick word."

"Right. Yes. Will do."

He turned back to Conrad but Conrad was now no longer listening. Frozen in place, by the mention of Liv's name he felt ice-cold sweat on the back of his neck whilst simultaneously rage started boiling up within him. His face flushed. Jonty was talking again and Conrad tried to re-focus.

"So, you see. There are many steps to this delicate and

complicated process, Mr Ho. And before all of that even starts, many stages of consultation and design review to ensure only the best materials are involved and only the finest products leave our factory with our blessing." He handed Conrad back his portfolio and sample book which he had been carrying with him. "And I'm afraid the designs you have here are just not in keeping with our processes and approach to quality."

Conrad stared vacantly at the folders he was holding. Unable to think clearly he stuttered a feeble protest. "But, I have worked on these designs with the express-"

"I'm sorry, Mr Ho." Jonty cut him off, the meeting now clearly over. "Perhaps some other mill might take them on… although I think all our competitors have become specialists in one particular area or other. Some will create the cloth, some will finish it for you, some will turn existing cloth into garments. I think we're the only mill which still acts as a one-stop shop ."

"But-" He couldn't reconcile his inner anger and this sudden becalming disappointment. The personal rejection was now swiftly receding into the distance and standing in the foreground of his mind, with a target playing over her figure, was Liv. He heard himself begging. "Are there none of my designs you could use? Any of them?"

Jonty pursed his lips and rubbed the back of his neck. "Perhaps the tartans?" He took the book from Conrad and flipped through it looking for the right page. "These here, that's along the right lines. But you'd need more of it, much more, and as I said, better quality material to make it from."

"I can get the material!"

"Not with us, you can't." Jonty handed the book

back, finally this time. "And can you work more tartan into your designs?"

"No." Conrad shook his head, sadly. He gave a heavy sigh and the part of his brain which had been wildly whirring now stopped and kicked him in the shin. *But I know a woman who can.*

The red light was winking on the disk drive when Dougie got to the server room so the system alert had been genuine and now he had a problem. Most of the company files were held on this network drive and it wasn't hot-swappable. He'd have to take it offline to restore the backup which would mean telling everyone to close their files and wait, then emailing them when everything was back to normal. Then, for the rest of the day (and probably tomorrow as well), he would get random calls from fellow workers letting him know that their mouse had stopped working, or they couldn't print, or they'd lost their wifi connection and "could it be connected to the problem with the network drive?".

No it fucking couldn't.

He didn't have time for this shit. Nor the genuine issues which would follow where people had forgotten to save their files when they closed them and so discovered, when the backups came online, that they'd lost *vital* work. *Through no fault of their own.* And what was IT going to do about it?

Arse-biscuits.

His phone vibrated in his pocket and when he pulled it out he could see it was a text from his brother-in-law: Job4u. BIG. Urgent. Call when conv.

Wtf? If it was urgent why call when convenient? DJ

85

was a crazy mother. Must be a footballing thing - none of them were too sharp. He called DJ straight back.

"Deej. Got your text. What's up?"

"Hey bro, thanks for getting back to me. Got something for you, think you'll be mighty interested."

"Cool. But Deej, I'm in the middle of something right now, can I call you later when I've got this sorted?"

"'Member that chat we had a while back?" His brother-in-law clearly wasn't listening.

"Deej."

"About Omar?"

"What?"

"Omar? Off The Wire, man! The guy with the shotgun and the scar? Mean nigger goes round topping drug dealers? You know."

Dougie's mouth went dry and his hands went cold and clammy. He knew exactly the conversation DJ was referring to. A drunken conversation, flagged as *in strictest confidence* between the two of them only. The one where Dougie had confessed to DJ that he wanted to be a killer. A hitman. A cool dude who no-one messed with, who came and went like Keyzer Soze, dealing death and living off the proceeds. A man who operated outside the law.

Unbelievably DJ hadn't known who Keyzer Soze was, but he did know who Omar was - which amounted to much the same thing.

"You still there, bro?"

"Yeah." Dougie could feel his heart pounding in his throat, his temple, his chest. "Yeah, still here."

"Cool. 'Cos I think I got you your first contract, man. How 'bout that?"

"Really?"

"Straight up! Fifty big ones."

"Fifty-?"

"'S'right, man. Five-Oh."

"Shit a brick."

"Say what? Is you up for this or not?"

His heart leapt like a tiger at a toddler and he suddenly felt more than a little sick. This was it. His opportunity. Was he up for it or was he going to spend the rest of his life rebooting servers?

"I'm in."

"Cool. I'll text you the guy's number. Told him you'd call."

"Right." Dougie's mind had stopped racing and he heard his voice in its own echo chamber, like someone else's. Time had suddenly slowed down and he couldn't think clearly. "What's the next step?"

"Say what?"

"Next step. What's my next move?"

"Shit, I don't know, man! This ain't my thing. I done my piece, the rest is on you."

"Right."

DJ hung up and Dougie stood frozen, unable to process what was happening. His phone buzzed again with a text from DJ containing a phone number.

Shit, this was really happening. He left the freezing cold of the air-conditioned server room and walked back past reception in a trance.

"Dougie? You ok?" Mandy on reception was looking at him strangely.

"Hmm? Oh, yeah. Yeah." He slowly returned to the real world. "Need to get everyone off the network drive so I can restore it. You wanna close your files? I'm just about to send an email out to everyone."

"Okily-dokily!"

He headed back to his desk to send the email that would bring the wrath of every stupid person in the building down around his head.

Stupid fuckers. Shouldn't be allowed computers if they didn't have the first idea how to use them. Surely there was some kind of "driving test" that existed which meant anyone - *anyone* - using a computer for work had to have a certain level of competence before being allowed to touch one, let alone use one. They didn't let you use a fire extinguisher or a chainsaw without some training, why were computers any different? Christ, you needed training these days to learn how to sit at a fucking desk properly!

Ah, but, you see. This "driving test", this training - who'd give it, hmm? Fucking IT, that's who. Him, muggins. There was no escape. You did the job, you took the abuse, you tried to keep your temper while some numpty prattled on about something they didn't understand and then they waited, hands outstretched, for you to give them a fucking resolution. *Now.* And not so much as a *please* or *thank-you*.

He clenched and unclenched his fists as he walked back to his desk. Fuckers were all going in his little black book. Anyone from now on who complained about something they'd done themselves, or wasted his time, or reported some problem they couldn't reproduce, or about the fact they'd not been given any training on the system, or...

His phone rang as he closed the door to his room.

... or anyone who called him to interrupt his train of thought.

He looked around the empty room and shouted to the ceiling "F-U-U-U-C-K!!!", let it ring three times then picked up the received and calmly said "Hello, IT?"

It was Brenda. Her name was going to be *first* in the fucking book.

No wait. The book could wait. First, he had a proper job to do.

FIVE

"I've been out walking the streets all fucking week! When is it going to be your turn?" Guy was nursing his bare feet, massaging his toes, his socks balled up and thrown in a corner.

"I have my photoshoot plan to finish. We each do what we do best."

"Seems what I do best is your donkey work."

"I am front of house. I agree the deal, handle the money, manage Mr Chu. You are rear of house. You find the car. Together - front and rear - we deliver to Mr Chu."

"Well, I'm relieved to hear that last bit. I expected to find that somehow, stealing the car would be what I do best as well."

"Together." Conrad assured him. "So, today, you find one?"

"Yeah, I think so."

"Excellent! Great news. Today is the day, I can feel it. I have a sick sense."

"I'm sure." Guy was too tired to correct his friend. "I need to double-check. It whizzed past me too fast. Plus we need to see the interior, make sure it's a match for the spec."

"Ok." Conrad closed the lid of his laptop and stretched in his chair. "Tonight?"

"Yeah, alright." Guy yawned. "First, I need a long soak and a good kip."

"Is that magnolia leather or butter-cream?"

The car was parked on the forecourt of a large Victorian villa, between two other, somewhat less desirable, BMWs. They were both staring into the car, hands hooding their eyes so they could see the interior without the glare from the streetlights.

"I don't fucking know." Guy was still moody after being woken up by Conrad at 2am. "You're supposed to be the car expert. *Whatever you need, Mr Chu.*" He spread his hands mimicking Conrad.

"I'm calling it butter-cream."

"Excellent. Now what?"

"Now? Now you steal the keys."

"Wha-?" Conrad had disappeared behind the gatepost to the house. Guy chased after him and prodded his chest, speaking in a loud whisper." You said together. Remember? We steal it together. Front and rear. Your words."

"Yes. That's right. You get the keys, I'll drive the car."

"And how do you propose I do that then, hmm?"

"You see that open window there?" Conrad pointed to a small window vent, propped open on the ground floor.

"I can't fit through that."

"You don't have to. You reach through, open larger window, climb in, grab keys, climb out."

Guy looked at Conrad, gritting his teeth. "You know, this isn't how I imagined the fashion business would be."

"Trust me. Five minutes and we'll be forty grand to the good."

"Right. Now try and start it quietly." Guy was nervously looking around, listening keenly for any untoward sound.

"How can I start it quietly? It's a fucking Lamborghini."

"Try, ok? For me? Pretty please?"

Conrad turned the ignition and the powerful engine growled like an approaching storm. He adjusted the rearview mirror and then squinted over his shoulder trying to see behind him. "Christ, these cars have zero visibility in the rear. How are you supposed to reverse?"

"Carefully?"

"I'll be careful." Conrad put the car into reverse, lifted the handbrake and slowly started to swing the car around and out between the gateposts. His neck was stiff from nerves and craning to see behind him. His foot slipped a little on the accelerator and the car lurched backwards.

"Don't forget the fron-!" Guy shout-whispered too late.

The car alarm of the BMW Conrad had just hit with the front wing of the Lamborghini went off like a firecracker. Lights in windows all around them started flickering on. Conrad planted his foot down hard on the accelerator and the Lamborghini shot out from between the BMWs and plunged with a sickening crunch into one of the gateposts.

"Shit!" Conrad cried, and thumped the steering wheel with both hands, stamping his feet like a toddler denied. "Shit, shit, shit, shit, shit!"

Guy looked passively on as the driver's airbag chose that moment to deploy.

Dick saddled up with a spring in his step and not a little excitement. He pedalled the wrong way slowly down Rosetta Road so that he could get to the High Street quickly and, from there, down to Tweed Green - their standard gathering point.

There were a few riders already there, enjoying the New Year sunshine when he pulled up. They chatted until they were close to their full complement of twenty, although the number was rising week by week. Initially, recruitment to the charity ride cause had been sporadic but, as the name implied, the network effect grows on an exponential curve rather than an arithmetic one, and a tentative two became a more healthy four, a nicely rounded eight and, then a fulsome sixteen. He did a quick mental calculation: six weeks until the start of the ride and he was hoping for a start-out contingent in the thirties and have it grow by ten or so for every day they rode, every stop they passed. By the time they reached Edinburgh they could be 100-strong, if all went well.

His fellow cyclists came from all walks of life - farmers, librarians, insurance salesmen, software testers - but all had one thing in common (apart from their love of cycling and their shared Facebook connections) which was volunteering. Between them they spanned the voluntary sector in the Scottish Borders like a collective colossus of acronyms and abbreviations: SCOOBYDOO (Scottish Charitable Organisation Outreach for Borders Youth Development & Ongoing Operations), SWETYSoc (Scottish Women Ettrick, Tweedsmuir & Yetholm Society), BAGSY (Borders Autism Group Support for Youth), and TSI:Borders. In fact it was only Anita who's voluntary venture (Men's Sheds) didn't have an abbreviation. From Broughton and Skirling in the west, to Melrose and St Boswells in the east, Dalkeith and Penicuik in the north, to Hawick, Duns and Kelso in the south. There was not a single voluntary organisation unrepresented by the varied and vested interests of this rapidly growing group of fund-raising cyclists.

Add in those members who were also fellow church folk - ministers, laymen, sermonisers, treasurers, secretaries, curates. Anyone in doubt that the Anglican clergy had withered and died on the secular bough of the 21st century need only cast a glance at this lycra-clad millipede as it wound its way through the Scottish countryside like a lurid, living worm. Dick had unknowingly tapped into a nascent nexus of do-goodery all willing to saddle up in the Lord's name. Inclusion was not just the norm, it was their watchword. One of them was even a Roman Catholic.

Dick waited for the church bells of St Peters to mark the hour and then walked his bike to the head of the group and mounted. With the echo of the bells lingering in the clear morning air, the yellow and blue bike train conga'd across the river Tweed and headed up the hill towards the High School.

Conrad looked vacantly at the bedside clock as it burped its alarm at him and realised he had no idea what he was going to do or say when they knocked at the door. He dragged himself out of bed, made a coffee, and sat at Guy's kitchen table looking out over the estate below. The sounds of people moving around in the flats above and below echoed in his head, ringing more deeply and slowly than they should, all ominously tolling like some imaginary church bell before he was led out to the noose.

The doorbell shrill chime made him start and reverberated through the flat. Conrad sat frozen and listened to impatient knocking on the front door. Rooted to the spot he heard a loud thud and splintering then heavy steps in the hall.

The man standing in the kitchen doorway was clad head-to-toe in motorcycle leathers, topped off with a glossy helmet, tinted visor down, bearing a shimmering green tiger leaping across the side. He didn't greet Conrad, or wait for a greeting, just stood, patiently removing his gloves to reveal heavily tattooed hands, one of which was missing two fingers. He held Conrad's own left hand at the wrist and pushed down hard so that Conrad had to instinctively spread his fingers out on the waxed tablecloth. From somewhere the man magically produced a cleaver.

With no announcement or preparation, the man brought the cleaver down on the little finger of Conrad's left hand and the severed portion bounced across the table with the impact. Blood pulsed irregularly across the smooth yellow surface.

The man picked up the severed finger gingerly, wrapped it in a piece of cloth and zipped it into his breast pocket. He turned to go, letting drips of blood from the cleaver mark his trail back down the hallway. Conrad watched, numb with shock, as the figure disappeared through the door. Not a single word had been spoken by either of them.

Ten minutes later Conrad received a text that read: one finger each week until you pay.

Tuppence was attracted to the stillness and echoing silence immediately she opened the creaking kirk door. The smells of old paper, floor polish, damp plaster and dust seemed to draw her in and she felt the hairs on the back of her neck prickle as she closed the door gently behind her. Stepping slowly behind the rear pews into the nave, something about this place sucked her in - a welcoming womb enveloping her. It wasn't warm inside but she no longer felt cold as she walked down the aisle, almost on tiptoe, afraid to leave a mark or make a sound.

She edged into the row of pews second from the front, smoothed her dress beneath her and sat down on the threadbare cushion. Up to her left was a large stained glass window depicting the crucifixion. She caught her breath as she looked up at it and, for a moment, saw her father's face in profile gazing up at the cross.

A harsh scraping sound off to her right jolted her to attention and she sat bold upright briefly, afraid, as a lycra-clad figure strode clumsily into the chancel and disappeared out of sight again, behind the pulpit. Shuffling and banging loudly she thought she heard faint swearing as the figure reappeared to reveal a bulky torso and a closely-cropped blonde head with red sweaty features. The man wiped his face with the back of his black sleeve, looked up - perhaps now with clearer vision - and started nervously as he saw her sitting there.

He cleared his throat. "Sorry. Didn't see you there. Were you waiting for me? In a bit of a state at the moment, I'm afraid. Just got back from, er,... Give me a moment, I'll... I'll. Let me just change quickly. And... and... and..." He withdrew hastily, retreating backwards to the door he'd entered from, holding a book of common prayer and a bicycle pump across his chest, bending over slightly as he shuffled towards the door as if protecting his groin from an imminent free kick.

Tuppence sat, non-plussed but smiling slightly at his embarrassed politeness. While she had no idea who he was, she decided that she would wait for him to return - she couldn't bear to imagine his flustered discomfort were he to reappear only to find her suddenly gone.

Even showered and freshly clothed when he came back into the chancel and saw her again, Dick couldn't help feeling like Sam Gamgee next to Galadriel. She stood as he approached and he could see she was almost a head taller than him, slender and willowy and impossibly beautiful. Standing in a beam of light angling down through the stained-glass window above her, she was immaculate and angelic; His emissary sent to greet him. *Oh God, please let her anoint me.*

As he got closer he saw her cheekbones and eyes, her wrists and neck, her eyebrows and lips. Nothing out of place, nothing so imperfect as a pore, a blemish, a spot. Her delicately freckled skin smooth, her long hair teased and curled into a delicious tumble, her green irises sparkling in samite white pools. *Oh God, please let her.*

Dick realised he was staring and couldn't stop himself. Neither could he stop his momentum, as he felt himself drawn towards her, body lurching ahead of feet that couldn't seem to keep up with him. Like a schoolboy who'd been kicked out of the house by his mother and spent the rest of the day falling forwards, he managed to keep himself upright as he reached the pew and held out his hand to greet her.

Then she spoke.

Oh God, please.

Silence.

He waited and then realised that, perhaps, she had asked him a question and was waiting on him to answer. "Sorry, what did you say?"

"I said Hello." She smiled kindly at him, showing perfect teeth and two wondrous dimples.

"Yes." His stomach dropped like an elevator from the fiftieth floor and he had to swallow hard to keep his concentration. "Hello. Sorry about... earlier. I was..." He stood, drowning in her eyes, completely, utterly, totally lost. *Oh God.*

"Are you the vicar here?"

"What? Yes. No. Yes. Er, No. I mean Yes I am but, but, but, er, No I'm not." Her smile widened, her eyes creased and shone, and he had to fight to retain control of his bladder. "I mean, I am the minister. Here. But, but, but I'm not a minister. Yet. Technically."

"I see."

"Are you, er... are you...?"

"I'm with the photoshoot."

"Ah. Right. Right. Right. Right." He tried to unstick his needle. "Of course you are. Of course you are. Erm, I'm Richard. But everyone calls me Dick." He offered his hand and she took it. His thoughts stopped as she shook it but awoke when she spoke.

"Tuppence."

He had no idea what she had said. "Sorry?"

"Tuppence."

"For my...?"

"It's my name. Tuppence."

"Right!" He was flooded with relief. "Oh, it's..." He wanted to say beautiful but instead said: "suits you."

"Thank you." The dimples appeared briefly again and then vanished as a wistful look passed over her face. "My father's choice. He had a friend who had a daughter not long before I was born, a friend who'd swindled him out of some money. His friend called his daughter Penny so my Father called me Tuppence as he said I was twice the girl she'd become."

"Ha." He smiled himself at the story, tried to add to it… and failed. "Good job, your father's friend didn't call his daughter… er, something else!"

"Yes." Tuppence released his hand and looked around the kirk, as if searching for a way out of the conversation. He decided he didn't want her to leave. Ever.

"Erm, sorry about earlier. I'd been out cycling and should've showered and changed before coming into the kirk but, well, there's usually nobody around at this time of day and I…"

"It's ok. They're manhandling lights and things and I just wanted a break. Somewhere to sit quietly. I don't know why."

He saw a look flicker across her face, a look he'd seen many times before in others. Sometimes it was loss, sometimes uncertainty, sometimes searching for something, anything.

"Well, it's a beautiful old building. Full of history and memories. Generations of worshippers who have come here, sat where you're sitting, seeking peace. A chance for reflection." He gave her what passed for his reassuring look. "You don't need to know why. You just need to be."

She sat down again, automatically smoothing the dress across her bottom as she did so, and he found himself transported, gazing at the material and how it folded and flowed across her like a living thing.

"I felt so calm." She looked up at the window above her. "I felt as if I was being held. As if he was here, holding me."

"He is here. He is always here. This is His house."

"No, sorry. I didn't mean Him. God." She gave a small, sweet frown as if by way of apology. "I meant my father."

"Ah." Dick nodded and sat down beside her, hands folded in his lap. "Would you like to tell me about him?"

Tuppence felt her eyes filling as she spoke. She had no trouble with the words, no um's and er's, no pauses to catch her breath and arrange her thoughts. It all tumbled out, unbidden, from somewhere deep within her. Somewhere that this quiet place gave her permission to access and then empty. She watched the dust motes bob and weave in the coloured light and heard her own voice, calm and clear, unwrapping herself to this man who didn't know her from Adam. Alright, Eve. Unafraid of his (and His) judgement, she felt as if she was speaking to the church, the space, the air; not him. He was just a witness.

Halfway through her story, he reached out for her hand and she held it. And all the time, like a disembodied soul, she was looking down on herself. I'm really doing this. This is me, she told his church. And I am telling the truth, the whole truth and nothing but the truth.

So Help Me God.

She had loved her father. So much. A Daddy's girl, she guessed. From the first, he had doted on her and she on him. He had called her his FD - favourite daughter - even though she was an only child. It was only much later she had realised the jokey nature to it; for the first few years it was her most treasured possession.

Even though her mother was the primary care giver and her father worked long hours, often away from home for days on end, in her memory he outshone her, a huge bursting solar flare of energy and light. When he was away, she had used her mother as a functional helper - they got on together as housemates rather than parent and child. When her father came home his brightness made her mother disappear only to reappear when he'd gone again, like the after-image on your eyelids if you looked too long at the sun.

A marvellous bear of a man, with patience and humour, wit and resourcefulness: he could fix anything that was broken, make a new toy from anything to hand, solve any problem, answer any question. As she grew, through those awkward teenage years and into adulthood, he had been her first port of call for advice. He never admonished her, never doubted her, never criticised her. And it was he who had encouraged her to try a modelling career.

When her career took her away from home she kept in touch by phone when she could and his baritone smoothness and hearty laugh down the line conjured images of his crinkly eyes and curly hair. Her mother, also on the line on another handset would ask about her health and the weather, a mechanical counterpoint to the emotional weight of the conversation she focussed on him.

She had loved him to breaking point. Until she thought her heart would burst. And then one day it did.

Her mother had phoned, unusual in itself, while she was on a shoot in the Maldives. She recalled it clearly, as clear as the blue waters she was ankle-deep in on the beach, stretching out to the reef where it merged with the inkier blues beyond and the storm-gathering sky in the distance. Tuppence had been standing, arms akimbo, allowing makeup to artfully sprinkle grains of sand on her arms when she saw Kara, from Wardrobe, treading down across the beach holding her phone.

At first immensely irritated to be interrupted at work, she had been looking out to the reef when her vision suddenly shrank like a shrinking iris. The sound of the sea disappeared and all Tuppence could hear was her mother telling her that her father had Stage 4 cancer, had been admitted to hospital with perhaps only days left to live. He had known, apparently, and not told anyone. He accepted it and wouldn't apologise for it. It was what it was. Tuppence had caught the next available flight home, weeping inconsolably all the way on the eighteen hour journey back.

He had died a few hours before she landed at Heathrow.

When she walked into the hospital room her mother was calmly sitting at his bed, holding his cold hand, staring at his fingernails. Although it was only a few months since Tuppence had seen her, she had aged years. Hunched and broken, she sat like a fragile bird in the chair, all feathery grey hair and brittle cheekbones. They hugged each other and Tuppence could barely manage to look at his face - the memory of his vitality was burnt so strongly into her retina that this lifeless husk seemed another being, another time.

They shared a cab from the hospital and before they

had even reached her parent's house, her mother had proceeded to break Tuppence's heart all over again. His passing had breached some dam inside her mother, broken some seal, and even at this most inappropriate time, she was now unable to prevent herself from spilling out the pent-up resentment which had festered inside her for so long. Tuppence listened in a trance as she dispensed the truth about him over tea and biscuits.

He had been a womaniser and an alcoholic. He had beaten her and slept around, staying away from home for nights on end coming back only to drink heavily, argue and beat her. Episode by episode, one anecdote after another, her mother wound back her story starting from before Tuppence was born, painting over treasured memories in black emulsion, obliterating all the love and light, leaving only a cold, empty blackness.

Tuppence had listened in shock, waited patiently for her to finish before turning on her mother and spitting in her face. Actually spitting. Even now, she couldn't believe she had done that. She had gathered her things, still not having unpacked, and left the house. She never uttered a word, never looked back. If she had she would have seen her mother motionless in the chair, the spittle still clinging to her cheeks, mixed with tears as Tuppence slammed the front door and disappeared.

She checked into a hotel and spent two days, curtains drawn, sitting on the bed, crying and thinking, trying to piece together her childhood memories and reconcile them with what her mother had said. Gradually, overlooked details started to float into her mind from somewhere and position themselves into the mental images she had treasured and recalled. Little by little, not all of what her mother had said began to gel, but much of it did. She slowly, painfully, recast her memories in light of this new perspective and, for the third time in as many days, her heart shattered once more.

She packed her bags and went back round to her mother's house and the look they shared when her mother opened the door told its own story. Together, they spent the next few days, in a mostly silent pact: gathering up photos and old cards, personal possessions and clothes, arranging the funeral. All the time she hid amongst the practicalities of the present while her brain refiled and reallocated her memories, rearranging her own personal narrative in an attempt to leave her with something she could keep.

The months had passed and time had worked it's magic: burying some truths, allowing white lies to grow and fill blind spots in memory, joining the dots in a less painful way whilst allowing occasional reflection to not be too painful. Within a year she had met Jack and his initial charisma and presence had overwhelmed her, just as her father's had, knocking her off her feet and making her scream with laughter, delight in affection and attention, and remember the peaks that life can bring which all too often get hidden by the troughs immediately surrounding you.

But the months and years had gradually revealed her husband's true self. Now familiar with the mask and secrecy which her father had wielded she saw the signs in Jack and tried to quell her untrustworthy heart when it jumped up and told her all was not well. This was not happiness. This was not true love. This was a mirage. She wanted to believe, so desperately, that everything was fine. But time and again she found herself crying and wondering why. What did her tears know that she didn't?

She had placed her trust and love in two men in her life. One had spent her childhood betraying her and now she felt it was happening all over again. She wanted to love and be loved; want and be wanted. To be cherished and be held and be safe. What this small quiet church seemed to provide was what she had missed. Feeling it here, now, pulled everything into focus.

And all the time, this man sat quietly and held her hand.

Dick sat entranced by the awful torment this beautiful woman was laying bare to him. As she spoke his brain flitted from one scripture quote to another, seeking one that might be suitable, adequate, true. He found none, and when she had finished she raised her face to the altar, took one slow deep breath and then turned to look at him. Her eyes were red and smeared with black, her cheeks and hair were wet, her lips seemed bruised and cracked. She was the most beautiful mess he had ever seen and now she was imploring him to say something - anything - which would acknowledge this terrible transmission of her pain to him.

And he had absolutely nothing - nothing - to give her.

He felt completely inadequate; a fraud. He attempted a thin smile and it was only when she reached out a finger and wiped a tear from his own cheek that he realised he had been crying with her. When he looked up, the kirk seemed quite a lot darker than before. Excusing himself, he rose quickly and walked over to the pillar behind the pulpit and flicked a set of switches. Small wall lights came on and two large hanging chandeliers threw some light onto the nave. The rain suddenly grew heavier outside and Tuppence looked up at him as he came to sit back beside her.

"Can I ask what type of cancer your father had?" he asked, softly.

"Liver cancer. It spread to his bones." She looked at him keenly. "Does it matter?"

"No. It's just... well, the cycle ride I am training for - when you saw me earlier in my cycling gear? I'm training for a marathon cycle ride to London - for charity - and, well, its meant to raise money for the upkeep of this place." His eyes rolled up to the roof where some drops of rain were starting to leak down onto the last row of pews. "But I don't see any harm in portioning out a small part of the donations to go to something like Cancer Research."

"No." She shook her head and gave him a quite fierce look. "That wouldn't be right. I am more than capable of donating to Cancer Research myself and -" she looked suddenly away, eyes moistening again. "And I don't know why I didn't think of doing that before." She held his gaze again. "I certainly will now, though. Thank you."

Tuppence stood up in the pew and straightened her dress as best she could. It had not survived the ordeal well. "And thank-you for listening. This place has helped me." She looked around the kirk, marvelling at the effect it had had on her. "And you have helped me. And here was I thinking I didn't even need helping. Ha."

She looked down at herself and winced. "I don't know how I'm going to explain this to wardrobe and makeup back there. Not sure, actually, why no-one has come looking for me."

She started to walk back down the aisle towards the door.

"Just say you got caught in the rain." Dick suggested. "They'll believe it."

"Yes." She turned to him and smiled. "They probably will."

Dick watched Tuppence as she left, entranced by every swing of her arms, the tilt of her neck, the arc of her shoulders, the curve of her calves. Not for the first time in his life, he realised that it wasn't just the Lord that moved in a mysterious way.

SIX

"Hello?" Guy pushed gently at the shattered front door and watched it slowly swing open. "Anyone home? Con?" he stepped in warily, wondering if he should go back down in the lift and call the police first. When he saw spots of blood on the carpet he made up his mind and turned, only to hear what sounded like Conrad's voice coming from the kitchen.

"Con?" he called down the hallway and, against his better judgement, stepped gingerly into his flat, pulse thudding in his temple. Conrad was stock still at the kitchen table staring out of the window, trance-like.

"What the hell happened to you?" Guy surveyed the blood spattered table and the red handtowel wrapped around Conrad's hand.

"Cut myself shaving."

"What?"

"It's a joke, dummy." He looked at Guy with lifeless eyes.

"What sort of joke is-?" Guy teased the towel apart and then stepped back in shock. "Bloody hell! You've chopped your whole finger off!"

"Yeah, it smarts a bit."

"What did you do that for?"

"I didn't. Someone did."

"What someone? Who?" Guy looked frantically under the table and around the kitchen floor. "Where is it?"

"Gone."

"Gone?"

"Yeah, he took it."

"Christ! We've got to get you to a hospital." Guy bundled the unresponsive Conrad up from the table and out to his waiting car. He put Conrad into the passenger seat and fastened his seatbelt for him, like dealing with a zombie. When they were on the move, Guy turned to Conrad again. "What the fuck happened?"

"I need to speak to my father."

"What?"

"I need to call my father."

"Your father did this?"

"No. I need to call him."

"You're not making any sense." Guy put his foot down and tried to keep one eye on the road, one on his passenger. "You're in shock."

"It was Mr Chu."

"Who cut your finger off?"

"Yes. He wants his money back."

Guy slowed at some lights, tapping the steering wheel in frustration waiting for them to turn green. "The upfront ten grand? Well, give it him-." He turned slowly to look at Conrad. "You haven't? You fucking haven't?"

Conrad stared balefully out of the front window. He couldn't look Guy in the eye and so simply closed his eyes as the car sped through the empty streets.

Dougie sat in his car, by the recycling banks in a car park in Dalkeith, wondering if this was as glamorous as becoming a hitman would get. He dialled the number his brother-in-law had given him and waited for an answer. When the voice came on the line, it sounded busy and yet simultaneously distant, detached. Vacant and engaged at the same time, Dougie smiled at his own wit.

"This is Jack. Who's this?" The voice was odd - some syllables punchy and then others faint and squeezed out - like someone talking while they were trying to force out a shit.

"This is-." Dougie stopped himself just in time. This was his first engagement and he needed to act professionally. Cool, calm, objective. Menacing and purposeful. "You don't need to know who this is. DJ gave me your number."

The voice on the other stopped momentarily, and Dougie could hear a brief, muffled exchange with what sounded like a woman's voice, then a louder harsher complaint, then a door slamming. Finally the voice came back on the line.

"Sorry. I was … entertaining. My name is Jack."

"You already said. And you didn't need to. Let's keep this transaction business-like shall we? No names, no pack drill."

"Ok. What should I call you?"

"Don't. I'll call you when I need to talk. It won't be often. You just answer. No need to use my name."

"Ok."

"Understand?"

"I said ok."

"Good. Now, we need to meet to discuss details."

"Face to face, you mean?"

"Perhaps." Dougie realised he hadn't thought this all through particularly clearly. He decided to improvise. "You may not see me at our rendezvous. Or you may. But if you do I will be wearing a disguise."

"Ok. When and where?"

"Tomorrow afternoon, 2pm. I will text you the

location later tonight."

"Right. Ah, no. Hang on, I have training tomorrow afternoon."

"Here are your instructions: 1 - Wait, what?"

"I can't do 2pm tomorrow. I have training."

"Training?" Oh, Dougie thought, he's a footballer too. Shit. This wasn't supposed to be how it went. He tried to recover. "Right. Ok, when can you do?"

"Erm, Wednesday is free - knocked out of Europe you see."

"Oh. That's a shame." Dougie found himself on the back foot, forced into a nodding conversation with his client when he had wanted to keep things all brusque and business-like.

"Yes. Last minute equaliser in Dortmund. Away goals rule."

"Right." Dougie had no idea what Jack had just said.

"And Friday. Day before a match, that's always free."

"Right. Ok, well Wednesday then. Here are your instructions: 1. Come alone. 2. Bring a down-payment - ten grand should do."

"Ok. I can do that."

Dougie instantly wished he'd asked for more. "And bring relevant material along."

"Relevant material?"

"Yes. Photos. Details of the usual movements, upcoming engagements. That sort of thing."

"Mine, you mean?"

"No, Jack. The target's." Christ, being a hitman seemed awfully like working in IT.

"Ah, ok."

"Anything I can use to build up a profile and start to track the vic-, er, target's whereabouts."

"Right, Ok. Er, that may take a while."

"Really?" Dougie was beginning to think this whole thing was a whole lot more hassle than it was made to appear in the movies. He didn't recall Jason Bourne ever having to haggle over arrangements. "Ok, Friday then."

"Fine. Whereabouts?"

"I told you, I'll text you later. And Jack?" Dougie thought he had better show he was in charge. "Discretion in this matter is vital. The phone I am using is disposable. Next time we speak I will be using a different one. You will not know where to find me unless I want to be found. I will not divulge anything about this matter to anyone."

"No. Neither will I."

"Good. Because if at any time - before or after our transaction is completed - there should be any mention of my identify or involvement of any kind in what is agreed, I will come after you. I will find you. And I will kill you."

There was a long pause sigh at the other end of the phone and Dougie smiled to himself. This was actually working!

"I understand."

"Good. Then we have an accord. Friday in Edinburgh. You will receive a text beforehand."

"Fine. Excellent."

"Good night, Jack."

"Yes. Good night."

Conrad was self-medicating on Guy's gin and, whilst his injury was now cleanly sutured and freshly dressed, his mood was filthy.

"Who needs fucking Borders mills, huh? It's all bollocks anyway isn't it?"

"Sorry, what are you talking about?"

Conrad ignored him and continued in rant mode. "Just bollocks. Look at Pringle, case in point. Based in Hawick for generations, worldwide reputation for product quality. Then snapped up by a company in - wait for it - Hong Kong!" Conrad waved his bandaged hand triumphantly. "Who promptly move production to Asia and shut the Borders site down. All that's left of two hundred years history - two hundred years! - is a factory outlet. They're all fucking history, is what they are." He put his empty glass down with an emphatic thud. "History, the lot of 'em."

"Con, what's this all about Pringle?"

"Bad management, poor designs, tired image. That's what it's about. Pringle was losing money hand over fist. Fucking prehistoric equipment, ancient working practices. They say it's about attention to detail, hand-finishing, quality craftsmanship. Fucking medieval inefficiency is what it is. Streamline production, move it to China, ta-da! That's the future."

Guy was still unaware of Conrad's rationale for this outburst but, if there was one thing he did know about, it was hand-making clothing. He enjoyed it, felt he was good at it and believed strongly in the artisanal model. If Conrad wasn't going to tell him what he was ranting about, Guy felt he should at least inject a note of factual accuracy into the fast-becoming-drunken-bombast

"Now hang on, Con. Borders mills are renowned for quality. Craftsmanship. Attention to detail. Always have been. But that costs. A lot. And there's only luxury brands can afford it."

"Pringle went abroad." Conrad sniffed.

"Yes, but Pringle aren't a luxury brand. Maybe you could describe them as high-end but not luxury. They're like one or two steps up from Marks & Sparks. They're not competing with the likes of Dior or Hermes."

"Who made you a fucking expert suddenly?"

"I did - by going to lectures that you've been skipping!" That shut Conrad up momentarily. Guy pressed home his advantage. "The market is segregating into luxury and bargain-basement. Anyone in the middle is going to get squeezed out: they can't make it cheap enough to compete with the likes of Primark, Zara, H&M; can't make it well enough to compete with Hermes, Chanel, Dior. Go abroad or go to the wall. Pringle went abroad."

"But it's not the money. It's the time."

"Time is money." Guy smiled.

"No, I mean I'm not arguing against Borders quality craftmanship-"

"Yes you are."

"Ok, I am. But I'm playing double's avocado. What I'm saying is that you can get Borders-quality stuff from elsewhere that's just as good-"

"No you can't. And it's *devil's advocate.*"

"Whatever. My point is - you *can* get it *and* you can get it faster. The Borders mills take ages. Antiquated technology. Old biddies peering through magnifying glass hand-finishing buttonholes and seams. Cramped, dated facilities which don't provide the bandwidth that a new plant does. Take it abroad, get it faster with the same quality."

"Con, you can't."

"Are you saying that you can't have good quality and

fast time-to-market?"

"Yes."

"Why?"

"Because the quality comes from the very time and care taken."

"Doesn't."

"Does."

"Doesn't."

"Oh, for fuck's sake, Con! What's this all about?"

Conrad looked up through his fringe and Guy realised his friend might have been crying. "The bastards rejected my designs."

It was an admission of defeat and honesty that had Guy, for a few moments, trying to recall if Conrad had ever confessed before.

"Pringle?"

"No. Merry & McKay." Conrad sloppily poured himself more gin and added. "I'm fucked, Guy."

"Because one mill said *No*? That doesn't mean you're... done for."

"It's discrimination is what it is. Discrimination of the worst kind."

"What kind is that?"

"The kind against me! They basically told me my designs were unmanufacturable. And the material was poor."

"Well, try someone else."

"Guy." Conrad looked his friend straight in the eye for the first time. "I have no money. Worse, I have no money and I owe money. I owe Mr Chu money and I owe money to all the people who just worked on my photoshoot. Billy, Ed, Tuppence. And I have no time for denial and error."

"Trial and error." Corrected Guy. "Who's Tuppence?"

"The model, you know?"

"Tuppence Lowry?"

"Dunno. Old pal of Liv's apparently." Conrad spat the name. "Anyway I owe her money too."

"I'm sure she'll survive."

Conrad looked inquisitively at Guy.

"Seriously?" Guy screwed his face up. "She's married to Jack-Jack?"

"The perfume guy?"

"Well, actually he's a footballer. Plays for Hibs. But, yeah, the perfume guy."

"Shit. They must be loaded. Nice that someone is." Conrad said, not at all convincingly. "But look, unless or until I pay Mr Chu his money I will end up with fewer fingers." He waggled his bandaged left hand. "And currently my only source of money, my fantastic father, has also told me my designs are no good and he will not finance them as they stand."

Guy looked at his friend sitting forlornly across the table from him.

"I have some money."

"And Mister Yeo, my Hong Kong supplier and potential manufacturing alternative wants more money - always more money - in order to equip his facility and procure raw materials."

"I said: I have some money."

Conrad looked at his friend, cocked his head to one side. "No, Guy. No."

"Look. It's not much. Few grand of savings I've scraped together. Probably." Guy mentally scratched his head. "Yeah. Something like that."

"Well." Conrad said, wavering.

"It might help save your fingers."

"Not unless I put it on red 17 and turn it into ten grand." Conrad brightened.

"No. Don't do that."

"You object to me risking your life savings?"

"Yes, I do. Plus I think you'll find 17 is black."

Stobo Kirk sits prettily, set back along a B-road that runs from Lyne towards Dawyck and Drumelzier. Technically in the grounds of Stobo Castle, a popular and successful upmarket health spa and hotel, it predates the Castle by some centuries. One of the oldest churches in Scotland, dating from as early as the 6th Century although the current building is a mere stripling built in the 1100's. The castle itself is a tremulous newcomer, finished in 1811.

A neat gravel path leads up from wrought-iron churchyard gates around the back of the kirk. The cemetery contains many old graves, the oldest nearest the gates, and as the path moves uphill, so the graves are newer until, right at the top, behind the kirk and out of sight, is a flat stretch of land bounded by stone walls, where present-day burials occur.

This morning, under a scudding sky of white and grey, kneels a figure in a cowboy hat with eyes moist. He has laid fresh flowers on the grave and trimmed the grass with scissors, removed the weeds. It's been a month or so since Cullen was last here and the maintenance was sorely needed. His hands shake, though, not in memory of his wife buried here but for the vandals who have caused him to pick up the pieces of the stone vase which lay shattered on the grave. Holding them in his right hand, now bloody from the sharp edges, he stares angrily at the headstone, cut in the shape of a Celtic cross. The leftmost arm, beyond the central ring, bears a ragged, damaged edge and several large chips from it lie on the ground.

He should have come sooner. He should have been visiting more often. He had no excuse. What excuse did they have for committing this, this outrage?

He stands and turns to leave, looking carefully around for evidence of other graves vandalised, other signs of damage, but sees none. Pinching the moisture from his eyes between his thumb and forefinger, he walks down to the kirk where he left his backpack leaning inside the porch. He tries the cedar wood door, which opens, as always but there is no-one inside. No-one around.

Cullen puts the stone pieces from the vase into an outer pocket of his pack, shoulders it, and stalks down to the main gates and the wooden signage board. He checks the time and day for the next scheduled service and then trudges back to the road, cutting across to the John Buchan Way and heading off towards The Glack and home for the night.

Jack had been balls-deep in Angelique when the call came in. He been resting his phone in the small of her back, on vibrate, and when it rang she gave an additional moan. He picked it up and held it to his ear with his left hand while he continue guiding himself into her with his right on her beautifully tattooed buttock. When he realised who was calling, to say it affected his libido would be an understatement. Angelique uttered a confused and disappointed "Hey!" as he withdrew his suddenly limp cock, slapped her arse and told her to get dressed. When she wheeled around to argue that she wasn't that type of girl, Jack had glared at her, threw her a roll of fifties bound with a rubber band and climbed off the back of the sofa, walking towards the window scratching his belly. Angelique scurried to pick up the wad of notes, scooped her clothes and high heels off the floor and flounced out of the room, but then must have had second thoughts.

When Jack got off the call, he turned away from the window. Angelique was crawling towards him, naked on all fours, purring loudly. By the time she reached his groin he was nearly erect again. Within minutes he was inside her.

"Oh, Jack."

"Unh."

"Jack."

"Unh."

She heard a different buzzing sound and felt the heel of his palm on her back vibrate as he continued to thrust into her. "Jack?"

"Unh."

"Jack?"

"Ahhhhhhhhhhhh." He collapsed onto her and she saw his phone fall onto the sheet beside her.

"Jack?"

"Sorry." He gulped air. "Text."

It said, simply: `IKEA car park, 10am`.

The last hour in the Coach & Horses, thought Guy, may have been the best hour of thinking he'd ever done. Perhaps the best hour of thinking *anyone* had ever done.

119

Ever.

He couldn't be certain, of course, because unfortunately he'd already forgotten it. Conrad, on the other hand, had now had so much to drink that he appeared to have wrapped himself around the drunk spectrum and was now intriguingly coherent.

Having finished off Guy's gin and flush with his newfound, albeit temporary wealth, he had suggested they pop into the pub to celebrate and plan the next steps.

"So that's agreed then." Conrad emphasised.

Guy was tried to communicate via the medium of controlled burping but Conrad just gave him a funny look so he tried to marshal his lips into emitting some form of speech.

"Run that past me again?"

"What we agreed?"

"Yep, that too."

"Right. OK, it's brilliance. Sheer brilliance. You and me, Guy. What a team!" Guy grasped this opportunity to participate by simply nodding and allowed Conrad to proceed.

"So, first we steal Liv's designs."

"What?"

"From the mill?"

"What?"

"Guy! You sound like Father Jack."

"What?"

"Will you stop it with the *what*!"

"What?"

Conrad looked sternly at his friend, admonishing him like a primary school teacher. "I'm beginning to think that someone's not been paying attention."

Guy looked around wildly for that foolish someone and then, seeing nobody behind him, slowly turned back to Conrad.

"OK, look. Let me run through it, uninterrupted. And then maybe you can get all your *what's* out of the way at the end, hmm?"

This sounded eminently sensible to Guy, so he nodded and tried to convince Conrad he was concentrating by staring hard at the bridge of his friend's nose. Conrad, slightly taken aback by this new fixed countenance, slowly moved his head from side to side. When he saw that Guy's eyes tracked his movement, he decided they were good to go.

"So, we steal Liv's designs from the mill. That's where they're making her samples up and I can't believe these old places have got anything in the way of security at all. Sure they protect the bales and yarns and such, but paperwork? Forget it. This will serve three separate and yet connected purposes: firstly, it means I'll have designs which can definitely be manufactured. My sneering father's words will crumble to dust when he sees my designs produced in double-quick time by Mr Yeo. And I will show him my worth!"

"With someone else's designs?"

"Shut up. This was your idea!"

"Was it?"

"Yes. Second, I debut my collection - actually hers - at London Fashion Week and make the garments available to buy and take away before the end of the show and all eyes will be on me and my new business model. I will have revolutionised couture!"

Guy nodded appreciatively at the plan's beauty.

"And third, and most exquisite joy, by using her

designs two days beforehand, I then force Chanel to abandon their marquee show and they have nothing to put up for London Fashion Week. Liv is a failure and loses her job and I steal her crown as the new Queen of Fashion!"

"Blimey!"

"You see? You see?" Conrad was beaming. "What a team."

"There is…" Guy was attempting to frame a question so Conrad gave him some space. "Something bothering me…" He burped again. "About the plan."

"Well, I think we've eliminated all the faults and burnished until it shines brightly, but go for it, brainiac."

Guy forced his thoughts into single file and checked the order. "Something about the stealing… and passing off the theft as your own work… something something?"

Conrad was appalled. "That's the best part!"

"Really?"

"Yes! Liv is ruined, I am triumphant. All it takes is a tiny, tiny, almost insignificant crime."

Guy wasn't big on the pecking order of crimes these days, not having it memorised like the ranking of poker hands, for example. But he thought maybe that theft, whilst maybe not as great as a full house was certainly more serious than Ace high.

"Are you sure theft is insignificant?"

"Well…" Conrad gave it some consideration. "It's certainly less weighty than kidnapping."

"Well, yeah." Guy thought, kidnapping sounds like a full house; maybe even four-of-a-kind. "But we're not talking about kidnapping are we?"

"D'uh! That's how we're going to raise the money,

idiot." Conrad looked deep into his friend's eyes. "I swear, Guy, sometimes it's like you're not even here."

"What money?" Guy's thought processes were still bringing up the rear.

"The ransom money! You do understand how kidnappings work?"

"Yes. Obviously." Guy breathed in deeply and slowly and felt a bit better. "But I've just given you money."

"Yeah, but that's not enough!" Conrad laughed and Guy suddenly felt hugely crestfallen. "That's nowhere near enough. We need big money."

Guy sat silently and Conrad seemed reluctant to let the conversation just end like this.

"So you're not happy about the kidnapping?"

"I thought we were talking about theft?" Guy pondered. "I could maybe manage theft."

"We were talking about theft. And kidnapping."

"And. You see, that's quite heavy isn't it? Seems heavy to me, anyway. Couldn't we at least downgrade it to theft *or* kidnapping?"

Conrad prodded him in the ribs, hissing. "There's no point in the theft if we don't have the money from the kidnapping. Do you see?"

Guy thought for moment and then simply nodded.

"Oh good, thought we'd lost you there for a minute. We need the money to fund the operation that turns Liv's designs into finished garments we can sell at London Fashion Week."

"The stolen designs?"

"The very same."

"So you kidnap someone-"

"We."

"We?" Guy mulled this over for a minute before

continuing. "So, we kidnap someone to obtain a ransom so that we can use that money to have the stolen designs turned into clothes that we later sell at London Fashion Week?"

"Knew it'd all come back to you." Conrad slapped Guy on the back. "It'll be a peach of cake."

"Right." It seemed to fall into place, although none of it seemed at all familiar.

"And who are we going to kidnap?"

"That." Conrad wagged the index finger on his good hand in front of his face, triumphantly. "That is the other genius bit!"

"Are you going to tell me, then?"

"No." Conrad teased. "I already told you and you've clearly forgotten. Perhaps you'll remember when you sober up."

Guy winced trying to see if he could winkle a name from his brain but all was foggy and indistinct. Although one thought did manage to make its way through the murk.

"Ok, But I do have one question."

"Fine. Shoot!"

"What about my rent?"

Where the fuck did she keep it? And how many fucking clothes did this woman have? Jesus, ok, she's a model and everything, but fuck me. He was rooting through her wardrobe when he heard a key in the door. Jack rushed into the living room and threw himself onto a sofa, grabbing the remote.

"Only me!" Tuppence walked over to him, bent down and kissed him on the top of his head. "Busting for a waz, as you would say!" She dropped her handbag heavily on the kitchen counter and skittered off into the downstairs toilet, shucking her skirt as she did so.

Jack saw an opportunity and dived for her handbag, rifling through the separate compartments until he found a small battered filofax, black leather with a clasp and a myriad of small brightly coloured post-its and tabs sticking out from its edges. He wrestled it free from the folds of the lining as he heard the toilet flush and ran back to the sofa, stuffing the diary behind a cushion. Mission accomplished.

Tuppence emerged from the cloakroom, starting to unbutton the cuffs of her blouse. She took off her shoes as she walked over and sat down next to him. He edged slightly away from her, wedging himself more firmly between her and the concealing cushion.

"That's better!" She kissed him again, this time on the cheek. "Didn't expect to see you here, babe. That's why I left the note."

"What note?"

"By the fruit bowl?" She pointed over to the glass dining table. In the centre was a large bowl full of oranges, grapes and kiwi fruit. There was a large white card leaning against it. "It doesn't matter. You're here now. I'm going away for a couple of days. Photoshoot. I need to make tracks. Cab'll be here in five and I haven't packed a thing."

"Didn't you do one just the other day?"

"Yes, but that was tiny. Favour for a friend of a friend." Tuppence stood up to go and started unbuttoning her blouse and skirt. "This is the real deal. Down at some mill in the Borders. Bankholm, maybe? Chanel anyway."

Jack watched her disappear into the bedroom and sat, looking forward to an unexpected freedom pass. She came back into the room, trundling a pastel roll-along case behind her, grabbed a raincoat from one of the coathooks by the door and shucked it on.

"Right, I think that's all." She flipped through her handbag to check she had everything and Jack froze. She rooted in each compartment and then again, a second time, seeming to go through each one again more carefully. He felt his mouth dry up as she looked up at him and then scanned the room urgently. "I don't suppose you've seen my address book anywhere, have you?"

PART TWO

THREE DAYS LATER...

.

SEVEN

Jack was banging his head against the black stone wall which had been dripping with sweat and condensation to which he was now adding his own blood. His right eye was jammed closed and felt a mile wide, throbbing and tender; through his left he could make out the DJ shouting unintelligibly into a speaker system which just reverberated pounding bass. The slave mistress who had chained his hands and feet and bound his limbs with stiff leather laces, licked his face and stared into his semi-vision like a rabid horse with angry yellow eyes rimmed with smeared mascara.

His head felt as if it would explode as the thudding beat degenerated into an insistent electronic pulse and Jack opened his mouth to howl. The woman slammed his face into the wall one more time and Jack woke up on the carpet with his phone beeping angrily

When he tried to focus on the pile and pattern of the carpet he realised his vision *was* blurry and his head *did* hurt like fuck. His hands and feet were fine but as he pulled himself up onto his knees his back arched and he retched and emptied the contents of his stomach onto the floor. There was some blood. He stared at it for a few seconds and then reached for the phone.

"Where the fuck are you?" A very angry voice.

"Who's this?" Jack remained staring at the blood in his vomit.

"This is the person you were supposed to meet in IKEA five minutes ago, fuckwit."

129

The IKEA store looked just like any other, a big blue box on the outskirts of Edinburgh. Jack pulled into a row of empty spaces far from the main entrance where he couldn't be seen and flashed his headlights three times as agreed.

On the passenger seat was his phone, a folded scrap of paper torn from a notepad and the brown bag from a McDonald's Big Mac meal he had grabbed from a drive-in en route. Having eaten it all ravenously, Jack had instantly brought it all back up into the same bag from which it had come.

Jack did a quick assessment of his condition: he looked like shit and his car stank to high heaven. When the phone rang this time the voice on the end was much calmer.

"Well done, Jack. Now go to Penicuik and park in the Lidl car park in the town centre."

"Where?"

"Penicuik."

"Penny Cook? Where the fuck's that?"

"Turn left when you leave here and follow the signs. It's not far. When you get into the town centre you'll see a Lidl on your left. Park in there and wait for my call."

"What f-"

"I'll be watching you. If anyone else is with you or following you I will know and the deal's off."

"Oh. Ok."

Jack followed the directions, found the Lidl and parked in a disabled spot - the only empty space in the car park. As he pulled up he realised he should have been keeping an eye out in his rearview mirror to see if he could make out the hitman's car, but he was too hung over to think clearly. Anyway, surely the whole point of this fucking charade was to meet the guy in the first place? He'd see what he looked like soon enough.

He opened the car door intending to drop his McDonalds Bag-O-Vomit into a bin when his phone rang.

"Follow me. I'm in a white Range Rover."

Jack saw the car pulling out into traffic and hurriedly closed the door again and reversed out of the space to give chase. An elderly driver honked his horn as he narrowly missed hitting him. Jack wound down his window and flipped him a V-sign.

"Can't you see I'm fucking handicapped? Wanker."

He spotted the Range Rover three cars ahead of him and kept it in his sights as they drove out of town, up a winding hill and into open countryside. To his left was a steep gash in the land which dropped away sharply into a narrow gorge; to his right, fields of heather and gorse, brown and purple with exposed rocky patches stretching out flatly towards mottled hills in the distance. The road dipped and lurched and then embraced a long straight section where Jack could see the white Range Rover clearly in the distance. He saw the car indicate left just as it vanished round a long bend.

Jack slowed and kept a lookout for a turning as he wound left along the road. The vista opened out in front of him as he did so, to rolling hills and the road ribboning through them into the clear blue distance. On his left was large lay-by with separate entry and exit points; the white Range Rover was parked up in the centre, indicators blinking.

Jack pulled in and parked behind the white car and

stopped his engine. Sporadic traffic zoomed past along the A-road, every now and then a lorry. His phone rang again.

"Come and join me."

Jack got out of his car and walked nervously up to the car, around to his left and got into the passenger seat.

"Hello." Dougie held out his hand and Jack gripped it in disbelief. This man was an eight stone weakling! Five eight at most, rake thin, spindly with piercing little eyes and a razor thin nose a little too large for his face. He had a scrawny neck and large sticky-out ears protruding either side of a scruffy non-descript baseball cap which was stuffed onto his head, and a gold ring through his right nostril. The outfit was completed by a camo jacket that looked long in the sleeve and combat trousers tucked into a pair of Doc Marten's that had seen better days.

"Is this some kind of joke?" Jack looked around wildly, imagining perhaps that the real killer was lurking somewhere on the backseat.

"No joke." His handshake was surprisingly tight and Jack's brow furrowed slightly as he wondered if perhaps he had judged this man too quickly. "Do you have what I asked?"

"Yeah, but-"

"No buts, Jack." He partially unzipped his jacket and pulled it to one side to reveal a gun holstered under one armpit. "Let's see what you've got."

Jack handed him an envelope from his jacket pocket containing the money and the slip of paper he'd written down the photoshoot appointment on. The man turned the piece of paper over as if expecting to see something on the back.

"Is this it?"

"Yeah, sorry." Jack felt as if he'd genuinely let the man down. "Couldn't get her diary."

"Fuck's sake. Tell me you've at least got a photo?"

"Er-" Jack rummaged desperately in his wallet, realising his error. "Yeah, here. Here." He handed over a slightly crumpled head-and-shoulders snap of his wife and him together at an awards dinner a while back.

A car horn sounded harshly somewhere and an angry incoherent shout carried on the wind.

"Beautiful." The man surveyed the photo and raised an eyebrow at him. "You sure this is what you want?"

"Yes." Jack whispered, feeling once again that he was letting the man down. "Yes." He managed more certainly.

The man flicked through the cash in the envelope and, satisfied, stashed it into a pocket in his cargo pants. "Ok, go." He nodded towards Jack car. "Drive off and don't look back. I'll be in touch when it's done."

Dougie watched Jack until his car disappeared and out of sight, then retrieved the envelope from his trouser pocket and started counting the money to make sure it was all there. He had been too nervous to count it in front of Jack and had wanted to hide the fact that his hands were shaking uncontrollably during their entire encounter.

It was all there. And here he was, now. Committed. Actually engaged to kill someone. A very beautiful someone too. He looked again at the photo of the woman and the hairs prickled on the back of his neck. He shivered involuntarily as he jammed the envelope of cash into his pocket, then almost had a heart attack as there was an enormous thud on the window right beside his head. He turned to stare right into the face of a blue-eyed, red-faced man wearing a cycle helmet, banging on the driver's window repeatedly shouting "Did you see it? Did you? Did you see it?"

Dougie's first thought was that a little bit of wee had escaped. His second thought was that this man might have seen him looking at the photo or counting the money in the envelope. Trying to calm his nerves while his heart still thumped loudly in his chest, he wound down the window halfway and immediately felt the sting on his face from the brisk breeze and the smell of sweaty exertion from the cyclist.

"Would you mind not banging on my window like that?"

The man was breathing heavily, through his mouth, and it took him a few moments to compose himself and calm down enough to respond. "Sorry. Shock, I think"

"Shock?" Dougie started nervously, on high alert. What had this bloody man seen?

"Yes. I'll be alright in a minute." The man tried to steady his breathing and took off his helmet to wipe his brow with his sleeve. "Did you see him, though? Did you?"

Dougie's eyes narrowed. "Who?"

"The bloody loony who ran me off the road! Stupid tosser in the HGV - 'scuse my French."

"Oh. Er, no actually." Dougie's flight-or-fight system was flooded with relief. The buffoon hadn't seen anything, he was after a witness to some minor road accident. "Sorry."

"Just came round that corner, sent me flyin'. All over

134

the road! Must have been doing 70-odd easy! These things are supposed to have speed-limiters on 'em, you know, but they fiddle 'em so's they can-. Sorry, what did you say?"

"I didn't see anything. Sorry."

"But you must have. It happened right there. You couldn't miss-"

"I'm sorry. I'm afraid I didn't see anything." Dougie started his engine and began winding his window up.

To say the man was crestfallen was an understatement.

"What about your friend? Perhaps he saw something?"

Dougie stopped his window halfway and felt all his senses go to Defcon 1. "What friend?"

"The friend who-" The man noticed, for the first time, that Dougie was alone in the car. "Who *was* sitting next to you." He looked around puzzled.

"There was no-one sitting next to me." He felt like Obi-Wan Kenobi trying to persuade the stormtroopers these were not the 'droids they were looking for.

"I'm sure I saw you talking to someone, sat next to you, when I was picking myself up over by the-" He turned to point to the spot on the road where he'd presumably come off his bike, but Dougie had already hit his window button again.

"I've been here alone the whole time. Maybe it's shock?" Dougie suggested to him as his window slid upwards

"I could have sworn..." The man shook his head from side to side, as if scanning the ground.

Dougie's window snicked into place and he put the car into gear as the man banged on his window again. He wound the window down, glaring now, intent on giving the man short shrift. Instead, the man handed over a crisp, white business card.

"In case you do remember something. Later on."

He smiled sadly and walked dejectedly across to his bike which he must have earlier lifted up out of harm's way and left lying high on the grassy verge. Dougie watched as he checked his steering, brakes and chain, remounted and wobbled slowly forwards, pushing hard up the slope to the layby exit. He lifted one hand in a parting gesture towards Dougie as he passed unsteadily by and Dougie noticed the small red camera light on his helmet slowly winking.

Recording.

He looked down at the name on the business card in his hand: Richard Money.

That Sunday morning, as Dick stood at the kirk door shaking hands with the members of the congregation as they filed slowly out, he noticed a tall figure in a cowboy hat hanging back. When everyone else had finally gone, Dick turned to the man with an enquiring smile.

"Can I help you, Mister…?"

"Cullen, Father."

"Please, there's no need for the Father. I am not yet a minister, Mr Cullen." He gave a hopeful smile.

"Just Cullen. No need for the Mister."

"Ahm, right. Ok, Cullen. I think I may have, perhaps, seen you before?"

"Perhaps." The man was, it seemed, in no mood for small talk.

"In church?"

Cullen remained silent and Dick started to feel more than a little awkward. He broke the silence.

"So, how may I help?"

"It's about my wife's grave." A ripple of sadness seemed to travel across the man's face and then was gone.

"I see. Would this be a new plot?"

"No." The man frowned. "Her grave is up on the back there. It's been damaged."

"Really?" Now it was Dick's turn to frown. "Would you mind showing me?"

Dick bustled after the man who's lengthy stride ate up the gravel path as it wound round the back of the kirk. Note to self, thought Dick, better step up the training program. This man had more than a decade on him and he wasn't even breaking a sweat.

They stopped at the foot of a neat plot on the end of a row closest to the surrounding stone wall. Dick noticed there was a small amount of damage to the wall, fresh stone chips and shards scattered in the grass beside the grave. He looked on as Cullen pointed out substantial damage done to the headstone and showed him the stumpy remains of the vase. To Dick, churchyards were sacrosanct and extensions of Gods' house - no place for the vandalism this appeared to be.

"I'm afraid I don't know what to say, Mr... sorry, Cullen." Dick bit his lip. "I'm not aware of anything ever happening like this before. Round here, I mean. You know, churchyards can attract kids at night - spooky playgrounds, games of fright, and all that. But... not around here." There aren't any kids for a start, he thought. Plus this looked like it must have required tools or metal implements of some kind to make so many chips and split the stone so cleanly. His thoughts started to wander but Cullen brought them to heel.

"Only my wife's grave is affected."

"Are you sure?"

"I looked."

"When?" Dick asked. "When did you say you discovered this… damage?."

"I didn't." He looked blankly at Dick. "Earlier this week. Wednesday."

"There's damage to the wall here too." Dick bent down to examine one of the larger fragments and then straightened, looking along the row of graves. "But, yes. It doesn't look like any other plots have been affected." He preferred the term plot over grave - especially when talking to relatives. It helped prevent unhelpful emotions.

He looked at Cullen now, trying to weigh up the man's mood. "I'm sorry to ask this, Cullen. But do you know who it might have been? Someone who, perhaps, had a grievance with you or your…?"

"No." An immediate retort.

"What I mean is…?"

"I know what you mean." Cullen interrupted again. "No-one but me knows this is here. No-one but me knows it is *her* grave."

"I see."

"No-one."

"Yes. Quite. Yes, I understand." Dick nervously tried to reassure this man he had unintentionally riled. While he tried to gather his thoughts, Cullen paced the area, searching the grass.

"There are marks."

"Really?" Dick scuttled over. At each end of the row of graves - plots, damn it, plots - there was a pattern of holes and indentations in the grass. The holes several inches deep, arranged in a rectangle or diamond shape. The grass along the back of the row, between each plot and the wall, was flattened and slightly muddy. There had been the traffic of feet and some… suddenly the penny dropped.

"The film crew."

Cullen looked at him, puzzled.

"The photoshoot! There was a photoshoot up here the other day." Dick announced, as if Cullen would have known all about it. "Cameras, lights, lots of heavy boxes and stands. Makeup people milling about. There was one of those large American trailer things parked by the gates - beautiful women going in and out dressed in all these costumes, having their pictures taken all over the place. It was really quite exciting." He was getting all worked up again, remembering it. Remembering Tuppence.

"Photoshoot?"

"Yes." Dick was really motoring now. "They'd been over at the castle, taking pictures and everything and they offered a substantial - I mean, substantial - donation towards the upkeep of the kirk in exchange for being able to use the grounds here as well. Although I haven't yet received it." Dick made a mental note to chase this up.

"Who?"

"What? Oh, sorry. Erm… not sure he gave me his name, actually." Dick tried, unsuccessfully, to recall some detail. "Chinese chap."

"Who was?"

"The head guy. Young fellow. Fashion Designer, I think. Seemed to be the organiser, anyway. He was the one who promised me the donation." That he did remember. Cullen's face appeared to be darkening as Dick wittered on. "That'll be it. They must have caused the damage. I'm afraid that, well you know, we're not insured for this sort of thing. Gra-, er plot owners must take care of their own, er, plots. Pay for their own upkeep, as it were."

"If this Chinese man caused the damage then he must pay."

"Well, you must take that up with him, of course." Dick wasn't sure he liked where this was going. "It is not a matter for the church to get involved in."

"Hmm." Cullen considered this for a moment, glaring at Dick. Dick, for his part, averted his gaze and found something interesting in one of his fingernails.

"Over at the castle you say?"

"Yes." A relieved Dick sensed this conversation reaching a peaceful conclusion. "Stobo Castle, over the way?

"Aye."

"Yes. They may even have been staying there as well, now I come to think of it. Perhaps their records will show who it was." Cullen didn't look too convinced but Dick pressed home his advantage. "Well, I am sorry for the damage here, Mr... Cullen. However, I hope you don't mind but I have another service to hold over at Broughton in half an hour so I really need to skidaddle. Do let me know if you do manage to track down our designer friend. I can see I will need to arrange to have someone repair our boundary wall as well, so if he is willing to offer compensation..." And with that, Dick made a hasty but, he hoped, still dignified exit.

"Night, Dougie. Will you lock up?"

"Am I last again?"

"Looks like it." Mandy nodded. "I'll check on the way down and call your phone if there's anyone else left."

He looked at his phone, surprised to find it was 6.15 already. "Isn't the big meeting still going on. Brenda asked me to hang around until they finished, in case anything went wrong."

"Oh, that finished ages ago. They're well gone."

"What! But I've been…" Mandy disappeared and didn't call back up. He was alone in the building.

He massaged the back of his neck and took a sip from his coffee mug which was stone cold.

"Fuck this."

He took out the photo of his intended victim from his wallet, took a photo of it with his phone and uploaded it to google image search. His jaw dropped as he surveyed the results.

Tuppence Lowry, top model, upcoming fashion icon. Most often seen on the arms of her husband Jack Something-unprounceable. He flicked through the many photos. Tuppence wearing evening gowns, slit to the waist; wearing outfits on the catwalk open to the navel; a photo of her from behind, wearing a sheer dress scooped down to the very top of her buttocks while Jack had his arms around her. The caption read: *Jack hugs his wife backstage.* Aye, thought Dougie, we can all see her backstage.

He popped to the kitchen to put the kettle on and made himself a coffee while he thought it over. Back at his desk, he googled some more trying to find out as much about this pair as he could. This man Jack, the man who'd sat in his car and given him ten grand to kill his

141

wife, was a high-profile footballer alright. Athletic and good-looking, he endorsed underwear, aftershave, haircare products, had his own line of football boots. His wife must coin it as well, looking at the catwalk appearances and magazine covers. Together they must be pulling in 7-figures a year.

He was mulling this over when his phone alarm went off. The message said: 6.45pm mass, Stobo.

Dougie dropped his unfinished coffee, grabbed his coat and headed for the door.

The last of the congregation were leaving as Dougie pulled up outside Stobo Kirk. A thin stream of pensioners wound unsteadily down to the main road where many of them had parked their cars. Dougie sat patiently in the early evening light, listening to the birds, waiting for the reverend to lock up and leave.

After some considerable delay, he eventually appeared in the porch of the kirk, locked the door and Dougie could now see why he had taken so long to emerge: he had swapped his dog collar, grey shirt and trousers for vivid lycra and his precious cycling helmet. The recording light on it was already winking and Dougie stiffened involuntarily in his seat. The lurid figure trod gingerly down the gravel path to the kirk gate and retrieved his bike from where it been waiting, partially hidden, locked up against the railings.

Dougie wondered if this was what the modern church had become: a place where even God's messenger had to chain his bike to the railings in case a worshipper nicked it. He waited as the cyclist wobbled down to the main road, and hung back for a while wondering quite how he was going to follow a cyclist in his car without being spotted. Then, panicking that he might lose the man if he turned off somewhere, followed on and saw him in the distance moving along at a fair clip.

Dougie overtook the cyclist and, when he reached a junction took a punt, turned left and parked up in a large layby from where he could keep an eye on traffic arriving at the junction in his rear view mirror. He turned off his engine and lights and waited for the man to reappear.

The vicar appeared a few minutes later and Dougie watched him turn right towards Peebles. He decided to take the same tack he'd just taken so he started his car, pulled out and overtook the cyclist and kept going straight until he found another junction a mile to so further on at which he could pull over and see which route the rider took. He repeated this overtake-and-wait strategy, pleased with himself that it was working so well, until he reached a car park on edge of town. When the cyclist passed him this time, he followed slowly at a distance, happy that the road had narrowed with cars parked on both sides making a slower speed unremarkable. Almost too soon, the bike turned left and the man disappeared from view. Dougie followed into a narrow one-way street and then saw the rider suddenly veer off to the right, between two parked cars, and swing himself off the bike as he braked to a walking dismount.

With another car's lights now behind him, Dougie had to keep going but got a clear look in his rear view mirror of the front gate the vicar opened and the metal railings which ran along the front wall to his garden. When he reached the next junction he made a note of the street name: Rosetta Road.

When he arrived back home, Dick showered and made himself a quick tuna salad. He ate it sitting at his desk while updating his Facebook page and blog with footage grabbed from his GoPro. He scrolled down the page to review his post before he submitted it and spotted a new photo pulsing amongst those of his collected friends. It was Tuppence. Disbelievingly, he clicked on it and was immediately transported back those few days to their first meeting and watched as her own home page grew on his screen.

She had accepted his invitation to be his friend! It had taken him no time at all to find images of her on the internet, and now he had started to see her everywhere. In the past two days alone, he'd seen her on a magazine cover, a poster on the side of a bus stop and, fleetingly, on the Daily Mail website's sidebar of shame. But whilst it had taken no time at all to find her, and then locate her again on Facebook, it had taken him an agonising age to pluck up the courage to send her a friend request.

He had sweated and tormented himself, acting like a shy schoolboy with a crush. Convincing himself first that this was somehow inappropriate conduct which betrayed the sanctity of the relationship he had immediately formed with her when she told him her story; then telling himself that he was a grown, mature man for heaven's sake and that communicating with her via Facebook was merely providing her with another channel to him, should she wish to repeat or add to her confession. Eventually, the latter had won out and he had hovered his hand above the mouse button before clicking it, letting go of the breath he had been unconsciously holding, and then slamming the lid of his laptop shut straight away, embarrassed by the sight of it and pretending that the removal of the screen from his sight would undo the deed.

It hadn't and now, feeling guiltily like a stalker, he wandered over her page, checking out her many photos, examining old posts looking for clues to her past, her state of mind, her feelings. For him? *No! Pshaw! Away with you!* This wasn't about him, it was about her. There was no mention of him on her page or in her recent history at all, and that was perfectly alright. Quite alright.

Absolutely no problem at all.

He wondered if he should, perhaps, send her a wee message.

EIGHT

When Cullen found the badger it was in torment,
tearing at the homemade snare digging into one of its
legs. In the quiet dusk there was no-one else around -
indeed, he'd been walking through the woods for some
time and hadn't seen anyone - but the badger's wound
was fresh enough and the animal was clearly in some
distress. He watched and waited from a distance, took
some nylon cord from his pack and made a large noose
with a slipknot. Sitting on his haunches, he grabbed a
dead branch from the undergrowth and started whittling
with a knife from his pocket. When he was satisfied, he
tied the noose to one end. After some twenty minutes,
when it looked like the badger had exhausted itself,
Cullen slowly approached it, newly crafted badger-
grasper in his hands.

He looped the noose around the badger's neck and let
it slowly tighten to the knot he had tied to keep it from
choking the animal. The badger shot forwards, towards
Cullen until held fast by the snare again. Snarling and
grunting in pain and fear it tried to shake free of the
noose. Cullen wrestled with it, giving it slack until the
animal started to tire again. Just as it looked ready to
drop, he reached around with his knife and cut the snare
on the badger's leg. Holding the grasper with his right
and another branch in his left, he began to wrangle the
bleeding badger onto the path. Like some demented
juggler with an enormous furry writhing diablo, he half-
followed, half-led the animal around in slow circles,

pushing it around the belly of the hill towards the Shieldgreen Centre and some relief for both of them.

The building was a white two-storey house in Glentress forest, just three miles from Peebles, accessible only by a gravelled logging trail that wound through the pine-clad hills. During a handful of weeks during the school year it was unlocked and its shuttered windows thrown open to accommodate groups of scouts or children from Rosshall Academy in Glasgow on outward bound trips. For the rest of the year, it lay silent, empty and cold - except when Cullen chose it as his shelter. Somewhat dilapidated - the Academy still raising funds to renovate and refurbish - it suited him well. He had no need for luxury or, if it came to that, comfort. All he required was somewhere dry and quiet where he could sit, eat, stay and sleep. Alone.

And now, hopefully for one night only, a badger.

All the rooms were simply furnished with several upstairs rooms laid out as small dorms sleeping 5-6 children each. These rooms also had the advantage of not having their windows shuttered so Cullen could read in natural daylight, although there wasn't much of that at this time of year. Downstairs was a living room with some tattered sofas and armchairs and a large fireplace. This gave onto a square hallway from which led doors through to a small kitchen, a toilet and a store cupboard with a split stable door. The lack of light on the ground floor made the whole place feel cold, damp and dirty but seeing the stable door lifted his spirits.

Quickly, he opened it and turned on the bare lightbulb within. He shepherded the badger into the store cupboard and threw the grasper in after it, quickly shutting the door. After a few minutes of crashing and thudding, he unlocked the catch and opened the top half of the door. The badger launched itself like a horse at a fence, but the length of the grasper hindered it in the small enclosed space, and the loss of blood from the snare and the energy it had expended trying to free itself meant it had no real thrust to get up from the ground. The animal gave a desultory snort and satisfied itself with sniffing around its new accommodation, like a grey-striped pig in a sty. Cullen watched for a while and then left it in peace, closing the top-half of the door.

Cullen had been at the Centre for a few weeks now and his natural inclination was that it was time to move on. He was a tall figure with intelligent grey eyes and a head full of curly salt-and-pepper hair which he usually hid beneath a battered leather cowboy hat. In his fifties, he still moved with an easy fluidity and there was clearly power and muscle beneath his scruffy walking gear. His face and hands were tanned and lined from constant outdoor exposure and age. Anyone coming up close would be able to see that he needed a shave and a bath, but it wasn't in Cullen's nature to allow anyone up close, and he'd bathe when he wanted to, thank you very much.

He was wearing a navy blue T-shirt which had once worn a logo but no longer. His trousers were plain grey with zippers at the knee so they could be converted into shorts. On his feet he wore brown leather walking boots, scuffed and stained, and on his back he carried a canvas rucksack with several exterior pockets from which protruded a water bottle and a lime green waterproof jacket stuffed unceremoniously into a ball.

As he walked up the path between the trees he reached once again for his knife. It held three separate blades of black steel which folded back into a handle made of zebra wood. Each blade - a serrated one, a smooth one, and a saw - was 3" long and locked independently, released by separate catches in the hilt. He handled it now, testing the sharpness of the smooth blade with his thumb. Satisfied, he pocketed it again and lengthened his stride. His aim now was to get back to where he had found the badger and lie in wait for the return of whoever had set the snare.

The next morning, Cullen woke beneath his tarp with a stiff neck. He hadn't meant to stay hidden there all night, but the susurrations of the woods had got to him and he'd nodded off. He'd eaten only a couple of cereal bars he had found in his pack, not wanting to make a fire and flag up his presence in the woods. There was no sign that anyone had been back to the site while he'd been asleep and now he was starving. He thought of getting back to Shieldgreen and cooking himself some breakfast. Rubbing the back of his neck, he looked around to see if there was anything he could take back to feed his badger - his, now, note to self - when he heard the sound of snapping twigs and clothes rustling against branches.

Cullen quietly took out his knife and watched as a large burly figure emerged from the trees over to his right. The hulking shape drew close to the snare but, rather than turning to go, moved closer as he noticed the snare had been cut. He bent down to examine the damage and looking around to see if anyone responsible was still there, came face-to-face with Cullen. The man's dark eyes widened in surprise and then his features split into a massive grin.

"Mate!" The man stood and held a massive hand out

in welcome.

Cullen sighed, blinked slowly and closed his knife. "Fuck sake, Beep."

"What? What's up?" Paul's innocent face dropped swiftly into brief embarrassment and then out again. "Just looking for a little organic something. For the dogs, and all."

"Your dogs partial to badger?"

"Fuck. Where?" Paul looked around expecting some demonstration of this. Seeing none, he looked back at Cullen. "You sure?"

"Sure enough." Cullen pocketed his knife and started packing up his tarp. "Come on, I'll show you."

Paul whistled sharply and, as if from nowhere, two Jack Russell terriers bounded from their hiding place in the undergrowth and scuttered around Cullen, sniffing and jumping. Paul helped Cullen pack away then stood and rubbed his stubbled chin.

"Don't suppose you got any coffee on the go, have you?"

Cullen looked silently across at him and nodded down the path. "Shieldgreen."

"Cool!"

Cullen slung his pack and together the pair trod slowly back down the hill towards the Centre.

Big Paul was a giant of a man, six feet five of solid muscle and brawn, with an olive complexion and close-cropped black hair thinning on top. Known to his friends - which was almost everyone - as Beep, he was a shambling, disorganised, lovable bear of a man with a loyalty streak a mile wide and fists only slightly narrower.

His neatly cut goatee, shiny black, was the smartest thing about him, apart from his two beloved Jack Russells, Ant and Dec. Always perfectly groomed, his dogs acted as some kind of fairground mirror on his psyche: a distorted reflection of himself, the more distressed his own appearance and prospects, the more beautifully turned out his pets became.

They had had been a gift from Cullen, magically appearing in a dog basket on his doorstep one morning after his first pair of terriers, Penn & Teller, had been butchered by a Russian thug. For a long time, while they were tiny, Paul had found it hard not to call them Penn & Teller as well, but as they grew and exhibited their own distinct personalities, so his own grieving had diminished and he had decided to rechristen them to distance himself from his loss and out of respect for their memory. No longer puppies, he found his dogs once again an extension of himself and the ultimate keepers of his sanity in an insane world.

As the party neared Shieldgreen, Paul broke the silence.

"Where'd ya put it?"

"In the larder cupboard thing."

Paul looked at him, caught between confusion and admiration. "Inside?"

"Aye."

"Blimey. How did you do that, then? Are you the badger whisperer or something?"

"Never mind. You just keep the dogs outside, ok?"

They sat in the shelter while Cullen lit a fire and got some coffee going. Paul let his dogs mooch about while together they watched the cold sun creep over the trees. When the coffee was ready, Cullen handed him an enamel mug and Paul sniffed appreciatively, then sipped.

"Early start today then?" Cullen prodded.

"Dogs wanted a run." Paul explained. "Plus, snares to check you know? Not the sort of thing to be doing in broad daylight."

"Hmm. Thought you were the lying-in type."

"Not anymore, mate. New leaf, and all that. Today, I have been sober for 10 days."

"Really?"

"Yeah, well, not like in a row or nothing. Just total, you know."

"Right."

"You?"

Cullen paused. "I don't drink. Anymore."

"Ah, yeah. Sorry, mate. Forgot."

"Helps you forget. Doesn't help you feel better."

"Ah, that's where you were going wrong, mate. Drinking against the grain. You gotta drink with the grain. Smoother you see." Paul smiled, his joke alluding to his occupation as joiner, carpenter, cabinetmaker, all-round worker of wood. Cullen, however, didn't smile so Paul decided to change the subject, albeit none too subtly. He nodded towards Shieldgreen Centre.

"What sort of idiot stays outside the house and lets the badger live inside?"

Cullen shrugged. "Inside was warm and safe. It was bleeding and vulnerable."

"Well." Paul threw his dregs on the fire and stood up. "Let's have a butchers, then."

Together they entered quietly through the back door. The house was silent but there was a definite musky smell. Cullen looked over the top of the stable door to find the cupboard was bare.

"Fuck." This in a loud whisper.

"Don't tell me." Paul looked over the door and saw no sign of the badger. "Steve McQueen's done a runner."

Cullen stood in the centre of the hallway, ears pricked, hoping to detect some indication of the animal's whereabouts. He started to pad slowly upstairs. "You stay here."

"What the fuck for?"

"In case it comes down."

"Can badgers even climb stairs?"

"Don't know."

Paul looked around nervously. "Why you going up then?"

"I'm not going to try and wrangle an angry wounded badger. I'm going to get my stuff together and move out."

"I've got the dogs." Paul indicated with his thumb to the back door.

"I didn't rescue it to kill it."

"Gotcha." Paul pursed his lips and nodded.

"Was thinking of moving on anyway. Just mind the door, I'll be down in a minute."

After what seemed like an age, Cullen crept back down the stairs with a large rucksack in tow. They slipped out the back door and Cullen left it ajar.

"We just goin' to leave it in there, then?"

"It'll find its way out in its own time." Cullen slung the pack on his shoulders and started buckling the straps. "I'll come by again tomorrow maybe. Make sure, lock up."

Paul didn't think he sounded convincing but let it go.

The party of men and dogs moved down the logging

trail and followed it over the burn and through the forest out into an open valley, with fields of sheep on either side. The track started a steady descent as the valley narrowed again and a collection of small wooden buildings appeared, clinging like rice terraces either side of tumbling, twisting Soonhope Burn.

This collection of large wooden huts, cottages and even an old re-purposed railway coach were built after the Second World War to provide opportunities for miners and ex-servicemen to enjoy the countryside and fresh air affordably. Some were now neglected but most appeared well cared-for and still occupied, brightly painted with well-tended verandas and gardens. A few wood burner chimneys poked shinily from bitumen-clad rooves. In the bright sunshine it looked like a newly opened model village.

"This is me, then." Paul spoke up, as they passed the first building on the right.

"Eh?" Cullen's mind had been elsewhere.

"Down here." Paul indicated a concrete path between two adjacent cottages which led down towards the burn and then angled off to the right. "I'm building a cabin."

"Oh aye. Who for?"

"Me." Paul said, proudly. "Land's owned by Soonhope farm, over the way. Said I could build a chalet here if I did some jobs for him on the farm over the winter."

Paul was technically homeless, primarily due to chronic cashflow issues brought on by absentmindedness, lack of business acumen and a perverse optimism that everything would come good if you remained cheery. Often he would sleep in his van, lodge with a friend, sometimes stay in an empty property minding it while the owners were away. Occasionally, if the gods were smiling on him, he'd have enough cash to fund a short-term let.

Occasionally.

"So you're going to live here?" Cullen almost smiled.

"Yup. Ain't much, but it'll be all mine."

"Right. Ok." Cullen looked around. "Facilities?"

"Um, not really, no. Gonna have to get water from the burn, but I've got a woodburner in, candles and battery power, cetera. Pit latrine, maybe get a composter. Don't know yet. The cost is starting to mount up already just with the timber."

Cullen surveyed the properties nearby. "Guy over there looks like he's got a satellite dish. May be some power supply you can tap into?"

"Aye, mebbe. Could be solar panels, mind. Anyway, first things first. Rome wasn't built in a day and all that. Got to get the structure up and waterproof asap. Rest'll have to wait." Paul looked up at the sky.

"Wanna beer?"

Cullen looked at him kindly. "Tea?"

"Aye. Whatever."

"Is she bonnie?" Cullen asked.

"Shirley?" Paul thought for a second. "She's big."

"Big?"

"Yeah. I like 'em big." He was sweating as he bashed the last wooden post into the ground with a sledgehammer. "Shagging a skinny bird is like trying to separate deckchairs with your dick."

"Lovely image." Cullen squinted into the low-hanging sun while Paul lay down his hammer, wiped his brow on his sleeve and slumped into a heap next to him on the decking. Together the two had been working hard since morning and now there wasn't much daylight left.

"Don't get me wrong. I'm not advocating being fat. Too much weight is bad for you."

"That's why it's called *too much*."

"Really?" Paul looked at him with eyebrows raised. "Well, I guess I'm no male model. Could probably lose a few pounds." He stood up and patted his belly appreciatively and arched forwards, stretching, supporting his back with both hands. "Tomorrow."

He wandered across the deck and disappeared into the half-built wooden hut which stretched out over the whole back half of this newly constructed platform. The cabin was about eight metres long and five metres wide, single storey, all made from brand new pine which winked and dazzled in the setting sunlight. Three sides were complete with the last gable end currently just an outline covered with tarpaulin. The roof was half complete, sloping bitumen sheeting nailed and glued firmly down. At the far, finished, end a chimney from a woodburner poked through silver and new. Midway along the cabin was an interior wall which separated the completed, liveable section from the still-to-be-completed work-in-progress half. A white plastic double-glazed door with frosted glass built into this wall acted as the main entrance and Paul emerged from it now holding a beer.

"Is that door going to stay there?"

"Nah. S'just acting as my front door the now. Once I get that gable end done and finish the roof that'll just be a dividing wall between the lounge and the bedroom. I'll put a wooden door there and move that one to here-" he pointed to a corner which was currently draped with translucent plastic sheeting. "That'll be my porch." There was pride and satisfaction in his voice as he saw the finished article in his mind's eye and took a hefty swig from a Budweiser. "Cheers."

"Cheers." Cullen watched Paul chug his beer and cast his eye slowly over the cabin and the decking. The valley sides were quite steep here and the decking gave Paul's home its foundation and a small veranda with steps down towards the tumbling brook which threaded itself down towards the Tweed. Beneath the deck was a large storage area where Paul was currently keeping his tools, building materials and anything which wouldn't fit into the two rooms so far habitable.

The sun was dipping over the low hills to their west, casting long shadows and making them squint.

"Anyway, you could say we're going steady."

"With Shirley? Good luck."

Paul grinned, white teeth flashing. "Don't need luck, mate. I'm on fire with Shirl. She may be built like a steakhouse, but she handles like a bistro, know what I'm sayin'? Although it's been a while, mind. Giving all my focus to this place, made me a bleedin' hermit. I wanna get it finished so she can move in proper like - but tonight's my night off. Put on my best T-shirt, splash on the old smelly stuff and mosey down to town. Don't wait up." He chugged the last of the beer and threw the empty bottle under the veranda. "You got plans?"

"Might go for a walk up Glentress. Might just sit here and watch the stars come out."

"Each to their own."

"Never do that?"

"Yeah…" Paul admitted, reluctantly. "Gotta be in the

mood, though. You know, mellow."

"Right." Cullen looked up at the sky, darkening but showing no stars just yet. "What if, amongst the billions of stars, we're all alone? What if the universe is just a barren desert, devoid of sentient life?"

"You mean like Innerleithen?"

Along a winding track high up in Cardrona Forest is a wide hairpin bend. At its apex, the bend recedes into the trees and splits in two: one path heads downhill towards a logging trail called Lower Kirkburn Road, a well-used path for hikers, bikers and dog walkers; the other penetrates into the forest, no longer a path but a ghost of a track which soon becomes boggy and overgrown. Venture some way down this path and you will find what looks like an abandoned caravan, mouldering in a small clearing out of sight.

Peeling and rusty paintwork, the original white now a rain-streaked grey. The windows dirty with grime and covered on the inside by old blankets and mouldy shower curtains with a seventies motif. Its two wheels blocked in and tyres flat, a faded blue Calor Gas bottle attached by a scabby hose to the towbar fitting. A dull padlock and chain bolting the only door. It looks like an abandoned caravan because that is what it is, albeit not permanently abandoned.

Not by Cullen, anyway.

And inside is a treasure trove of the useful, the useless and memories of what used to be. Piled high with boxes, sacks, books and folders. Here a tray of bottles and jars filled with screws, brackets, nails, nuts, bolts and other odds and ends; there an old cassette player and a portable black and white TV. Barely room to manoeuvre and not tall enough to stand up in. There is a bed, just. It's usable if you move stuff out of the way. Cullen has, before now.

He doesn't like to stay here, really. Brings back too many memories. Every time he comes here it takes him slightly longer to leave, makes him a little sadder than on his last visit. Every time he tells himself he won't come back and every time he needs something useful, this is where he comes.

His itinerant lifestyle - from choice - doesn't allow him to carry much. He has what he needs to exist day to day, and more besides, given his resourcefulness. He might stay in a barn, or a fishing hut, or a bothy, or camp beneath his tarp - wherever it may be, he generally has what he needs to survive and subsist. But now and then, he needs something unusual. Today is one of those days, and today's need is for a net. Or something.

Something he can use to re-capture a loose badger.

NINE

The slip of paper Jack had given him was less than useful, merely stating Chanel Photoshoot, Bankholm Mill, Feb 8. What time it started, when Tuppence would appear, where Bankholm Mill was; these were all facts noticeably absent from the communique. Dougie decided to plan as best he could and cover all the bases. He told work that he would be "working from home" and did some research.

Bankholm Mill was the last working mill standing of the many mills in Hawick which had once crowded along the banks of the tumbling River Teviot in the 18th and 19th centuries. Blessed with endless supplies of local wool from hillside sheep and a number of fast-flowing rivers with crystal clear waters, the Borders had boomed from the industrial revolution through to Edwardian times as a centre of excellence in Britain's textile industry.

During the 20th century, however, with the advances in technology, cheaper offshore labour, and globalised supply chains providing cheaper higher quality wools like cashmere at a fraction of the price of home-grown wool, the mills had slowly reduced production or been forced into closure. Some had re-focussed on finishing and designing only, providing the last stages of processing for textiles which were woven abroad and shipped to the UK. So Hawick still retained its name synonymous with high-quality woollens and silks, and still supplied many of the world's most exclusive and expensive fashion labels, even while most of its once-proud factories stood idle and empty.

Today, the mill stood serenely on the sunny side of the river, its three-storey walls dressed in glistening yellow sandstone, its long rows of tall sad windows staring balefully out at the brown river as it foamed and seethed its way along the rocky bed towards the sea. The morning was beautifully clear, with a sharp frost which was slowly melting where the sun hit the ground as it rose. The sky was a cloudless cornflower blue and Dougie's breath felt mint-fresh on the brisk, bright air.

Between the mill and the river was a towpath, and between this and the mill was the mill race, a straight channel dug into the riverbank which diverted the water towards the mill and, in particular, to its 14-foot diameter waterwheel which had once powered the entire operation. Today it stood enclosed in a dry-dock as a visitor attraction, occasionally activated by water from a sluice, its former labours now performed effortlessly by electricity from the national grid.

Dougie read all this from the visitors' guide as he surveyed his surroundings for some vantage point. Between the mill and the mill race was an octagonal lawn, criss-crossed with gravel paths and enclosed by a low sandstone wall. And here, already, Dougie could see roadies and photographer's assistants clad in black, humping trunks of equipment, cabling and stands from a side door which led into the ground floor of the mill building proper. This must be where Tuppence's photoshoot was to take place and without somewhere nearby, secluded and high up, from which he could take a single shot, all the tourist guff in the world wasn't going to butter any parsnips as far as he was concerned.

161

Across on the other side of the river was a smaller, derelict building - it's walls now sooty grey, its upper windows broken, the lower ones boarded up. Dougie decided to check it out and see what view and seclusion he could obtain from one of the windows facing Bankholm mill.

"Not sure this look suits me." Guy said, contemplating himself.

"Too late now, matey boy." Conrad pulled uncomfortably at his own turtle neck. "Time and tide something something."

"I feel as if all I'm missing is a beret and a string of onions."

"Or a bag that says SWAG." Conrad chuckled to himself.

The pair were dressed all in black: long-sleeve, turtle neck tops, black jeans, black gloves and lightweight climbing shoes. Like two mimes waiting for their cue, they sat glumly in the car, keeping out of the way of the real camera crew and roadies who were setting up the equipment for the shoot.

"Why do they dress like this anyway?" Guy was genuinely mystified, as well as trying to keep his mind off the job in hand.

"No idea. Union requirements?"

"Hmm. You're sure we're not over-reaching ourselves here?"

"Dream big, Guy. Shoot for the moon, aim for the stars."

"Land in the gutter."

"Tut-tut-tut. Negative, negative. Look, is the glass

half-empty or half-full, hmm?"

"Depends if you're emptying it or filling it up."

"Guy, Guy, Guy. What sort of friend are you, you talk like that?"

"The sort of friend who's just about to steal something for his friend while his friend sits here and spouts platitudes."

"I'm not just sitting here. I'm keeping guard." Conrad looked genuinely wounded by Guy's implication.

"I could keep guard."

"You could. You may not. Now, check your walkie-talkie." Conrad pressed the transmission key down and spoke gently into his. When Guy pressed his own button down there was a deafening squawk of feedback. "Not here! Go round the corner, move away. Someone will hear!"

Guy reluctantly got out of the car and went around the corner of the yard, temporarily out of sight and heard Conrad say what sounded like "Alpha Charlie Dibley Enterprise Fruitcake."

Guy pressed his own button down. "You're supposed to say *over.*"

"Over."

"Galapagos Hurricane Instagram Jackdaw. Over"

"Good. Ok, now you know what you're doing. If I see anyone coming your way I'll use the codeword… Kowloon. Ok?"

"You mean over?"

"No, Kowloon. Over."

"Ok. Kowloon. Got it. Over."

"When you have the designs use the code word… Tanktop. Over."

"Tanktop. Got it. Over."

"And when you are on your way back, let me know so I can make sure the coast is clear down here. Use the codeword, er, … Marzipan. Over."

"Marzipan? You sure this is the official radio alphabet? Over."

"Yes." Conrad hissed. "Now, synchronise watches. 9:19… now." He waited for Guy to confirm and when he didn't he pressed his comms buttons again. "You get that, over?"

"Yes. Over"

"Why do you not confirm, over?"

"'Cos you never said over. Over."

Conrad sighed. "Ok, good luck. Over and out."

Guy crept up the wide stairwell to the second floor, nervously ducking under the windows overlooking the courtyard in case anyone should look up. The courtyard at Bankholm mill was getting busy now, with scurrying figures humping camera equipment or pulling polythene-covered clothes rails down the ramps of the assembled trailers and artic's which now crammed the loading area. Conrad had considered the photoshoot would be an ideal time to steal the designs since there would be plenty of open doors and loads of strangers walking around. Who would notice anyone peeling away to pry into areas of the mill otherwise off-limits?

Guy had been unconvinced and wasn't about to take any chances. He pushed through the large double-doors from the stairs and tried unsuccessfully to walk silently down the wide corridor in front of him. It was flooded with light from tall windows arrayed down one side. The polished wood, yellowing with patina and age, creaked with every step he took echoing like gunfire.

Along the right hand side of the corridor were a series

of wooden doors, all numbered and bearing little metal sliders to show whether the occupants were in or not. He moved down until he found one which read Design Studio and tried the handle. To his surprise, it opened onto a large area several tennis courts in size, with windows down the right-hand side. Thick iron pillars dotted the floor, supporting the weight of the storeys above. Large cutting tables and other work surfaces were arranged in L-shapes around the space, scattered with various fabrics, paper patterns and photos, partially unrolled bolts of cloth. Under each of the surfaces were stacked cardboard boxes with holes cut out of them and protruding from each hole was more fabric, tape, rolls of buttons and fasteners - all manner of assorted bits and bobs used in constructing clothing. The far wall was entirely covered with bookshelves, packed with box files with handwritten labels: A/W 16, DIOR-SS-17, and others in a similar vein.

Guy scanned the rows, looking for some indication of content from either Liv or Chanel, but found none.

At the end of the row of bookcases was a battered, head-height metal cabinet, several feet deep, with large metal scrolling doors which met in the middle. The doors were locked. Frustrated, Guy perched on the edge of the nearest desk and looked around the room. This cabinet had to be where they kept current or protected designs. It seemed the only thing in the room that was locked or not lying open in plain view. He checked the desk drawers he was sitting on, looking for keys and found a small bunch of keys in an old tobacco tin in the top drawer.

Hands shaking, he tried each key in turn.

Guy gave a little gasp of delight when the sixth one

turned in the lock and he was able to peel back the metal doors. The cupboard held six metal shelves, all dinged and bent in places. Each shelf was piled high with large portfolio folders and books, secured in landscape mode by clips or bindings. On the far left was an index card taped to each shelf with handwritten annotations of the contents, in various hands and coloured biro, some crossed out and over-written. Guy traced down each card until he found one that read *NEW* Liv Night. 16/17. A and B designs.

He pulled out all the books on that shelf and hefted them onto the desk nearby. Each was an inch or two thick of heavy paper, A2 or A1 size, with post-it notes and bits of fabric sticking out from between some pages. He checked the front covers of each until he found one which matched the shelf label and put it to one side. He replaced all the others back on the shelf and then lifted the cover from the one on the desk.

There were something like thirty pages in all, covered in drawings of stylised mannequins in various outfits. Each drawing was annotated and accompanied by fabric swatches and button or zips, some small samples of hand-stitching or linings. At the top right of each page was Liv's signature scrawl of her own name and the year 2016. At the back of the book was a large pocket containing folded pieces of pattern cutouts and tracing paper. He closed the book, extremely pleased with himself and picked up his walkie-talkie. What was the codeword again? "Er, haemorrhoid? Over"

There was a short silence and then a clearly frustrated Conrad said "What?"

"You're supposed to say over. Over."

"And you're supposed to say the codeword. Over."

"Is it not haemorrhoid, over?"

"No! It bloody is not. Over."

"Er, Kowloon. Over"

"Christ's sake, man. Kowloon is what I say. Over."

"Oh, I don't know!" Guy was fed up with this stupid game. Considering how successful he now was when he had initially assumed this assignment was inevitably going to involve a substantial stay at one of Her Majesty's residences, he decided he'd had enough of codeword bingo. "I've got them, ok? I've got them and I'm coming down now. Over."

"Ok. Coast is clear. Wait at the bottom and contact me again before coming out. Is that clear, over?"

"Yes. Over."

Guy closed the cupboard, replaced the keys and did his best to make it look like he'd never been there. He hoiked the unwieldy portfolio book under one arm as best he could and walked quickly out of the design studio and down the corridor to the stairwell. At the top, he looked out over the courtyard again to see what level of activity was still in evidence. It was now quiet and he looked at his watch, shocked to find that more than half an hour had passed since they'd synchronised watches. He felt like he'd only been gone minutes. Guy stepped carefully down the stairs and stood with his back to the courtyard door, breathing heavily from the effort. He called Conrad again, blind now and relying solely on his friend for instructions. "I'm down. Over."

There was no answer.

"I'm down. Over."

Static.

Fuck, thought Guy. He raced back up the stairs to get a good look out over the courtyard. He couldn't see

Conrad or the car.

"Conrad. Will you fucking come in, over!"

More static. Then, trying to break through, came: "Chhhh…. fucking name…. chhhh… radio…. chhhh."

"Where are you. Over?"

"Chhhh…. fucking car… chhhh."

"What?"

"Chhhh… -ait there… chhhh."

Guy sat on the stairs and looked morosely out at the empty courtyard. Then he saw the car, Conrad driving gingerly and extremely slowly, meandering between the trucks and vans which had been parked willy-nilly on the cobbles. He pulled up by the far corner of a loading bay in the shadows, away from pretty much everything else. Guy watched as Conrad stepped out, looking around him before ducking back into the car. Not suspicious-looking at all to anyone watching, thought Guy.

The walkie-talkie crackled back into life.

"Ok. All clear. Ready when you are. Over."

Guy leapt down the stairs, picked up the portfolio book he'd left by the door and bolted out into the yard, head down staring at cobbles as he hustled awkwardly for the car.

"Any answer?" asked Brenda.

"Not yet." Mandy put the receiver down. "I've left him two voicemails. Don't see any point leaving a third."

"He's left me in a bit of a pickle, you know. Really."

Mandy looked at Brenda's cheeks, reddening under the stress she was experiencing. She was a well-meaning soul, always offering praise and encouragement to others. But she took too much on herself and she was also, quite unfortunately, as flaky as hell. Disorganised people looked up to her as some kind of role model for the instinctively random. Time and again, she seemed to leave things to the last minute, unable to grasp the concept of forward-thinking or contingency-planning. Time and again, some important - crucial, even - task would need doing at the eleventh hour and time and again, some IT aspect of it would come to thwart her. These were the times when she called, ever-so-gratefully, on Dougie. But today, he wasn't here and he wasn't answering his phone.

"Would like to see if I can print it out for you?"

"Could you, Mand? That would be tremendously helpful." She ran her fingers up and down the edge of the reception desk, fretting.

"It looks like you've been Dougie'd." Mandy added. "Perhaps it's your turn."

"My turn?"

"Yes. You must have been Dougie'd before?"

"I'm… not sure." She frowned, puzzled.

"It's what the girls upstairs call it. When Dougie has let you down, or broken something that previously worked. You've been Dougie'd."

"Oh." Brenda's fingers played a faster arpeggio on the desktop. "But he's the best IT person we've ever had, isn't he?"

Mandy looked at Brenda sympathetically. "Best. Only. It's a fine line."

Dougie looked at his phone: 3 missed calls, 2 voicemails. Bollocks. He tried to access his voicemail but had no signal. He'd try again when he found a nest by a window. Phone reception in this old building seemed patchy - maybe it was the thick stone walls, or the iron supporting pillars supporting the heavy floors over the open-plan layout.

The derelict building had been surrounded by metal fence sections, chained together, occasionally tagged with "DANGER. KEEP OUT. AUTHORISED PERSONNEL ONLY" signs. Here and there the sections had been blown over or sagged in their concrete footings and it had been a simple matter to clamber over and look for a way in to the old mill. The west side of the building was hidden from view, invisible from the river unless you were in direct line of sight between the mill and the warehouse next to it - a narrow alley separating the two, probably almost always in shade. Weeds grew tall and empty beer cans and broken bottles littered the alleyway along with fly-blown carrier bags and soggy bits of cardboard and rusty tins. Along this side of the mill one of the boarded-up windows had been attacked by kids or vagrants in the past and a substantial section torn from it. Dougie had hoisted himself up to it and dropped into the darkness inside without a problem, although as he landed on broken glass fragments he had immediately wondered how easy it would be to get out again. Scouring the floor with a torch he had pulled from his bag, he had gathered together some empty tea chests and broken pallets to construct a rickety escape staircase of sorts which would provide an easier escape route back out through the window, should it be necessary.

On the first floor and above, the windows had been left unboarded and each dusty floor was well-illuminated by the bright morning sunlight, even though the river-facing windows were currently in shade. Scattered

170

machinery lay neglected and rusting - cogs, arms, sprockets, frames - a giant Meccano set waiting to be assembled. At both ends of each floor were large sets of double doors and broad wooden stairs wide enough to drive a coach and four up. Dougie zigzagged through the building, crossing each floor and up the opposite stairs until he reached the third and final floor and started to descend again. He was looking for the best window position which would give him uninterrupted views of the photoshoot on the other side of the river.

In the end he settled on a first floor window, near the western end of the mill. This gave him a good vantage point almost directly opposite the octagonal lawn as well as being very near his escape route. It also meant his elevation wasn't too high above that of his target - the greater the vertical distance between the source of the bullet and its intended destination, the more he'd have to allow for changes in its trajectory and so he'd have to adjust his rifle sights so that the crosshairs reflected where the bullet would actually hit. To this end, he'd brought along a small notebook with hand-written adjustment tables that he'd researched and tested out on his various practice runs in Cathkin Braes.

Pleased that he'd planned carefully and thought things through to the best of his abilities, he hunkered down to the left of the windowsill and started assembling his rifle and stand. Out in the sunshine, the crew were putting the finishing touches to what was now a large assortment of tripods, light reflectors on stands, banks of cabling and even what looked like an automated dolly track which ran half the length of the mill race with a camera arrangement mounted on it. He watched as the crew tested this out, running the camera unit by remote back and forth along the track.

As the morning wore on, word must have spread and a small straggle of locals were hovering around, gawping from the towpath. Keeping one eye on the crew preparations, Dougie checked his phone again, found he had some reception now, and dialled his voicemail. Sighing as he listened, he pulled his laptop from his bag, tethered it to his phone to get a 3G connection and logged onto the office VPN. A few minutes tapping later, he closed the lid of his laptop and texted a quick message to Brenda saying "Pls try again now."

Conrad looked at his watch. "I think we should make our move."

"Now?"

"Why not? Why wait?"

"Well, that's a good question actually. Because I genuinely don't know what we are waiting for." Guy looked at his friend earnestly. "When you outlined the plan you did, sort of… leave that bit out."

"Look, we can't grab her while everything in full swing! We need to wait until near the end. Everyone packing up, people hang around, fag break, cetera cetera. See if we spot her all alone, no-one paying attention. Bang!" Conrad clapped his hands together.

"You do know chloroform doesn't go bang, don't you?"

"Metaphor, dummy."

"Right. And remind me again - why am I the one who has to wield the metaphor?"

"Because she knows me! She'll see me, I distract her attention." Conrad nodded, as much to himself as to

Guy, confiding his plan one final time to them both. "Lure her away. You sneak up behind. Whammo!"

"Right. Right. Ok." Guy breathed out deeply. "Hang on. She knows me as well!"

"What?"

"She knows me, idiot."

"How does she know you?"

"Duh. She's seen me loads of times."

"Really?" Conrad was astounded. "Ok, well it doesn't matter. As long as she knows me I can distract her. She won't even see you."

"OK." Guy shrugged. "Let's get on with it, then."

"Come with me."

"But I thought you were going to scout her out, separate her from the pack so to speak. Before I-"

"You watch. You learn." Conrad wagged a finger in Guy's face. "You see me ready. You pounce!"

"Alright, Jackie Chan. Can we get on with it, then?"

"Ok. And remember, don't let Liv see us."

"How're you going to distract her if she can't see you?"

"Huh?"

"Liv! How're you going to distract her if you can't let her see you?"

"I don't want to distract Liv! I want to distract Tuppence."

"Is she here as well?" Guy was beginning to realise that Conrad had only shared a tiny part of the big picture with him.

"She'd better be. Otherwise we won't be able to kidnap her will we?"

"Hang on, I'm confused."

"No shit."

173

The penny in Guy's head finally dropped. "I thought we were kidnapping Liv!"

"Is Liv married to someone rich enough to pay a ransom?"

"Well, no."

"So why would we kidnap Liv?"

"Well, I don't... I mean I thought because we were stealing her designs..." Guy tailed off weakly.

"Ok. Ready?"

"I guess."

"Right, let's go."

And they burst out of the car like Butch Cassidy and the Sundance Kid.

"He wasn't best pleased, I can't lie." Liv blew a cloud of cigarette smoke into the air and Tuppence tried to subtly wave it away. "But then he never bloody was, was he? I mean, this is my big break Tupp! Fucker should have supported me, not shot me down."

They were standing in the corridor which led from a quadrangle inside the mill where the loading bays were, to the outside lawn where the shoot was taking place. The corridor was harshly lit by the sunlight streaming through the tall windows on one side. The opposite wall was crammed with coat racks and rails, hanging with outfits that had not been worn, and chaotically strewn with discarded costumes which had.

Tuppence was only half-listening to Liv's monologue. She had just noticed a new Facebook message from Dick and she found herself feeling a little guilty and yet somehow excited. Aware that she was now distracted from her friend's monologue, she put the phone back in her handbag, and made a mental note to read it later.

"Did he really shoot you down, though, Liv? He loves you, doesn't he?"

Liv snorted, forcing smoke from her nostrils. It writhed up with motes of dust dancing in it, the exhaust from a real flame-haired dragon. "Funny way of showing it. So ok, technically no, he didn't shoot me down. But he did tell me I shouldn't take it. Not take it! Think of us, he said! Think of himself, more like." She puffed on the cigarette again and turned her head to blow the smoke away from Tuppence, towards the open door. "Fuck him. We're over and, you know what? It's a fucking relief!" Liv swept the array of clothes in front of them with her hand. "I mean, all this is mine. All these designs. My photoshoot. My models. I am on my way!" She nodded meaningfully at Tuppence, and then turned to shout at a passing crewhand. "Can you close that door, please? Fucking freezin' in h-."

Liv felt the breath solidify in her lungs and found herself falling backwards as the sun fell down through the facing window, sinking as she sank. Achingly, beautifully slowly. Watching as every speck of dust on the window, every stitch in Tuppence's coat, every strand of her own hair, played footsie with gravity and time. And all amidst an echoing silence, that total emptiness caused by a sudden absence of sound sucked from the air. Her eyes rolled back as her head fell, and when it hit the polished wooden floor all was blackness.

The models emerged onto the octagonal lawn in a slow procession, long hair flowing beautifully in the breeze, exquisite fabrics clinging to their enviable shapes.

They slinked along the gravel walkway, long legs flashing in heels, calves tennis-racket tight. Dougie thought if they didn't get a good meal inside them, their legs were at risk of snapping with the next sharp frost.

As each one reached the end of the path, a camera hand passed them a floor-length puffer coat, in British Racing Green, which they stepped into and zipped to keep themselves warm in the bright February chill. Through his telescopic sight, he scanned the faces until he found Tuppence. Nervously, he double-checked the photo Jack had given him and a folded printout he had made himself with selected images grabbed from the web. This was a woman of a hundred hairstyles; he didn't want to shoot the wrong one. Satisfied, Dougie trained his sights on her and checked the adjustment of the crosshairs in his notebook. He patiently followed her movements as she came and went, occasionally looking up from his rifle to see if he could work out when would be the best time to take his shot. He needed an opportunity where she was not the centre of attention, when the eyes of the photographers and onlookers were elsewhere.

Time ached by and he felt a burning need to adjust his position to avoid cramp. Dougie stood up and walked around, away from the window, pressing one foot firmly into the floor until the discomfort went away. He paced more gently up and down the floor a few more times, until he felt he'd made better amends to his circulation, then went back to his perch.

As he did so, a phalanx of cyclists, riding three or four abreast, appeared along the towpath and slowed as they approached the mill race and the small crowd of onlookers. What the fuck? Did every moron decide to cycle in the Borders? Was it some condition of citizenship or something? Fuck sake, people, get a grip. Seemingly out catching the best of this beautiful morning, the cyclists stood as one, their bodies steaming in the sunshine like stallions in the winners' enclosure.

Dougie looked through his rifle sight to find his previously perfect view now obscured by a forest of shocking yellow, orange, blue and black. The extreme magnification flattened the depth of field to the point where he was unable to work out what was in front of what, who was behind whom, or what distances were involved. He played his sight left and right trying to make out what was happening but in the end resorted to looking up above it from a distance to make sure Tuppence was still where he'd last seen here. There she was! But it was clear, now, that he could no longer see a fucking thing from where he sat. If those cyclists weren't going to move, he would have to.

Fuming, he picked up his stand and bag and hunch-crawled along the floor, one window to his left. The view from here was only marginally better so he went down a further two windows to regain an uninterrupted line of sight. When he settled down in this new perch and looked through his sights, Tuppence was nowhere to be seen. Taking deep breaths to calm himself, he swept the rifle scope slowly this way and that. Panic rose in his chest until he thought he spotted her disappear behind some brickwork and then reappear, half-obscured by a window with her back to him. She was speaking to another, flame-haired, woman - both swathed in their puffer coats.

Dougie's right leg started to spasm with cramp again and something inside him rose, unbidden, and insisted:

Now! He gritted his teeth as his leg shrieked in protest, returned his gaze to the rifle sight, and placed the crosshairs on the back of Tuppence's head. As the flame-haired woman turned away to exhale extravagantly from her cigarette, Dougie pulled the trigger.

The recoil made him blink and when he looked again, the window was empty of both women, and he could no longer withstand the cramp shaking his leg. He stood, and slammed his foot repeatedly into the floor until it subsided, grabbed up his rifle and stand, quickly and expertly dismantled them, stuffed them back into his bag and walked quickly across to the stairs and down to his escape route.

He exited into the quiet morning sunshine, crept down the alley to the back of the derelict building and strutted down the opposite towpath. Heading out of town, he whistled gently to himself, imagining how he would spend his just-earned fifty thousand pounds.

Tuppence looked on in astonishment as Liv crumpled in front of her very eyes. Mid-sentence, she collapsed like a demolished smokestack. Tuppence stared down at her feet and then, from nowhere, Conrad appeared. Skidding in from the right of her vision, dressed in black, like a street mime on ice.

"Liv!" He shouted, trying unsuccessfully to catch her head before it thwacked on the wooden floor. He cradled her head, smoothing the hair from her face, checking to see if she was still breathing, moving his hands over her puffer coat until he brought it away a vivid, ugly red.

"No, no, no." Robotically, over and over again, rocking as he stroked her head.

Conrad looked up at Tuppence and his expression changed from shock to... confusion? It was almost like he was looking past her, incomprehension spreading across his features.

"Conrad?" she asked.

"NO!" He protested as she sensed a strange smell welling up from the floor towards her, felt a hand clutch her face, tilt her head back and then... nothing.

"*No*, I said!" Conrad was trying to scream in outrage and whisper for fear of discovery all at the same time. It came out like a strangulated mewl. "What the fuck don't you understand about *No*?"

Guy pulled a roll of tape and a sack from his pocket, smacked a section of the tape over Tuppence's mouth and then threw the sack over her head. "I thought that was just another one of your *No-no-no*'s."

"What?"

"Look. No time for arguments, come on!" Guy was hissing at Conrad, petrified that someone might suddenly appear from either end of the corridor.

"What the fuck you doing?"

"The plan, remember? Your plan?"

"Not now!" Conrad nodded down to Liv, unconscious in his arms.

"What d'ya mean, not now?" Guy pointed to the sack over Tuppence's head. "It's a bit fucking late for *not now*!"

Conrad looked at him in disbelief but Guy, for perhaps the first time in his life, felt the adrenalin surge required to take charge. "Leave her and come on."

"I... can't.... leave her!" Conrad was doing his *Do-I-*

179

have-to-spell-it-out-for-you-again-fuckwit face but Guy felt his heart thudding in his throat, brooking no arguments. If someone saw them now they would need one hell of an explanation to save them.

"We have to." He thought of appealing to Conrad's better nature, then abandoned it mid-thought. Far better to appeal to something baser - like greed. "Look. Someone will be here soon. They'll find her. She's not going to die. Whereas this one." He nodded at Tuppence, fast becoming a sagging weight in his own arms. "She's your meal ticket. She's the one who's going to get you money to pay your debts and get your career launched."

Guy watched the emotions roil around Conrad's contorted features: greed and fear, love and guilt, hope and hopelessness.

"But she needs me." Conrad sat, motionless, clearly torn and Guy knew they were on borrowed time.

"Does she?"

"Yes." Some uncertainty there, Guy felt. He pressed harder.

"She didn't see you did she? She doesn't know you were even here."

"True." Guy watched some colour return to his friends cheeks. "But *she* does." He looked up at Tuppence.

"Yes, but she's coming with us. And-" Guy felt this was the trump card. "All she saw was you coming to her rescue!"

Conrad almost sat bolt upright, a calculating decision sweeping through his body. "Ok. Let's move." He almost dropped Liv's head back on the floor in his haste. "I'll call 999 when we're on our way."

"Right. Grab her feet. She's heavier than she looks."

They hustled Tuppence down the corridor between them. As they passed the last coat rail, Conrad grabbed a loose dust sheet and draped it over her body. "Just in case" he explained to Guy. They staggered out into the sunshine and Guy felt as if time had been standing still and just suddenly sprang forward several hours. Like emerging from the cinema into broad daylight. He looked around the loading bay area and saw a handful of crew busy loading up, no-one paying them attention.

"Put her in the boot." Conrad prompted as they reached their car.

"What! No!" Guy was outraged. This was his brief taste of being in charge and he wasn't going to let it go so easily. "She'll rattle around in there, smack her head on metal, who knows what."

"What then?"

"She can sit in the backseat." Conrad looked at Guy askance. "With me." Guy kept adding ideas until he felt he'd won the argument. "I'll sit next to her. Keep her upright."

"She's got a bag over her head." Conrad was already back to his usual demeanour of explaining to a small child.

"I know. Duh!"

"People will see."

"What? People will see what? A body completely covered head-to-foot in puffer coat and a sack?" Guy was adamant, this was going to be his way or no way. "Will they fuck. They'll see a mannequin. A dummy. A statue. Whatever. Who gives a fuck."

Conrad was taken aback by his friend's sudden new vehemence and mutely assisted as Guy bundled her into the back of the car and got in beside her. Conrad plonked himself at the wheel and looked in the rear view mirror at a tall blonde mime seated next to a be-sacked mannequin. Well, whatdyaknow?

"Now drive. And let's get the fuck out of here."

Guy tried to look serenely out of the window but winced when Conrad put the car in gear and screeched out of the loading bay area, causing one or two heads to turn. Fortunately he had hired them a nondescript 4-door saloon in a difficult-to-describe shade of dark red that no-one would remember. They skeetered out onto the street and headed up to the junction with the main road.

Just as they reached the junction, a string of pushbikes shot out from the left of Guy's vision and the lead cyclist almost hit the car. Conrad managed to swerve just in time as the cyclists braked sharply and several of his follower piled into the back of him. Guy watched the cyclist dip his head and shake his fist at them as they fishtailed up the road towards the roundabout and all routes out.

Some of the cocaine had fallen into the crack of Melanie's arse and Jack was doing his level best to snort it *in situ* while she was wondering whether the anaesthetic effect would give her trouble going to the toilet later. She wriggled with delight as his stubble scratched her thighs and his tongue wiggled into her, hot and wet.

He tried a snort, found himself simultaneously struggling for breath and gagging on a stray pubic hair. He sneezed all over her backside.

"Jack!"

He sat up and wiped his nose and mouth with the

back of his arm. "Sorry. Better try that again." He looked at the mess on her buttocks and tried to smear it away.

"Nuh-uh. Excuse me while I go shower." She reached around to feel the stickiness and pulled a face. "I'm starting to numb up and now my arse is like -" She smelt her fingers and bulged her eyes. "Not nice."

"Mel!" He whined to her retreating back as she walked unsteadily to the bathroom. She closed the door, ignoring him.

Jack rolled over onto his back and looked at the ceiling. Flecks danced across his vision and he tried to catch them in focus but every time he moved his eyes the flecks moved with them, floating over the patterned swirls in the artex. He idly checked the time on his phone and was surprised to find it was 7:30 in the morning and he had an unread text message. He opened it and read: Job Done.

TEN

"You're not going to abandon me here, are you?" Guy said. "Jet off to Hong Kong?"

"Of course not." Conrad poked at his phone with his index finger, inefficiently texting. "Although can't rule it out."

"Why?"

"Why? Because Yeo wants more money. As usual. And I can't wait until I have the money for ... her. I'll miss the window for London Fashion Week. I -" He hesitated for a moment, trying to think of what to type next. "I need to persuade him that he doesn't need the money up front."

Guy sucked his cheeks in glumly, then sighed. "My friends cousin almost went to Singapore once."

"And?" Conrad looked up and sneered, frown lines appearing on his forehead

Guy shrugged. "Just sayin'."

"Just saying what? That someone you don't know, didn't go to a different place to the place I'm talking about?"

Not for the first time, Guy was crushed by his friends withering retorts. He mumbled apologetically "Only trying to make conversation."

"Well don't, ok? Save your breath. Maybe might need it later to blow up your date."

The pair were sitting on floor cushions in the living room at Shieldgreen. A sullen fire spat in the hearth shedding the only light in the room, the windows blanketed with heavy curtains to hide the fact that anyone was home from the prying eyes of any passing walkers. Tuppence was bound and gagged in the room next door, lying on a stained mattress shivering with cold.

The pair sat in silence for a while - Conrad texting and swearing every time he made a mistake, Guy trying to think of a conversation starter that Conrad wouldn't immediately ram back down his throat.

"Can't fucking get the hang of predictive text." Conrad swore again and hit the backspace key several times. "Why the fuck you can't turn it off I don't know."

"You can. Let me show you." Guy reached for Conrad's phone and received a sharp jab in the ribs in return.

"Fuck off! I'm in the middle of a text."

"Why don't you just call him?" Guy massaged his chest with his palm, wincing.

"Because, cretin. A, I only got one bar. Fucking reception out here sucks big time. And B, do you know how much it cost per minute to call Hong Kong on a fucking mobile?" He paused far too briefly for Guy to answer. "No? A shit load. That's how much. And, unless you have not been keeping up, the reason why we are here sitting in the dark in middle of nowhere, nursing this excuse for a fire, is because we are potless."

"If you've only got one bar, how're you gonna call Jack?"

Conrad looked anew at Guy. "Fuck!" He got up, held the phone aloft and walked slowly around the room, checking the signal.

"I saw an episode of QI once." Guy recalled. "Stephen Fry said that the bars on a phone don't bear any resemblance to signal strength at all." Conrad ignored him. "Said each manufacturer used a different algorithm to give users the impression that it does. Reassuring, apparently."

Conrad slowed his pace and moved deliberately to the window. He peered through and, seeing no lights or movement, parted the curtains slightly and pushed the handset up against the glass. "Three bars!"

"How are you going to call him with the phone held like that?" Guy wrinkled his nose. "Do you want me to hold it there while you stand outside and talk through the glass?"

"Oh yeah, that'll work. Christ, I wonder what's worse: me losing another finger or me having to keep listening to your stupid ideas." Conrad gave him a saddened look and nodded towards the bedroom. "Why don't you go check on her? See if she's awake."

Tuppence lay on her side, her nose pressed against the dirty mattress. Her mouth was clamped with some heavy-duty tape which someone had wound clumsily around her head, pinning her hair and the bottom of her ears in a single loop. She snorted hungry breaths through her nose, smearing snot on her shoulder as she struggled to sit up.

Angry smears of mascara lip gloss and eye-shadow streaked her face, intercut by trails of her tears, making her look like Heath Ledger's Joker. If only she'd had a mirror to see herself in. She was cold and uncomfortable, her head buzzing like a bad hangover. She wondered if she'd been hit and then, immediately afraid, suddenly checked her clothing and legs for marks, trying to sense her groin and thighs. Had she been assaulted? She couldn't be sure but she didn't think so. And why hadn't Conrad helped her? He'd been nursing Liv's head in his lap and just shouted "No!". Why hadn't he done something? Perhaps he had contacted the police? Perhaps they had taken him as well? Maybe he was in another room. She looked around her dim and filthy prison and wondered where she was and how long she'd been unconscious.

Her hands were painfully crimped at the wrist, bound by cable ties which gave her no movement other than her fingers. She felt the tightness of the ties giving her pins and needles in her hands and held them down below her waist in a bid to get circulation to them. One of her shoes was missing and her watch had been taken. She didn't know where or when she was but she was instantly ravenous and her stomach complained in confirmation. As her breathing slowed and the pulse in her head quietened, she wondered if she was imagining faint voices - mens' voices - from the other side of the door. She stood slowly and moved quietly over to the door, listening, but couldn't hear anything. When a key rattled in the lock she gasped involuntarily through the tape and hurtled herself back onto the bed, facing the wall, hoping to feign sleep. Her heart was thumping in her chest as the door opened and someone entered.

Tuppence felt a hand gently stroke her jawline and couldn't stop herself from stiffening in fear. The man instantly snatched his hand away but sat down on the bed beside her.

"Sorry." A quiet voice, gentle like the hand, but somewhat muffled. "I was just seeing if you were awake." She felt him move slightly away from her. Slowly she turned and, as she did so, closed her eyes tightly shut. From somewhere, some instinct kicked in telling her not to look at him, not to see him. *If you don't know who he is, he won't have to kill you* was the charming thought. Yes, perhaps. But not having to kill you wasn't the same as not killing you. She faced in what she assumed was his direction, eyes still defiantly bunched closed, flicked her head exaggeratedly from side to side, and made deliberately loud but indistinct noises through her tape gag to show that she was simultaneously annoyed, afraid and desirous of speech.

"Hum-mum-uh-huh." *Of course I am.*

"Sorry?"

"Hu-huh, Hum-mum-uh-huh." *I said, of course I am.*

"You can open your eyes, you know. We're not going to hurt you."

We. She had heard voices. There was more than one of them. She fought between the discomfort and fear of keeping her eyes shut and the trust she was sensing from his soothing voice. A delicate southern accent, soft. Posh almost.

"I'm afraid I can't take the tape off - not now, anyway - in case you make a noise. But, honestly, I won't hurt you. You'll be more comfortable if you open your eyes."

It was the *honestly* that did it. Something told her that hardened criminals - kidnappers, terrorists, or whatever - didn't use words like *honestly*. Wondering if this was the most stupid thing she'd ever done - and perhaps, now, ever do - she opened her eyes and looked directly up at the face of George Clooney.

"Uh-huh-UGH!" *What the FUCK!*

"Look, I'm sorry I can't understand what you're saying." The Clooney mask mangled some of his words

188

but she got the gist. She could see blue eyes and pale lashes in the mask's eyeholes. "Just please try and stay calm and everything will be alright. I'll get you food and something to drink and hopefully it won't be long before you can go home."

"Huh-um-uh-mmmhh-uh-mum-ugh-uh-mum?"

She tried to sneer at him but all she could see were the blue eyes smiling at her. "You know, with that tape on I can't make out what you're saying but I could swear you just said to me *How I am going to eat with this on?*"

She opened her eyes wide and nodded her head at him. "Uh-MMM!"

"You did?"

"MMM!" More violent nodding.

Clooney smiled and then, amazingly, attempted a half-decent Humphrey Bogart impression. "Hey, sweetheart, looks like we got ourselves a dialog goin'."

She looked at him as if to say *really?* and let her shoulders sag. His willingness to make light of the situation didn't cheer her or provide relief, but merely clarified, for her, their different perspectives on her situation: he was amused and saw it as a game; she was an inch from tears and petrified that this mask and this room would be the last things she ever saw on this earth. And on her gravestone, her last words: "Uhm!"

Clooney looked back through the open door, checking to see if they were being observed. Carefully he padded over to the door, and quietly closed it with a click. Then he came back to the mattress and sat down next to her. "Look, if I take the tape off will you promise to be quiet?"

Eagerly she nodded, her heart leaping at this small gesture; this tiny nub of hope. He turned her upper body away from him so that he could fiddle with the tape at the back of her head. After a long while of pulling and hair tugging he turned her back to face him. "Look, I can't get it off."

She wrinkled her forehead, asking a question.

"Sorry. I've got no nails and it's all tangled up in your hair."

She looked at him with large sad eyes, pleading, and he thought for a moment. "I could cut it off. Might ruin your hair though."

That grain of hope grew again. He was *worried* about her hair. Not the mark of a killer, she felt sure. She uttered a "uh-huh" and nodded to the door in what she hoped was the universal sign language for *go on then*.

Whether he understood or not she wasn't entirely sure but he stood up, said "Ok, stay here. I'll be right back." and left the room, locking it behind him.

She heard half the argument through the locked door.

"What you want scissors for?" A loud, annoyed Oriental accent she couldn't quite place. This voice penetrated through to her, the quieter tones of Clooney just sounded like murmuring. She wondered what mask the loud man was wearing.

"It not a fucking hair salon!"

"..."

"Why do you want to take tape off? She'll cry for help!"

"..."

"Well, who says she needs to eat just now, huh? You hungry? No. Me neither. She can wait too."

"..."

"I don't have time or crayons to explain right now, guy. Ok?"

"…"

"Look. Your job, keep her in the room. Alive. End of."

"…"

"No."

"…"

"No."

"…"

"No! Look, I could agree with you but then we would both be wrong."

"…"

"Fuck sake, guy. For the last time. You. Leave. Tape. On." Conrad checked his watch, exasperated. "It's dark now, there won't be anyone around. I'm going to go outside and make the call."

She heard a door slam and then silence. There was something about the way he said *guy* that seemed familiar and she continued listening to the silence while she tried to dislodge a memory. Clooney didn't come back.

With his left hand, Jack was playing Candy Roulette on his phone for £1000 a spin, with his right he was pulling anal beads from Melanie like he was trying to start a lawn mower. He looked confused when the phone rang in his hand. It was an unknown number. For a split-second he thought of not answering it, then the thickness in his head started to sway, his vision began to blur and he decided to use the call as something to focus on. That last blast had made him woozy and the room was still spinning.

"This better be fucking good."

"Is that Jacek B-jock-ge-vic? Jo-back-je-witz?"

"Close enough. Who's this?"

"A friend."

"Oh yeah? What do you want, friend?"

"Actually, ha, I have something I think *you* might want."

Jack looked down at the the hooker giving him a blowjob, the half-empty bag of cocaine on the coffee table, the four empty champagne bottles upended in their ice buckets and, through the open double-doors, the emperor-size bed strewn with £500 notes. "Don't think so, pal."

"Erm, yes. Jack. May I call you Jack?"

"Fire away."

"Jack, I have your wife."

Jack waited uncertainly for the end of the sentence. He imagined it might be ...*as my screensaver,* and it took him a while until he realised it wasn't coming. He slowly re-parsed the sentence to ascertain it's meaning and gave up. "Huh?"

"I have your wife, Jack. Here. With me."

"Right. Yeah. Good one."

"I assume you would like to speak to her at some point?"

"What?"

"In the future? Tonight or tomorrow perhaps?"

"Look, pal. Can you get to the point - I assume you do have one? I mean, I'm a busy man and I can't afford to waste precious time listening to a wanker like you if you can't-"

"Enough!" Jack had managed to break the patience of the voice on the other end. Throughout his life, he had invariably managed to do this. Sometimes it went well, sometimes it didn't. Didn't bother Jack much either way, truth be told. He just couldn't stop himself doing it and it was now something of a conversational touchstone for him. A badge of pride. If he couldn't piss off the person he was speaking to then something, somewhere had gone terribly wrong. Like when he went more than three games without a goal, it was a drought and something to be rectified.

"Right then, friend. State your business - in no more than five words - or I'm hanging up."

Jack waited, listening to what sounded simultaneously like silence and panic, before the voice spoke again: "We have kidnapped your wife."

The room waited.

"Jack? Did you hear me Jack?"

Jack watched Melanie continue to attend to his erection, the scene now seeming to take place underwater. Everything slow and quiet and deafened by the sound of his own heart in his chest.

"Jack. Do you want to see your wife again?"

Silence. The walls of the room expanded outwards at warp speed and then zoomed back in on him. Jack struggled to breathe.

"Jack? A hundred grand, Jack. What do you say?"

"Hold on." Jack managed, and pressed the mute button. Whilst Melanie continued her ministrations, gradually Jack felt the pulse in his neck slow and the throb in his penis increase. After another minute he felt he had regained himself enough to think clearly.

"You still there?"

"Of course, Jack. Are you ok?"

"Yes. You say you have my wife?"

"That is correct. And for one hundred thousand pounds she will be returned safely to you."

"You have my wife." Jack repeated.

"Yes, Jack. We have your wife. Would you like to see her again?"

Jack stared vacantly at Melanie's bobbing head and then, coming finally to his senses, flipped a coin.

Cullen crept round the back door to Shieldgreen, holding his badger catcher in front of him like a tightrope walkers pole. He stood with his feet far apart, making sure he was well-balanced and in a firm stance before he lifted his rear foot off the ground and swung it forward. Like a shaolin monk on a rice paper floor, Cullen quietly and slowly stalked down the hallway, eyes and ears alert for his prey.

He saw the badger snuffling away to his left at the far end of the hall, just as he heard the voices.

"What do you mean, keep her?"

He stopped and listened. It didn't sound like the Scouts and he hadn't seen any vehicle outside. Two voices, both men. Arguing now about something one of them had said. He edged up against the hall wall and inched himself along towards the door until he realised he was also closing in on the badger, still oblivious and intent on whatever it had found to eat on the floor. The door to the room with the voices was ever so slightly ajar and Cullen decided discretion was the better part of valour. Still with his back to the wall, he inched back slowly, feeling his way until he felt a door frame with his hands. He leant into the alcove just as the door ahead of him opened, bursting a shaft of light into the hallway. A figure stepped out and Cullen could only make out the man's back. Blindly, Cullen tried the knob to the door behind him and turned it. As it opened and he walked backwards into the room, he heard the man in the hall shouting and running back to the room he'd come from. Then the sound of slamming and banging and furniture moving and one voice saying over and over: "A badger. It's a fucking badger."

Cullen turned into the room and found himself looking at a beautiful woman lying on a bed, eyes wide with shock, her face covered with freckles and gaffer tape, with her hands tied behind her back.

Even though his first words were a polite "Hello", Tuppence couldn't help feel wary of this tall stranger in a cowboy hat carrying some kind of snare-on-a-stick device which she fervently hoped wasn't electrified or meant for her. His eyes cast around the room, possibly trying to work a way out, possibly trying to establish quite what he had walked into. It looked very much like he was as surprised to find her here as she was to find him.

"Are you with them?" He inclined his head towards the adjoining room.

She nodded, sadly.

"Willingly?"

She pulled a face which she hoped was a clear *'What does it look like?'*. When he didn't respond, she frowned and earnestly shook her head. The stranger approached the bed and shook it violently, perhaps attempting to drag it towards the closed door. The metal frame shrieked in protest and in the other room she heard voices again.

She looked anxiously at the door. The stranger put a

195

finger up to his lips - with no trace of irony - and then slipped out into the hallway.

Tuppence let out a muted "Umm" from behind the tape and slumped her shoulders in disappointment.

"Hello? Hello?" Conrad had answered his phone but couldn't hear anyone at the other end. Standing in the hallway, alert for the badger, he shook the handset in the hope that he could shake loose the missing voice at the other end.

"Hello." Said a quiet voice behind him. And Conrad shot out of his skin. "Masks is it?"

Conrad whirled around and found a tall man staring down into his eyes. For a moment he forgot he was wearing a mask, convinced this stranger could see him fully revealed. Whilst being several inches taller than Conrad was not unusual in itself, the confident way the man held himself made Conrad uneasy. Plus the cowboy hat made him seem even taller. He looked like he owned this place and could handle anything anyone threw at him. Conrad had no intention of starting anything. At all.

"Having a party?" The man inquired, his eyes a cold smile.

"Erm…" Conrad attempted speech but nothing would come. He could feel the fear grip his throat and his stomach dropped alarmingly.

"Mind if I-?" The man reached for Conrad's mask and as he instinctively turned his head away, he caught sight of the badger trotting around the corner. Seeing the two men, the animal bolted forwards. Conrad lurched to his left and the cowboy, holding some kind of noose-on-a-stick in his right hand, lunged to his right to try and catch the badger as it barrelled towards them. With the practised skill of long-forgotten games of British Bulldog gone wrong, Conrad squirmed away from the stranger's grasp and made a dash for it. Getting as far away from this animal and this man as he could, he pelted up the hallway towards the back door which was half-open and through which the cold air of freedom was clearly detectable.

When he reached the doorway, Conrad risked a frantic glance back. It looked as if the man had been wrested to the floor by the force of the badger hitting the noose full-on and dragging them both along the hallway. Man and badger wrangled together, each clawing and hissing; the man having the better of it and managing to move the feral animal to arm's length and more, as he leveraged the pole to push the badger up against the wall and the noose tighter.

Conrad didn't wait to see any more. He dashed out into the cold night air and pelted through the knee-length grass at right angles away from the house until he found himself on the stony track. Stumbling in the dark he kept the track beneath his feet and ran until his breath gave out, pounding and rocking along the track until the house was out of sight and he was enveloped by the forest.

Guy waited for Conrad to re-appear and realised he was holding his breath.

"Con!" He greeted when the door flew violently open but it wasn't Conrad that thundered towards him. Guy could see the badger was wearing some kind of noose around its neck, attached to which was what looked like a long fishing rod. Attached to the other end of this was a tall man wearing a lime green waterproof jacket and a leather cowboy hat. Guy couldn't work out whether the man was leading the badger or the badger was dragging the man and before he had time to find out he was knocked backwards, hit his head on something hard and felt the blackness falling up towards him.

ELEVEN

Dougie had made a note of the service schedules on the parish noticeboard at Stobo Kirk and chosen this time in the evening so as to be sure the reverend would not be home. He knocked on the front door anyway, just in case, and when there was no answer he scanned the street up and down and disappeared through the side gate into the back garden. All the windows were locked but there was a key under one of the flowerpots arrayed on the rear decking. It opened the patio doors and he slipped inside.

The vicar's "office" was actually in the hall. The front door opened onto a narrow hallway with stairs leading up off to the left and the space under the stairs held a desk and a corkboard. On the desk was a PC with a large monitor, a printer and an external disk drive. Dougie sat back in the reclining chair and turned the computer on. The vicar's screensaver was a group of cyclists in a race, all black and white except for the cyclist in front who was in colour and the legend THERE CAN ONLY BE ONE LEADER. He started searching for video files, found none of interest, so plugged in the external drive and repeated the search.

There were hundreds of them.

He sorted them by date and started viewing them from the day he had met Jack and soon found the one he was looking for. The rider was pulling slowly up an incline and in the distance, off to the right, Dougie could see his own white Range Rover. The camera drew closer and closer until it was almost level with the car and then a large blue HGV swung straight into shot, travelling over the centre line and filling the screen. The camera suddenly fell off to the left and picked up grass and tarmac before righting itself and then panning right to follow the offending truck off into the distance. Dougie didn't think much of the vicar's chances of picking up the number plate from this footage.

The view returned to the lay-by opposite the grounded cyclist and Dougie froze as a clear image lingered on the screen for several seconds showing him and Jack chatting in the front of the car. The picture then went all wonky and cut to black, presumably as the vicar removed his helmet and turned the camera off.

Dougie stared at the black screen and tried to decide on what to do. Should he delete just this clip or all the clips for that date? Or all the clips? No, not the latter, that would only indicate someone had broken in and deleted the files. And if he deleted just that one clip the vicar might be able to work out that it was him by a process of elimination. No, best to delete all the clips for that date and hope the omission wasn't spotted. He selected the clips with that date, moved them to the recycle bin and then emptied it.

Breathing more easily now, he clicked on a few more at random and watched them out of interest, turning the volume down so that the wind noise didn't crackle through the PC's speakers. This was one angry reverend. It looked like these files had been heavily edited down from the originals which, Dougie guessed, would have filmed an entire cycle journey lasting an hour or more. These were snippets of a minute or two each, showing pertinent road rage incidents and real (or imagined) traffic violations by the many drivers the vicar had encountered. Some clips showed the cyclist on his own, others were with a larger group all clad in bright colours.

There was something familiar about one of two of the riders in this group and it was only when he saw a clip of them coasting to a stop and having a break and a chat that he realised this was the same group of cyclists who had temporarily blocked his view at the Hawick mill yesterday. His heart skipped a beat and he scrolled down to the most recent clips and watched them through. What if he'd been inadvertently caught on camera at the shooting? There were three separate clips and he watched all of them the whole way through, face pressed close to the monitor to make sure he didn't miss anything vital. He slowed the footage down as they cycled along the towpath but the derelict mill passed out of shot without incident. When the group came to a halt they had obviously stood and watched the photoshoot for a while and Dougie watched along with them now, looking to see if Tuppence or the shot itself appeared. Neither did.

The final clip showed the group setting off again and the camera wobbled as the vicar moved to the front of the group and then came to a juddering halt as a speeding car leapt out of a side road and nearly smacked into them. The vicar had obviously braked and so had the car. The camera dipped down as the vicar stooped to catch the eye of the driver and Dougie looked to see if he knew who it was. He didn't - and why should he? But something caught his attention and he rewound back to before this last incident and ran it again. As the camera dipped to peer inside the vehicle he slo-mo'd it and watched carefully.

The driver was a Chinese guy who was glaring at the camera as the cyclists fist slowly appeared into shot. The camera panned right to take in the backseat and between the front seat headrests Dougie could make out the figure of a blonde man sitting bolt upright in the middle of the backseat. Next to him was a figure with what looked like a sack on its head. He rewound this split-second shot a few times and then zoomed in on the backseat figures and freeze-framed.

The figure on the back seat was wearing a dark green puffer coat.

Dougie was intrigued for a time, idly contemplating this new criminal underworld he had himself come to inhabit and marvelling at the others who might also be residing alongside him, unnoticed, as the hurly-burly "normal" world went about its business. He rocked back in the vicar's desk chair and saw yachts and fast-cars, beautiful women and suitcases full of fake passports and stacks of cash.

Here he was, taking his first steps into the glamorous world of assassins and hitmen and here were these people - the Chinaman and the Blonde, he had decided to christen them - performing what looked distinctly like a kidnapping on a bright, bustling morning as ordinary people milled all around. What larks, Pip!

Dougie was all too aware that he had not so much dipped his toe into this new world of elicit murder-for-hire, but rather belly-flopped into the deep end - taking on a contract from a premiership footballer to kill a famous model in broad daylight. He wondered whether these kidnappers were old hands or first-timers like himself and then wondered who it was they had chosen to kidnap.

He opened the vicar's browser and was greeted by a Facebook homepage called God's Own Peloton, loaded with photos and videos of cycling and cyclists. Googling *hawick kidnap* he found plenty of hits but nothing recent or relating to the photoshoot except for the BBC news story of the shooting. Out of interest, he clicked on this link and scrolled idly down only stopping when he saw the sentence:

Police have still not named the victim, said to be a woman in her twenties, who is in Borders General Hospital in a stable condition.

Oh Christ, thought Dougie. Tuppence was still alive.

He read the sentence over and over, feeling his mind dance nimbly around the two sharp swords sitting crossed at his feet, to wit: (1) Tuppence wasn't dead so he still had to find a way to kill her (2) he had already told Jack the job was done, when it clearly wasn't, so he would either need to 'fess up to Jack and confirm that he would finish the job somehow, or gamble that Jack was unaware of all this and get the job finished before he found out. Either way, he needed to visit Tuppence in hospital and finish what he had started. Whether he should tell Jack first was the question.

Dougie closed the tab and stared blankly at the screen. Images and text swam into focus and out again. Images of men on bikes. Everywhere.

He took a closer look at the homepage which was sitting in front of him and realised that the vicar had been posting clips of his road rage incidents on his Facebook page. He scrolled down for recent posts but couldn't be sure from the thumbnail images which clips had been uploaded. And whether - the thought now gripped him - the clip showing him and Jack in the Range Rover was one of them.

Aw, fuck. He'd failed to kill the target, had told his employer she was dead when she wasn't and now it was a distinct possibility that some god-botherer had plastered a video of him meeting his employer on the internet. Fuck, fuck, fuck. Perhaps this hitman business wasn't going to be as easy as he'd thought. With a heavy heart, he called Jack's number. It took some time for him to pick up and when he did Jack sounded quite, well, spaced out.

"It's me." Dougie said.

"Hello me."

"I, er, thought I'd better call." Dougie swallowed hard, wishing he'd rehearsed what he was about to say. "There have been some developments."

"No shit, Sherlock." Jack interrupted.

"I mean, with regard to your wife-"

"S'what I'm talking about."

Dougie wished the bastard would let him get the words out, this was difficult enough as it was. "Yes, you see, erm, she's - well, she's still alive."

"I know."

"You see, I thought-. What?"

"I just spoke to them."

"What?"

"I. Just. Spoke. To. Them."

"What? Who?"

"The kidnappers."

"Who?" Dougie wasn't entirely sure he and Jack were sharing the same conversation.

"The kidnappers who have kidnapped her."

"What?"

"I swear to fucking God-"

"Ok. Ok. Sorry. Hang on, let me recap here. Make sure I understand." Dougie took a deep breath and tried to speak slowly and calmly. "Someone has phoned you up and told you they have kidnapped your wife?"

"Yes."

"Right." Dougie couldn't have chosen a more inappropriate word to summarise his current state of mind. "So she's not in hospital then?"

"Huh?"

"Your wife. Is she not in hospital?"

"Not unless the kidnappers are there with her, dickhead."

Dougie found himself shaking his head, literally trying to worry his thoughts loose. "Ok. And you said?"

"I told them to fuck off."

"Because?"

"Because I thought it was a wind-up because you told me she was dead!"

"Ah."

"Which she clearly isn't because they've kidnapped her! Unless this is some new, cutting edge crime: kidnapping corpses."

"Right. Right. Right." Dougie was completely out of ideas, talking to himself now as much as anything. "So, who's in the hospital then?"

"What FUCKING hospital?"

"Never mind."

"So, what now, Einstein, hmm? You think you're gonna lie to me and take my money? Think again."

"I am thinking…" Dougie willed his brain into gear. "Did they say where they were? The kidnappers?"

"What? Oh yeah, they gave me their address. I've got it right here… No Fucking Way, Stupid Motherfucking Central, Nowheresville." Dougie was scrabbling for a pen before he got Jack's point. "Of course they didn't say where they were, they're fucking kidnappers. Cretin. Although, if you were a kidnapper instead of a hitman you'd have given me your address, wouldn't you? That's how fucking useless you are!"

"Look, let's calm down shall we? Try to think clearly."

"Listen, shitforbrains. I don't have to think clearly 'cos we're done. See, these fuckers are going to do your job for you. And it won't cost me a penny."

"Jack. Jack. Be reasonable, here."

"I am being reasonable. I'm not even going to ask you for my ten grand back."

"But you don't understand!" Dougie was struggling to keep traction in this discussion now, feeling it all slipping away from him "They're kidnappers! They don't want to kill her, they want you to give them money!"

"But I'm not going to give them money. I've told them to fuck off."

"But do you think they're just going to give up like that? They're desperate enough for money that they've kidnapped someone!"

"That's rich coming from somebody so desperate for money they're prepared to kill someone."

"Touché. But what do you think they're really going to do? Just kill her, dump the body and find someone else to kidnap? Of course not. They'll cut off an ear and send it to the papers, or put video of them torturing her online and ask for more money." Dougie started to warm to his theme and felt a gathering silence on the line as he ran with his imagination. "There'll be a nationwide manhunt, police search parties, vigilantes. You'll probably have to put a reward out for her safe return. Press Conferences. Like Madeleine McCann, you'll be constantly in the papers. You may even get accused of orchestrating it yourself. You'll end up paying a fortune to get her back. And then, with all the publicity, you won't be able to bump her off without arousing suspicion. And at the end of it all, Jack, you'll be stuck with her. For years and years. Forced to appear happily married. Is that what you really want? Is it?"

There was a long pause and then a very quiet: "No."

"No, of course it fucking isn't." Dougie had reacquired the whip hand.

Jack surrendered. "So, what's the plan?"

"Give me a minute." Jack waited silently while Dougie tried to think. "Ok, here's what we do. Call them back and tell them you've had a change of heart."

"A change of heart?"

"Yeah. You made a mistake. You were in shock. Whatever. Just tell them you really DO want her back and wait for them to propose the handover."

"But that means I'll have to pay the ransom."

"No, It'll be our secret. You pretend to go along with it so that we can find out where they propose to do the handover. I get there ahead of time and, when they turn up with Tuppence, I shoot her. She dies. You don't spend any more money. I get my fee. They get fuck all. Everyone's a winner!"

Jack was silent for a while before giving a quiet chuckle. "Not too shabby."

"Thank you." Dougie smiled to himself. "And Jack. The kidnappers? When you spoke to them did one of them sound Chinese at all?"

"I only spoke to one man."

"Did he sound Chinese?"

"He did a bit. Why do you ask?"

"No reason."

Well, Dougie thought, all things considered, that probably couldn't have gone any better. So it had been Tuppence he'd seen in the back of that car with the Chinaman and the Blonde. Fancy that. Which just left the question: who was the poor fucker in hospital?

Confused, he sat at the desk tapping his fingers when he heard a key in the front door.

The phone lying on the hallway floor said "One missed call." Cullen picked it up, looked at it somewhat disbelievingly and wandered back into the room where Tuppence sat. As he walked over to her she could detect the smell of dampness, mud and sweat. Chokingly rising above it all was badger musk which he must have had all over his hands because as he grabbed the tape at her mouth she reflexively pulled her head away and felt her gorge rise in her throat. He pulled, she turned and the tape ripped away from her face just as she projectile-vomited across the room, dregs of spittle and sick flecking her clothes as she coughed and breathed properly for the first time in a long while.

"Round here, we normally just say 'hello'." He said.

She finished coughing and rasping, clearing her throat and swallowing bile before looking up at him beneath her damp mop of hair. "Sorry. It's not you, it's the smell."

"Of me?"

"No. Well it's the smell of the badger, on you." She nodded at his hands and he lifted them to his own nose and inhaled deeply.

"Fair enough."

He looked around as if for something to wipe them with, imagining that would be sufficient to remove the stench. She couldn't understand how he could sniff his hands and not at least wince. She felt a sharp, cold pull on her wrists and released he had cut the cable tie binding her hands. She brought both hands round in front of her and rubbed her wrists with relief.

"Thank you."

"Recognise this number?" Cullen said, showing her the screen.

"Yes, that's Jack. He called you?"

"Not me. The kidnappers."

"Well, call him back then."

Cullen looked uncertainly at the phone and then Tuppence but, seeing her steadfastness, decided to hit the call button. It was picked up after two rings.

"This is Jack."

"Jack, this is the kidnapper." Cullen deadpanned. "I am returning your call."

"Oh, yeah. Hi." Jack sounded weirdly cheerful and Cullen couldn't but help stand outside himself for a moment and look at how unreal this conversation was even while he was having it. Jack continued. "Listen, I, er, may have been a bit, er, hasty when you first called."

"Yes? Well. That is all very well and good but certain wheels have been put in motion."

"What are you doing?" Tuppence hissed in disbelief.

Conrad covered the mic with his hand and looked impassively at her. "Sorry, what was that?" he said into the phone.

"I said, 'what wheels'?"

"Certain, erm, steps have been initiated which may... not end well for your wife. I am afraid it might be no longer possible to guarantee her safety."

Tuppence's eyebrows shot up in alarm.

"Aw, shit." Said Jack.

Cullen felt instinctively that Jack's reaction was wrong. This was the response of a man who had just missed his last train home and not of a man who was about to lose his wife. He pondered for a moment. "Please stay on the line." Cullen covered the mic again, looked at Tuppence and slowly counted to ten. "Jack, are you still there?"

"Yes, I'm still here."

"You are a lucky man, Jack. Your wife is unharmed and at no further risk until I make another call. Would you like me to make that other call?"

Tuppence crossed her fingers.

"No." Jack exhaled. "No. I would like to... accept your original offer."

"A hundred and fifty thousand?"

"No. No. A hundred thousand."

"One hundred. And fifty." Cullen repeated.

"You robbing -"

"Is this sum beyond you?"

"No, no. Not at all. Ok, £150,000. Do we have a deal?"

"We do." Cullen gave Tuppence a single thumbs up.

"But I'll need some time."

"Excuse me?"

"To get the extra money. I'll need more time."

"How much time?"

"Er, a few days. Just a few days, is all."

Cullen thought on his feet. "You have until Friday."

"Er, wait. Hang on." Jack sounded like he was panicking at the other end. "Hang on... how about Saturday?"

"I said Friday."

"Yes, but you must understand I have commitments - training, matches, personal appearance, all that. I can't just drop everything and get that much money together by Friday."

"Then you must say Goodbye to your wife. Shall I put her on the line?" As soon as the words were out of his mouth, Cullen bit his lip. Shit, he'd said that a call was required to make sure Tuppence was still alive. Why would he say that if she was here beside him ready to speak to Jack. He held his breath waiting for Jack's response.

"No! No, that won't be necessary." Cullen breathed a sigh of relief. "Look, I'll be in Edinburgh for a game on Saturday. Cup Tie, actually. That's only one day later. Can we make it Saturday?"

Cullen thought for a second. "Ok. Saturday. Call this number when you have the money and we will arrange the details of the exchange. Are we agreed?"

"Yes. Sure. Yeah." Jack sounded relieved.

"Good." Cullen was too. "Goodbye, Jack."

"Hey!"

When Dick entered his hallway he saw a leg disappear through into his living room and quickly surveyed the scene. His desk area was always a bit of a jumble at the best of times but he definitely made a habit of turning his screen off and unplugging his external hard drive. Both were currently attached. The intruder had been looking

211

through his files and Dick's Facebook page was shining at him on the monitor. He quietly opened the tall cupboard by the door where he kept coats and boots and stuff and searched with his hand for the old seven iron he kept in there. There was no sound coming from the living room as his hand fastened on the golf club and he felt himself straighten his back, readying his defence.

"I'm calling the police!" He yelled down the hall, knowing it would carry into the large open room beyond. God knew the postman had no trouble attracting his attention when he was deeply buried in a casserole recipe over the stove, which was the furthest point from the front door the builders could have arranged.

There was no answer so Dick trod slowly down the hallway towards the door.

"I'm warning you. They'll be here any minute."

When he got to the door he stood against one jamb as he had seen policemen do in films and shoved the door open in one quick movement whilst leaning back out of the way.

There was no-one there. He cleared his throat.

"Blessed be the Lord, my rock, who trains my hands for war, and my fingers for battle. Psalm 144:1"

Dick looked back at his desk, reassuring himself that he wasn't going mad and that someone had been here since he'd gone out. Had he seen a flash of disappearing leg?

"Hello! I know you're here." His eyes scanned the room but not only could he detect no sign of an intruder he could see no suitable place where one could hide. The sofa was side onto him so he could see front and back. No-one there. The table which served as both kitchen and dining table was unadorned and he could see right beneath it and the through the various chair legs. Same for the breakfast bar which helped divide his kitchen area from his living space.

"I'm armed you know. There's no use in hiding from me. Might as well reveal yourself. *Or else I will stretch out my hand, that I may smite thee. Exodus 9:15.*"

The patio doors to his small back garden were closed and so was the door to the utility room. That was the only place he could be, but there was nowhere to hide within it, so the intruder was either waiting on the other side of that door ready to pounce or was a figment of Dick's now hyper-alert imagination.

He stepped slowly towards the utility room door, his hand twisting and tightening around the golf club's rubber grip, only to hear a movement behind him. He turned and saw a shock of pink hair and then the barrel of a gun inches from his nose.

"I'd like to introduce you to two new members of your congregation: Smith and Wesson."

The intruder had short blond hair, thinning on top, and a streak of it had been dyed a bright pink, cutting a strange swathe across his head. One nostril and one earlobe were pierced with identical gold rings and he was growing an ostentatious looking Van Dyke beard, with what looked suspiciously like a waxed moustache. He looked familiar and yet, at the same time, utterly other-worldly.

"Do I know you?"

The intruder just looked bored and shrugged.

"*And the Lord said: Cursed be he that smiteth his neighbour. And all the people shall say, Amen. Deuteronomy 27:24*" quoted Dick.

The stranger looked at his watch. "Yeah? Well the

213

Lord can suck my dick. Me 7:45."

Dick could tell that this man was not going to be much influenced by the scriptures.

"What do you want? I don't have any money."

"I know. You're just a lowly priest. Blah blah blah."

"Not a priest, actually. More of-"

"I want your Facebook password."

"What? Why?"

"Because I want it. So…" He waggled the gun under Dick's nose, motioning him back out to his desk in the hallway. "Render unto Caesar that which belongs to Caesar."

"It doesn't belong to-. Ow!" The gun jabbed Dick's adam's apple and *really* hurt. "It's Ecclesiastes7:9."

The intruder looked unimpressed. "Enlighten me."

"*Do not be quickly provoked in your spirit, for anger resides in the lap of fools.*" Dick parroted.

"Huh." The man sat down at the computer and laid down the gun. "How do you spell Ecclesiastes?"

"Upper case E, lower case: c, c, l, e, s, i, a, s, t, e, s, seven colon nine." Dick felt dirty and watched the man type the unfamiliar sequence uncertainly on the keyboard, two fingers pecking at the keys.

"Couldn't you have chosen a quote from Job or something?"

The man zoomed around Dick's Facebook page and went to his uploaded files section, scrolling up and down to see what was there. He selected a swathe of files and deleted them.

"Hey!"

"Sorry, reverend. Don't have time to check 'em one by one." He quickly logged back off and turned round to face Dick again. "Chin up. You can upload the ones you want again at your leisure. Now, just sit here quietly for a wee while and I'll be out of your hair forever. Toodle pip!"

The man disappeared out of the front door and let it click softly behind him. Dick looked at his monitor and the homepage of his Facebook profile the man had left displayed. His latest post read: *"Too many Christians treat the Bible like a Software License Agreement. They don't read it, they just scroll to the bottom and click Agree."*

Tuppence watched from through the open bedroom door as the cowboy expertly went about his business. First, he lifted the heavy table up by one leg and looped the "badger stick grasper" around it. Lowering the table effectively tethered the badger to it, leaving it able to prescribe an arc of some six feet and no more. The badger jerked and struggled, trying to free its neck from the tight grip and, when that failed, clawing and biting at the loop around the table leg. As it fought, it pissed, and the foul smelling odour exploded into the bedroom. Tuppence tried not to gag.

Now with both hands free, the cowboy swiftly manhandled Clooney into a sitting position and then tied him tightly to a chair with some rope. When he had done this, he dragged the chair on its back legs to the far end of the room, away from the badger and removed the Clooney mask.

He moved back over to the bedroom door midway between Tuppence, sitting on the mattress, and Clooney unmasked at the far end of the living room. The cowboy leant against the door jamb and took off his hat. His grey curly hair was clamped to his head where the hatband had been and he was sweating heavily. He wiped his brow with his sleeve and looked over at her.

"Recognise him?"

Tuppence looked at the kidnapper and scrutinised his features. Reluctantly she shook her head and looked around the room as if for the first time and through the open door. "Where's the other one?"

The cowboy shrugged off his coat and let it fall to floor. He was perhaps six feet tall and rangy, perhaps even a little gaunt. Middle-aged, greying hair and hard features: sharp nose, creases on his forehead and around his eyes. His ears stuck out a little and he wore a few days stubble.

"Dunno." He shrugged. "Gone."

Tuppence was worried. "What if he comes back?"

The creases around his eyes appeared briefly and his grey eyes twinkled. "Little fella. Probably piss himself when he sees the badger again."

"Do you know him?"

"No. But I know his type. Amateur."

Tuppence looked at him with new interest. "Who are you?"

"You can call me Cullen."

"Why? Is that not your name?" She asked innocently.

"No. It's my name." He raised his eyebrows at her, enquiringly. Tuppence started.

"Oh, sorry. Tuppence. Tuppence Lowry?" He looked as if he was waiting for something more. "Do you know who I am?"

"Tuppence Lowry." He said, slowly, as if to a small child.

"Right. So, you're not here to rescue me then."

Now it was Cullen's turn to frown. "But I have

216

rescued you. See?" He held his palms out and upwards, offering the room and its contents as his witness.

"So why did you just ask my husband for £150,000 for my safe return? Not the act of a traditional rescuer I'd say."

"Well, you're right there. I don't know who you are and I wasn't sent here to rescue you. I was just -" He thought for a moment. "In the area."

"You don't know who I am?"

"No."

She wondered, suddenly, if she should be more worried than she was. "Do you live nearby?"

He ignored her question and asked one of his own. "Do you know where you are?"

"No." For the first time since she'd come round she realised she had absolutely no idea where she was.

"Does anyone know you're here?"

"I don't think so."

"Then you're not rescued." He smirked. "Yet."

He led the way out of the house through a back door which opened onto an overgrown, uneven patch of grass surrounded by a low, derelict picket fence. On the other side of the fence were nettles, weeds and thistles and then a dilapidated dry stone wall. Behind that was a looming pine forest which stretched away to her left and right as far as she could see. He pushed through the long grass around the side of the house and she followed him closely. The wet grass soaked through her clothes and she realised she was unsuitably dressed for her new location.

They walked out onto a path with the forest to her left and a burn running down below them. On the other side was a single cinder track road which wound right past the house and away around a bend and to the left followed the burn downhill. Behind the road more forest rose up to the sky, dark and dense and green.

The path followed a gentle descent and gradually opened out until it too became a cinder track. They crossed a footbridge and then up a wooded incline, through a gate and emerged out into open moorside, the valley widening considerably but still topped on both sides by conifers.

"Where are we?"

"This is Glentress forest." He indicated to her left and then to her right. "And that is Venlaw. And this-" he waved at the path they were taking. "Leads to Peebles."

"Is that where we're going?"

"No."

"O-o-o-kay." She stopped walking and waited until he stopped to and turned to face her. "Well, where are you taking me then?"

"Somewhere safe."

She held her ground, looked sceptical and waited.

"Look, until either of us know what is going on I think it's probably best if we put you somewhere safe where no-one knows where you are."

"Well, I don't agree." Tuppence put her hands on her hips and stood firm. "I would like to know what the hell is going on. And call my husband, tell him where I am and have him come and get me."

Cullen looked at her, sorrowfully. "I think, perhaps, we need to have a little talk."

TWELVE

Big Paul was busy hammering in the last nail with a brick when Cullen poked his head around the corner and gave him a start. Paul looked at him sheepishly as he finished hammering and Cullen led Tuppence into view.

"Tuppence, this is Paul. Solving today's problems with yesterday's technology."

Paul's jaw dropped, and the brick went with it.

"Paul, this is Tuppence."

Tuppence held out a hand while Paul continued to stand agape. Cullen coughed and Paul put out a hand, saw it, spat on it, wiped it on his overalls and offered it again. Tuppence smiled and declined.

"Wha-?" Paul began.

Cullen ignored him, talking to Tuppence. "You'll be safe here for a few days." Then to Paul: "Won't she?"

"Wha-?"

"It may not be much to look at." Cullen scanned the half-finished interior of the cabin. "But you couldn't get much safer."

"It doesn't, erm, look safe." Tuppence offered then, turning to Paul. "No offence."

"It's as solid as he is." Cullen nodded at Paul who was still mute and then smacked the wall with the side of his fist. A curtain pole rattled briefly but held.

"Got to tighten that up." Paul stirred and smiled apologetically.

"I didn't mean like that."

"Ah, but the beauty of this place is that it doesn't

technically exist." Cullen said. "It's not on any registers, doesn't appear on any maps, doesn't have a number or a postcode, isn't served by any utilities or known by any council."

Paul chipped in. "Yeah. Half the neighbours don't know it's even here yet."

"I see." Tuppence looked around the dishevelment and bravely tried to see it as a finished safe haven. Relenting, she turned to Paul again. "Is there a toilet or - dare I dream - a shower?"

"Shower? Not yet. Toilet? Through there." Paul hitched a thumb at a door to his left. Tuppence excused herself and disappeared through it, struggling with whatever lock was on the other side of it. Paul took some time to come to his senses while Cullen plonked himself on the sofa and took off his hat, inspecting and testing the stitching.

"Do you know who that is?" Paul finally managed.

"Yes." Said Cullen. "Tuppence Lowry."

"You say that as if you don't know who Tuppence Lowry is."

Cullen pushed his bottom jaw out disappointedly. "Who is she?"

"Ever heard of Gille Santerre?"

"No."

"Christa Tuscan Wilde?"

"Nope."

"Lucille Grande?"

"No. What are they, fonts?" Cullen was close to losing what little interest he had in this conversation.

"Supermodels."

"Supermodels?"

"Yes. You know, beautiful women who model

clothes? Pin-ups? Cover girls?"

"I know what a supermodel is."

"Really? You don't recognise any of their names." Paul was aghast not just at how little Cullen knew but how little he cared about not knowing. "These are some of the most beautiful women. In. The. World."

"And Tuppence is …?" Cullen persisted.

"New kid on the block. Flavour of the month. All over the papers."

"Huh." Cullen acknowledged.

"Huh! Is that all you've got - huh! How the hell did you hook up with her? How… What… I'm just chock full of questions."

Cullen shrugged. "I just picked her up."

"You picked her up?"

"I mean I found her."

"What, you mean you were just walking through Glentress and you found her?" Paul's face could not have made his disbelief more profoundly apparent.

"Pretty much."

"And then brought her here?"

Cullen nodded. "Yeah."

"Mate. This is my home. It may not be finished yet, but it's my home. It is not your knocking shop."

"Oh, I don't think she likes me." Cullen looked offended by the idea. "Actually, I made her sick."

When Liv woke up it was dark outside but her room was full of fresh flowers and a large bowl of fruit with a card in it. She couldn't read it from her bed and she was connected up to at least one drip so decided the information on it could wait until later.

221

Her shoulder felt like it'd been stomped on by a horse and her head throbbed like a bugger. And she was immensely hungry. She looked around her bedside for a button or some other means of summoning a nurse when one appeared, smiling sheepishly.

"How are you feeling?"

"Starving." She tried a smile. "I assume that's a good sign?"

"You're doing fine. Your wound should heal nicely."

"Wound?" She looked down at her shoulder, bandaged beneath her gown.

"Yes. Gunshot wound. They took the bullet out, but you will have a scar. A very small one.""

"Bullet?" Liv couldn't quite comprehend what the nurse was saying to her. Her brain felt... mushy.

"Could you sort me some food out, please? I really could eat a dog with a scabby head right now."

The nurse gave a wincing smile. "I'll see what I can do. There's a policeman here to see you."

"Policeman?"

The nurse left and a sheepish-looking young man in uniform shuffled in, brandishing a small notebook

"Ms. Nightingale?"

"Yes. What happened? Who shot me?"

"Well, that is what we are trying to establish. I was hoping you could tell me, actually."

"Ha!" Liv couldn't help the outburst. "I didn't even know I'd been shot until about thirty second ago. You're talking to the wrong person."

"Well, perhaps then we could start with what you do know. Can you tell me what you remember?"

Liv lay back into the pillows and tried to piece together what had happened at the photoshoot. She remembered standing in the corridor chatting to Tuppence and then just some strange sensation of falling backwards for an eternity. All the sound dying in the air and she remembered seeing the individual motes of dust as they danced in the light streaming in from the window, then a gentle feeling of warmth wrapping itself around her as her vision dimmed. Then waking up.

"I don't know. I was… standing in the corridor talking to Tuppence, smoking a fag. Then I fell. Backwards, I think. Then I woke up here." She screwed her face up at the policeman as if the physical effort might dislodge some additional memory. It didn't. "The end."

"I see. And do you know why anyone would want to shoot you?"

The nurse brought in a tray of some pasta and Liv started to wolf it down. After a few mouthfuls which diminished the hunger pangs, she started to slow down and feel better. She looked up at the policeman.

"I'm sure there are plenty of people I've pissed off in my time - pissed on and pissed off, in fact - but I'm not sure there are any who'd be driven to take a pop at me." She wrinkled up her nose as she thought. "Though there's plenty I wouldn't mind taking a pop at myself. Was anyone else shot at?"

"Not that we are aware of."

"But didn't Tuppence say anything?"

"Tuppence? Who's Tuppence?"

"She's a friend. A model who was on the shoot. She was right there when it happened."

"No. I'm sorry, I don't -"

"Tuppence Lowry?"

The policeman made a note in his book.

"Yes. I was talking to Tuppence when I fell down. She was right there. Did she go and fetch help?" Liv played the memory back, testing to see if Tuppence was still there in her head. Suddenly an image of Conrad popped into her head. She had been chatting to Tuppence and seen something out of the corner of her eye at the end of the corridor, glanced to her left and seen Conrad walking round the corner, dressed in black. Hadn't she? Why would he have been there? She heard the policeman talking again and tuned back in.

"- no witnesses that we know of. The lady who called us was…" He consulted his notes. "Selma Hatchard."

"But what about Tuppence?" Liv didn't understand. "Or Conrad? Was he there?"

"Conrad?"

"Never mind." She stopped chewing for a moment and shook her head from side to side, trying to dislodge the real from the imaginary. "I'm sorry. That's all I have, I'm afraid."

The policeman closed his notebook and gave her a business card. "Please. Once you have had time to rest and reflect, please let us know. Anything. At the moment we have nothing to go on really."

When he had left the nurse reappeared to take the tray away.

"Is my phone here?" Liv asked.

The nurse rummaged around in the handbag under the bed and retrieved it for her. Liv entered her PIN and dialled Tuppence's number, but all she got was her voicemail.

Tuppence re-appeared holding a door handle

apologetically. "Sorry. It came off."

"No worries." Paul took it from her. She looked tired and drawn, her freckled face pale and stretched. A million miles away from the magazine cover images of her he'd seen. "I'm sorry I don't have a shower yet. Soon." He apologised.

Tuppence looked around for Cullen and, not seeing him, raised her eyebrows at Paul.

"He's ... gone." Paul said. Then, sensing she might be alarmed by this, tried to reassured her. "He'll be back. At some point. He does that."

"Right." She was wandering around this unfinished structure, running her fingers over the few sticks of furniture he owned. "And what do you do?"

"Chippie. Er, carpenter." He clarified. "Joiner actually."

"Is there a difference?"

Paul snorted. "God, yeah."

"Oh sorry." She bit her bottom lip as if in atonement for her ignorance and Paul instantly forgave her everything.

"No, no. I should apologise. You don't need to know the difference. It's... no biggie." He felt a little like a schoolboy on a first date, unable to make conversation. "What do you do?"

"I'm a model."

"Right." He continued to feign ignorance. "I thought maybe you looked familiar."

"I've been in magazines, you know."

"Right. Yeah, I may have seen you in a magazine. I read those sometimes, you know. Not *those* sort of magazines, you know? I mean, I'm not implying... I mean I don't..."

"It's ok." She laughed delightfully at his embarrassment, dimples appearing in both cheeks. "I know what you mean."

"Can I get you a beer? I mean, while I'm getting one myself?"

"Sure." She said it as if the idea of drinking a beer was a complete novelty she'd always been meaning to try and never got around to. When he handed her the can he made a show of opening his own, in front of her, slowly, in case she had never done it before.

She watched him glug down the entire can and then reaching for another. He saw her watching him and felt the need to explain himself.

"Needed that."

"Do you, um, always drink this much?"

This much? Two cans? Who's idea of too much was this? How the hell do you reply to a question like that? "No. Yeah. Sometimes." Paul looked at her. "I'm having a bad week."

"Me too. Why's your week bad?"

"Well, I'm working on a kitchen refit, for a friend, and laying this floor - solid oak. And somehow, someone- don't know who, don't know how - but the measurements I had were wrong. So I spend ages laying this floor - it's gotta be glued down too. And then I got to a certain point I had this nagging feeling that something wasn't quite right. And I looked at what I'd done and what I had left and realised I'd laid it wrong, so I had to spend more time I don't have lifting it all back up and reordering more wood. I'll have to swallow the cost too. Solid oak." He whistled.

"Huh."

"How 'bout you?"

"Well, one of my best friends was shot - right in front of me - and then I was kidnapped by two men who put a bag over my head. Then I was rescued - so it wasn't all bad - but then my rescuer tells me that the kidnappers contacted my husband for the ransom and my husband told them to ... fuck off. *They could keep me,* he said."

Paul sighed heavily. "Well, it's a big kitchen floor you know? Lot of wood. Did I say it was solid oak? 'Cos... you know... it took ages... and it's going to cost me... ok, you win."

And she hit him with a megawatt smile. Although with a few tears added.

"Listen, you've had a very bad week." He offered. "I've had a pretty bad week. What say we both just drown those blues away, hmm?" He raised his beer and she wiped a tear away and chinked hers against it

"Right. Ok." She brightened. "Tonight's forecast: alcohol with low standards. Judgement, poor."

For someone who thought two cans of beer was a lot, Tuppence kept up with Paul's alcohol consumption pretty well. Perhaps, not in volume per se, but they continued chatting and drinking and seemed to be getting drunk at about the same rate as each other. The colour had returned to her face too.

"You married?"

Paul let out a belly laugh. "Look around you, what do you think?" He looked at her thoughtfully. "You are though, right? What's it like?"

"It's... well, I thought it was... ok. Now I don't know at all."

"Well, thank you Ms Lowry, for that deep insight into

the state of matrimony."

She elbowed him in the ribs. "I don't remember telling you my full name." She tilted her head to one side, eyes narrowing. "Wait a minute, you knew who I was the whole time!"

"Guilty." Paul nodded, sadly.

"Why did you do that?"

"Nervous, I guess. We don't get a whole load of beautiful women round here." He hung his head in mock shame. "Sorry, should've said."

She smiled and looked him in the eye. "Paul, you are... a charming man."

"And your husband is a very lucky man."

"Huh. Well. He is lucky. But he may not be my husband for much longer" She contemplated this novel observation for a while in silence. "But you seem like a nice man. Funny, considerate, honest."

"Yeah, well I was married once. In a relationship for a long time and then..."

"What?"

"Then I suddenly wasn't." His eyes creased at the recall. "She decided she didn't want me anymore and things went downhill pretty fast from there really." He swigged his beer to try and shake the memories free but it didn't work. "I must have made one teeny huge mistake. Thing is, if I did, she never told me what it was." He got up from the sofa. "Another beer?"

"Sure."

"But look at me now! Turned the corner, building my own place, money coming in. Beautiful woman in my living room. Happy Days!"

"And do you have anyone right now?"

"Maybe. Yeah, I think so. Usually, though, it's just me

and Ant & Dec."

"Ant & Dec?"

"My dogs."

"Right." She looked around for them, unsuccessfully. "But are you happy?"

"Sure." Paul answered, unhesitatingly. "I mean I may have squandered much of my potential, but I'm getting by alright ekeing our what's left of it."

She opened her new beer. "I think you're lovely!"

"Well that's very nice. But you are, I suspect, in a rather small minority. I mean, don't get me wrong, I agree with you. I think I'm a great catch." He swallowed a burp. "Sometimes I really wonder what the fuck is wrong with people. Women in particular."

"Is this one of those times?"

"No." He said emphatically. "Fuck other people, I say. If I'm good enough for you, I'm good enough for them."

"Hear, hear!" She looked at him, full in the face and he blushed. "You know, we're both in the same boat aren't we? Unappreciated, when we shouldn't be."

"Absolutely." He tried to give her a meaningful look. "You're not suggesting that we…?"

"No." She replied swiftly.

"Of course, not. No. Just checking."

"Are you really planning on building this whole place yourself?" Tuppence looked around and, for the first time, saw the work it might take and the skill it might involve.

"Sure."

"It seems awfully daunting. Wouldn't it be easier to

229

just, you know, buy somewhere?"

"Easier, yes. Cheaper, no."

"Ah, right. Money's an issue then." Spoken like a conclusion she'd independently arrived at, rather than a question. He thought about this for a moment.

"You know, it's funny hearing someone phrase it like that. I guess I've never thought about it, and that's the problem: it's *not* an issue for me, which is why it *is* an issue for me. Money comes in, money goes out. Like the tide. Sometimes the tide is high, sometimes it's so far out all you can see is beach. Trying to catch the tide and keep it, it's kinda pointless."

"Have you ever had a lot of money?"

"Nope. Being in debt's kind of a lifelong hobby, I guess. You, on the other hand, I bet you're loaded aren't you?"

"Yeah." She sighed, embarrassed at the truth of it. "Seems wrong when I see you like this, though. You're at least working for your money and, even if it isn't much - maybe, because it isn't much - I bet it feels hard won doesn't it? Me, I just stand there looking pretty in someone else's clothes, in photos someone else is taking, and they can't seem to stop me throwing the stuff at me."

"Plus, hubby? He's probably more loaded than you isn't he?"

"Probably." She sighed again, and then sparked suddenly into anger. "But, you know what, the man's got an awful lot of explaining to do - money or no money."

Paul softened his tone. "Does he love you?"

"Well, I don't know how to answer that right now, do I?" She tried to calm down and uncover her true feelings, beneath this beer-fuelled indignation. "Sometimes I'm sure he does. He *says* he does. Sometimes. But sometimes I think he's just… using me."

"You mean, sexually?" Paul's interest was immediately aroused.

"Yes." She dropped her voice to almost a whisper. "You know, sometimes, it's like I'm not even there." She stared off into the distance and Paul waited to see if his silence would draw more out of her. "Can I ask you a very personal question?"

"Huh-uh." Paul managed, now struggling unsuccessfully from becoming erect.

"What do you do immediately after sex?" She looked up into his eyes with such open and confiding innocence he thought his heart would break. He couldn't bear this genuine intimacy so back-pedalled into his default mode.

"Usually delete my browser history."

She snorted beer out her nose and drunkenly put her head on his shoulder. "You're funny."

He waited, delighted to be bearing her weight. It was as if he could feel her beauty, inside and out, through the heat of her on the cloth of his shirt. She lay still for a minute or two, then roused herself.

"I have three questions."

"Shoot."

"What time is it and where is Mr Cullen?"

"It's 11:20 and I don't know. Guess he'll appear in the morning." Paul counted off two fingers. "You said three questions. What's the third one?"

"Do you have anywhere where I can throw up?"

The bright morning light glared off the patch of lino Paul was using as temporary flooring in his temporary kitchen. Tuppence padded in wearing only one of his brushed cotton workshirts and he took one look at her and thought he was going to come in his pants.

"I think I've stubbed my toe."

There was a smear of blood between the toes on her pedicured, but dirty, left foot.

"Ok." He pulled himself up from where he'd been lying on the sofa and padded over to a kitchen cupboard. "Gotta second aid kit in here somewhere."

"You mean first aid kit?"

"No, first aid kit's in the van. Where I usually need it. This here-" he pulled a zipped bag about the size of a phone book from the cupboard and opened it. "Is a second aid kit. Let's see…"

She nosed over his shoulder into the contents. "What've you got?

"Plasters…" he handed her one. "Some booze. Chocolate?" she declined. "Floss. Duct tape. Spare undies, a, er…" He took the condom out of the bag and shoved it into his pocket. "And… bacon!"

"Bacon?" She looked him disbelievingly. "How long has that been in there?"

Paul sniffed the unopened vacpac and waved it at her. "Bacon! Never goes off, man."

"Right. I'll… just take the plaster if it's all the same."

"As you wish." He shoved everything back into the bag and returned it to the cupboard. "Waste not, want not." Tuppence applied the plaster to hide a perfectly painted toe-nail and, somehow, made it look sexy. Paul decided to busy himself with her out of sight. He poured water into a kettle.

"Tea?"

"Please." She felt a chill and hugged herself to try and

generate some heat. "What time is it?"

"Dunno. Ten-ish? Why?"

"I'm wondering where Mr Cullen is."

"Look, two things I'll tell you for free. One: don't call him Mister Cullen. Really gets his goat. Two: don't go expecting him. He doesn't do expecting. In fact, he's so bloody arse-y that the more you expect him the more likely he is to fail to turn up, just to annoy you."

"But I thought he was your friend?"

"Oh, he is. But he's also a fully paid-up member of the awkward squad."

"He saved me." She presented this as prima facie evidence that he didn't know what he was talking about. "Said he'd help me."

"Did he?"

"Yep."

"Well, then he will help you."

"Good." she smiled, happily.

"Just don't expect the help you get to be the help you want."

"Why not?"

Paul considered this for a while, not having ever had to explain this to anyone before, and poured the boiling water into two mugs with teabags in them. "He doesn't work like that. He's not a big one for rules - unless they're his rules. He mostly just tries to keep out of the way. And every now and then, he kind of appears, and things go a bit wonky for a while."

"Oh." She seemed crestfallen as he handed her the tea. "Thanks."

"I mean he won't open the can for you. But he will give it a bloody good shake, so you need to be careful when you open it that you don't get it all over you."

She took a sip and looked out of the window at the trees on the other side of the valley. "He seems nice enough."

"Yeah, doesn't he."

Dougie put the phone down and typed the details of Lindsay's problem into the IT ticketing database. Under the section marked "Problem Diagnosis" he typed PICNIC. All user issues were logged and categorised so that the CEO could see monthly stats about the health of the company's IT, illustrated in simple Red/Amber/Green pie-charts on a Powerpoint slide. Each month the slides showed a healthy percentage of issues raised and resolved relating to the PICNIC system, which the CEO knew to be the company's IT system responsible for payroll, health, holiday/overtime pay, and National Insurance contributions. But it wasn't. PICNIC was Dougie's code for user error: Problem In Chair, Not In Computer.

His mobile rang and when he picked it up he could see it was Jack. Dougie got up from his desk, closed the door to his room and then answered the call.

"Your plan is on."

"Oh, Hi Jack. What is this, no pleasantries anymore?"

"You shoot her. In return you get to keep the ransom money."

"Right, so the kidnappers were happy that you changed your mind?"

"They just raised the ransom."

"Huh. Cool." Dougie was impressed. He could learn something from these guys, he thought.

"No, it is not cool." Jack was slurring, but clearly

234

annoyed. "Not fucking cool at all. However, given your plan it won't fucking matter will it? So. I am going to get the money they asked for, put it in a locker and keep hold of the key. You are going to arrange a meeting with them at the match on Saturday. They'll bring Tuppence and I'll bring the key. You kill her and you'll get the key. And the money. Job done. I just want this over. Can you do that?"

Dougie took a deep breath. "Yes."

"Good. Here's their number." Jack recited some digits and Dougie scribbled them down and repeated them back to Jack to make sure he'd got them down right.

"Wait a minute. What did you say about the match on Saturday?"

"That's where I said I'd be when they asked for the exchange to happen."

"At a football match?"

"Yes. We're playing Hearts in the Cup. They wanted the money sooner but I can't -"

"It's a fucking cup tie?"

"Yeah. Big one. Edinburgh derby."

"Shit! There'll be TV cameras and all sorts."

"There's always TV cameras at matches." Jack said, not unreasonably.

"So, you want me to shoot someone in the middle of a football match?"

"Is that a problem?"

"Well, not if you pretend it's possible to sneak a firearm into a football stadium. Or if you ignore the cameras and the forty thousand potential witnesses."

"There won't be that many people there. The capacity is only 20,000 something."

"Oh, that's all right then." Dougie snapped.

"Look. You work out the details. That's what I'm paying you for, right?"

"Well, yes and no. Nothing was ever said about a bloody public execution."

"Didn't think of that."

"Really. Is that something you do often, thinking?"

"I think… you should have killed her by now." Jack said. "Listen. The ransom money is more than your agreed fee. Three times as much now, in fact. And you can keep it. You can keep it all if you'll just get this over and done with. At the game on Saturday. Deal?"

Dougie felt something inside him fall on its side. "Deal." he agreed.

"Good. Call them and set it up. Call me when you need the key. And then we are done. Are we clear?"

Dougie felt swept along by circumstance, unable to get his head into gear while Jack was motoring along at ninety in the fast lane. All he could think to do was relent

"Crystal."

Dougie got himself a cup of tea and then devoted his attention to this new brainteaser: how to arrange a fake moneydrop and shooting of Tuppence now that he had agreed to have it played out in front of a stadium full of people at a Scottish Cup tie. What sort of idiot was Jack? God knows, Dougie liked a challenge - that was why he was in IT in the first place: diagnosing problems and fixing them, learning new skills along the way. But this was something else; an order of magnitude beyond the usual cluster-fuckery he had to deal with. He put his phone onto divert and bent his will to the problem at hand.

It was the smell that woke him, Guy reckoned. It was a very bad smell. Very bad. And it wouldn't go away. It reminded him of when he was a child and his pet dog would disappear behind the sofa where no-one could see it and silently fart, over and over, almost orchestrating the arrangement so that each one drifted across the room causing his father to curse and close his eyes, crying "What in the name of Christ… ?" before the next wave hit.

This wasn't a wave, this was a fog.

He couldn't at first tell where the smell was coming from. Tied to the chair as he was he had a pretty good view of the room, and he was wedged almost into a corner so the smell couldn't be coming from behind him. In front of him was the bed - empty - where was Tuppence? The plain wooden table and chairs and what looked like a discarded hood she'd been wearing lay on the floor beside it. The windows were boarded and closed, as was the door.

"Con?" He called, hoping for a response.

The response he got was that the discarded hood moved and turned towards him, revealing itself to be the badger. Woken by Guy's cry it glared at him and then charged, launching itself towards him like a shaving brush missile. Guy leant back in his chair and almost wet himself with relief when the badger's charge was brought up short by a rein around it's neck attached to one of the table legs. The table moved ever so slightly as the badger was jerked off its feet in surprise. It span and charged again, this time with less slack in its rein, and the table definitely moved, scraping the floor an inch or two in Guy's direction. The badger sensed progress and had at it again, and the wooden burping sound from the leg

237

dragging on the floor rasped its encouragement to the angry animal.

"Con? Con? You there, mate? Con!" His shouts echoed emptily around the room and seemed only to encourage the badger to redouble his efforts. Guy could see the rage in its eyes and the sputum around it's black-lipped muzzle, its flashing teeth and claws claggy with wet earth and dried mud. "Con! Help!"

Guy took his eyes off the threat and tried to look over his own shoulder as he wrestled with the rope tying his hands together. He could buck himself in his chair but this only moved him right into the corner of the room, gaining him maybe an inch or two. There was nowhere further to move without reducing the distance between himself and the badger, no window or skylight or shelf above him, no weapon in reach.

Christ, this badger could menace for Scotland, Guy thought. He counted seconds as the animal made another lunge, inched forward, spun on its leash to untangle itself and then repeated the process. Ten seconds between lunges. Say two inches per lunge. He reckoned the badger, at full extension, was about eight feet away from tearing his throat out - or at least giving him a nasty bite. Two inches every ten seconds was about a foot a minute. He had less than ten minutes to get himself free.

Guy stared at the floor, then at the ceiling, closed his eyes and began to silently cry. The snuffling, scraping, struggling ball of fur, fleas and energy that was going to kill him, edged remorselessly closer. The air was hot with the animal's musk and Guy's own fear.

Guy wet himself.

"Hello again, George." *George. Who the fuck was George?* For a minute, Guy literally didn't care. Here was rescue, albeit in an unexpected form. The man with the cowboy hat who owned the badger had returned and was standing in the open doorway, leaning against the jamb, arms folded, one leg crossed over the other. "Or should I call you Mr. Clooney?"

The badger was momentarily alarmed, then confused as to which way to turn. He made an exploratory foray in the direction of the new entrant, but did so by shooting under the table which was not between it and the door. The badger was immediately caught up in a tangle of leash and chair and table legs and found itself struggling to free itself without choking harder on the noose around its neck.

"Please." Guy begged. "Untie me. Let me go. This things going to kill me." The man showed no signs of having heard him at all, continuing to stand there casually observing him. "Did you hear me?"

"Yes." The man replied, smiling calmly. He looked over at the badger which was freeing itself from the tangle and readying itself once more at Guy who, it had clearly decided, was the closest and most vulnerable target currently in the room.

"Well, can you untie me then? Before this crazy animal has my bollocks for its breakfast."

The eyes stopped smiling. "Not so fast there, George."

"My names not George!" Guy wrestled with his bonds, illustrating his seriousness and panic. "Will you just untie me? Please!"

"What is it, then?"

"What?" Guy's mind whirled briefly, wondering what he should tell the man. "Ok, it's George. You can call me George. Or anything else you like, as long as you get me out of here!"

The man leant up off the jamb and turned to go. "I'll help you when you tell me your real name."

"It's George. Ok? George."

"Bye, George." The man disappeared out of sight, down the corridor to the left leaving the door open. The badger was now only about five feet away.

"Ok, ok. It's Guy, ok? Guy! My name's Guy!"

There was no sound from beyond the door and the man didn't reappear.

"It's Guy! Honestly, that's my name. Guy Hence." His head sagged onto his chest as his tears started again, defeated. "Guy Spencer Hence. 13.11.89."

"And what are you doing here, Guy Hence?"

Guy jolted up and saw the man back in the doorway, scratching his stubble.

"I'm being attacked by a badger, now please get me out."

"I mean: what are you doing here, with an accomplice, kidnapping a woman and holding her in a derelict house in the middle of a forest?"

"I think kidnapping's a bit strong." Guy protested.

"Really? Let's see. Kidnap: an infringement of the personal liberty of an individual involving the taking or carrying away of one person by another, by force or fraud, without their consent and without lawful excuse." The man briefly hummed and haw'ed to himself. "Nope. I think you've ticked all those boxes, don't you? The sack over the head was a particularly nice touch."

"It wasn't my idea!"

240

"Ah. Well, in that case Guy, you are free to go." The man disappeared down the hallway again leaving Guy to stare the badger down. They were very close now.

"It was Conrad's idea! Conrad! I helped, ok? I helped. But it was his idea."

The man's head appeared around the door jamb. "Conrad…?"

"Ho. Conrad Ho."

"Friend of yours?"

"Yes." Guy was pleading with his eyes as the badger loomed closer.

"Little guy?"

"Yes. So?"

"Currently not in danger of losing an appendage to a raging, wild mammal?"

"No!" Guy was desperate now. "Yes. No. Ok, he was here, alright? I don't know where he is. If he's fucked off and left me here with … you and …. this thing… I'll - "

"What?."

"I don't know! Oh, please! Look I'll answer all your questions. I'll tell you everything. Just - PLEASE - get me out of here and I'll tell you all you want to know."

"Why did you kidnap her?" The man hadn't listened to a word he'd said and time was now very short.

"For money?"

"Who from?"

Guy was leaning back into his chair, shrinking from the snapping teeth and foul breath of the filthy animal. His voice was at a strainingly high pitch.

"Her husband."

"Who's he?"

"Famous footballer."

"Called?"

"Jack."

"Jack?" The man looked at the badger inches from Guy's face. "The man who wouldn't pay up."

"What?" Guy was momentarily shocked.

"He refused to pay, didn't he?"

"How did you know?"

"I just do." The man moved swiftly into the room and sat on the table. "Although he appears to have changed his mind. Why do you think that might be?"

"What?"

The badger took a while to realise that its forward movement had been halted and looked around to work out why. The man took advantage of this split-second lull and dragged the table a few feet away towards the door pulling the badger with it, buying Guy a few more minutes. He turned to leave the room again.

"Hey, wait! What's going on? Where are you going?"

"I'm going to make a cup of tea." Said the man with a smile. "Then I'm going to dispose of a badger."

Guy sighed with relief. "Any chance of, erm… two sugars?"

The man stared at him, emotionless.

Tuppence had piled the empties into a binliner and taken them out onto the decking when a shadow fell across her feet and she looked up with a start to see Cullen watching her.

"Heavy night?"

"Good morning." She straightened her back as if she'd been told off by her father. He strode across the decking and into the unfinished cabin without knocking. She heard a muffled brief conversation between Paul and

Cullen and then the pair reappeared, Cullen holding a steaming mug of tea.

"Time to talk." Cullen gestured to the deckchairs and she obediently tiptoed over in her bare feet and sat down. Paul admired her movements from the door and then, once she was seated, ducked back inside.

"So you were kidnapped." Cullen started off as if this was some kind of official interview.

She rolled her eyes. "Happens all the time."

"Really?" He seemed genuinely concerned.

"No! Sarcasm." She raised both eyebrows.

"Ah, I don't do sarcasm." He continued as if nothing had happened. "Tell me how it happened."

Tuppence told him what little she could about the photoshoot and the sack. While she spoke she tried to recall any details she might have subconsciously tucked away but the truth seemed to be that there were none.

"So, recap. You were talking to your friend, Liz."

"Liv."

"Right. And then you smelt a strong chemical smell. Next thing you wake up and you have a sack over your head and when someone comes to take it off, he's wearing a George Clooney mask and you're on a dirty mattress in a derelict room where I found you?"

"That's it."

"And you don't know who George Clooney is and or why he took you?"

"No, I know who George Clooney is."

"Do you?"

"Yeah, he's a Hollywood actor."

Cullen sighed. "And the man behind the George Clooney mask?"

"Ah. No idea." He looked at her, narrowing his eyes.

"Honestly, I don't know who the man wearing it was."

"You might do."

She examined his expression, intrigued. "Why do you say that?"

"Does the name Guy Hence mean anything to you?" She shook her head, trying to make the name mean something but failing. "What about Conrad Ho?"

"Conrad?"

"You know him?"

"Conrad! Conrad wouldn't kidnap me, silly!" She scanned his face again, to check if he was being serious. It looked like he was. "Really? Conrad?"

"So you know this Conrad then." Cullen digested this for a moment. "Who is he?"

Tuppence gathered her feet up under her long skirt and tucked her knees under her chin, about to tell a tale. "Well, he's a friend... no, he's not a friend. He's a long-time boyfriend of a girlfriend of mine. Studying fashion. Thinks he's a bit of a hot-shot." She wrinkled up her nose delightfully. "I helped him out on a photoshoot recently - mate's rates - just so he could get a portfolio together for some new thing he's working on." She looked quizzically across at Cullen. "I think you're barking up the wrong tree if you think he had anything to do with it.." Cullen just sat there giving nothing away so she pressed him. "Why *do* you think he had anything to do with it?"

"'Cos his accomplice named him." He threw this out and she could see Cullen's mind was wandering. She sat in silence until he focussed on her again. "Do many of these photoshoot things do you?"

"Enough. They tend to come in bunches - as some seasonal deadline approaches, you know Spring/Summer catalogues, that kind of thing?" Cullen was looking at her with the blank expression again. "Anyway, this was my last one for a while. I did that one last week for Conrad, two more before that - although those two were down South."

"Where was the one you did for Conrad, then?"

"Oh, it was round here somewhere. Nice hotel with a spa somewhere in the countryside. Funny name. Can't remember it now."

"Stobo?"

"Yes, that's it! Stobo. Funny name, isn't-" She stopped herself. "How did you know?"

"This Conrad guy. Is he short? Chinese?"

"That's him."

Tuppence had been aware that the temperature on the deck had been dropping as he had followed this line of questioning and, as she looked at him now, there was hardness forming in his eyes, which she thought was more than just his discomfort with the cold. There was a setting to his features which made her look anxiously around for Paul but when she turned back to Cullen he was staring out across the valley.

"Look, would you like some more tea?" She stood up and nodded at the empty mug he was still holding in his hands. When he didn't respond, she prodded him again. "Mind if I get another one?" She waited for some acknowledgement but when he remained motionless she stepped gently back across the deck and into the cabin, in search of Paul and his reassuring presence.

Paul had his back to her and was scraping some burnt toast into the sink. He looked round when she coughed gently. "Want some?" He gestured at the toast.

"No, thanks." She smiled awkwardly. "Black toast

245

intolerant."

"I can do you another lot. Promise I won't burn them."

"No thank you." She crept closer. "I'm a model, remember? Can't just eat anything you know."

"Ah, right." He slathered butter onto one slice and shoved it into his mouth, crunching almost half of it in a single crispy bite. "What do you eat, then?" He managed through the mouthful.

"Lot of salad." She made a mental list. "Chicken. Fish. Some pasta - not much. Superfoods - you know, like kale." She checked the flask to see if there was any hot water left in it.

"Kale's a superfood?"

"Hmm-hmm."

"What's its superpower - tasting bad?"

"It is an… acquired taste, I'll give you that." She smiled and then leant into him, whispering. "Could you come out on the deck and sit with me? Please?"

Paul looked at her questioningly and she glanced back over her shoulder before confiding "I'd rather… not be alone with him."

"Cullen?" Paul blurted.

"Yes." She hissed, grimacing at his volume. "He's gone a bit… funny and he's scaring me."

Paul watched her as he swallowed the last of his toast. "Ok. You go back out. I'll bring your tea."

"Thank you." She squeezed his arm gently and then tiptoed back out of the door. Paul made her tea and then followed her out.

Cullen was sitting in his usual deckchair and had taken his leather hat off. He had it resting on his lap and was ruffling his hair with both hands as if waking himself up.

"Everything ok out here?" Paul said, handing Tuppence the mug.

"Yup." Cullen replied brightly and reinstated his hat. Tuppence sipped cautiously at her tea and looked apprehensively across at Paul, who tilted his head at Cullen and waited expectantly.

"I have a new project." Cullen proclaimed proudly.

"Ah." Paul sighed. "Bollocks."

THIRTEEN

Easter Road, Hibernian FC's ground in Edinburgh, is a monstrous assemblage of four metallic stands painted green and white, the teams colours, squatting amongst dirty wind-blown streets in the Leith area of the city. But here in Flat 12, 11 Albion Place, Dougie could see he had a cracking view of the stadium. Dirty windows on the third and top floor of this tenement brownstone gave clear sight of large sections of the East stand, perhaps 200 yards away on the other side of the glass.

Dougie had googled for images, seating plans and maps for Easter Road after his conversation with Jack. Hemmed in on all sides by an array of old tenements and new apartment buildings, his attention had been immediately drawn to sight lines which must exist at the corners of the ground, in the gaps between each of the four stands, and realised he would have to go down and survey it for himself. He had engaged in banter with the letting agent and left fake details. Now, on his way down the communal stairs and out into the cold, he opened the Amazon app on his phone and ordered the highest rated "lock pick set and practice lock" for next day delivery.

On a whim, he nipped into the official merchandising store beneath the Famous Five stand and bought himself a Hibs home shirt. It would allow him to better dissolve into the crowds on match day should any escape become necessary, and he congratulated himself on starting to think like a professional hitman - covering all the angles, making contingency plans.

When he got home he pulled up a detailed copy of the seating plan for the East stand, and cross-checked it with the photo he had taken from the flat's window. Satisfied, he texted Jack to request 3 tickets for the match in section 43, somewhere around row R, tickets to be collected from the Ticket Office on match day in the name of Renshaw. While he thought about it, he sent a second text with instructions as to what to do with the locker key on Saturday.

When all this was done, he surfed the net for several hours looking at ways he could spend one hundred and fifty thousand pounds without arousing suspicion.

"But I don't understand!" Whilst this three-way conversation with Cullen and Paul been taking place for a while now, Tuppence felt as if she had stepped out at some point and missed an episode or two.

"Well I don't understand all of it." Cullen said, attempting to reassure her.

"Never stopped you interfering before." Paul muttered, out of Cullen's earshot.

"The point is." Cullen added, "I am now... incentivised to help."

"Who are you helping? You're not helping me - I'm going to the police." Tuppence resolved.

"Let's not be so hasty." Cullen spread his hands. "I am... not a big fan of the police."

"I was kidnapped, remember? Who else do you think can help?"

"Me?" Cullen replied. Tuppence looked at him doubtfully so he ploughed on. "I rescued you, didn't I? Not the police. Me. And now we both have an interest in finding this Conrad fellow."

"We do?"

"Yes. You, because he kidnapped you. Me, because I am interested in why he did so and, more importantly, why he damaged… some personal property of mine."

"What property?"

Cullen hesitated. "Let's just call it something of significant emotional value."

"Did he?"

"Oh, yes."

"How can you be so sure?"

"I can smell it. He did it."

"And his partner. What did you call him, Guy?"

"Don't know if he did it as well."

"No, I mean, where's he?"

"I have him - on retainer, you might say."

"He could be lying to you." Tuppence suggested. Cullen ignored her.

Paul nodded. "So how are you going to find this Conrad bloke?"

"Well, he obviously wants the ransom money. I'm going to stick with the other fella, arrange the money drop and sit on the money until Conrad shows up." Cullen smiled to himself. "Follow the money, as they say."

"And what're you going to do when you find him?"

Cullen thought for a moment. "Ask him to atone."

"Atone?"

"Make amends."

"Huh." Paul nodded. "How?"

"Haven't worked that out. Yet."

All three were silent for a while, until Tuppence came to a decision.

"Well, whatever. I'm not going to try catching Conrad. I'm going to the police."

"No." Cullen's tone was enough to make her stop in her tracks. "I will deal with Conrad. You will deal with Jack."

"Jack?" Tuppence said. "What do you mean, deal with Jack?"

"Don't you want to know why he didn't want to pay your ransom?"

"I… but, I… it must have been the shock! Of finding out I'd been kidnapped. As soon as it had sunk in, he realised…" Tuppence trailed off, suddenly feeling the cold out on the deck.

"Perhaps." Cullen said, gently. "Either way, there's only one way to find out."

Conrad had booked a taxi to the airport, showered and hurriedly packed a bag. The options open to him now were extremely limited, but that just made his choice all the easier. Time to put the petal to the medal.

The whole operation was now a grade one clusterfuck. The cowboy and the badger simply put the tin lid on the whole thing. There was no way he could see Guy standing in the way of a deranged animal or a mean stranger. And Tuppence was now an irrelevance. Either her husband wasn't going to pay the ransom or the cowboy was going to free her.

And ignoring all this, the bottom line was: he didn't have the money. Correction: he didn't have enough money. He had Guy's money and he had the designs. And he still had all the photos and videos from the Stobo photoshoot. Perhaps there was a way to get these editted or Photoshopped or something so that it could be made to look like Tuppence had been wearing the new designs? Something to think about there with London Fashion Week now barely a week away. He had a show tent slot and no content for it. And that would require money too. Fuck!

Perhaps, if he could just appear in front of his father with the new designs he would cough up just enough to keep Yeo sweet until there were some finished garments to sell. Once he'd got to that point the whole process would bootstrap itself. This was still all to play for. No pain, no gain.

And on the subject of pain, there was absolutely no point in sticking around here any longer. Conrad unconsciously flexed the fingers on his left hand and grimaced - his next finger payment to Mr Chu would be shortly due. It was Hong Kong or bust. This was where the rudder met the road.

"Why's it so warm this morning? It's February but if feels like June." Tuppence was sitting in one of the deckchairs, feet up on the rail in the bright sunshine.

"It's an ab-err-a-tion." Paul enunciated slowly, turning to her and smiling.

"Is it now?" Tuppence smiled back.

"I love life's little aberrations: warm days in winter, four leaf clovers, gingers."

She poked her tongue out at him. "Strawberry blonde, actually."

"Look, be safe ok? Here's some cash." He counted out some crumpled notes from his back pocket. "Get you back to civilisation."

"I thought you didn't have any money?" She was genuinely touched.

"It's *his*, ok?"

"Thank you." She reached up and kissed him on the cheek. "That doesn't diminish the gesture."

"And here's my number." He handed her a slip of paper with a mobile numbers scrawled on it.

"Great. Thanks. Oh, wait - I don't have my phone!" Tuppence suddenly remembered having it in her hand, about to reply to a text from Dick when Liv was shot. She was instantly distraught.

"Here." Paul pulled her handbag from behind his back. A magician revealing his favourite trick.

"What! How? Where did you get this?"

"I didn't. He said the talkative kidnapper had it."

"Oh, fantastic! Thank you so much." She rummaged in the bag for her phone and found it out of battery. "What about his number?"

"He doesn't give out his number. Not sure he even knows it."

Tuppence nodded, of course. "So how do I get in touch with him? Tell him about Jack?"

"He'll call you."

"And if he doesn't?"

"You call me."

"And then what?"

"Then we wait."

"For what?"

"For him." Paul shrugged. "He'll turn up. Sooner or later. My money's on sooner."

Cullen sat snoozing, rocked back on the chair legs, hat

over his face like a cowboy on a saloon bar boardwalk in the old West. His phone lay on the table, waiting. When it rang, Cullen lifted his hat and eyed it warily. He got up and walked over to where the phone was skittering across the table and put it on speakerphone. He looked at Guy and put a finger to his lips.

"Hello?" said a voice.

Cullen shook his head and they both waited, Guy holding his breath.

"Hello? Hello?"

"Who is this?" Cullen asked.

"I'm calling to arrange the exchange."

Cullen silently mouthed *Jack?* to Guy who shook his head.

"Is this Jack?"

"No. I'm his… representative."

Cullen looked at Guy again, who shrugged. "Ok, go ahead."

"Let me speak to her, first."

Cullen didn't hesitate. "She's asleep."

"Then wake her."

Cullen looked at Guy for a moment and then back at the handset. "No."

Guy held his breath and there was silence on the line for five seconds or more. It seemed like an hour. The voice came back on again as if this exchange hadn't happened.

"You are to go to Hibs football stadium off Easter Road, this Saturday. I have arranged for three tickets in the name of Renshaw for you to collect at the Ticket Office. Two for you, one for her. Kick-off is 3pm. Be there much earlier. Take your seats and watch the game."

"Then what?"

"If the girl is with you, I will call this number again at half-time."

Guy signalled frantically to Cullen, hands waggling in panic. Cullen stood motionless, staring at the phone, waiting to see if there was any more but it seemed there wasn't. "Is that it?"

"That's it."

The caller hung up and Guy exhaled sharply, looking at Cullen. "What are we going to do?"

"Go to the game." Said Cullen.

"But we haven't got Tuppence."

"So?"

"So he said we have to bring her." Guy appealed to him. "He's in control."

Cullen glanced at him in disdain. "No-one's in control. And no-one controls me. Half the time I can barely control myself."

"But he'll see she's not with us."

"Then we need a plan. We have to get to him before he gets to us."

"Us?"

"Me and You."

"But... you mean, you're going to go along with this?"

"Yes."

"Why?"

"I want the money."

"This is mine and Conrad's money."

"Oh, you can have it when we're done."

Guy's shoulders slumped. "This was our thing. You've just... messed it up."

Cullen put his hat back on, wedging it down onto his head. "I haven't started yet."

What was she going to do? What did she want to say to Jack and what answers did she want? If Jack had told her kidnappers he didn't want her back, it not only meant he didn't love her. It meant he was passing a death sentence on her. That wasn't a lack of love - bad enough - it was naked hatred. He didn't just want her out of his life he wanted her out of life period.

What she'd been told had the terrible ring of truth about it. But she also knew that it would only be when she looked into Jack's eyes and asked him point blank that she would truly believe it.

Tuppence sat in a coffee shop on Peebles High St, charging her phone from a wall outlet. It buzzed and pinged as it came to life and a slew of missed messages, emails and notifications filtered through. There were several messages from Dick, all politely ignoring her lack of response. The last one listed his phone number, inviting her to call him if she wanted. Everyone was giving her their number all of a sudden!

Even as she caught up on what she'd missed, a new message came in from him: Cycle ride starts 2day! Out of contact for a few days. Wish me luck!

She pondered a response for a few minutes and then, exhaling sharply, called his number. He picked up straight away.

"Hello?"

"Hi." Now she had him on the phone she didn't know what to say to him. "It's Tuppence."

"Tuppence! Wow. Hi! Erm, how are you? Did you see just my message?"

"Yes. I... I wanted to wish you luck but couldn't work out how to word it, so I thought..."

"Are you ok?"

"Yes?"

"You sound... sad."

"Well, I... Yes, I am sad."

"Would you like to talk about it?"

"Well, you must be in the middle of things and I shouldn't take up your time. Maybe-"

"You *should* take up my time - if I can help."

She smiled to herself at his kindness. "I really shouldn't. I'm not even one of your parishioners." She smiled again at the awkwardness of the word.

"I look upon the world as my parish. John Wesley said that. Why are you sad?"

She took a deep breath and told him. To his credit - and she assumed this was something that the church trained into you - he took it calmly and didn't interrupt until she'd finished.

"But you must go to the Police."

"I'm not sure that telling kidnappers they can *fuck off* is actually a crime." She reddened as she realised she had sworn out loud, even if not to him.

"Perhaps not. But kidnapping clearly is."

"Yes but Jack didn't kidnap me."

"I understand that. But someone did and they need to be caught."

"But I got away." Was all she could think of saying. She didn't want to mention Paul and Cullen's reluctance to come into contact with the constabulary.

"And I'm very pleased about it." She smiled at his matter-of-fact tone. "But what if they try and kidnap someone else? Or come after you again?"

The idea had simply not occurred to her and she felt a shiver at the back of her neck. "You're right. Gosh. I will. Of course, yes." But what about Cullen and Paul? And what about Jack? "But I need to face Jack first."

"Are you sure?"

"Yes. What if this is all a mistake? What if Jack knows nothing about this? What if he didn't tell them to keep me?" As she said the words out loud she felt something heavy inside her swing down and hit the truth. She knew, right there. All the subliminal moments, the unregistered glances, the unconscious feelings, flooded up from somewhere and overwhelmed her. It hit her like a cold wave and she shivered again.

"I'm sure that must be the case." Dick reassured.

"You are?" I'm not, she thought.

"Tuppence, listen to yourself. What husband doesn't love his wife? Want her by his side?"

"Plenty, if you read the Daily Mail."

"I don't" He snorted. "And I suggest you don't either."

"But... it has the ring of truth about it!" She protested to him, wanting to be talked out of her new certainty, worrying her forehead between her thumb and fingers

"But it's all made up!" He blurted.

"How can you be sure?"

"Well, I can't. But the infamy of the sidebar of shame has reached even-"

"I'm not talking about the Daily Mail!" She covered her mouth with her hand, trying to stifle a sob. "What have I done to him that he could hate me so much?"

Dick's reply was immediate and heartfelt. "More to the point, perhaps, what has he done to himself?"

Steffi didn't look exactly like Tuppence but Jack realised he was splitting hairs. What with the wig and the copious amount of amyl nitrate he would have popped by the time she showed up - not to mention that he only intended viewing her from behind. She would be a dead ringer and that was all he cared about. All the years his wife had deprived him of anal sex - he was now about to enact it, dream-like, with a look-a-like and he had a diamond cutter.

Since his final instructions to his incompetent hitman, Jack had become a man possessed. Tuppence was not coming back and he could indulge his whims and fantasies now without limit. Suddenly he was full of ideas and being constrained to only two possible decisions at a time was suffocating. He had abandoned the coin and returned to the dice for his decisions. Now he was free; now he could breathe; now he could really live like The Diceman.

Many of his ideas were bizarre, sometimes impractical, sometimes just plain stupid. But as he wrote each one down against the numbers 1 to 6, they became more real. And each time a bizarre option was avoided he would replace it with another, even more outrageous. With each roll, he was ratcheting up the options and his excitement. You always had to have one or two sensible options, otherwise that would be going against the spirit of the book: you couldn't have six options all requiring you to murder someone in different ways until you'd chosen the "murder someone" option. You had to have choices like "pay the paper bill" or "Eat only cream cheese for a day" in amongst the daredevilry.

By Sunday, two things had happened: firstly, his options for each roll were insights into the mindset of a madman; secondly, Paw was getting on his fucking nerves and something simply *had* to be done. So now he had:

Rolling a one would have him defecating onto the glass coffee table in front of the next person who rang his front doorbell.

Rolling a two had originally been "give Paw a kick in the knackers" but this had seemed both too minor and also likely to damage his shooting foot. He'd upped it to microwave for 5 minutes on full power (which had required him to not only read the manual but also search the internet to see how long it might actually take to kill a cat in a microwave. Google told him that he was far from original in this idea and that there had been several instance of people having done the exact same thing).

Rolling a three meant he had to take the bins out.

Rolling a four would cause him to hang himself by a belt from the landing while whacking off.

Rolling a five was "Take a Tuppence look-a-like up the arse".

Rolling a six simply said "Shag Paw".

Feeling lucky, he took another snort on a popper, turned up the volume on the hifi until the windows rattled and picked up TWO dice. Standing naked in his living room, he shook his fist and rolled the dice out onto the floor.

Six and Five.

Jack did a little leap of joy, called Steffi and then went in search of the unlucky animal.

"Why's your cat …?" Steffi asked when Jack opened the door only to be silenced by the sight of his enormous erection, the central feature of a bloody, lacerated pubic area which looked like he had tried to give himself a sack and crack wax with a Flymo. "Oh my God! What the hell have you done to yourself?"

She looked down to see a spattered blood trail leading from the living room, loud music reverberating through the open door.

"Don't ask." Jack said ushering her in, grabbing both her shoulders and pushing her down so she fell to her knees. "It looks a lot worse than it is. Main thing is that *this* still works." He thrust his cock towards her mouth.

"How can you even think about it?" She protested, struggling back to her feet. "I'm not touching that. You need your whole groin bathing, dressing and maybe even stitches! How come you haven't passed out or anything? Doesn't it hurt?"

She looked him in the eyes and realised that he was so high on whatever-it-was that he wouldn't feel anything if a white rhino tried to shove it's horn up his rectum. "Jack, are you ok?" He was standing like a zombie, staring into the middle distance, and she gently manoeuvred him down the hallway into the living room and lowered him onto a sofa. The music was deafening in here and she could see the speakers but no sound system or control panel. "Can we turn the music down?"

Jack stared in her direction rather than at her. "I'm self-medicating." He said woozily.

"On what - heroin?" She was shouting to make herself heard over the thudding bass.

He laughed. "No! Yeah! Actually mostly amyl-nitrate and Jack Daniels."

"The music, Jack?"

"Remote's in the bathroom." He waved vaguely off to his right.

"Right. Come with me." She swung him up off from his sitting position and led him slowly over to a doorway on the right. He had left a bloody Rorschach smear on the cream sofa.

Steffi sat him down on the toilet seat and took a closer look at his wounds. Christ, it looked bad. She opened some cupboard doors under the His and Hers sinks at random until she found a flannel and some plasters. That was all there was.

"Where's the remote?"

Jack looked blankly around. "Not this bathroom."

"How many have you got? Never mind. Sit still." She could at least hear herself think in here so she ran the flannel under a hot tap and then started dabbing at his bloody mess of a crotch. Jack didn't even flinch. Instead, her ministrations merely seemed to stiffen his erection - and his horniness. He started clumsily pushing her hands towards his dick.

"What the fuck happened, Jack?"

"Fucking cat." Jack tried to push her head down into his groin. "Not the most co-operative sexual partner I ever came across."

"Huh?" She couldn't hear him clearly, his hands almost clamped over her ears, so she concentrated on not getting impaled on his cock while trying to bathe his angry-looking cuts.

This wasn't quite what she had anticipated when he had called her but a gig was a gig. Hers was not to reason why, hers was just to do as she was told and trouser a cool thousand pounds for her pains. If he had wanted her to play Scrabble she'd would have obliged - although she felt he would have found it poor value for money, given her dyslexia. Plus he paid for the outfits and the wig and the other paraphernalia. She just turned up, made sure she'd showered and shaved beforehand and put on her face. Ready Steady? Blow.

Tuppence stood at her front door, took an enormous breath, and pulled her key out of her handbag only to realise that the door was slightly ajar. She poked it with one finger and watched it swing slowly open.

The first sight that greeted her was that of her beloved cat, struggling painfully to free itself from a coat hook where it hung suspended by its diamond-studded collar. The poor animal was mewling and choking, writhing as it tried unsuccessfully to release itself, shaking with fear.

"Paw!" She ran to it across the marble tiles, ignoring for now the music thudding from the living room. She picked him up gently and nursed him in her arms, shushing and smothering him with kisses. "My baby, my baby! What has he done? Are you ok? Are you? Are you?" She checked his coat and eyes, saw what looked like blood on his claws but could see no wounds anywhere on him. Paw uncurled, relaxing into her embrace like a submariner on shore leave.

Tuppence's resolve shot through the roof. She had come here, telling herself the whole time that there must be mitigating circumstances. Someone, somewhere had got the wrong end of the stick. And in her mind's eye she would confront him. Look him straight in the eye and force out the words: "Why, Jack? Why did you tell them you didn't want me back?" And in that instant, he would have the chance to say he didn't know what she was talking about, or express bewilderment that she might have been kidnapped, even ask who the *they* were she was referring to. In that one moment she would see the truth in his face, feel it in her bones, and know.

But now there wasn't going to be any such confrontation. Now she knew. If he could do this to the thing she loved most in the whole world, what kind of monster was he? This man she was married to. A branding iron burnt into her heart and for a moment tears obscured her view. Then she straightened, holding Paw tenderly in her arms and strode into the living room and into the wall of bass pounding through the house.

The room was empty. The only signs of life, apart from the music, were two shiny dice lying on the gleaming floor and a huge red smear on one of the sofas. A spotted trail of blood led across the floor towards the cloakroom door which was open. In the floor-length mirror opposite she could see Jack sitting on the toilet with a strawberry blonde woman kneeling between his naked legs, her head bobbing slowly up and down.

Tuppence blanched, her mouth a tight red weal across her pale features. Her wet eyes blazed, a toxic mixture of incomprehension and utter betrayal roiling inside her. She could taste bile in her throat, but she swallowed hard, hugged Paw close, turned on her heels and marched out of her house.

FOURTEEN

"Olivia? This is Daniel Tyson-Wright. I am the COO of Chanel, UK Limited."

"Hello! Oh, call me Liv, please. No-one apart from my mother calls me Olivia. And only then when I've done something to earn her displeasure."

To say she wasn't expecting the call was an understatement. Discharged from hospital the day before, she had set up her office in her bedroom which was currently strewn with cloth and A2 sketches. Her laptop was currently burning through a bar of chocolate she had left on the dressing table alongside a fifth of scotch - empty - and a pack of Camel cigarettes - ditto. Her left arm was in a sling and she had abandoned the laptop unable to type with one hand. She had been pacing the room smoking her last Camel when the phone had rung.

"Liv it is, then." The man's accent was difficult to place - a touch of Eastern European about it, she felt, but that didn't tie in with his ever-so-English double-barrelled name - but it transmitted the honeyed tones of money and authority effortlessly down the line. She had never been introduced to the COO before, having been recruited by the Design Director and Chief Creative Officer, but she knew his name. "How are you? Is there anything you need from us?"

"Oh no. I'm fine, really. Bit tired but nothing... really. Thank you for asking."

"Not at all. Not at all." He purred. "I was just calling

to check that everything is still on schedule."

She felt herself immediately bridle at the man. *Who the fuck-?* She choked down her indignation and put on a bemused expression.

"I'm sorry? You will be aware, no doubt, that I have been shot."

"Yes" He sounded amused. "And you are, as you said, fine?"

"Yes but-"

"So we are still on track then? All will be ready on time?"

"Well, yes, it will be ready on time." *Fucking nerve of the man,* she thought. *Of course I'll be ready on time. Professional pride. Can't you see I'm working when I needn't be? Well, no he couldn't, obviously. But why call me up just to push my fucking buttons when I'm still recuperating you fucking heartless -.* What she said was "Despite the fact that I was shot."

"In the shoulder."

"Yes." *Ooh, get you, Mister I-have-all-the-facts-at-my-disposal.*

"Not in the heart. Or the head."

"Well, no." *Nor in my dick as you appear to have been.* "Although I am still restricted in my movements which-"

"No doubt is an inconvenience, but perhaps not one which need hinder an artist and professional like yourself."

Speak for yourself, tosspot. "Of course, I am doing everything I can to maintain progress on our agreed schedule." She wondered if he would pick up her emphasis on the word *agreed.* He did.

"Excellent. And progress against our original schedule?"

Will be shoved up your arse if I ever knowingly come within a

266

million miles of you. "Yes. That too."

"Good. Well, don't let me detain you any longer, Liv. I will wait, along with the rest of the world, agog as to what excellence you can put before us next week."

"Yes." *Go fuck yourself, wanker.* "Thank you."

"Goodbye."

She threw her phone across the bed, winced from the pain in her shoulder from the rotation and threw her head back to scream at the ceiling. *Fucking... men!*

The doorbell rang and Liv shuffled out of the bedroom and down the hallway to answer the door. A courier held out an electronic pad for her to sign and she did so gingerly and then brought the large box he'd given her into the kitchen.

It was a large bouquet of flowers in a vase and a card in an envelope.

The flowers were beautiful - lilies and orchids, whites and blues, her favourites - but she struggled to scoop the vase from out of the box and ended up cutting the box away brutally, stabbing with scissors using her one good hand. She lay the envelope flat on the kitchen counter and extracted the card inside.

GET WELL SOON, HOPE YOU'RE FEELING BETTER & QUICKLY BACK ON YOUR FEET. LOVE CONRAD.

What the - ? She stared at the message and cocked her head this way and that, like a bird trying to figure out the best way to insert a twig into its nest. What was Conrad playing at, the clingy creep? Or maybe she should be flattered that he was thinking of her and not be so mean-spirited? Hang on, though... how did he know she'd been shot? Had it been on the News? Even if it had, how did he even know she'd been at the photoshoot? Had she told him? She thought perhaps she had. Had Tuppence told him? And where the fuck was Tuppence anyway?

But no, Tuppence wouldn't have told him would she? Not since they'd broken up, a fact which Liv distinctly remembered telling her. No, wrestle with this as she might, she couldn't avoid landing on the conclusion that the truth was that Conrad *had* been there, she *had* seen him, and he *had* seen her get shot. With Tuppence there as well. She wasn't hallucinating.

So why had he been there? And where was Tuppence? She tried her number but it went straight to voicemail again.

Conrad sat on the plane flipping through Liv's design book. Christ, these were good. He was angry and jealous but couldn't stop himself turning the pages to find the next image again better than anything he could come up with.

The only criticism he could make of them was that tartan predominated. It wasn't a favourite look of his but even he could see that these looked like custom tartan designs - he wasn't familiar with the full range of tartan designs available by any means but the subtle colour combinations and off-kilter structures of squares and lines seemed like a new take on the traditional format.

And the material was clearly cashmere or some cashmere mix - although assuming what he'd been told by Jonty from the mill was correct, this probably represented finest quality, pure, cashmere. Liv was never one to spare the expense and if this was now being bankrolled by Chanel then one could only assume money was no object.

Dejected though he might be as to the originality and quality of her designs, these designs were now his. This was now *his* challenge. If Yeo could get the completed garments back in time for the end of London Fashion Week he would take the show, and the fashion world, by storm. Being able to sell catwalk garments to the buyers while they were still at the show? Couture-To-Go: the words would be on everyone's lips.

He closed the book and called Yeo.

"My flight arrives 3pm Hong Kong time. Can you have someone meet me there?"

"Of course, I will have a driver waiting for you." Yeo was silky smooth, as always. "But I told you there was really no need for you to come over at this moment."

"I know." Conrad had his father's words ringing in his ears. "But I would like to run through the process you have in place - so I understand my obligations as part of it and what I can do, if anything, to make sure there are no obstacles to our planned timeline."

"What you can do." Yeo injected. "Is make sure the money we require is available when it is required, so that we can progress to our planned timeline.

"Yes. Yes, naturally." Conrad did his best to sound insouciant. "And the new design? Your thoughts on them?"

"They are impressive, yes. But injecting new designs at this stage, when a lot of investment has already been made on the existing designs… well, this will incur additional cost as I explained."

"Mr Yeo. I have explained - repeatedly I believe - that the money is not a problem. My father, you are aware, is fully behind my business venture." He breezed, fingers crossed.

"Yes, but credit will get us only so far. We have invested time and money in setting up the supply chain, sourcing materials and dyes, and so on. Not to mention, reverse-engineering the designs and preparing programming models for looms and knitting machines."

"Look, you can't keep asking for more cash every time I speak to you." Conrad again felt the pinprick of his father's opinions regarding Mr Yeo needle his spine. "It's not right!"

"Why ever not?" Yeo purred.

Conrad clenched his left fist, feeling the fingernails biting into his palm. "It's not fair!"

"It may not be fair. It is business." Yeo paused. "We are all here to make money, are we not? You and I, both. How can I make money if I am paying money out and not getting a return? Where is my profit?"

"Where is mine if I have to keep finding more money?"

"Finding?" Yeo's voice seemed to tighten somewhat. "Find. You not *have* money? We still have some way to go, Conrad, before we ship finished designs - whether they change again or not." He insinuated. "Do not be surprised that more money is required at each stage. I can almost guarantee it will be necessary."

"Please do not misunderstand me, Mr Yeo. The money is available. We are not talking about not making a return. We are talking about a highly profitable enterprise here. This is just cashflow. When the orders come flooding in, we will all have a feel day."

"As long as the cash flows, I agree, we will all be happy."

"Agreed."

Yeo hung up and Conrad looked forlornly out at the grey blanket hiding the earth from view.

The day was bright with clouds skimming the sky like a skinned knuckle, and God's Peloton was ready for the off. Huddled together outside the Houses of Parliament, Dick had organised a photo opportunity with the MP for his own Dumfries, Clydesdale and Tweeddale constituency. Passers-by and tourists looked on curiously at the cyclists in their lurid outfits and slender race-bikes. A convoy of two Transit vans, both stencilled with hashtags and publicity markings stood ready, laden with camping equipment, food, bike spares and a copious amount of First Aid kit.

A single photographer wandered in and around the group, snapping away and Dick sat straddling his cycle now waiting only for the ITV camera-van to show up before they could make their way north. He bit the side of his thumb, anxiously, contemplating the conversation he'd had with Tuppence an hour or so earlier, unable to shake the mental image of her as a Weeping Madonna and him kneeling to kiss her feet.

When the camera crew eventually arrived, Dick acted as master of ceremonies and gave a short interview to the reporter making sure to mention the kirk roof and plug the Facebook page for charity donations. The producer said she'd like a shot of them receding up the road, all riders abreast, and then would ask them to stop so that the van could overtake them and take a short sequence from the front, while they rode in a tight bunch. Dick corralled his teammates with the requisite instructions and then, with a few watery cheers and waves from the assembled onlookers, they staggered up to a slow but steady pace, each rider trying to get into the zone and pace themselves, ignoring the scenery of the capital and focussing instead on the steady pulse of one foot down, then another, as they pedalled gradually towards home.

"I'm not exactly comfortable in your company you know." Guy fidgetted in the chair, nervous and agitated, as he had been for their entire time since Cullen had dragged him from Shieldgreen to here, wherever the hell here was. Some half-finished log cabin on a hillside.

"The feeling is reciprocated." Cullen sighed, gazing idly out of the window.

"I mean, if you're so set on getting the money, why don't you go on your own and let me go?"

"You're my insurance."

"I'm your prisoner."

"Is that right, kidnapper?" Cullen didn't turn from the window.

"Listen, you." He protested. "I am an innocent party in all this and don't take too kindly to being called names." He narrowed his eyes, trying to appear threatening. "I could call the police and have you arrested for kidnapping me."

Cullen reached into his pocket and Guy flinched briefly. "Here's the phone."

Guy crossed his arms, bluff called, and stared at his shoes.

Cullen put the phone back into his coat and exhaled slowly. "Tell me about this Conrad friend of yours."

"Why?" Guy sulked.

"I'm interested." When Guy showed no indication of being talkative, Cullen gave him a shove with his shoulder. "We're stuck with each other until Saturday. Might as well make the best of it. Might learn something to your advantage."

"You mean, you might learn something to your advantage don't you?"

Cullen was quiet for a while, then resumed. "You think I'm interested in the money?"

"You said it."

"That's right, I did." Cullen nodded, remembering. "But it's only true up to a point."

"What do you mean?"

"I want the money so I can get to Conrad. Once I've got Conrad, I don't need the money." Guy didn't respond so Cullen elaborated. "You can have it."

Guy turned to face Cullen and the man raised his eyebrows ever-so-slightly, his face otherwise deadpan. "You want me to sell out my friend, is that it?"

"For a hundred and fifty thousand pounds." Cullen said, making it sound not unreasonable.

"He's my best friend."

"Are you his, though?"

"What do you mean?"

"Nothing." Cullen turned back to the window, idly wondering out loud. "Don't suppose he's ever used you, persuaded you to do stuff you don't want to do. Ever taken you for granted. Anything like that."

Guy bristled and felt his face redden. "I've known him for years." He protested. "Every now and then, … if he's in a bind or a scrape… we help each other out… he'd do the same for me."

"Would he?"

"Every time." Guy retorted, and then sat thinking quietly.

Cullen stood up. "It's up to you, Guy. You need to decide whether you're going to be a doormat all your life or an independent man with a future and money in the bank."

Guy nodded absently and watched as the man padded through to the kitchen. He looked around at the unfinished walls, insulation foam and polythene lining leaking out where the ceiling joints. A metaphor for his relationship with Conrad he wondered. Cullen was gone what seemed like a long time. When he came back, he put a mug of tea down in front of Guy and just sat staring at him.

"Alright, alright." Guy spluttered. "No need to go on about it!"

Cullen silently sipped his tea and turned to stare out of the window again.

PART THREE

LONDON FASHION WEEK

FIFTEEN

Tuppence scrolled slowly down the Facebook page, reading the comments and clicking on the short videos. It looked like God's Peloton had grown to a quite substantial size already and they were only just past Birmingham. There was a link to Dick's Justgiving page and she clicked on that to see how the donations were going, wondering whether she should donate and, if so, how much.

She was surprised and delighted when a small Facebook chat window appeared with a message from Dick. Before she knew it, she was engaged in a conversation with him.

Dick:	Hey, how are you? Have you seen how well we're doing?
Tuppence:	Yes, I have! Well done. Keep going! How are you managing?
Dick:	Not so bad, really. Thighs ache like nobody's business and my bottom - ouch :-) But the wife of one of van drivers is a masseuse and she gives everybody a good seeing to at the end of each day - oo-er,missus!
Tuppence:	Ha! It sounds like a quite professional setup. I think you've done a great job of organising and coordinating all this. I hope your parishioners appreciate you.
Dick:	Thanks, but it is kind of my

job really. I mean, it should be all our jobs to do what we can but if I have to be the one to start the ball rolling, so be it. *Let no one despise you for your youth, but set the believers an example in speech, in conduct, in love, in faith, in purity. Timothy 4:12.* Although, not so sure I should use the *youth* bit!

Tuppence: You're fine! I don't know your age but I certainly wouldn't describe you as *old*.

Dick: 38

Tuppence: Oh, that's not old at all.

Dick: Old enough to be feeling the pain of riding 60-70 miles each day.

Tuppence: Well, I couldn't do it so there! You're putting me to shame, making me wonder what I can do instead of just standing, pouting and having my photo taken.

Dick: *Do not neglect the gift you have, which was given unto you. Timothy 4:14*

Tuppence: Well, this Timothy seems to have a lot to say for himself, I must say.

Dick: :-) Actually, it's Paul. Paul wrote letters - epistles - to Timothy, amongst others. He wrote so many that the ones included in the bible are identified by the recipient; hence Timothy.

Tuppence: Oh. Ok.

Dick: Sorry. Didn't mean to come over all bible studies lecturer there. It doesn't

	matter who wrote what to whom, the sentiment is what's important. And the message here is: you have a gift and it makes you special. You should use it without shame.
Tuppence:	Is it a gift to just be pretty?
Dick:	You're not pretty. You're stunningly beautiful. A gift from God.
Tuppence:	Thank you.
Dick:	If you feel you want to help in a more personal and direct way, maybe you could find a way to use your modelling to raise money or awareness? Then you'd be using your gift to help others.
Tuppence:	(pause) Yes.
Dick:	Are you ok?
Tuppence:	(pause) Yes.
Dick:	It's just that you've gone monosyllabic on me. Have I upset you?
Tuppence:	(pause) No.
Dick:	I'm sorry.
Tuppence:	What for?
Dick:	I think I've upset you.
Tuppence:	No. You haven't. Not at all. The opposite in fact.
Dick:	Oh.
Tuppence:	Now who's gone all monosyllabic :-)
Dick:	Sorry, I'm a bit confused. I'm sorry for quoting The Bible all the time. Habit. I didn't mean to belittle you or your lack of faith.
Tuppence:	You didn't. And I'm not hurt. I'm flattered. No-one's ever called me stunningly beautiful

	before.
Dick:	But it's true.
Tuppence:	You're making me cry.
Dick:	Please don't… you'll make a mess of your makeup :-)
Tuppence:	Jack never said anything like that to me.
Dick:	Never?
Tuppence:	Well, only when he was … in the mood. You know.
Dick:	Ah. Could we perhaps talk about something else?
Tuppence:	Sorry.
Dick:	Tuppence.
Tuppence:	Yes?
Dick:	Are you sure you're ok?
Tuppence:	I wonder now if I ever loved him at all.
Dick:	Well, sometimes feelings can be difficult to decipher. Wouldn't it-
Tuppence:	I just want to know what's the right thing to do. Then I can do it and know I'll be alright.
Dick:	*So whoever knows the right thing to do and fails to do it, for him it is sin. James 4:17.* Shit, sorry! Said I wouldn't do that again.
Tuppence:	Dick, it's ok. I don't mind all the bible stuff. I've actually been wondering if a bit of bible stuff might not be what I need right now.
Dick:	Would you care to elaborate?
Tuppence:	What is right? For me? What do I want? What should I do with my life? I feel… lost.
Dick:	I'd like to help. If I can.
Tuppence:	Will you?
Dick:	If you want.

Tuppence:	Yes. Please. You seem to have your life sorted. Know what's what. Is that what God did for you?
Dick:	No. I did it for myself. But I needed God's love to show me how to do it.
Tuppence:	That's what I need.
Dick:	God's love?
Tuppence:	Someone's love.
Dick:	Will God's love do?
Tuppence:	It's a start :-)
Dick:	Ok. Well, look. Maybe we can continue this conversation later? I'd rather do it face-to-face - it's easier and better - but I'm in the Midlands and you're.. Actually, where are you right now?
Tuppence:	In my hotel room off Euston Road. Listening to the traffic outside.
Dick:	London?
Tuppence:	Yes. London Fashion Week starts tomorrow. I'm not back home until .. Well, maybe I'll never go back home now.
Dick:	Right. Ok. Well, look. I'm sorry but I really need to get some sleep if you don't mind.
Tuppence:	Of course. I'm sorry. You must be exhausted.
Dick:	I am. But you have brightened the end of my day. Renewed my energy.
Tuppence:	I'm sure I don't know how. But you have told me I'm beautiful-
Dick:	Stunningly beautiful.
Tuppence:	Yes, that. So… Thank you.
Dick:	You're welcome. Can we chat

```
                      same time tomorrow?
Tuppence:        Ok.
Dick:            Ok, goodnight.
Tuppence:        Goodnight.
```

Tuppence closed the lid of her laptop and lay it on the empty side of the bed. Her bedside clock said 23:59 and she sat for a while, watching it, waiting until it ticked around to 00:00. Then she shuffled down under the quilt and went to sleep.

On Wednesday, Liv had flown down from Edinburgh and checked into a hotel just down the road from Kensington Gardens. Chanel had erected a warehouse-sized marquee in the park, dedicated to their fashion shows for the week, one of which was Liv's own. There she'd met up with her team - dressers, hair makeup artists, choreographer, model reps, stage hands and director, dressmakers, tailors, Chanel PR girls and reps. Clothes racks ran along one wall, the other wall was a series of floor-to-ceiling mirrors. A set of portable tables were arraigned along the top wall, and a small table of cups and ashtrays - already overflowing - sat alongside a water fountain and a pyramid of diet cokes. A large section of the awning had been pulled back nearby, allowing those in the team who smoked (the vast majority) to do so without polluting the cavernous interior.

The tables at the far end were strewn with clothes, rolls of material, zips, buttons and other assorted odds and ends. Two sewing machines sat at the end of the table, their power cables stretched to their fullest extent, straining to reach the power strips which were fed by a thrumming generator running constantly outside. A flipchart with broad red numbers and markings on it stood in one corner and it was to this that Liv bullishly strode. She was wearing a pale cashmere turtle-neck top over a boldly geometric pencil skirt and open-toe flat shoes. Her left arm was still in a sling.

"Right, this is the running order. Carl? Can you make sure you have the timings down so that the music changes synch with the girls run-ins please? I want to rehearse this tomorrow in whatever spare time we can manage to grab the girls from the show. This is NOT a time for Mr Cockup to pay a visit."

"But we'll miss the early shows." This was Fliss, her assistant.

"Can't be helped." Liv brushed her aside. "Nothing worth seeing anyway. Ours is the only show to be seen."

"It's not just about what you get to see. It's who gets to see you."

Liv frowned. "Huh?

"You want to get your photo taken wherever you can. Sitting next to the great and the good." Fliss explained. "You need a profile."

"I'll have all the profile I need when we've finished the show."

"No." Fliss said, horrified. "It doesn't work like that. When the show finishes, everyone moves on. Paris. Milan. New York. If you don't make a buzz this week, you may miss your chance."

"But I'm not on until Day 3!"

"Which is why you need to be seen beforehand." Fliss explained. "There's no real time afterwards. Day 4 is really people packing up and winding down. You can't afford to waste this opportunity. You have to get out front whenever you can, Day 1 and 2, and press the flesh wherever you can."

Liv took a long drag on her cigarette and bit her lip. "Shit." She looked at her watch and expelled the last of the smoke through her nostrils. "Can you crack the whip here for me, then? I'll go and change and then try and catch people's eyes for the last hour?"

"Perfect." Fliss smiled. "Relax! Try and enjoy yourself. Talk to whoever you can and push your show, your ideas. Build it up."

"Right."

"And take notes. See how the fashion editors react to what you're telling them and try and interpret it. Then you can come back here and make some tweaks if you need."

"Ok." Liv stubbed out her cigarette in one of the ashtrays and took a deep breath. "Thanks."

"You're welcome!" Fliss said in a sing-song, waggling her blonde head from side to side.

Two hours later, Liv made her way down to the main LFW venue in Soho and strode brashly in through the Brewer Street entrance, brandishing her credentials on the lanyard around her neck.

Held, twice a year, in an iconic art deco building in the heart of Soho, London Fashion Week, to the uninitiated, looks like a charming riot of beautiful people, famous people, outlandish people and madly-dressed tossers all being chased to ground by khaki-jacketed hyena photographers and loner fashion bloggers on selfie-rampages. Spanning two floors of the building locals know as Brewer Street Car Park, built in 1929.

Tuppence's cab had to stop several hundred yards away due to the volume of traffic and parked vehicles and other lorries attempting to go about their normal loading and unloading business in the midst of all this fashion hubbub. She walked to the main entrance and looked up at the huge banners and advertising signs rippling in the air before showing her id to the security guard at the main entrance who directed to a side door and stairs up to the main floors.

One floor was the Show Room - a cavernous but intimate space divided into grandiosely elegant stalls, booths, shops and installations highlighting (and selling) the works of fashion designers and stylists from around the world.

White. White everywhere.

Clean lines, with lots of empty air emphasised by semi-transparent dividers. Laser-cut cubes, glass, chrome, and other assorted designer flotsam were deliberately positioned to look as if they weren't there. Oodles more white and floating shelves acting together to create a sparkling setting in which high-end, top-end and very top-end items of clothing were artfully draped, hung or folded in front of monochrome minimalist logos; designer pearls nestling in the midst of this translucent oyster shell of chic.

The second floor, dubbed the Show Space, had as its main hub a 70 metre long catwalk running the length of the space. Tiered rows of modernist white benches sit either side and the central runway is lit by natural light flooding down from huge windows in the vaulted ceiling directly above and then augmented by the strategic placement of large angled mirrors which reflect the light, and the models, as they shimmer up and down. Spangled flashes from cameras, loud dance music and an amplified narration from each presenter add the finishing touches to a jostling, hectic scene. The bustle only increased between shows as the models, dressers and makeup people hustle in, shuffle around and mingle with those trying to make their way out while keeping to the announce schedule.

Behind the catwalk was the preparation area, cordoned off and hidden from view by more white. It was here that Tuppence entered into a whirlwind of swirling hair and costumes, hairspray and nakedness and immediately sought out a helpful runner who could fetch her a cup of peppermint tea. Her watch said 12:50 and she had shows at 2.00 and 3.30 - not ideal, having them so close to each other as there could be significant make-up and hair changes required between shows - changing outfits was the easy bit. She did her best to find a quieter corner of the bleached out changing arena in which to shelter and calm herself in preparation.

The 1,600 square metre open space layout was also home to a number of corporately sponsored pop-up eateries, a large champagne bar and a smaller non-alcoholic one serving a mass of herb, grass and vegetable juices, smoothies, yoghurts and milks. Across all the various menus on offer, it seemed only carbohydrates were the omission from the range of food groups available.

Between the eating areas and the Show Space was a set of marquees - white again - themselves pop-up homes for digital presentations for smaller design houses, independent designers or future attractions being trailed by those with shows elsewhere.

Whilst Brewer St was the main hub of LFW, the events themselves were spread over a number of different locations across the city. One, at the ICA, was used by as a presentation venue where fashion houses could showcase their ranges on the big screen, or transmit the catwalk shows to those unable to get tickets to Brewer St themselves. Other, more independent minds, had hired their own venues and hooked them into the agenda creating a so-called fringe, enlarging the network of to-be-seen at locations across the capital. Chanel had an enormous marquee at Kensington Gardens, Burberry at the South Bank, with others in Bloomsbury and Hyde Park.

Around 5pm, all her duties done, Tuppence wandered down to the front of the Show Space and mooched about amongst the pop-up tents. The open plan area was awash with people chatting in small groups, posing for selfies, drinking champagne or journos doing pieces to camera. A tuxedo'd waiter circled with a tray full of glasses, and, unprompted, placed a champagne flute in her hand whilst her eyes were elsewhere.

She poked her head inside the first tent but the music swirled too loudly for her and the flashing images reflected on the white canopy started to strobe. Tuppence retracted her head and looked over to the opposite tent. Through the sides of the translucent material which formed the sides of this marquee she could see a large presentation underway of a catwalk show, models proud-footing down the runway, posing, turning and stomping back. She saw a few faces she recognised but a lot of the models were oriental and the whole set had a strange foreign vibe she couldn't quite put her finger on. The sound mix was a little off and she couldn't hear the voiceover for the music, so she stepped over and brushed past some hangers-on at the entrance to sneak inside.

The narration was a little clearer now and a familiar oriental accent occasionally cut through the buzz. Something about ready-to-wear haute couture, she thought. The images on the screen then changed and she had to look away slightly as the new setting was a landscape with an enormous bright sky. The camera panned across scudding clouds and china blue and slowly dropped onto a country church surrounded by a dry stone wall. Jump cut to a huge close-up of a girl's face.

Hers.

A slow zoom-out showed her draped elegantly over a gravestone in the shape of a large Celtic cross. That was the shoot she'd done for Conrad a few weeks ago! She watched, fully engaged, and tried harder to pick out the narration which she now realised must be Conrad's own. The presentation was very slick and well done and the message seemed to be that here was new concept in designer fashion. Top-end styles, on show now, available to order now and ready to take home before the end of LFW. Couture-to-Go he called it, and the CtG logo bled onto the screen at the end along with dates and times at which this presentation would be re-run during the show. The screen faded to black and a number of young Chinese women, dressed as schoolgirls, moved among the crowd handing out small flyers.

Tuppence took one. It was elegant monochrome, black predominating, and all it contained was the CtG logo and a QR code beneath it. She scanned it in on her phone and was taken to a CtG app which she downloaded and launched. Now, this was pretty neat, she thought. The app showed full-screen images of all the items she'd seen in the presentation, including the ones she'd been wearing. You flipped through them, tinder-style, and when you found one you liked, you selected a size and any colourway options - if there were any - and got immediate text confirmation of your order and a pickup date/time from the Brewer St Show Rooms. Pay on collection. Item will be personally handed over by Conrad Ho.

A small gear clicked in Tuppence's brain and she flicked through to her contacts and sent a text to Big Paul.

"This is some weird, fucking twisted joke." Guy attempted to pull down the hem of the dress below the knee, feeling and looking completely uncomfortable in his new outfit. The best adjective he could summon right now was *unflattering*.

Cullen's mouth turned up, ever-so-slightly, at the edges as he surveyed Guy's appearance. "I think it suits you."

Guy was wearing a dark green, knee-length woollen coat, beneath which was a tight-fitting bodycon dress in pale green and white. Beneath that, albeit hidden from the naked eye, was a bra and panties from Marks and Spencer and a pair of American tan tights which reached up past his belly-button and made him feel pregnant. He tottered on shiny black high-heels like a baby giraffe having a drink.

Cullen sat with his feet up on the arm of the chair. The floor was strewn with garments which Guy had tried on and deemed even more ill-fitting than his current garb. What he stood up in was all that was left.

"Nothing's my size." Guy whined like an overweight, body-conscious teen.

"Yeah, well Shirley's a big girl. Apparently."

"Who the hell's Shirley?"

"She is the current squeeze of the owner of this establishment." He waved airily at the room around them. "But never mind that. Have you managed to get hold of Conrad yet?"

"No." Guy put his hands on his hips, the model of an outraged teen. "I've left loads of voicemails but he hasn't called me back."

"We need to find out where he is." Cullen sucked his teeth. It was at that moment that Big Paul entered.

"What the fuck?" Paul stared first at Guy and then, pointedly, at Cullen. "I can't keep up with you. One minute it's supermodels, the next its trannies! Who the fuck's he?"

"Guy this is Paul. Paul this is Guy. Our friendly neighbourhood kidnapper."

"Oh, that reminds me." Paul smacked his forehead with a meaty palm. "Your mate - Conrad. He's in London. Fashion Week apparently. And Tuppence says 'Hi'."

"Of course!" Guy realised. "D'oh. I should have known. He's exhibiting his clothes!"

"What?" Cullen screwed up his face but before Guy had time to explain, Paul exploded.

"Here, hang on! Is that Shirley's clobber you're wearing? Oh, Christ on a bike."

"It's ok." Cullen reassured him.

"Oh, it might be ok for you. It's not your balls she's going to have in a sling!"

"Calm down, Beep. How would like to earn some serious money?"

Paul's mood softened immediately. "How serious?"

"Deadly."

Guy wrestled and wrangled with the dress and underwear, all uncomfortably riding up and restricting him every which way he position himself. Nowhere was comfortable. The heels didn't help.

"I can't even walk properly."

"Practice." Cullen said. "Pretend it's a catwalk."

"I'm not some fucking supermodel!"

"She is."

"Yes, well I'm not her am I?" Guy fizzed, jaws clenched.

"Well, tomorrow you are. One performance only. Tonight Matthew, I will be-"

Paul leant across to Cullen. "He's not exactly a lookie-likee is he?"

"Look, it's either him, me or you. What do you reckon?"

Paul turned back to Guy. "You'll be fine, mate. Chop, chop! Let's see you wiggle those hips."

"You're all fucking enjoying this!"

Cullen sighed and threw Guy a carrier bag bundle. "Put the wig on."

"Where do you get the wig? Shirley doesn't have a wig." Paul frowned. "Does she?"

"Caravan." Cullen said, as if that explained everything.

Guy spent more than fifteen minutes parading up and down, pausing every now and then to pose in front of the full-length mirror and make adjustments to his straps, his dress or his wig. Cullen and Paul watched in silence, waiting to see if there would be a request for matching accessories.

"Now who's enjoying it?" Cullen offered.

"I don't even look feminine." Guy complained, regarding his reflection in the mirror once more. The lighting didn't help. "Didn't you think about makeup or anything?"

Cullen grimaced. "Sorry. Maybe I could pop out and get some in the morning?"

Guy sighed and tried smoothing his dress down over the bulges and valleys of tightly fitting underwear, examining his silhouette in the mirror, for all the world like a woman in a changing room. Finally, unhappily, he stood and put his hands on his hips.

"Is this even what she'd wear to a football match?"

"No idea." Cullen scrutinised Guy and thought for a moment. "Maybe you could be a, whatdyamacallit, transsexual. You know? All the rage now I believe."

"Unreal." Guy shook his head, a beaten man. "Unfucking-real."

SIXTEEN

"Con?" Liv was standing in the Show Space staring at the back of the man she immediately recognised.

Conrad turned sheepishly towards her and tried on his best smile. He looked nervous and scared and Liv strode straight up to him.

"Hey." His eyes strayed to her shoulder and arm still in a sling, and Liv instantly bristled.

"Never mind, Hey. You were there, weren't you?"

"What?"

"I saw you. Just as I was shot." She scrutinised his face closely, alert to the merest hint of a lie. "You were coming around the corner of the corridor towards me. I looked up, saw you and then - bam! - everything went black."

Conrad shoulders sagged. "Yes. I was there. I saw you. Watched you... fall."

"Why?"

"I... wanted to see you. Wanted to apologise. Make up." His big brown eyes were moist and his mouth twitched involuntarily and she simply didn't believe him.

"Is that why you didn't stick around? Didn't call an ambulance? Left me to be found by someone else, in an empty corridor?"

"I... I... I wasn't supposed to be there. I was afraid." Conrad turned his face away from her and thrust his hands in his pockets. "I should've called for help."

"Damn right." She was angry and suspicious. There was something wrong and she couldn't work out what it was. "What the fuck are you doing here, anyway?"

Conrad had persuaded her to grab a coffee, not least so she didn't clap eyes on his pop-up show with her designs being paraded around in it. This unexpected development had thrown him hugely and he needed every second he could get to work out how to play this now. Why hadn't he thought of this? Of course, she'd be there if she had her own show to orchestrate. Had he really thought he could put on his show at Brewer Street and magically escape her attention? Idiot!

His mind cycled, like a hamster in a wheel, as he shepherded her out of the main building to a coffee shop around the corner. By the time they had ordered and were seated he had decided that, while revenge may best be served cold, here he was with a still-warm serving. But he had better make the most of it, because this was as chilled as it was going to get, now that she'd seen him. It was time to go for full gloat.

He was wondering how to broach the subject when Liv saw the tartan samples in his bag on the seat next to him.

"What are those?"

"Hmm?" Conrad's feigned cool was immediately supplanted by his heart pounding and he was sure he must be blushing.

"In your bag? There?" Liv pointed and he hurriedly grabbed the mouth of his leather shoulder bag and tried to tuck it under his chair out of sight.

"If you must know." He began, his pride urging him on. "They are design samples from my new range which I am debuting - in full - tomorrow at the show."

"What!" Conrad watched as her face went through a series of emotions in rapid succession, eventually settling on astonishment. "How on earth-?"

He smiled and sipped his glass of water. "Contacts, Liv. Contacts."

"Yours or daddy's?" She sniped, immediately on the attack.

"Mine, if you must know. All mine. In fact, my father was less than complimentary about my business dealings but…" he rubbed his hands together and flexed his fingers like a magician preparing for a particularly tricky sleight of hand. "I have just come back from Hong Kong, actually."

"But…" Liv was momentarily lost for words. "How did you…?"

"It is the future, Liv. Wake up and smell it." Conrad couldn't resist beaming at her. "I have a number of presentation slots at one of the pop-up marquees in the Show Space. The British Fashion Council have set them up to provide a platform for new designers to market and sell their goods and promote them at LFW. All part of a drive towards expanding across social media and digital platforms." He parroted.

"Huh." She tried to appear unimpressed. Conrad didn't notice, wrapped up in his oft-rehearsed sales pitch.

"I am leveraging this precious opportunity to showcase my Couture-to-Go concept and range. Bringing ready-to-wear to haute couture."

"May I see them?"

"No." He snapped, too hastily, and Liv's hackles rose instinctively.

"Why not?"

"All in good time, my dear." Conrad twirled an

invisible moustache theatrically.

"Oh come on." She pouted. "It's not like I'm going to steal them or anything!"

Conrad started and reddened. "They, er, need a few finishing touches. I'd rather you see them when they're complete."

"But you said they're in the show tomorrow?"

"Well, not these exact ones. A video."

"A catwalk video?"

"Sort of. Some shot here, some in Hong Kong, modelling my whole range." He leant forward, warming to his theme. "There's a QR code on the programme. You download the app to your phone and the app's in sync with the show - as each garment is modelled it appears on your screen. You swipe right to choose it and then state your size and place the order. Tailor-made item is collected on the last day of the show. Couture To Go. CtG!"

She pursed her lips, impressed that he had managed to deliver his vision wondering if she had underestimated him. Gazing at him with renewed interest, she wondered if perhaps she had been too harsh on him; too judgemental. Perhaps.

"However did you manage it?" She asked, an eager gleam in her eye.

"Bloody hard work is how." Conrad boasted, puffing his chest out.

"But I thought the mill had knocked - er, dismissed your designs as unsuitable for manufacture?"

"Yes. In Scotland." Conrad huffed. "But like I have told you many times, Hong Kong is not Scotland. Different rules. Different ways of working. Hong Kong has no time for pre-madonnas."

"So, all done using the exact same designs as before?" She sniffed an evasion.

"Not the exact same, no." Conrad had reddened again and she knew he was hiding something significant. "I had a little help. My manufacturer in Hong Kong wanted something less fussy, so he could produce them quicker and in a more streamlined way."

"Ha! Told you." She gulped a slug of coffee and flicked a strand of her behind her ear triumphantly. "Who from?"

"An, er, up and coming new designer, actually." There was something the matter with his smile. She thought he was being cute.

"Who?" And when his smile widened she knew something was up. "Anyone I might know?"

"Might do." He was beaming now, a gleaming grin a mile wide.

"Don't tease, Con. Who is it?"

"Well, if you must know." He paused for dramatic effect. "It's you."

"I- I don't understand." She smiled, not getting the joke.

"You." Suddenly Conrad's smile was cold, his eyes gloating. "I stole your designs."

"My designs?"

"From the mill."

"You stole them?" What he was saying to her still refused to compute. Was this a joke at all?

"Well, borrowed them." His manner had switched from revenge-at-last to oleaginous. He was relishing this, she could tell. "Or borrowed from them, shall we say."

"Borrowed from them?" Liv's voice rose, beginning to boom throatily across the restaurant. "You mean copied!"

"No, I mean borrowed from them." Conrad pursed his lips. "Heavily."

"You… BASTARD!" Suddenly the whole room was silent, the other customers intent on not looking at them. "How could you?"

"Revenge is a dish best served cold, my sweet."

"Give them here!" She lunged for his bag and wrestled it from him, pulling fabric swatches and samples and dumping them on the table. Rifling through them they looked familiar but she couldn't be sure they were all, or some, of her own. She couldn't understand why he would lie, but she also couldn't understand why he would steal them in the first place. "I don't get it. What do you mean, revenge?"

"For your Chanel post." Conrad raised an eyebrow, coolly, explaining the obvious.

"I… I still don't get it."

"Don't you? I win."

"You win?"

"Yes." Conrad smiled. "Check mate."

"Is that what this was, for you. A competition? You and me?"

"Of course." Conrad condescended. "Don't tell me it wasn't one for you too?"

"No! It wasn't a competition. Not for me." She spat the words at him. "How could it be, hmm? When you were never going to be good enough to beat me. You were never going to win. What would be the point of a one-man competition, hmm? Or should I say, one woman?"

"It is too late to withdraw, Liv. You have lost and I have won."

"You have won!" She laughed. "How have you won? You've had to use my designs to get your ideas off the ground! Doesn't sound like winning to me. It sounds like cheating. Sounds like theft."

Conrad gave a stilted smile, the shine perhaps taken off his victory slightly. "Prove it."

"I will." She sneered. "I'll-"

"What? What will you do?" Conrad leant back in his chair. "What do you have? Some designs with my name on them that look awfully like some designs with Chanel's name on them? Big deal, happens all the time. It's called fashion! And when my designs come out tomorrow but Chanel's don't come until - when - Sunday? Monday? Then who's going to look like they copied who, hmm?"

"You fucking bastard." Liv sank in her chair. Then a new, more shocking thought hit her. "I'll have to cancel my Chanel show!" She put her head in her hands and looked up at Conrad with wet eyes. "I'll have to tell them!"

"That is up to you."

"They'll fire me!"

Conrad shrugged.

"You bastard." She dropped her gaze from his eyes to the tablecloth.

"So you've said."

"I hate you."

"This is about winning. It's not a popularity contest."

"How can you be so fucking calm and cold about this?" She looked up at him, imploring. "Doesn't my livelihood matter to you? Don't you care about what happens to me?"

"Not anymore." He gloated. "I win."

"What am I going to do?" She wailed, lost.

A waitress came over. "Would you care for a top-up?"

After several cigarettes and rehearsals of what she wanted to say, Liv had called Daniel Tyson-Wright's mobile number. With shaking hands she waited for him to pick up. When he did, they were off to a good start at least.

"Olivia? This is a nice surprise." His voice sounded far-off, maybe he was on speakerphone? "I understand everything is ready for Sunday? I am on my way to the airport now to make sure I'm there in plenty of time. Want to get a front row seat, you know?"

He laughed at his own wit and Liv took a deep breath before plunging straight in.

"Actually, that's why I'm calling Daniel. It's about... the show." She realised mid-sentence that her mouth was drying up and her hands were sweating. She had to swallow hard to continue. The COO picked up her discomfort like a shot.

"Is there a problem, Olivia?" The air temperature dropped noticeably.

"Well, yes. Actually. I'm afraid there is. You see, last night I was told that there had been a leak-"

"A leak?"

"Of my designs." She left it there and waited for a beat, two beats. It seemed ages before he spoke.

"Go on."

"I have been led to understand that a competitor has - somehow - erm, got hold of my designs and, erm, used them to-"

"Used them?"

"Copied them."

"Copied?"

"Essentially, yes." She swallowed again, difficult though it was to do so. "To base their own work on which is, erm, obviously then clearly derived from, erm, and remarkably similar to…"

She didn't know how to finish and tailed off in the teeth of the eerie silence on the other end. She waited several seconds for him to say something but there was no sound.

"Hello?"

"Yes, I am still here Olivia."

"Right. Sorry."

"Sorry I'm still here?"

"No. No. Look, Daniel. I'm sorry. I'm really sorry. I don't know how this has happened but it *has* happened and these designs are being shown at LFW tomorrow, before mine. Yours. Ours." She bit her tongue. "Chanel's. And so I thought I'd better let you know so you could make a decision as to the best-"

"You're fired."

"What?" Despite her worst fear being realised, Liv hadn't been ready for it.

"Ms Nightingale, you're fired. I will cancel the show and arrange for you to be paid up until today."

"But-" She tried to protest, even knowing that the formality of using her surname consigned her to history.

"You will receive full written confirmation and remuneration details from our HR department early next week."

"But it wasn't my fault!" She cried, eyes filling with tears.

"It was your show, Ms Nightingale. *Your* show. *Your*

designs. *Your* project. *Your* responsibility. All of us in senior positions must sometimes pay the price for the mistakes of those below us."

"Then why don't you resign!" She huffed, immediately regretting her outburst.

"Ms. Nightingale-"

"I'm sorry. I'm sorry. I didn't mean that." She begged. "Please, you have to understand-"

"Goodbye, Ms Nightingale."

"But the people at the mill should- !"

Daniel Tyson-Wright had hung up and Liv was left keening into an unheeding dial tone.

"It's all a complete and utter *fucking* nightmare." Liv groaned, fingering a beermat with her chipped nails

Tuppence looked on, concerned, at her friend who was now almost nose down in her fifth champagne flute. Liv's nest of tangles she called a hairstyle had lost its lustre and sat uncomfortably atop her head, as if disconnected from their owner. Thrust at odd angles, pointed here and jagged there, they advertised her tipsy status whilst, at the same time, almost beckoning to others around her - goading them - as if to say "Come on then, arseholes, if you want some!"

"What am I going to do?"

Tuppence really didn't know what to say and wished Dick was here with some words of kindness and wisdom. Feeling obliged to say something - anything - she said "It's really not as bad as all that, you know. Things'll look brighter in the morning."

"This is the morning!" Liv slurred. "Yesterday everything went tits up, today it's still tits up. Why should it be any better tomorrow?"

"Time heals all wounds." Was all Tuppence could think of and she winced as she heard herself trot this tired cliche out to her friend, clearly hurting. Tuppence felt helpless.

"Well, it won't heal *his* fucking wounds when I get hold of him." Liv spat. "He's fucking ruined me. Ruined me." She gestured wildly around, sloshing her glass, at anyone within hearing distance.

"Conrad?"

"Of course, fucking Conrad!" she hissed. "Who else?"

"I thought you might have meant Mr... thing at Chanel." Tuppence apologised.

"Him!" She snorted. "Well, he can go and take a fucking running jump as well. Bastard!" People around her were now either staring or moving carefully away. Liv straightened, suddenly, and tried to look her friend in the eye, giving Tuppence the benefit of her wisdom. "Mark my words, Tupp. In this day and age, it is still possible to be decent and civil, chivalrous and polite, and still - still! - be successful at business. What does fucking Daniel fucking Tyson fucking Wright know about anything like that, hmm?"

Tuppence looked on, downcast, at her distraught and dishevelled friend. The people milling around, drinking casually and chatting animatedly, were already starting to give Liv more space, recognising a clear difference between their amateur drunkenness goals and those of someone who looked semi-professional.

Liv was wearing a loud tartan ensemble, riddled with large intentional holes, some woven into the fabric, others hacked out and hemmed in contrasting colours. Her shoulders and left side of her midriff were exposed and the rest of the dress fell loosely to just above knee height, asymmetrically. The large checks of the tartan enhanced her already ample bosom, split as it was by a heart-shaped hole at the centre of her cleavage. Bunched up theatrically with a huge belt which owed its visual cues to a post-modern sporran, the outfit was bottomed by bright orange heels on which she now tottered, and topped by a back-combed, teased and spiked helmet of vivid red which had orange neon highlights shredded through it, to pick up the same notes as her shoes. Sober and statuesque, Liv would have looked gorgeous; shambling and half-cut she looked like a wounded hit-and-run after an Old Firm match.

"So, what now?"

"Now? I'm ruined aren't I? Sacked by Chanel, who's going to want me, hmm?"

"Talent will always shine through." Tuppence tried to reassure her.

"Yes." Liv nodded ruefully. "Yes. I thought I had talent."

"You do!"

"Hmm." She sighed. "Mister Tosspot-Wanker doesn't think so. Never did. Do you know, he called me." Liv looked into Tuppence's eyes, her gaze unsteady. "He called me, after I'd been shot. Still in pain. Struggling on. With his *fucking* collection. To make sure I was still *on track*. Not feeling better, *on track*. Fucking bean counter."

Tuppence's face turned serious. "That reminds me. When you were shot, I think he kidnapped me."

"Huh?" Liv raised an eyebrow and turned her head side-on to Tuppence, as if to hear better.

"I think…" Tuppence lowered her voice and glanced briefly around. "He kidnapped me."

"Mister Tosspot-Wanker?"

"No! Conrad."

"Conrad kidnapped you?" Liv snorted.

"Shhh." Tuppence insisted, looking around again.

"Conrad kidnapped you?" Liv repeated, quieter this time. "Nah! He's got a wishbone, not a backbone."

Tuppence shrugged. "Apparently."

"Seriously?" Liv was incredulous and then, immediately, aggressive. "Let's report him! Arrest him! Lock him up and throw away the fucking key!"

"No!" Tuppence protested and then, realising her own voice was raised, she hunkered down again.

"I don't understand you, Tupp." Liv looked earnestly at her friend. "I don't understand why you're so laid back and relaxed about this. Your marriage is essentially over and you were *apparently* kidnapped but you don't seem to care about catching the people who did it, getting revenge or anything. What's that all about, hmm?"

"Revenge just… isn't my thing." Tuppence sighed. "I'm not mad about Jack so much as sad. He needs help and I really hope he gets it. He's just not going to get it from me." She looked into her friend's eyes, honest innocence emitting from every pore on her face. "I've spent my life loving others when they didn't deserve it and not enough time being loved myself. Life's too short and I want to be loved. I deserve to be loved. And poor unfortunates like Jack - and Conrad - well, they'll get their rewards whether I administer them or not. Let them look after themselves, and let me look after me."

"Oh I get it." Liv smiled. "Blessed are the meek. Turn the other cheek. Blah blah blah. He's really got to you, hasn't he?"

"It's not like that."

"Isn't it, Tupp? Isn't it? Wouldn't you like to turn his other cheek, hmm?"

"Liv!" Tuppence protested, blushing. "I'm not talking about turning the other cheek. In either way you are implying. Jesus said: I desire mercy, not sacrifice. I'm not sure I want them to be granted mercy, but I certainly don't want them sacrificed."

"Well I bloody do! Conrad at any rate." Liv huffed. "You can go about your new god-bothering business without me."

"I'm not a god-botherer!" Tuppence was wounded.

"No, sorry. I didn't mean to be snippy. You've found someone and... something, perhaps. And I'm really pleased for you. I hope it works out. Really." Liv placed her hand on Tuppence's and squeezed it gently.

"Anyway, it's all in hand. My *friend*, is going to get his money."

"Conrad's money?"

"Yes. Well, Jack's money really."

"Jack? I thought you said it was all over?"

"It is."

Liv snorted and then sat in silence, gazing into the crowd, nursing the last bit of champagne in her glass. Eventually she looked back at Tuppence. "Men, huh?"

"Yeah." Tuppence reminded herself of her own situation, sniffed, and agreed with her friend. "Bunch of pricks. Excuse my French."

"Correct!" Liv raised her glass. "Men! A bunch of complete and utter pricks. Let's cut their balls off and kill them all!"

They chinked glasses and then Tuppence, thoughtfully, added: "Perhaps not all of them."

Tuppence:	Hi. Glad to see you're still up.
Dick:	Hi. You must be a mind-reader. I was just going to try and call you!
Tuppence:	Really?
Dick:	Yes. I wanted to ask your advice.
Tuppence:	Ooh! That makes a change. Ok, shoot.
Dick:	Really? Well, I… wait, what's happened to your status? It says *No longer a couple*.
Tuppence:	Yes. Jack and I are over.
Dick:	Are you ok?
Tuppence:	Yes. No. I don't know. He's a … prick!
Dick:	What happened? Do you want to tell me?
Tuppence:	I went to see him. To talk to him about what happened to me? He was … you don't want to know.
Dick:	Oh, I'm so sorry Tuppence.
Tuppence:	I'm not. How could I have been so STUPID! He didn't love me!
Dick:	Did you ask him about-
Tuppence:	No. Stormed out. Didn't seem much point.
Dick:	Of course.
Tuppence:	I don't know what he could have done to hurt me more.
Dick:	I'm sorry.
Tuppence:	At least it looks like Paw clawed him. That's some justice.
Dick:	(Pause). Sorry, is that auto-correct or something?
Tuppence:	What?
Dick:	You wrote *Paw clawed him*. It

307

```
                       doesn't make any sense.
Tuppence:              Paw's my cat.
Dick:                  Ah, right. Is he ok?
Tuppence:              Paw?
Dick:                  No, Jack.
Tuppence:              Who cares! Bastard deserved it.
                       Hope it REALLY hurt!
```

Neither of them wrote anything for a minute or two.

```
Dick:                  Are you still there? Are you
                       ok?
Tuppence:              Yes. I'm working tomorrow and
                       part of me feels completely
                       embarrassed and ashamed and
                       wants to just curl up in bed
                       until this is all over, and the
                       other part of me wants to shout
                       it from the rooftops and tell
                       the world he's a complete
                       arsehole.
Dick:                  Could be cathartic :-)
Tuppence:              Can't though, actually. You're
                       under contract - as a model -
                       to not say anything or do
                       anything which might bring your
                       clients into disrepute or
                       attract unwanted attention.
                       Just have to pout and pose and
                       keep shtum.
Dick:                  Doesn't that include Facebook,
                       then? Shouldn't you change your
                       status back?
Tuppence:              I don't think so. It's only
                       when I'm wearing their stuff,
                       or appearing under their
                       banner. They don't OWN me!
Dick:                  Sorry.
Tuppence:              And that bastard doesn't own me
                       either.
Dick:                  Nobody owns anyone. Not even
```

	God. He may have created us in his own image, but he gave us free will.
Tuppence:	Free will to sin?
Dick:	For some, yes. For Jack, perhaps. For you? He created you to be beautiful so that others may delight in your beauty.
Tuppence:	I've got a good mind to sin as well! Get my own back.
Dick:	And who would that benefit? Would you feel better for it?
Tuppence:	(Pause) I might.
Dick:	Tuppence, I know you must be hurting right now. And I can't honestly say I've been in the same position and know how to deal with it. But time does heal, and things will get better. And you are good and kind and deserving of so much more.

Dick waited for a response but there was none. After a long silence he checked to see if she was still there.

Dick:	You ok?
Tuppence:	What advice did you want?
Dick:	Well, I'm not sure I should bother you right now. My… difficulties, don't seem to compare with yours really.
Tuppence:	Dick, honestly. It's fine. I have some tissues here. And I have Paw to cuddle. HE loves me. HE won't let me down.
Dick:	God loves you. He won't let you down.
Tuppence:	He has a funny way of showing it.

Dick:	Are you sure you're ok?
Tuppence:	Yes. Fine, really. What did you want to ask me?
Dick:	Well. Deep breath… I'm afraid that I am become a victim of my own success!
Tuppence:	What do you mean?
Dick:	Well God's peloton is attracting bigger crowds, and more and more publicity. I'm getting daily requests for radio and TV interviews. Even TV stations sending cameras on motorcycles to cover sections of our route. It's all getting rather intrusive.
Tuppence:	Ah. That might be my fault actually.
Dick:	What do you mean?
Tuppence:	Well, I did tweet about it and send links to my friends to help publicise it. Sorry, didn't think it would get out of hand. But, well, the circles in which I move do attract the more fame-hungry. Some of them are awfully well-connected.
Dick:	I'm not sure you should take all the blame. Or credit, whatever. I suppose I can't complain about the media if it is sending our total raised soaring! I don't want to sound ungrateful.
Tuppence:	No, I understand. I don't think anyone really can anticipate what it's like to be in the full glare of publicity until it hits and then, well, it's too late.
Dick:	Yes, it does feel a bit like being caught up in a whirlwind

where everyone but me is
setting the agenda. I don't
mean to sound like a control
freak but, well, I don't feel
I'm in control anymore! It's
grown arms and legs.

Tuppence: Welcome to my world :-)

Dick: And it isn't helping
            camaraderie much either.

Tuppence: What do you mean?

Dick: Well, I've become the
            figurehead for the whole thing.
            Natural, I suppose since I
            started it. But all the
            attention, it feels like it's
            on me. I think the others are
            starting to resent it.

Tuppence: I'm sure they're not.

Dick: I don't mean the attention
            thing. At least, I don't think
            I do. But because of it I have
            to be seen to be in the lead.
            When we get to photo
            opportunity spots, you see?
            It's my face they want to see
            leading the pack when the
            cameras are there. Continuity
            as much as anything, I guess.
            But it's my face they want. So,
            its become like this big
            logistics operation. I can't
            lead all the way, I'm not fit
            enough for that. Don't think
            anyone is.

Tuppence: Sorry, I'm not sure I see the
            problem.

Dick: Well, it means that they have
            to give me special treatment.
            The whole way. So, everyone has
            to know where the photo spots
            are first of all, so that I
            have time to be reminded and

311

get out of wherever I am in the middle of the pack and out front ready in time. And then, I need to slip back into the pack so that I can save some energy ready for the next one. So I think everyone feels they're all just acting in a supporting role, making sure I am the one treated with kid gloves and they all have to ride as best they can while I get wrapped in cotton wool when no-one's watching, get wheeled out for the cameras, and then put back in cotton wool for the next time.

Tuppence: Oh, I see.

Dick: Yes. And I feel as if they all resent it. Talk about me behind my back. Scowl for the cameras, that kind of thing.

Tuppence: No! Surely, not. Aren't you all men of the cloth?

Dick: Well, we're all men. It's all getting too much for me, I think. I'm riding all day, arse hurts like crazy. And then you get calls from the police and councils, wanting to know about road closures or crash barriers or something else. Bad enough riding on its own, without having to take a call and mentally consult a map and talk and not crash into anyone. And when you get to the end of the day, you've got just enough energy to eat like a zombie and you're completely exhausted. But you can't go to sleep until you've done social media

	updates, interviews, worked out details for the next days route-
Tuppence:	Spent half an hour chatting with someone on Facebook.
Dick:	That too! Sorry, I'm ranting aren't I?
Tuppence:	I understand. I think I do anyway.
Dick:	So, constant attention, friction with my fellow riders, interruptions, other duties. I feel like I'm snowballing down a hill and can't stop, and that I'll come crashing to some horrible end all worn out and wounded and wishing I'd never started the whole bloomin' thing!
Tuppence:	And then you'll see the size of the cheque.
Dick:	Yes, but even then I'll be the one with my picture in the paper. I'll be the name everyone remembers. And all my attempts at forming ties with other clergy across the country will seem like some self-aggrandising vanity project and no-one will speak to me again.
Tuppence:	Come on! I think you're melodramatising a tad.
Dick:	Maybe. It's just, right now, in the middle of this whirlwind, it seems like everything's spinning out of control and it's all going to end… badly.
Tuppence:	Ok. And this is why you want my advice?
Dick:	*sigh*. Yes. Please
Tuppence:	Well. How do you think you'll feel when you see your

	parishioners' faces when the roof is mended and the churchyard's repaired, hmm? And how will your fellow riders feel when they get their share of the proceeds and are able to spend it on their pet project? Won't it all seem worthwhile, then?
Dick:	Perhaps.
Tuppence:	And, when time has passed - your fifteen minutes are over, if you like - won't you all have kept in touch? Maybe get together once a year to reminisce and catch up?
Dick:	Maybe.
Tuppence:	So, here's my advice. You know it'll all be worthwhile when it's over, because that's why you decided to start it in the first place. And maybe your image is more prominent than others, but it was your idea and your energy that has kept this thing on the road - literally. And so it's only natural that you'll be associated with it. But it IS just your fifteen minutes of fame. It happens so fast, it's all so fleeting. You will - and you do - feel caught up in something bigger than yourself. But if won't last. And one day you might even look back on it and wish you could revisit it. When you're back in relative obscurity and you'd give your right arm for a bigger profile or some way of drawing attention to an issue - and you

	will want to, at some point, won't you? There will be an issue and you will want to do something about it?
Dick:	Aye.
Tuppence:	So this is your apprenticeship. You're learning the ropes and taking the hard knocks. But it could serve you in good stead in the future. And it won't be long before you're tomorrow's chip-wrapper - a few more days is all! - and no-one will care. Apart from those who will have benefitted enormously from what you've achieved. So, hard as it might be, try and enjoy it! It won't last long and you'll miss some of it when it's gone. Fame isn't all good, but it certainly isn't all bad.
Dick:	I suppose. (pause). At any rate, I do feel better so thank you for that.
Tuppence:	You're welcome :-)
Dick:	Have you ever thought about a role in the Church?
Tuppence:	Give over! I'm just doing for you what you have been doing for me. Least I could do.
Dick:	Well, thank-you anyway. You're right. Two more days and I'll be back home and hopefully counting the money. And nursing my groin.
Tuppence:	That's the spirit. Good night, sleep tight.
Dick:	Good night. I don't suppose you'd be interested in nurs-

But she'd gone.

SEVENTEEN

At breakfast, Cullen just had coffee while Guy sat opposite him, making short work of a full English breakfast that Paul had raided his second aid kit for.

"Go easy." Cullen said, not looking up.

"Are you telling me to watch my weight?" Guy hissed.

"No. Just that we've got a big day ahead of us. Might need to be... light on our toes."

"Light on our-?" Guy bristled and dipped his head down attempting to catch Cullen's eyes. "In fucking high heels?"

"You look a lot better in that gear than you did last night? Is it me?"

"No." Guy grinned sheepishly. "I made a few... alterations."

"What?" Paul shot up from the table.

"It's ok!" Guy panicked. "Just tacking stitches kind of thing. I'm a dab hand with a needle and thread."

Paul sat down slowly, only partially mollified. "Might come in handy once Shirley's finished with me."

"Ok." Guy asked, breakfast finished. "So now what?"

"Now? You go back to the room and... change." Cullen winced. "I'll go and find some makeup."

Paul exhaled slowly and loudly. "Then what?"

"Then? Tickets."

Cullen came back half an hour later with a carrier bag bulging with tubes, jars, packets and boxes. He offered it to Guy along with a large pair of dark glasses, "Just in case", and left him to it.

Dougie sat in coach D on the 11:45 to Edinburgh, gazing idly out of the window. He had his laptop open and was checking tickets on the IT system to see if anyone needed any assistance. An egg and cress sandwich sat half-eaten in its plastic wrap on the table in front of him. A partially dismantled rifle and ammunition were in his luggage on the seat beside him.

At the other end of the carriage were a group of football fans who looked and sounded as if they might be on the way to the same match he was. He kept an eye on them and thought of blending in for a moment, then decided against it. Surreption was the key - he didn't want to attract attention, good or bad. He was wearing his newly acquired Hibs top under his camo jacket, wondering now whether buying the shirt had been such a good idea. He zipped his camo jacket up high, hoping his scruffy jeans and trainers cut him an anonymous figure.

From Waverley, he walked down Leith Walk, cut across Brunswick Road and down to the junction with Albion Road. The roads on this side of the stadium held rows of polluted sandstone terraces, four or five storeys high. Narrow and winding, they funnelled the wind effectively so that it formed eddies and mini-tornadoes on street corners, litter and dust whipped into little whirling dervishes.

Here and there were pedestrian barriers along the pavement, and rows of parked cars interspersed with large, commercial wheelie-bins of different colours. Finding a place to cross was tricky - pedestrians needed to make a choice, pavement or road, and stick to it until you were well away from the stadium itself.

Past the ticket office, merchandise store and main entrance the road widened and led away out towards another main artery to the west of the stadium. Here, pedestrian barriers were ranged across the road, closing it off with tabarded stewards diverting traffic down through a small industrial estate to a lower junction with Easter Road.

Still several hours before kick-off, fans were thin on the ground, although he had passed at least one pub with hardened green-and-white clad smokers huddled outside, football tops and the odd meagre scarf their only protection from the bitter February wind, clenching their pints as if their very lives depended on them.

He finished reconnoitring and turned back towards Albion Place. When he reached number 11 he methodically pressed the buzzer to each flat in the tenement, starting at the top, allowing twenty seconds until he proceeded to the next one down. The third buzzer opened the door, no questions asked. Dougie climbed the dingy elliptical stairwell, navigating bikes locked to the bannisters on each landing until he reached the top floor. With an enormous skylight directly above him illuminating this whole landing, he knelt down and proceeded to put his hurriedly-practice locksmith skills to work.

It took him twenty sweat-stained minutes. Each one stringing him taut as he waited for one of the other doors on the landing to open. When the lock finally snicked open he mouthed a silent prayer and fled inside, closing the door by leaning back against it. Dougie remained there for several minutes, breathing heavily and trying to regain his composure.

The living room it led onto was scruffy with a torn,

faded carpet and grey net curtains adorning the windows. He pulled back the nets and looked once again gratefully out at the East stand. Then he sank cross-legged to the floor and coolly assembled his rifle and sight from his holdall. Happy, he then started the process of training his telescopic sight on the seats T164-166 and consulting his pocketbook for adjustments. He turned on his newly acquired laser sight and watched the pale dot move as he adjusted the trimming on the rifle to align the dot with the crosshairs. This was going to be walk in the park - from here he could almost make out the individual seat numbers. He was leaving no room for error like last time, no need for last minute re-adjustments. He checked his watch, texted a reminder to Jack about the locker key, and resumed his cross-legged pose, closing his eyes and focussing on slowing his pulse.

"That fucking cat." Jack considered, as the team coach pulled out of the car park. "Fucking. Fucking. Animal." How much had it cost him?

He'd pleaded with the physio as he'd been manipulated on the treatment table, protesting into the vinyl as he was massaged and pummelled, trying desperately to hide the considerable pain caused by his wounds now that all the drugs had worn off. Christ, he couldn't even walk without wincing but he had to get a game. He tried appealing to the man's better nature and, when that didn't work, had even tried to bribe him. That had been a bad idea. The man had fingers like vices, arms like a Lithuanian tractor-puller and a cherry-red complexion partially hidden by a reddish neckbeard, but he was as incorruptible as fuck. *I just express my professional opinion, provide medical information. It is up to the coach to make the decision. Nothing to do with me. Fuck off with your money.*

So Jack had pleaded with the manager, arguing down from starting the game to coming on at half time, to getting a run-around for the last fifteen if things were looking a bit iffy, to being on the bench at all. As far as his manager was concerned, Jack was a pain-in-the-arse primadonna whose behaviour was becoming more and more erratic and difficult to tolerate, but who had the ability to turn a game with a moment of magic, even when he wasn't 100% fit. He said he would think about it, and Jack had had to settle for that.

And now, to cap it all, his fucking hitman was bandying around orders to *him* as if he owned the place. He looked at the texted instruction he'd received from him: Fasten key to underside of seat T164, East Stand, before the game.

He'd texted back straight away: How the fuck am I supposed to do that?

The swift response had been: No idea. Work it out.

He'd sat there fuming, initially trying to come up with six different ways he might achieve it so that he could let the dice decide. When he realised that he wouldn't be able to come up with that many he decided to let the coin decide. When he realised he couldn't even come up with one, he abandoned the idea and had to do something which he hadn't done for an awfully long time.

Think for himself.

That hadn't worked and here he was, on the way to the match, with still no idea how he was supposed to get the key under the seat. He moved down towards the back of the coach and joined the card game, budging up gingerly on the rear seats to give himself some real estate at the table for his chips and seatroom to keep his legs apart. He played absent-mindedly and randomly, betting loose on nothing and folding blind, as the mood took him. A few of the other players around the table soon went from wariness at his original arrival to relaxed anticipation of taking him to the cleaners but Jack just kept buying in when he ran out of chips and ignoring the growing audience for the game.

At some point, the chatter around the table, gave him an idea about the key. In a flood of relief, he went all in and promptly lost the lot. He didn't care. All he had to do was find a ballboy or some other lowlife who worked at the ground, bung them £50 and ask them to put the key under the right seat. Easy.

"Right, lads." He proposed to the table in general. "How about we quadruple the blinds?"

Dougie lifted himself up to window height and poked his nose through the net curtains. The weak sun came streaming in through the dirty glass while below, the streets around the ground were starting to hum. A few hawkers and vendors had set up stalls selling scarves and hot dogs, awaiting the arrival of the crowds. Some locals in Hibs tops straggled down the street, many abreast, pushing irritatedly at the crash barriers as though they were an unusual novelty deployed solely to restrict their freedom of movement. A few rebels, unwilling to be contained on the pavement by the parked cars and bins, wheeled into the road, stepping casually on and off the kerb as traffic honked by. A queue had formed at the ticket office directly opposite him and Dougie watched as it shuffled slowly and silently into the brown sandstone building.

Further down the road, out of Dougie's view, the gates to the ground were being opened, shutters on the turnstiles and shop being lifted, a street sweeper slowly chuntered by, circular brushes caressing the kerbs, small water jets helping move the dirt and rubbish out of sight. A large white, outside-broadcast juggernaut sat on legs in the corner where The Famous Five and Main stands met. Fat cables ribboned across the tarmac and disappeared out of view. One of the windows slid open and a hand threw the dregs from a mug of tea out, splashing onto the ground. A dog sauntered by, cocking its leg now and again, stopping to sniff and then lap at the slick of discarded tea. Bouncing off the echoing walls of the tenement canyons could be heard the faint intermingles cries of "Hi-bees" and "Jam-bo's"

Edinburgh was almost ready for a fifth round derby in the Scottish Cup.

Dick knew he was becoming something of a liability on this charity ride and, whilst he realised what the cause of it was - Tuppence - he was powerless to do anything about it. During the day he would daydream incessantly, recalling their conversations, their online chats, the sight and smell of her in his dim and dusty church, the way she moved and the way she'd confided in him. Her tears and words had moved him and now his imagination was calling up all manner of NSFW images which no amount of pedalling was preventing.

In the evening, after eating, discussing tomorrow's

route and stopping points with the rest of the group, ensuring all arrangements were in hand and that any media interviews and fund-raising opportunities had been seen to, he would attempt to update his increasingly tired-looking blog, and then - and only then - when he was happy that he had sacrificed himself on the altar of generosity to everyone around him, would he dare search for her online presence. His heart palpitating, his hands moist, his brain awash with eye-widening chemicals he would find her and chat to her. The hour or so she had would fly by and the minute she hung up, the chemicals fled and exhaustion claimed him.

At night, then, sleep overtook him earlier and earlier as the ride progressed and his nervous exhaustion burnt him out. He would fall into her welcoming arms and get just about the best night's sleep he'd had since the previous night. The only niggle seemed to be that these night-times passed in a moment - one minute his head was hitting the pillow, the next his alarm was jerking him awake and his dream's reveries evaporated by the time he was in a sitting position, even if his erection didn't.

The discomfort of days in the saddle was not helped by this tendency of his loins to spontaneously spring into rigidity, causing him to try cycling and covering his groin at the same time. A hunchbacked look that surely gave the game away but which his fellow riders were perhaps all too diplomatic to mention to him.

And so the days passed and the donation totals kept rising and Dick found himself in the middle of something capturing the country's imagination. Social media was loving it and #savethekirks and #Dickwantsyourdosh were regularly topping out the Twittersphere. His weight may have been dropping spectacularly away - and his fitness correspondingly accelerating - but he couldn't help feeling that he was gaining two years' worth of worry lines with every pound he lost. And all the time the money was rolling in. As Tuppence had reassured him, if he made a thousand pounds sterling for every pound avoirdupois he lost, he could consider himself fortunate with the bargain he had struck. She had even gone searching through the bible for a relevant quote:

Whoever is generous to the poor lends to the Lord, and he will repay him for his deed. Proverbs 19:17.

It was gestures of hers like this that made Dick realise he loved her all the more and his anguished days of pedalling and nights of dreaming now revolved around this one immovable question: *how to tell her?*

The tickets under the name of Renshaw were there as promised and Cullen pocketed them and strode back out into the light to see Guy ill at ease, practising his lady stance. Weight on one leg, the other kinked inward at the knee so as to not to place any strain on the hem of the dress. His coat open and moving slightly in the gentle breeze. Paul was standing off to one side, within reach of Guy if need be, but far enough away to appear to be uncomfortable in his company. From a distance, Cullen thought Guy would more than pass muster as a woman. Up close he had his doubts - Guy's makeup looked as if it had been applied with a shotgun. In the dark.

The three of them made their way to their allotted seats uneventfully, the ground only slowly filling up with over an hour still to go before kick-off. Cullen left Paul to sit with Guy while he went to scout the layout and check exit routes. Guy sat, head down, pretending to read the programme and wondering how many people who'd seen him this morning were talking about him, even now.

Dougie had been fiddling with his rifle and sights again, and made himself comfortable sitting cross-legged next to it, binoculars in his lap. He had a perfectly clear view of the East stand where the seats were and whenever he detected some movement or spot of colour moving into the view he raised the binoculars to his face and scrutinised the scene.

He didn't need to do anything right now. His plan was to wait until the game was in full swing, plenty of action and excitement to detract attention from what he hoped would be a single shot to the chest. In his mind's eye, Tuppence would slump unnoticed in her seat while everyone focussed on some goalmouth action, leaving some minutes perhaps before anyone suspected something was wrong. He hoped he wouldn't need a time delay to make his escape, given that he was barely yards from the ground, but he wanted no mistakes, no fuss, no attention. A simple, clean kill leaving no trace, executed by a professional.

There was a woman in a green coat sitting in the middle of the three target seats with a swarthy, olive-skinned hulk of a man next to her. After a few minutes a tall man in a leather cowboy hat appeared, shuffled along the row which was slowly filling up, and sat next to Tuppence. Neither of these two men resembled either the Chinaman or the Blonde. Perhaps they were just some hired muscle? Dougie considered the kidnappers' approach, pondering their professionalism. First they had bumped up the ransom demand at the first sign of delay from Jack; now they were avoiding personal risk by not attending at a handover when they needn't. He could definitely learn something from them, he thought.

He kept the binoculars to his face, scanned the parts of the ground he could see, and then returned to the trio in the designated seats. The Cowboy was scanning the crowd, oblivious. Tuppence was reading her programme. The Hulk was looking at his phone.

Dougie checked his watch and waited for the game to start.

Satisfied that he had his bearings and a decent assessment of the ground's layout, Cullen tried to relax slightly and idly watched the going's-on around him. The problem was, as the crowd had filled up, so the noise level had steadily risen. The Tannoy system spat random messages every now and again and there was a real sense of excitement and expectation, palpable within the ground. Worse though, was that a large section of the stands, sitting all around them had started bursting into orchestrated chants or sequences of claps. These interjections seemed to originate from nowhere, punch through the growing hubbub and echo around the stadium, before ending as suddenly as they started. Cullen tried to detect a pattern to them but couldn't.

Alcohol was everywhere and the stink of body odour and deep-fried food assaulted his senses. Becoming agitated, he tried to focus on the random activities taking place on the pitch below. Players in different tops where running and stretching on the turf, some kicking footballs to each other, others simply skipping and sprinting along one of the many white lines painted on the grass. Three figures in yellow and black, one holding a ball, were conferring in the centre circle.

Guy, sitting between his minders, was mildly amused watching Cullen and after a silent few minutes leant into him to attract his attention in the ever-growing din.

"First time? At a football match?"

"Hmm?" Cullen was distracted. "Yes. Not sure I-"

"Ok, that's called the dugout - those seats under the glass cover." Guy pointed at the foot of the stands. "That's where the managers and subs sit during the game. All the players will take up their positions once the captains have tossed a coin to see who gets which end. That's what they're doing now, see? Now, those supporters behind the goal over there?" He pointed to the stands to their left. "That's the away team fans. The rest of the ground, including where we are now, these are all Hibs supporters."

A sharp whistle pierced the din, one of the players in the centre circle kicked the ball and the noise in the stadium suddenly intensified. On cue, a huge roar erupted around them and, from nowhere, a big bass drum started pounding rhythmically and a brass instrument wailed across the top of the raised voices. A staccato chant, rich in consonants but otherwise unintelligible, echoed around the stand where they sat and a large green banner was unfurled a few rows below them and to their right, held aloft by five or more men who stood up from their seats. It obscured much of Cullen's view of the pitch.

He looked at Guy like a dog who hadn't noticed he'd been thrown a ball to chase.

"You know what?" said Guy. "I think we're sitting in the singing section."

Jack sat on the subs' bench nervously playing with a small crumpled piece of paper in his hands. It was a message from the ball-boy confirming the job was done. He looked up at that section of the stand opposite but couldn't make out any faces or figures he recognised or that stood out in any way. He wasn't sure where the seat was and no-one up there looked like Tuppence from where he sat.

But she'd be done for soon enough.

Assuming his twat of a hitman didn't fuck it up again. Couldn't rule that out, given his track record. Whichever way this went, when it was all over he was going to have some harsh words for DJ when they next met.

He had signed a few autographs walking from the tunnel to the dugout, waved at the sections of the home support and tried to turn a blind ear to the frequent chants from the Hearts fans of *Tuppence takes it up the arse* - a favourite taunt from opposition fans at pretty much every game he attended, which he continued to resent. Because, apart from anything else, she didn't. Now he sat awkwardly, periodically adjusting his seat to avoid the discomfort from his groin and cocking an ear to a dissonant chant he hadn't heard before. The echoes around the ground made it difficult to make out but it sounded for all the world like they were singing:

Que sera, sera
What ever will Jack soon see?
D-I-V-O-R-C-E

Que sera, sera.

At his window perch, Dougie couldn't believe his eyes. The game had started and the whole section of the stand he was training his rifle on had erupted out of their seats to urge their team on. A few had sat back down but the majority remained standing, waving banners to taunt the Hearts fans, punching the air in anger or holding their heads in despair. A large proportion of the fans were holding their hands above their heads, chanting and clapping their hands in unison. And there was a big fat bastard on the steps right next to the kidnappers' seats, banging merry hell out of a huge bass drum, swinging it this way and that.

Somewhere in the melee was his target and he couldn't see a fucking thing.

Cullen sat resolutely in his seat, arms crossed, while all around him stood. Including Guy.

"Come on! Don't be a stick-in-the-mud."

"You do know why we're here, don't you?" Cullen intoned.

"C'mon man!" Paul said, also standing. "Lighten up, can't you? Until we get further instructions we might as well enjoy the game. We've got free tickets to a Scottish Cup tie! How about that?"

"You've changed your tune." Cullen regarded the shenanigans going on all around him with visible distaste. "It's odd, don't you think?"

"What is?" asked Paul.

"This. Our... predicament."

"I'm the one in a predicament" protested Guy.

"Dressed like this. I don't see you two in any predicament." He sat back down.

There was a goalmouth scramble at the far end and the entire section rose to its feet again, as one, urging on Hibs. Cullen remained seated with the air and grace of an off-duty gravedigger. Guy threw himself up and back down, landing harshly on the hard plastic seat and wincing, rubbing his bottom.

"I don't like it." Cullen kept his eyes moving around the crowd. "It's odd. Sitting at a football match, surrounded by people, waiting for a phone call."

"And TV cameras." Paul prodded.

"Yeah." Cullen looked across the row they were in, then at the rows in front and behind, and then up again at the stands, the rooftops, the floodlights. "And why here?" Why these seats?"

"Dunno. Only ones left, maybe?" Guy shrugged. "You know, sometimes there just isn't a reason. Oh, referee!" He jumped to his feet again, only to twist an ankle in his high heels in the process. As the ref took out a yellow card, there was a low rumble of discontent. Guy looked forlornly down at his feet.

"Oh look." He bent down and picked up a small key off the floor.

He held it up for Cullen to see, just as the referee pocketed the yellow card and took out a red one.

The crowd all around them erupted in foul-mouthed and righteous anger.

EIGHTEEN

On the sixth day, God's Peloton toiled up the A68 towards Edinburgh. Their stated plan was to finish early on this penultimate day, rest up well and then cycle a gentle, ceremonial last leg on Sunday back down to Stobo for the official finish. There had been some complaints to Dick about having to cycle on a Sunday - the Lord himself had rested on the seventh day, was the gist - but Dick had seen no choice. The peloton had all agreed that the route needed to take in each and every rider's home base or church in order to show their appreciation for all the local support. And Dick himself was adamant that, as the organiser of the whole thing, Stobo should be the official finishing line. So, if they had to call at a handful of churches in Edinburgh that meant overshooting Stobo on the way North and then trekking back down South afterwards. Couldn't be helped.

The weather today and yesterday had been kind and Dick had even gone so far as applying some SPF50 - in February! - to keep any risk of sunburn at bay. He was increasingly mindful of his appearance since an ingénue mistake on a nightly news bulletin in Peterborough when he had done an interview to camera with an unsightly damp patch on his cycling shorts.

The peloton was now at its fullest extent. 67 riders, of whom 34 were actual clergy, 25 various priesthood trainees and a few laymen hangers-on mostly allowed for their specialisms in assisting the group: there were mechanics on hand to tune and repair bikes and race to cycle stores to track down spares; masseurs and physios to provide relief to aching muscles at the end of each day and help the cyclists keep tired limbs moving; a team of caterers who had brought their own van and would run up snacks during the day and full meals each evening. They also had some general purpose volunteers to act as runners who would fetch drinks, provide water en route, pass messages to and from riders, coordinate with the local police forces or liaise with the press to set up interviews or provide quotes, as well as updating social media during the rides themselves.

At Doncaster, thanks to one of their number who had a brother-in-law in St John Ambulance, they ended up with the own ambulance and crew following them along and attending to injuries, dizzy spells or simple exhaustion and, in one sad case, actually having to take one of the riders to hospital in Bishop Auckland when he missed a sharp turn following a diversion off a busy road and ended up ploughing head-first into the side of an ice-cream van.

To complete the picture, they also had the service of four motorcycle outriders. Friends of the Reverend Sidney McDermott from Holy Trinity in Melrose, they had been with them since Day Two, and usually rode two up front and two at the rear, each pair keeping a distance of a hundred yards or so clear of the cyclists, acting as advance warning of upcoming holdups and a barrier from finding themselves stuck behind slow-moving vehicles or streets unexpectedly closed off for market day or sudden protests.

The Fire Brigades in each county had also been informed and had a coordinator working with local traffic police on the ground and one of the outriders.

Their "Green Wave" systems allowed them to plot routes through traffic ahead of ambulances and fire engines, triggering traffic lights at junctions to make sure they were always on green as required in an emergency. Dick constantly marvelled at the feeling of celebrity as his peloton were able to sweep without stopping through busy junctions, passing queues of stationary traffic which had been held up on red while the cyclists had priority. He had to keep reminding himself that this was all in the name of charity and not some superpower that had come into his possession. *Proverbs 16:18: Pride goes before destruction, and a haughty spirit before a fall.*

As far as Dougie was concerned, that drummer was going to be first up against the fucking wall come the revolution. Right after Brenda. Here he was, simply trying to kill people cleanly and without fuss and this fucking clown was going absolutely spare, marching up and down the steps, banging his drum. Dougie could hear it thumping from here - God knows how loud it must seem in the seats around him.

And the twats with that big banner. They'd be next as well. Every time that went up, the people several rows behind it had to stand to see what was going on. Up and down, up and down. Like a fucking Mexican wave with St Vitus's Dance, the crowd couldn't - wouldn't - keep still.

Effing and jeffing to himself, he tried to keep a bead on Tuppence in the hubbub. If she wasn't being obscured by those around her jumping to their feet, she was pointing enthusiastically or jiggling in her seat or, standing up herself to get a better view. Or like right now, bending down out of sight behind the man standing in front of her and coming back up for air holding… the fucking key! Oh Christ, she'd found the money key! *Shit.*

Dougie watched as she handed it to the Cowboy beside her. He, in turn, regarded it carefully and then started to look around the ground, then raised his eyes to take in the rooftops and floodlights, then around, looking towards the tenements between the stands, scanning them up and down. Through his scope the world of bobbing, swearing, shouting supporters fell silent and Dougie could swear the man briefly stopped his gaze staring right down the rifle barrel into his own eyes.

He pulled away, blinking, and grabbed for his binoculars on the floor beside him. When his focus settled back on the three seats they were empty.

Buggery bollocks!

He panned across the stand swiftly with his binoculars, searching wildly for the Cowboy, the Hulk or Tuppence. There! Heading down the steps, about to disappear into an exit tunnel. The Cowboy was on his phone while Tuppence seemed to be having trouble keeping up with the Hulk's loping stride, teetering on her heels as went. Was the Cowboy calling the real kidnappers? Had they seen him?

Dougie took a deep breath and decided he had no choice but to act now and beggar the consequences. He scrambled back to get behind his rifle and swiftly zoomed onto the trio as they retreated into the shadows of the tunnel. He squeezed off two quick shots only to see a powder flare from the concrete walls beside them and the three figures vanish from view. Two shots, one puff of dust. Had one of his shots landed? He had no way of knowing now.

Bastard! Bastard! Bastard!

Dougie stared dejectedly through his scope as the crowd, unaware of the drama, were still caught up in the action on the pitch. He breathed in and out deeply for a minute or two, trying to consider his next move, unable to believe his misfortune. After a moment he stood, pausing almost as an afterthought, and casually shot the bloke with the drum in the right knee.

Guy pulled up sharply in the dark of the stairwell, feeling a stabbing pain in his buttocks. Attributing it to the twisted ankle he was struggling with, he removed the stupid heels in disgust. He resumed running after Cullen and Paul in his stockinged feet, the two figures rapidly receding in front of him, but drew up suddenly again with the same stabbing pain. He reached around to feel his backside and his hand came away red.

"Cullen!"

Cullen's head appeared from around the corner of the stairwell. He was still on his phone. "Come on!"

"I've been shot!"

"Well, come on faster then."

Guy turned the corner, narrowly avoiding stepping on the scattered remains of what looked like a mobile phone which had been stamped to death. The other two were waiting for him by a double-wide fire exit, doors thrown open.

"Let's see?" Guy turned and poked his derriere at Cullen, who contemplated it for a whole second before declaring it a "flesh wound."

"Maybe, but it's my fucking flesh!"

"Come on, hurry up." Cullen led the way out into daylight and the broad pathway which led away from the back of the stand down to the road. Guy threw his heels in a nearby bin and found his best means of locomotion without hurting too much was to almost skip along, favouring one leg over the other. He caught up with Cullen and leant on him, bending over to catch his breath. Ahead of them, manning the pedestrian barriers, two stewards in hi-vis tabards were gesturing frantically to their colleagues, walkie-talkies squawking in their hands.

"Why are we running away?" Paul panted.

"He's been shot."

"Yeah. But we were running away before he was shot."

"Yes, well now we have to get out of here pronto."

"But what about the money?" Guy was trying to whine while struggling for breath. It didn't work.

Paul was looking around at the increased activity amongst the stewards. Behind them the stadium had grown suddenly quiet. "What's going on?"

Cullen replied without turning to look at him, keenly scanning the area. "Bomb scare."

"What?" Guy wasn't sure he'd heard correctly. Paul was.

"They'll be evacuating the ground any minute."

"What?" Guy tried to shake his head clear.

Stewards started appearing from everywhere, throwing open entrances, gates and fire exits.

"Come on."

"But what about the money?" Guy repeated.

"We've got the money."

"We have?"

"Well, we have the key to the money."

"Ah." Said Guy, catching on at last. "Right. Ok."

Slowly, masses of people started to appear from the various exits. Some fans in festive mood, thinking this was all some kind of lark, others severely disgruntled at the loss of an afternoon's entertainment, hectoring or arguing with the stewards even as they were being directed out of the main gates. Police started to appear from the main road, adding weight and officialdom to the stream of bodies pouring from the stadium.

"Straight down to the very end of the street, please." One policeman with a megaphone was gesticulating with his left hand, conducting the crowd. "No rush. Orderly please. Please keep inside the barriers."

Cullen, Paul and Guy joined the mass of people, losing themselves in the torrent as it swept down the winding road away from the stadium. Hemmed in they shuffled along, in a crowd of eight or ten deep, into the shadows cast by the tenements next to the ground. Cullen looked up at one of them, as if seeking a sign.

Dougie packed away all his gear, wiped the place down for prints, and eased himself out of the flat and down the echoing stairwell. When he emerged onto the street some kind of mass exodus was clearly underway. A flood of fans were being herded past his building and away from the stadium. A handful of police officers were clustered near the ticket office coordinating events. Automatically flinching whenever he saw a uniform, he kept his holdall close to his body angled away from any officer, unzipped his jacket to display the fullest extent of his Hibs top he could manage, and attempted to walk against the tide towards the ground.

Within a few strides, the impossibility of this goal became apparent. The police had already closed off some roads and the obstacles arranged along each kerb effectively funnelled the crowd spilling from the stadium so that it bore all before it. Dougie was one small man, standing against a tide of humanity and a small battalion of officials who could see immediately if anyone was attempting to deviate from the desired flow.

"You there! Go the other way!" A sweaty policeman, his cap exasperatedly askew, was pointing at him above the heads of the crowd and jabbing his fingers in the desired direction of travel. "The *other* way!"

Detected, Dougie attempted to simultaneously turn around and vault between two large blue bins at the kerb. The difficulty of moving himself in two contradictory directions at the same time, along with the weight of his bag, made him miss his mark and he hit himself squarely in the knee with his bag, smacked his face into the side of one of the bins and fell gracelessly onto the cold tarmac. Technical difficulty: 5.9; Artistic impression: minus two million.

Kneeling, sore, as the crowd passed by in the road he was now at least out of visibility as far as the police were concerned. And he did indeed now have the pavement pretty much to himself, so would be free to move in any direction as long as he kept to a crouch. But now his knee hurt and his cheekbone was raw. He rubbed it and stared dumbly at the legs and feet of the crowd as they marched in procession past him, an endless sea of trainers, boots and … a pair of bare feet?

He watched as the bare feet, wearing nylons, padded -

no, limped - along, partially carried by the tide of people, stuttering as they encountered stones or came too close to the feet of others. By their side strode a confident pair of walking boots beneath scruffy combat pants and a shiny pair of Doc Martens. He'd found them!

Dougie turned around and scooted along the side of the parked cars, staying low, keeping Tuppence's feet in sight. The crowd's pace slowed and people started to bunch, voices starting to rise. Above the growing clamour he heard an unintelligible megaphone, presumably requesting patience, and saw two mounted policemen appear from the right, both carrying long batons.

Dougie skittered along, still safely on the pedestrian-free pavement. As he reached the end of the horde of fans he could see that there was some sort of hold-up at this T-junction. There were barriers across the road, penning the crowd from the stadium in place. He watched as the kidnapper's feet wangled their way slowly through the stationery crowd, working their way to the front where this blockage was. Two separate groups of officers were arguing amongst themselves and talking into walkie-talkies, waving this way and that.

It dawned on Dougie after a short while that the traffic lights here were all stuck on red. Traffic in both directions was building and the mass of people pouring from the ground towards this junction was steadily piling up pressure. Frustrated fans started vaulting the barriers to try and find their own exits, while the megaphone continued to blare vacantly and scuffles broke out amongst the harassed policemen on the barriers, trying to keep the crowd in their place.

Dougie had a clear view of proceedings here and he

watched as the two men and Tuppence finally made their way to the head of the crowd. Belatedly realising that none of the policeman at this junction would know who he was, Dougie rose from his crouching position and stood up, for all the world just another passer-by wondering what the hell was disturbing a normal Saturday.

He snatched a glance again across at Tuppence and, just at that moment, the Cowboy caught his eye and held it for a few seconds. Dougie felt some bizarre electricity pass between them and he momentarily froze in place. In that split-second, the Cowboy shouted something to the Hulk, then leapt the barrier and pulled Tuppence over after him. Taken by surprise, Tuppence's hair fell off and lay on the ground like a wounded animal. The policeman nearest them lunged after her/him and missed. The pair, hand-in-hand, raced across the empty traffic lanes to a road island, the cowboy hat whirling left and right as he tried to identify the best escape route. The Hulk turned and stared directly at Dougie

In that split second, Dougie made a decision.

PC Alex Whitstable was on the fifteenth hour of a double-shift and none too happy about it. Traffic duty was predictably mundane and non-taxing in the brain department, but then he hadn't joined the police force in search of mental stimulation and it was a Saturday afternoon, for chrissake. Come six pm he'd be away and have all of Sunday and Monday off to recover from what he hoped would be the mother of all hangovers from tonight. Might even pull, if he was lucky.

He realised he was daydreaming when he was roused

by a shout from his Sarge. Looking towards the sound he saw him point towards two figures leaping the barrier on the far-side of the junction and quickly covering the gap to the traffic island. Alex was on point on the north side of the junction, awaiting further instruction. This, he reckoned, was further instruction.

He roused himself only to experience a bizarre sensation of time suddenly slowing to a crawl, one he'd last experienced when he was twelve and knocked off his bike while doing a paper round. And here it was again. Slo-mo. And in this slo-mo, everything was clear. Each little detail shone, standing proud from its blurred background like a film which poorly converted to 3D.

Here were two figures standing alone: one holding the others arm, turning his head this way and that in the scene; the other looking like a bloke in a dress and a bright green coat.

Here was a third figure, vaulting a barrier over to Alex's left, away from the flailing grasp of a large bearded man. Sprinting in slo-mo towards them, one arm raised holding what could only be a weapon of some kind, in the other a holdall.

Behind it all, over it all, a backwash of shouting in deep drawn-out syllables, like a worn-down tape coming to the end of a reel. A megaphone intoning something and nothing in booming echoes containing no consonants at all.

He felt himself start to step off the kerb, his right foot searching for the tarmac. And then a flash and time wound back up to normal speed.

A brush on his shoulder and a sheet of bright orange and blue, green and red. A whirr of colour as one speeding cyclist buffeted him into the path of the oncoming pack. The stream of spinning wheels and hustling shoulders parted around him, skidding as they did so. Some riders mounting the kerb and parting company with their bikes, others manoeuvring skilfully around him like a chicane and pouring like a vivid tide onward.

Urgent and relentless, the shiny metal wave, ridden by lycra-clad surfers, swept imperiously past in a swarm of gears and helmets. The leaders, perhaps congratulating themselves on avoiding a terrible crash with a stupidly wayward copper, ploughed straight into the man with the holdall who was caught midway across the road. Like a storm surge, the shimmering tide broke upon him. Cyclists and their bikes flew this way and that, some skidding horizontally across the road and into the barriers, police officers scattering to avoid being caught in the tsunami as it hit. The road, awash with wheels and bodies; loose water bottles bobbing about like so flotsam and jetsam coming to rest, plastic driftwood on a tarmac beach.

As the peloton had dug in for the final sweep towards the city centre, the group had been unexpectedly forced off their intended route by a patrol car waving them right and they found themselves having to follow their motorcycle outrider as he sent them along busy shopping streets and side streets trying to get them back on their route. One of the outriders pulled alongside to explain that there had been some large-scale evacuation and certain roads were being sealed off. When the outrider dropped back, Dick started to slowly climb back up the order and get closer to the front. He saw a sprinkling of barriers along the roadside grow to a thicket, and the shouts and noises from a large crowd begin to overwhelm the background sounds of traffic. Distracted, he had brushed the jacket of a uniformed policeman who had just tried to step off the kerb next to him.

Dick's front wheel wobbled and he worked hard to right it, casting his glance down onto his handlebars and the tarmac to make sure he had not lost control of his bike. When he looked up again, he found himself careering straight for a figure who had suddenly appeared in front of him crossing his path from left to right. Wearing a hooded top and carrying a holdall, his right hand was extended into a shooting position with a pistol in his grip. As Dick was almost upon him, the man turned and their eyes met. At that moment of collision, as he mowed down his victim and the following pack buried them both in a pile of spinning metal, lycra and flesh, Dick recognised the man with the gun.

With the scrum of bodies and cycles, sirens and uniforms, crowd control and traffic honking, the T-junction had looked like a warzone. The police had eventually relented and opened up a pathway between barriers on opposite sides of the road so that people could cross and slowly start to filter away from the confusion and overcrowding. And it had been assumed that as each cyclist and bicycle was removed from the pile, like some giant game of ker-plunk, stranded at the bottom of the heap they would find the armed perpetrator, squished and blackened, helpless and immediately under arrest. Alas, this had not been the case and the bodies were removed one by one to reveal nothing more than slightly oil- and blood-stained tarmac and a realisation that no-one was aware of any shots having been fired, or what had happened to the man and woman the gunman had been thought to be aiming at.

Now, Dougie stood sheltering in the doorway recess of an abandoned shop on Albion Road. Away from the clamour and chaos, he leant against the graffiti'd door and nursed his battered pride. He had cuts and grazes from the collision and assumed he'd be plenty bruised tomorrow, but right now he was able to limp and that was what he had done to extricate himself from the melee. His ribs hurt and his right hand had been stamped on several times but he could flex his fingers. Just. Although it didn't matter now since he no longer had his rifle or holdall.

He closed his eyes to calm himself and think of his next steps. When he poked his nose out to look right he saw a tide of Hearts fans barrelling down the road, filling its width, chanting and gesticulating as a handful of policemen tried to corral them into Albion Terrace and a narrow footbridge which led away from the streets around the stadium. He looked down, saw that his exposed Hibs top would identify him as an enemy and struggled with his injured hands to pull the zip up on his jacket.

That was when he felt himself sledgehammered in the face.

The door behind him gave way and he fell backwards, clutching his bleeding nose. A cloud of dust and debris rose from the floor as he landed heavily on his back in a dim and damp-smelling room. Standing over him was a giant, silhouetted in the daylight coming through the broken doorway.

Dougie looked into the Hulk's face as he felt himself hoisted up by his elbows and plonked ceremoniously into a sitting position on some kind of counter. His attacker whipped Dougie's jacket up around his shoulders and secured it somehow like a straitjacket over his head. Before he knew it, his entire top half was immobile and he was gulping lungfuls of his own B.O. in through the close weave of his camo jacket. He could make out a moving shadow and shape in front of him but nothing concrete. Neither he nor the Hulk had yet made a sound.

"Right, Cinders. You shall go to the ball. But only if you reveal to me which lock the key fits."

"Wha-?"

Dougie felt the breath forced out of him as a punch collapsed his midriff. He almost retched, then sucked in air gratefully as the pain from his stomach hit him.

"Key." The voice instructed.

Dougie tried to steady his breathing. He focussed on the background buzz and hum of vehicle exhausts, motorbikes passing by, car horns, footsteps. He waited to see if another punch would land or another word would be spoken but he stayed slumped in silence on the counter top, listening to what sounded like soft metallic clicking.

"Key, sunshine. Now." A hand grabbed him by the throat and started to squeeze. "Haven't got all day."

Dougie felt himself starting to pass out. His body went all limp and the hand loosened round his neck.

"Fuck's sake." The voice said and then Dougie felt a searing pain splinter up into his left armpit and out to his shoulder blade. The pain came again, worse this time, as whatever weapon was being used was twisted and pushed further into the wound. He felt a hot trickle down his left side and cried out in pain.

"Shhh now." Said the voice. "No need for that."

Dougie started to sob, strangely aware only of the pain in his armpit and his legs dangling uselessly off the counter.

"You have a large pair of pinking shears inserted into your left armpit." The voice said. "If you don't tell me where the key fits, I will insert another pair into your right armpit."

"I don't know." Dougie managed tearfully. "Don't know what you're talking about."

"I think you do."

Dougie shook his head. "I think you've got the wrong man."

"Yeah?"

"Yeah." Dougie grasped for an alibi. "My name is... Omar."

"Omar, huh?" Dougie felt the man's face come in close to his own, the man's breath filtering through his jacket. "My name's Renshaw. Three tickets for Renshaw."

When the piercing pain came again in his right armpit, Dougie passed out.

NINETEEN

Conrad sat at the back of the pop-up show tent and surveyed the audience with a massive grin on his face. First showing of the day and his hired Chinese schoolgirls had harried and cajoled a good crowd in, plying them with champagne and helping show the unschooled how to download and use the CtG app.

There was genuine interest in the room he could tell, and he watched carefully as the garments came up on the screen, looking for those which attracted the most swipe-rights. On his iPad he had an administration app and he watched as orders were collected and categorised. There were several ooh's and aah's as some of the more Liv-heavy designs emerged and, looking at his tablet, he could see (because of the way he had categorised them) that items based on her designs were selling much better than his own.

Never mind. A victory was a victory, and still as sweet.

By the start of the second showing, word of mouth - for ever the ultimate marketing tool at LFW - had done its job and the tent was bursting with people. By the end, his phone had journos and bloggers queueing up to interview or get quotes from him. By the end of the day, the place was humming with the news that Couture-To-Go was *the* new thing and that a certain Conrad Ho was a new star in the fashion firmament.

Media duties done, Conrad sat quietly at a small metal table in the far corner of the champagne bar watching the staff clear away and wipe down ready for tomorrow's fresh assault. Alone with his thoughts as the huge open floor gradually emptied of people, the noise levels attenuating, he consulted his order screen and contemplated an excellent day's results. Could he rely on Yeo to fulfil all these orders? What was the risk that he'd want more money up-front, with a glorious victory now within reach? Conrad picked up his phone pondering whether to call Yeo, check how the order pipeline was looking from his end. He spotted more missed calls from Guy and tapped the phone thoughtfully with his finger.

Now that he was in a good position, perhaps he could give Guy his money back? He had, to all intensive purposes, left his friend in the lurch. But, sitting where he was now, he was no longer sure he could take their friendship for granite.

Let's not be so hasty, thought Conrad.

"Well?"

Cullen barely looked up from tending to Guy's wounded backside when Paul entered.

"Fuck, Cullen. You spend more time in my place than I do."

Cullen ignored him. "I assume you got him."

Paul loped over to the coolbox and reached for a beer.

"He'd got away from the bike race thing. Crash. Whatever. Found him sheltering in a doorway, hiding from Hearts fans." Paul fell into his armchair and swung his legs over one of the arms, swigging from his can.

"And did he offer up the information we need?"

"Well, he was reluctant, so to speak. Ergo, I

incentivised him. Slightly."

"Ergo." Pondered Cullen. "Huh. And?"

"Not sure."

"What do you mean, not sure?"

"All he said was Ormiston."

"Ormiston?"

"Yep. Training ground at Ormiston."

"Which training ground?"

"I guess whichever training ground is in Ormiston. Google is your friend."

Cullen gave Paul a look. "My mistake." Paul grunted. "Google is my friend."

"Where's Ormiston?" asked Guy, gingerly moving his leg to see how it felt now the wound was dressed.

"Dunno." Cullen shrugged.

"Near Tranent." Paul offered, fiddling with his phone. "Hibs training ground, Ormiston, East Lothian."

"Ah." Cullen smiled. "Jack's locker. Makes sense."

"So…" Guy screwed up his face. "How do we get the money from Ormiston then?"

"Don't have to." Cullen said, standing. "I know just the woman who can do that." He turned to Paul. "Can you send her a text?"

"Just did." Paul grinned and moved back across again to his beer store.

"Tuppence!" Guy nodded, impressed. "But isn't she still in danger?"

"From?"

"This bloke with the gun."

"I'd like to see him shoot anyone with two wounded armpits." Paul broke off from chugging his second beer. "He's not going to be raising his arms or putting a rifle butt to his shoulder any time soon."

"Armpits?" Cullen was intrigued.

"Yeah." Paul grinned again. "This abandoned shop thing. Where I found him? Looked like some kind of tailoring adjustment place, dry cleaning, all that. Loads of boxes lying around. Buttons, zips, hangers. Pinking shears."

"Imaginative." Cullen nodded appreciatively.

"Right, then." Chirped Guy, rubbing his hands together. "So, we're done! It's over."

Cullen stared at him. "No so fast. Still have a little outstanding business with your friend Conrad."

"My Hero." Tuppence cooed as she gave Dick a peck on the cheek. Dick blushed, wiped away a tear and waved to the crowd who were all cheering and clapping. Both his knees were swathed in gauze and dressings and his cycling jersey had a big rip down it, from his left nipple to his waist, the gash showing a dirt and blood-streaked torso. Bowed and bloody he might be but, as Tuppence kissed him and the crowd applauded, he felt like Alexander - weeping, as he had no more worlds to conquer.

These were his people, here at Stobo, the people he'd started the whole venture for. He realised he might look a state after yesterday's calamitous crash - and there had been plenty of buckled wheels to replace and sutures for the paramedics to stitch - but no-one seemed to mind. This slightly ramshackle homecoming reception was a genuine heartfelt gesture from his parishioners. And Tuppence's surprise attendance had left him on the verge of tears.

Some local BBC news reporter thrust a microphone

under Dick's nose: "Dick, how does it feel to have completed your marathon journey in front of your own flock, having raised so much money?"

Dick had thought long and hard about what he would say when he had finally finished. He had imagined, given the coverage en route, that at some point he would be asked for a quote or some pithy reaction to his week in the saddle. He hadn't envisioned it quite like this, nor having Tuppence at his side, but he forgot, for a moment, his aches and pains and his bruised appearance. With all the sincerity and composure he could muster he looked straight down the camera's lens and said:

"As the Bible says: *I have fought the good fight, I have finished the race, I have kept the faith. Timothy 2, Chapter 4, Verse 7.*"

Next to him, in shot, Tuppence stood beaming at his quote from her old friend Timothy, and tenderly squeezed his hand.

Daniel Tyson-Wright stood at the back of the pop-up marquee with his arms folded, surveying the carnage. He'd been avoiding visiting the CtG presentations since the mauling he'd had at the hands of the board on a specially arranged conference call two days ago. Clinging on to his composure, and his job, while he listened, they had made it clear in no uncertain terms that he would be held personally to blame if this season's revenues missed the targets due to this *unfortunate cancellation*. Their words.

Now, while the catwalk show and location shoot video played on the large screen at the back of the tent, in front of him was a full-on scrum of irate women dotted with microphone booms peering from the top of heads and the odd video camera being hustled shoulder high through the crowd. It looked like the first day of the sales in reverse, garments being flung up and out of the melee, many discarded to be trampled in the rush. The general trend of movement was towards the exit to his left. Four oriental young women dressed as schoolgirls stood demurely to one side, looking on dispassionately.

Daniel checked his phone. His twitter feed was alive and rampant. He had subscribed to #CtG and #ConradHo and scrolled now through sarcastic tweet after tweet, disparaging comments, swearing and a rapidly burgeoning series of memes showing dishevelled tramps holding up white placards, Bob Dylan style, saying #CrapToGo and #ConradNO.

He looked again at the fashion show up on the screen and paid closer attention to the clothes the models were wearing. Tartan predominated, and custom tartans as well to his keen eye, but whilst there was a certain flair to many of the styles on display, nothing was jogging his memory. He had paid close attention to all of the designs, samples and submissions that Liv had produced and it didn't look to him as if any of these garments were copies at all. Maybe he was wrong.

He picked up a CtG leaflet that had been discarded on the floor, covered in dusty footprints and scanned in the QR code, downloading the app. He then left the tent and the Brewers St car park and headed for one of the VIP parking bays where his driver was waiting, slouched against his Mercedes reading a newspaper.

Dick stood awkwardly as Tuppence delicately cut the torn top from him and threw it on the bathroom floor.

He could see his reflection in the mirror and grimaced as she traced her hands gently across his cuts and bruises, gasping as she touched a nerve and then grimacing again as his gasping hurt his ribs. As she bathed his cuts with a warm flannel he became embarrassingly aware of an erection in his lycra shorts.

Either Tuppence hadn't noticed, or she was pretending not to notice. He didn't know which was worse.

This was all a complete surprise and he had been uncomfortable with it from the moment Tuppence had bundled him into a cab which had appeared from nowhere. The driver gave him a knowing grin in the rear view mirror and had moved to pull away when Dick had started from his numbness and realised he was being taken away from his fellow pelotoneers.

"Wait!" he cried and leant over to pull down the window.

Tuppence put her hand on his shoulder and pulled him gently back into the seat. "Don't worry." She said. "I've left instructions. They'll be taken care of."

"What do you mean?" Dick asked, confused. "Where are we going?"

"My treat." Tuppence smiled.

The phone woke Liv who reached to grab it still mostly asleep and unaware what day or time it was.

"Ms Nightingale?"

"Speaking."

"Ms Nightingale, this is Daniel Tyson-Wright. I wonder if I might have a quick word?"

"Is this a call to offer me my job back?" Liv was

suddenly wide awake.

"I'm sorry, but no. I'm afraid things were said which can't be unsaid."

"Then you can fuck off." As she moved to cut him off she heard him still talking and thought she heard the word *theft*. She hesitated and put him back to her ear.

"… at all. Of course I may be mistaken, but that it how it very much looks to me."

"Sorry, could you say that again?"

"Yes, well it was quite a surprise to me as well, I can assure you."

"Sorry, what was?"

"The theft of your designs? I'm afraid it was only in your imagination."

"Look, Daniel. Sorry, I've only just woken up. Bit of a night owl rather than an early bird, you see. Could you start again? I'm not following you."

"What I am saying is that I do not think your designs were stolen. Have you actually seen these CtG designs which you say are copies of your work?"

"Well, no actually." Liv was taken aback by the simplicity of his question.

"Well, I have." Daniel purred. "And I may not be a designer myself but I am pretty sure - *quite* sure - that these designs you say are copies, cannot be copies. I have looked at them and compared them to your pieces. There are similarities, yes. Do they borrow from your designs? Perhaps, but not overly. Do they say Liv Nightingale or Chanel to me? Absolutely not."

Liv sat up in bed, silenced by what she was hearing. Daniel was still talking.

"I suggest you download this CtG app and see for yourself. I imagine you will be able to tell instantly whether they have your hallmark in them or not. And, furthermore, proof - if indeed proof were needed." He continued, burbling now cheerily. "If what I saw yesterday was any indicator, the finished garments are of inferior quality, finish and fabric. I would also add *fit* but I'm not sure anyone got as far as actually trying them on before walking out in disgust."

Liv listened dumbstruck.

"Are you still there, Ms Nightingale?"

"Erm, yes. Yes, I'm still here."

"I'm afraid you and I may have our professional differences, and those will no doubt remain. However, I am happy to say that these so-called copies - if they are indeed copies which, as I say, I doubt very much - do not reflect well on CtG, which I think we will now have heard the last of. And more importantly, in no way impair your personal or my companies reputation or brand."

"Are you saying what I think you're saying?" Liv finally managed.

"Ms Nightingale, I think - for what I suggested would be a quick word - I have said rather a lot. To summarise, I do not think your work has been copied. At all. If you still think it has I suggest you download the offending app and see for yourself."

"Right. Ok. Thank you. I will."

"Good day." Daniel signed off. "And good luck."

Liv switched straight to the app store, downloaded the app and spent the next few minutes swiping intently left.

"I can't move." Dick winced as he lay in bed, aching

all over.

"I know. Good wasn't it?" Tuppence was lying next to him, propped up on one elbow, her face fresh and shining, freckles glittering beneath a glorious bedhead of tousled strawberry blonde curls. She smiled coyly at him, two dimples popping in and out of view, and he thought she was the most beautiful thing he'd ever seen.

"This is awkward." He sighed.

"Is it?" She pouted.

"I'm a man of the cloth and you're a married woman."

"Technically you're correct - on both counts." She bent her head to kiss his chest. "Technically."

Dick looked at her perfect shoulders, the curve of her neck and clavicle, the slope of her back. He was in bed with an angel and being tempted by the devil.

"I might need to pray for forgiveness." He murmured. "After."

"Perhaps we should prepare first. Together." She slid on top of him and started kissing his chest as she worked her way down his torso.

"What for?" Dick asked, not caring anymore as he felt his body respond to hers.

"The second coming." Tuppence whispered.

Dougie woke up in a hospital bed, on a drip, and his first reaction was panic. He looked around wildly for clues as to where he was and whether anyone was watching him or, indeed, guarding him. There was no-one else around and he had this small ward of six beds to himself. No more than a large layby situated off a wide main corridor, he watched for a minute as various members of hospital staff strode purposefully past, blithely ignoring him.

The walls were uniform hospital drab; the smell a mixture of floor-cleaner, rubber and faintly overcooked vegetables; the staff dressed in standard coloured tunics and trousers and crocs. All he could see out of the window was a grey and white sky with the odd flat rooftop. Presumably he was several floors up but, apart from that, he could be anywhere.

There was a clear drip in his left arm and a red one in his right - they'd given him blood. Beneath the standard blue-grey gown he had professionally affixed dressings under each arm and, whilst he only had limited movement in his arms, there was no pain when he moved his shoulders so he assumed they'd dosed him up with some substantial pain relief.

There was nothing near or around his bed in the way of clothing or personal belongings and, as far as he could remember, he had made every effort to make sure he had nothing identifiable on him when he'd set off ... today? Yesterday? He realised he had no idea *when* he was either.

He lay back and looked up at the ceiling, wondering what to do.

"Ah, you're awake, then." He lowered his gaze to see a young nurse bustling towards him wearing a green tunic which seemed quite snug in places, and a welcoming smile. "Mr...?"

"Little." Dougie said out of nowhere. "Omar Little. Where am I?"

"Western General." The nurse said brightly. "Tea?"

Dougie nodded and she clipped a thermometer onto one of his fingers and disappeared back out into the yawning corridor again, reappearing shortly afterwards

357

with a polystyrene cup and sweet brown liquid which he gratefully cupped. He realised he was starving.

"How long have I been here? What happened?" He blew on his tea.

"Two days and don't know. In that order." The nurse breezed, checking his temperature. She briefly examined each drip and scribbled something on the chart clipped to the foot of his bed. She smiled eagerly at him again and leant in to fluff his pillows. "We just get you better. Don't want your bloody life story." She whispered in his ear. "Save that for the old folk."

"What time is it?"

The nurse nodded over to a large wall clock in the corridor. "How's your eyesight?"

"Quarter past two." Dougie sighed.

"Perfect." She lifted the tea out of his grasp and put it down on the bedside table to check his dressings and then handed it back to him. "Unusual that. Your wounds."

"Thought you didn't want my life story?" Dougie grimaced at the hot tea.

"Don't. Just wondering how you ended up with two large stab wounds in your armpits. Fall on some railings did you?"

"Something like that."

"Well, it's none of my business of course. Just - you know - you lost a lot of blood and there's some infection. Antibiotics in there." She nodded towards the clear drip.

"Right." Dougie was hoping to kill the conversation now.

"I mean, they couldn't be self-inflicted so…"

She looked at him, tilting her head like a teacher wondering what had happened to his homework. Dougie

358

calmly returned her gaze. "Let's just say, I'm a fashion victim."

Tuppence had noticed Dick's erection and smirked with her head down as she continued to trace her hands and flannel over his upper torso. He was in good shape, presumably from all the riding and the training he'd been doing, and his injuries seemed superficial to her untrained eyes. She had once seen Jack's knee after a bad tackle and, it had looked a whole lot worse than anything Dick was showing.

She gritted her teeth briefly at the unbidden memory of Jack and then exhaled slowly, calming and continuing to move, both hands now, down his body. She reached his shorts and cupped his buttocks with her palms.

"I think you should probably take these off." She said quietly.

"I… I'm…" She felt his whole body tense as he struggled to speak.

"Shhh. It's ok." She whispered and kissed his ear. "It'll be ok."

And it was.

Dougie had discharged himself after haggling with the nice nurse as to how much codeine and spare dressings he could take away with him. He spun her a white lie about needing - absolutely vitally needing - to get to a funeral the following day. Ok, not a white lie. Still. Needs must.

Sitting on the train back to Glasgow he watched the fields blur by and thought hard about his life. Decisions had to be made and, maybe it was the morphine in his system - the nurse had told him that the reason codeine was such an effective painkiller was that the liver converted it into morphine in the body - but his options seemed much clearer now; his decision easier.

I mean, when you looked at it - in the cold light of day - it was ridiculous, wasn't it? Him, a simple nobody working in IT, thinking he could become some big-time assassin. What had he been thinking? This wasn't The Wire, this was real life. His life. He only needed to look at hmself. He was barely able to board a fucking train without wincing, had lost all his weapons, nearly been caught by the police. Been captured and beaten up, missed his first and only target. Twice. Been seen - and filmed - meeting his client. Fuck! Toenail was right, he was a loser. A tosser. A nobody.

This adventure was over. He picked up his phone, walked down to the connecting section between the carriages and made a call.

"What do you want?" Jack hissed, ignoring any pleasantries. "I told you, we're done."

"No. I'm telling you I'm done." Dougie set his voice low and as threatening as he could make it. He wanted this conversation to be the last he had with Jack. "Your wife is still alive and, as far as I'm concerned, she is going to stay that way."

"What? You can't do that, you fucking cretin."

"Can. Am. Have."

"Now look. We have a deal. I pay you for ... services rendered. You render those services. It's a contract." Jack sounded all lawyerly familiar all of a sudden and Dougie briefly wondered if he should be at all worried. "You try and break this contract and-"

"And what? What exactly, Jack, are you going to do?"

"I'll take my fucking money back for a start!"

"Don't have it. I'm assuming it's still in the locker where you left it."

"Well, where's the key?"

"Dunno. Someone dressed as your wife has it."

"What the fuck?"

"Don't know Jack. And don't care. About you, about your wife, about the money. I don't have it, don't want it and, if you don't have it - well, at least I guess you can afford to lose it."

"Listen to me, you little shit. If you don't go through with this - money or no money - I will hire someone else. Someone who is not an incapable cretin, to hunt you down and do to you what you should have done to my fucking wife!"

"Jack, Jack, Jack." Dougie purred. "You will do no such thing. How do I know this? Because I have some rather nice video footage of you and me meeting, in a lay-by, where I agree to your request to kill your wife. And it would be so easy - so, super simple - for me to release that footage to the press."

On the other end, Jack was silent. "Now, sure, we're both identifiable in this footage and maybe - maybe - they could trace me. If I hadn't changed my hairstyle. And shaved off my beard. And hired a Range Rover with a false ID. But you? Well, you're immediately recognisable. No-one's going to be in any doubt. And your car. Pretty distinctive I'm sure you'll agree."

"You fucker. You wouldn't."

"Watch me."

"You fucking-"

"Farewell, Jack." Dougie interrupted. "Our deal is null

and void. If you can still get the money, good for you. But I am out. If you wish to hire someone else to hit your wife, that is up to you. Good luck with that. But I am out. I don't want to see you again. I don't want to hear from you again. I will not be calling you again. And if I suspect anyone is coming after me, whether arranged by you or anyone else, I will drop you in it with such speed, and from such a height, that you will never, ever see the world outside a prison cell again. In short: I am out."

Dougie listened intently as the silence on the line lengthened. He wanted to hear agreement from Jack. Some acknowledgement that, hard though it was, their arrangement was over. When Jack came back on the line, his whining gave Dougie all the confirmation he needed.

"You don't have the money. You don't have the key. You haven't finished the job. And now you're walking away. What fucking kind of pathetic hitman are you?"

"Retired." Dougie hung up, pulled down the train window and threw his phone, as far as his injured shoulder would allow, out into the disappearing countryside.

TWENTY

Henrietta Learmont-Jones had been working with Conrad for exactly four days. Four days in which she had learnt to dislike him intensely and come to fear his temper. *So random*, is how she had described him to one of her friends at the end of Day One of the show. Emphasis on the *so*.

"I mean, he's like totally out there? One minute, sweet as pie, the next he wants your blood. Like *NOW!* Ranting like this? Plus he's definitely got halitosis, I think."

She was an agency temp who spent her young working life working short-term assignments for fashion houses, design agencies, PR companies - anyone who needed a well-spoken bit of posh totty to front a small project. The missing adjective here was non-critical and, if Conrad had known, he would have baulked at the daily rate quoted for her and immediately looked elsewhere. Small didn't necessarily mean unimportant and Conrad's project was most definitely - as far as he was concerned - not just important but vital. Critical. Crucial.

Hen - to her friends - was not used to crucial. Her last assignment had come to a somewhat abrupt end when the gaggle (she was unsure of the appropriate collective noun) of penguins she had been charged with acquiring and marshalling for an ad shoot had stunk the place out so much that the actors had to have Vick rubbed under their noses. The creatures had then bolted to a fire escape during a costume change where they had been unable to descend the stairs and resorted to crapping everywhere, defending their new nesting platform with ferocious beaks and flapping fishy flippers.

The director decided he would add the penguins later in CGI and she had been kicking her heels for a fortnight, surviving on Costa and Pret until the agency called and told her to be at LFW Day One, 7.30am sharp. Short skirt, high heels, the usual.

At first it had been a breeze. Handing out flyers, mingling with the fashionistas, helping those few unfamiliar with their own phones how to download and use the CtG app. Conrad had been happy. Ecstatic even. Order numbers were good and their shows were attended by ever-increasing numbers as the week went on. They had even run out of flyers half way through and Henrietta had had to contact the printers and arrange a special rush job of extras to keep the event running smoothly.

She wasn't sure about the gang of Chinese schoolgirls she had inherited and had wondered about the clash between their dress and appearance and her own, but Conrad had pooh-pooh'ed her concerns and reassured her that she was the General and they were the troops - only fitting that they wore different uniforms. She hadn't been able to understand a word they'd said, but she had always found that a broad smile and boundless (if unearned) confidence would see her through, and LFW had thus far been no exception.

As the week had worn on, however, Conrad had seemed to get more and more agitated and easier to rile. Forever with his phone clamped to his ear, he had barked answers at her polite questions and at one point been actually spitting - real spit - with rage at a teeny-tiny problemette when she had accidentally dropped someone's phone and cracked their screen. I mean, everyone who had an iPhone had a cracked screen didn't they? And who was the woman anyway? Editor of Harpers or something, apparently. Whatevs.

So she had taken to avoiding him whenever possible, knowing that merely doing nothing would arouse his temper. And as the final day had approached, and the ordered garments had arrived for her to sort through and match to orders, she been looking forward to a long weekend off and the chance to binge-watch Extreme Beauty Queens.

Alas, it was not to be.

Conrad was screaming at her, spitting fury.

"Look at it! Just look at it!"

He held up one of the garments to the light.

"What am I looking for?" she frowned.

"The stitching detail? Along the hem? Here." He rippled the fabric to highlight one section. "And here."

"I can't see it."

"Are you fucking blind? Look here. And here." He kept inching the fabric through his fingers. "And here. And-"

"OK! I get it! I just don't know what you want me to do about it!"

The simple question appeared to calm him down - slightly. He at least seemed to come to his senses. He took a deep breath.

"Man the doorway. Try and stop more coming in. I need to speak to Yeo."

"I'm not a bouncer. I'll get trampled to death!"

"Do what you can. If all the items are like this there's going to be fucking pandemonium."

"Mr Ho. I'm not being paid enough for this." She pouted and shook her head.

"Just do your fucking job."

"I am doing my job." She almost stamped her foot.

"No. Your job is to do what I fucking well ask you to do. And I am asking you - telling you - to man that doorway and prevent anyone coming in until I say otherwise. Do. You. Under. Stand?"

Henrietta turned on her heel, tears in her eyes, and stormed over to the doorway. Conrad flicked to Skype on his iPad and called Yeo.

"He's still not answering or returning my calls." Guy said plaintively. "I've lost count of how many messages I've left him."

"Keep trying." Cullen sat impassively, picking lint off the arm of Paul's musty armchair.

"And what do I tell him when he finally deigns to pick up?"

"Tell him you have the money."

"But I don't!"

"He doesn't know that."

"But what makes you think he even wants the money? He ran away and left me with Tuppence, hasn't shown any interest in what happened to me since, hasn't returned any of my calls."

Cullen remained silent, studying the threadbare material on the arm of the chair.

"Maybe he's actually taken London Fashion Week by storm!" Guy grew animated as his imagination roused itself. "Maybe he doesn't need the money anymore? Maybe he's packed his bags and gone back to Hong

Kong? Maybe he's dead!"

Cullen lay back in his seat, folded his arms and put his hat over his eyes. "Maybe you should let me do the thinking."

Yeo clawed at the iPhone on his bedside table and checked the time. It was stupid o'clock and his phone was trilling loudly. He pulled it in front of his face and hit the green phone icon. The bright light from the display hurt his eyes, but not as much as his ears when Conrad came on screen.

"Yeo. What are you doing to me? Are you deliberately trying to fuck me over?" Conrad screeched.

"Good morning, Conrad. Nice to see you."

"Don't you fucking dare *nice-to-see-me*. Have you seen the shit you've sent me?" He didn't wait for an answer and pushed a scrunched up dress onto the screen. "The finish is unacceptable. That's what they're saying. They're all saying it! And they're fucking right. I wrote down what one customer said: *The finish is unacceptable for a high-end garment at this price. I will not be paying and I will not be buying again.*"

"I'm sorry, I can't see-"

His question was cut short as his view of the dress was shaken and then replaced with a jumble of shoes and trousers and skirts. A struggle of some kind was jostling Conrad's tablet this way and that. The microphone burping and squawking - some feedback, perhaps from another mike close by - and voices, overlapping and blurring. Here an argument, there a complaint, now a question, then a statement. He gave up watching the shaking images giving him motion sickness and strained his ears to try and catch what was going on.

"Can we have word, Mr Ho? ... Excuse ME! This is NOT my size, nor MY order and I will NOT ... No, I will not give you my credit card details, young lady... One moment, *please!*... Can we have an interview?... ... I'm not paying for this! It's an absolute dis-... Can I have quote please, for the BBC?... Can you close the tent somehow? Try and stop- ... This is London Fashion Week, not Primark! ... Hello? .... I will not be jostled like some common ... Mr Ho? Mr Ho? Is that you- ... I know, I know. Twitter's alight with it... Stop that! Stop that at once, please!... Mr Ho?...It's an absolute disgrace. Look, there's a whole rack of them- ..."

The hubbub continued and there was a loud smack as the tablet fell to the floor and showed a brightly lit ceiling, very far away, being partially obscured by footprints, soles and heels.

"Give me that back!... Hello, Mr Ho?... No, that's my order. I think this is *your* order... Mr Ho? ... I'm never a size 12, how dare you! ... Wait, please ... You can read my opinion in The Telegraph tomorrow, young lady... Mr Ho? Can I have a word- ..."

Yeo ended the call and went back to sleep.

Conrad sat amidst a sea of discarded tartan clothing, garments trampled and tossed aside, inside the empty show tent. Head bowed he looked in despair at the CtG admin app on his iPad. It looked like the FTSE 100 on Black Friday. A sea of red orders - unfulfilled, cancelled. A mere handful of open, to-be-paid-for, blue orders - one of which winked to red even as he watched. A small pie chart showing a summary breakdown of his trading position showed him in the hole to the tune of just under £85,000.

Just over £85,000.

Now £87,000.

Conrad closed his iPad cover, closed his eyes and wished himself elsewhere.

"Hello, Mrs Imbrochovs…, Ibrojovs…, Ibrok…, Mrs Jack!" The guard on the front gate beamed at her as she pulled up in her Audi.

"Hello. Arthur isn't it?" Arthur blushed, proud and humble to be recognised by a beautiful woman. His wife would be jealous when he told her - which, of course, he wouldn't. "It's a lovely day."

"It is, it is." Arthur nodded, looking up at the clear sky. "Don't know why I'm shut up in here when I could be out walking the dogs. Oh, I know why. The money!"

Arthur stooped slightly in his gatehouse to take a look at Dick in the passenger seat. "There's no-one scheduled in today, you know? Rest day, it says here." He ran his finger down a sheet pinned to the wall by his sliding window to confirm.

"Yes, I know. But Jack left some stuff behind in the changing rooms? He's got a signing today and he's got a load of photos and other stuff all signed and sitting in his locker." Tuppence shook her head, smiling again. "He'd forget his head if it wasn't screwed on."

"Right. Know the feeling. My missus is the same. Head in the clouds half the time." Arthur shook his own head, eyes creasing. "What can you do? Can't live with 'em, can't live with 'em!" He chortled at his own joke.

"Absolutely." Tuppence said, agreeing more than he

knew.

"And your guest...?" Arthur lifted his chin towards Dick.

"Don't you recognise him?" Tuppence teased. "He's newly famous. Almost. Dick Dosh!"

"Dick? Oh, the man on the bike!" Arthur's eyes widened.

"The very same."

"Thought you looked familiar!" Arthur exclaimed. "Guided tour is it?"

"Kind of." Tuppence said. "Won't be a jiff."

"Take your time. I'm here all day." Arthur raised the barrier and gave her a mock salute as she drove through to the car park.

Tuppence was barely familiar with the layout of the training facility and led Dick through the empty building following her nose, their footsteps echoing down the long corridors, his a steady amble, hers a habitual catwalk sashay. Through windows on their right Dick could see a couple of training pitches, nets and benches, all surrounded by tiered seating on two sides and thirty foot fencing on the others.

"Going to be around her somewhere" she theorized.

"What are we looking for?" Dick asked. "Forgot to ask."

"Changing Room. Lockers I guess."

"You don't know?"

"Just following orders." Tuppence shrugged and showed him her phone screen. "Ormiston locker? Paul."

"Who's Paul?" Dick scrunched his face up as he continued to look around as they walked.

"Friend of Cullen's."

"Ok. And who's Cullen?"

"Cullen? Another friend." She looked at him and shrugged again. "Well, a white knight."

"Cullen." Dick considered. "Rings a bell. How come he's your white knight?"

"He rescued me from my kidnappers."

"Good of him." Dick agreed. "Yes, I'd say that was the action of a white knight. What's in this locker then?"

"Don't know" She grinned at him conspiratorially. "That's what we're here to find out."

"Ha! A treasure hunt!" Dick laughed. *"If thou seekest her as silver, and searchest for her as hidden treasures. Proverbs 2:4"*

"Her?" Tuppence arched her eyebrows and lowered her head to look up at him.

"Her. It." Dick blushed slightly. "Depends on your translation."

"Well. In my albeit limited experience of Mr Cullen, I feel as if this is a little adventure he has gifted me. Well, us."

"*Mister* Cullen." Dick recalled. "The chap at the grave!"

"Sorry?"

"I think I've met him. Does he wear a leather cowboy hat-type thing?"

"Yes! Yes he does." Tuppence remarked, surprised.

"Small world." Dick nodded. "Is that the place?" He gestured to a sign on the wall of a corridor to their right.

"Only one way to find out." Said Tuppence and strode across. She scanned a row of smart lockers with polished wooden doors. Small numbers and names engraved in little bronze plaques on each. "Here we are. The moment of truth."

Dick was suddenly very apprehensive and felt the

hairs on his neck prickle. "You're sure this isn't some kind of trap?"

"Don't say that." She admonished, picking up on his nervousness and becoming anxious herself at his suggestion. She took a deep breath and exhaled slowly, thoughtfully. She held the key up between them. "You know what this is? It's life. Uncertainty. Excitement. Risk." She dared him with her eyes. "You in or out?"

Dick locked eyes with her, hesitated for the shortest perceptible moment, and then grasped her hand as she put the key into the door and turned it.

Five gin and tonics in, and it still wasn't enough to douse Conrad's shame. All he wanted now was to get as far away as possible from the disaster that was CtG.

And the small matter of saving his fingers from Mr Chu.

Whichever way he turned, his predicament still came up looking like shit. He had exhausted all his options. He had alienated Liv and Guy, taken money he couldn't pay back, still owed Tuppence and others for the Stobo photoshoot and the staff he'd employed at LFW for the week, Yeo was after a six figure sum for the garments he'd shipped, and he had angry customers calling him fit-to-burn all over social media - his name and hoped-for brand was now mud in the fashion world.

As far as he could see, he literally had nowhere left to turn, and no-one else to turn to, other than his father in Hong Kong. Which would mean showing up at his father's door in abject humiliation, swallowing his prize. He had no idea what reception he would receive but he saw, finally, that his misery was complete.

Until his phone rang. It was Guy.

At his lowest point, with nothing further to lose, Conrad sighed and silently took the call.

"Where the hell have you been?" Guy whined. "I've been trying to contact you for ages. Why do you never pick up?"

"I am ruined." Conrad's lament was a thin, wispy reed in a wash of echo - nothing but defeat in his tone.

"But we have the money!"

"Huh?" Conrad was preoccupied by his own doom.

"The ransom money? We have it!"

He stirred, slowly. "We?"

"We. Us. You and me. In this case, me. Definitely me."

"What?"

"Yes! I have it. I have it all!" Guy was gabbling madly. "And a gunshot wound if you're interested."

"A what?"

"A gunshot wound. I've been shot!"

"You've been shot?" Conrad was not picking up the pieces of the conversation as quickly as Guy was laying them down. "Um, who shot you?"

"I don't fucking know!" The increase in volume from Guy almost caused Conrad to drop his phone. "Someone with a gun."

"Jack?"

"No! Not unless he can be in two places at once and shoot someone in front of 20,000 witnesses without being noticed."

"20,000...? What are you talking about?"

"Long story. Look, someone contacted us - me - on behalf of Jack and arranged a meeting where we - I - assumed we'd - I'd - get the money. Anyway, look, none of this is important right now. What is important is that I have the money! You can have it! Plan A is back on track!"

"Yes." Drawled Conrad. "I'm afraid I've travelled a lot further down the alphabet now than that, though."

"Well, never mind. I have the money. Do you want it?"

"Yes! Yes, of course." Conrad was in no mood to look a gift hawk in the mouth. "Plan A! Why not?"

"Well…"

Guy hesitated and Conrad's gratitude was instantly replaced with suspicion. "Well what, Guy?"

"Well. There is, um, one condition."

"A condition?"

"Yes. You see, while you may be happy with all this… I mean, it was all your idea in the first place…"

"Go on." Conrad prodded, getting the distinct feeling that he was not going to like what he heard.

"Well, I was hoping that we could draw a nice neat line under all this, you see? And I never wanted the money anyway. But we've done all these… bad… things. And I'd like to be able to rectify them so we could… walk away. With a clear conscience."

What on earth was he babbling on about, thought Conrad. "How can any of this be rectified?"

"Well, we can put the stolen designs back. Before anyone notices."

"I'm afraid it's too late for that. Liv knows."

"Oh. Ah. Well, perhaps if we put them back quickly there'll be no evidence to connect us to them?"

"No evidence? I have - well, had - a shedload of cancel.. orders for designs which I stole!"

"But they could be your own! It'd be her word against

374

yours."

"If no-one else knows."

"Exactly."

"No, that's not what I meant. Half of London's seen them by now!"

"But you haven't told people they're stolen - have you?"

"No! Of course not." Conrad protested. Ironically, if he had told people they were stolen the failure of his CtG range would not have felt so stingingly personal.

"Well, then. If Liv - or anyone else - claimed they were, you could protest your innocence! And when anyone questioned the mill they'd find the designs still in place. It would just be a case of unconscious thing."

"Unconscious thing? What are you on about?"

"You know! Like when two people come up with the same idea at the same time. Make the same discovery or invention independently? Two people invented TV at about the same time, didn't they? Newton and Liebniz invented calculus at the same time! And didn't someone else come up with the idea of evolution when Darwin did? Happens all the time!"

"You're putting me in the same bracket as Newton and Darwin?"

Guy purred down the phone. "There is no off-position on the genius switch, Con."

"Hmm. Maybe." Conrad softened and felt himself burnish under the compliment. "Maybe. Wait! What about the girl?"

"The girl?"

"Tuppence!" Conrad rasped. "The girl we kidnapped?"

"Oh yeah. Well, see, she escaped."

"Escaped?"

"Yeah. Ages ago. Not long after you left for Hong Kong actually. So, no harm done!" Guy explained as if he had forgotten to get a loaf from the shops and would have to go back for it. "And we wore masks didn't we, so she doesn't know it was us!"

"Escaped?" Conrad repeated, feeling more than a little lost.

"Yeah. I don't think that's why I got shot though."

"Oh, you don't?" Conrad was gaping in the wake of Guy's blithe assurance, unsure how to continue the conversation.

"No, 'cos I was dressed up as her and-"

"You were dressed up as her because she'd escaped?"

"Yes. Now you're getting it. Oh, and I got an extra £50,000 ransom money!"

"What!" Conrad was very far from getting it, he thought.

"Yep." Guy preened. "£150,000. Cash."

Conrad couldn't quite take it all in. What Guy was telling him seemed too good to be true. But right now, like a rope to a drowning man, it was all he had and he wasn't going to ignore it. "Look - tell me all about it when I get home. If you want to put the designs back - if that is really your only condition for giving me all the money - I'm in."

He was already mentally counting the cash, realising he would be able to pay Yeo and Mr Chu - as well as Tuppence and all the other people he owed money to - and still come out ahead on the deal. Or - and now here's an idea - how about he just took all the money and disappeared? He couldn't risk going back to Hong Kong but what about Malaysia or Indonesia? Or Vietnam?

There was no end of places were £150,000 would allow him to live like a king and start a business empire by running a sweatshop at minimal cost, churning out his own designs for high-end customers.

"So, you'll come straight up?" Guy sounded relieved.

Conrad's cogs turned and his mind whirred, already elsewhere. "You bet your sore arse! I'll be there tomorrow."

"Well, it's actually not that sore, really. Kind of went right through, if you see what I mean. More like a sort of flesh-. Hello? Hello?"

They had been driving back to the hotel in silence for over ten minutes when Tuppence was finally able to bring herself to speak.

"What does the bible have to say about this, then?" She looked in the rear view mirror and then glanced over at Dick before returning her eyes to the road ahead.

"I don't think it says anything about one hundred and fifty thousand pounds explicitly. Nor about large sums of money in general. Our friend Timothy was told by Paul that money is the root of all evil. Matthew says you can't love both money and God, and that it is easier for a camel to pass through the eye of a needle than it is for a rich man to enter the kingdom of heaven." Dick looked across at her. "There's plenty more but I think you get the gist."

"So, to paraphrase: what does God say about money? He's against it."

"Yes." Dick nodded reluctantly. "Money makes people blind to where true value lies. Divest yourself of it and you will start to see that humanity, love and mercy are worth more and cost less."

"So I guess there's not much prospect of forgiveness for people like me?" She mused.

"No, that's not true." Dick considered. "God recognises that some people will always have money and some will have more money than others. I don't think he's a communist!" Tuppence kept a straight face as she pulled up at some lights. Dick continued. "What he is saying is that it is how you come by money and what you do with it once you've got it. If you come by it honestly and give freely of it, then you are a good man - woman; if you single-mindedly pursue it and grasp at it and use it to try and build yourself an earthly paradise, you are foolish and ultimately doomed, because love lies with Him in heaven and not in material things here on earth. True value is not the same as value for money."

"And charity? Taking money from others and using it to for the glory of God - that's alright isn't it?"

"Of course. Especially when the charity glories in his name"

"I think this money should be a donation to your cycle ride."

Dick was stunned. "What?"

"A gift to God." She trilled. "Who has worked harder for this money? Jack, me or you?"

"But…" Dick was dumbstruck. "But we don't know where it came from. Who it belongs to."

"It was in my husband's locker, therefore it belongs to him. He has donated it to me - he just doesn't know it yet. And he can afford it anyway. I-" She grinned a decisive grin. "I, in turn, am donating it to you."

"Well I-"

"Once I've allocated some sundry expenses from it."

"Of course, of course."

A dog shot out from between two parked cars and Tuppence braked sharply, glad to see it complete its way to the other side of the road, unaware of the danger it had been in. Shaken, she looked up in her mirror to see if anyone was right behind her and thought she caught a glimpse of a man in a cowboy hat walking on the pavement. She spun around in her seat but there was no-one to be seen.

"Sorry." Tuppence said, absently. "You were saying?"

"I…" Dick sighed. "Thank you. It is a tremendously kind gesture and one I will gratefully accept - as will He. You're sure you want to do this?"

"Yes. I think so, yes." She put the car into first and pulled away.

"How do you know Cullen?" She wondered aloud.

"Hmm? Oh, he came to see me recently. His wife is buried in one of my churchyards and there had been some damage to her grave. I think it was him."

Tuppence's grip on the wheel intensified and she swallowed hard.

"That settles it then."

"Is that it? You're going to give away a hundred and fifty thousand pounds because we both barely know a man who's wife's grave was damaged?"

Tuppence relaxed in her seat as the sun briefly burst through cloud cover and lit up the wet streets. She smiled broadly at Dick. "The Lord moves in mysterious ways."

"God loves you, Tuppence." He said, and then swallowed hard. "And I think love you too."

Tuppence looked at him, tenderly. "Well, that is plenty of value for my money right there."

The grounds of Bankholm mill were in darkness apart from the small gatehouse, lit by a small strip-light silhouetting a guard hunched over a small TV screen. The large wrought-iron double gate was the sole entry point. The perimeter was made up from the stone walls of several outbuildings, the spans between them bridged by a tall wall topped with metal spikes. Where the buildings ran into a stretch of woodland, the wall was replaced by a chainlink fence which ran along the edge of the woodland down to the towpath along the river where the wall began again.

Conrad and Guy had climbed the fence easily enough, hidden from view by the trees and bushes. They had also chosen to wear dark trousers and tops. Guy wore a black bobble hat, *sans* bobble; Conrad allowed his naturally black hair to act as sufficient camouflage.

They had walked calmly across the main quadrangle, partially lawned, between the gift shop and the main reception, then forked right and into a cluster of buildings, one of which led to the design studios up on the second floor. When they climbed the stairs out into a corridor leading to the studio, Conrad realised Guy was no longer behind him. He stopped and listened, worried that his friend had abandoned him.

"Conrad?" Said a voice.

Conrad nearly shat his pants and turned to see a figure standing at the end of the corridor holding a torch which was flashing across Conrad's face, blinding him.

"Guy? Is that you?"

"No."

"Who are you?"

"I'm with Guy." Said the man.

"Where is he?" Conrad turned to see if he could see his friend.

"He's with me." The man said and the unmistakable shape of a sheepish-looking Guy appeared around the side of the dark figure.

"Hmm. Are you the *we* that Guy was referring to?" The figure started walking towards him and Conrad tried to put on a brave front. "I'm not impressed."

"Neither am I." The man said coolly, and as he approached Conrad could make out the shape of a cowboy hat on his head.

"You're the badger guy!"

"And you're the scared kidnapper who ran away."

Conrad started backing down the corridor as the stranger and Guy drew closer. He ended up with his back to the door, no escape route available except the one behind the advancing cowboy.

"Guy!" Conrad appealed to his friend. "What's this?"

Guy stayed silent.

"What's going on? Why is he here?" Then to the stranger, now almost upon him. "What do you want?"

"Atonement." The man's face was an angry mask and he grabbed Conrad by the wrist and wrenched it smartly up and behind Conrad's back

"What do you mean, decoy designs?" Liv struggled with the phone between her shoulder and chin as she signed the check-out summary at the reception desk.

"It's standard practice." Jonty explained. "In our company anyway. I imagine other mills do the same, to minimise industrial espionage and so forth."

"Industrial espionage?" Liv was incredulous. "You are

381

a mill, correct? Not a nuclear power plant?"

"Liv, what is the most valuable thing you own?" He didn't wait for her to answer. "Your IP - your intellectual property. Or, to put it another way, your designs. You'll know yourself in this business you can't patent a look; can't copyright a sleeve or a weave. Everything's up for grabs - it's actually what makes fashion such a vibrant industry. Designers acting as magpies, taking inspiration and ideas from here and there and creating something new and wonderful."

"Well, of course."

"So we make a habit of producing a dummy set of designs for every set we are tasked with manufacturing. Our designers take the originals and change them - adapt them, alter the cut or the fabric or the details, or all three - and produce a similar, but obviously inferior set of patterns, drawings, instructions, specifications. The whole nine yards. These are the in-house designs. If anyone - employees or otherwise - attempts to steal ideas or complete designs, having these helps not just protect us but also helps identify the culprits if such a theft takes place."

"So they're what was taken?"

"Yep. We don't tell anyone, any more than we tell them we created the in-house designs in the first place. Kind of defeats the point. But we do monitor things internally. Your in-house designs were stolen several weeks ago and have not been returned. We have no information or indication that any employees - past or present - were involved and, so far, no evidence of them has surfaced anywhere."

"It has now." Liv chortled.

"Really? Where?"

"London Fashion Week."

"You're joking?"

"Not at all. For a while they were actually one of the hottest properties in the whole show. Until the finished products started appearing."

"Hmm. Well, I'm not surprised. Both sets of designs were very intricate and… well, rather demanding if you don't mind me saying so. The decoy's would probably have been more expensive and time-consuming to manufacture than your own."

"Apparently. So, does this mean my real designs are still safe? With you?"

"Naturally." Jonty sounded offended.

"Super." She paused before taking the plunge. "I don't suppose you could arrange to have them couriered over to me could you? Now that the show's over."

"Well, of course. I'll arrange that now. To Chanel Head Office?"

"Ahm, no actually. Would it be possible to get them across to me at my home address? I'm working from home for a while, recovering from an operation."

"Oh, I'm sorry to hear that. Yes, no problem. If you could let me have your home address I'll take care of it. I hope you get well soon."

Liv thanked him, told him her address and hung up with a broad smile.

TWENTY ONE

They descended back down the stairs and pushed through a fire door out into the chill night air. Cullen led them across the courtyard in silence and into an outbuilding, through large sliding double doors. Just inside the doors was a large noticeboard, a set of pigeonholes mounted on the wall, and a bank of display panels bearing swatches of different fabrics, patterns and designs - mostly tartan.

"Hey look at these!" Conrad momentarily forgot his situation and pointed to the swatches. "See them? Which ones are mine, do you think?"

"I like this one." Guy said abruptly. "This one, not so much."

Conrad's lip curled and he snarled. "That-" he pointed at the one Guy liked. "Is mine. And that-" now pointing at the one he didn't. "Is mine also." He waggled his head at the entirety of the display. "What we have here is a display largely made up of my designs. Mine!"

"Your point is?" Cullen piped up drily.

"My point, Mr Badgerman, is that this mill is displaying my designs here. In this dye shed. Where they dye wool to produce specific colours for their yarns." This last sentence he uttered with patronising disdain, as if explaining to a simpleton. "Designs which they told me - criticised me for - were un-manufacturable. Wouldn't work, they said. Poor design, they said."

He switched his attention to glare at Guy, and continued. "Remember? And now look. Up on the wall for all to see. In here, presumably, so that the dye-hands have a reference point. What the yarns should look like before they're woven into the fabric. My fabric. My designs."

"Designs you made or designs you stole?" Cullen asked quietly.

"Designs I made!" Conrad hissed. "My designs. Mine." He glowered at Guy. "They lied to me, Guy. They lied! I could have been a success!"

He was shouting, voice rising up to the rafters in this large space. A corrugated iron roof, several metres above them, no soft edges or materials to absorb the sound, the shed was all hard surfaces and metal machinery. Two large cylindrical vats over to their left raised up on a wide metal walkway, their lids standing upright as if waiting for their next meal.

"Con, come on." Guy urged. "It's too late for all that now."

"Yes it is." said Cullen. Guy looked at Cullen questioningly and Cullen rolled his eyes exaggeratedly towards a large industrial control panel on the wall to their right. Guy went over to it, surveying the buttons, handles and dials.

"Come on!" protested Conrad, suddenly sensing a different atmosphere in the room. "No harm done, hmm? Let's put the designs back. Everyone go home, hmm?"

"No harm done?" Cullen growled. "What about the damage to the grave?"

"What grave?" Conrad screwed his face up and pulled his chin in at this sudden comment from left field. "What are you talking about?" Conrad looked pleadingly at Guy. "What grave is he talking about, hmm?"

Guy shrugged theatrically and looked in turn at Cullen, who ignored him.

"Let's see if the green button refreshes your memory." Cullen nodded to Guy who looked at the prominent large green and red buttons, as big as his fist, on the left of the control panel. Guy stood rooted to the spot, unaware of what the button would do, and torn between loyalty to the memory of his old friend and some new fealty to this strange cowboy with blood in his eyes.

"Do it." Cullen insisted and, obediently, Guy crossed his hands together and leant down heavily on the button.

Three a.m. and the pile of chips in front of Jack had grown and shrunk, shrunk and grown. At one point, he'd been seventy-grand to the good, tipping the waitress, high-fiving others around the table, flirting outrageously with the female croupiers.

But now the open space of the casino floor seemed to be expanding rapidly as the number of punters fell and Jack felt his cash and himself shrinking correspondingly. He had moved away from the roulette table over to Black Jack, trying to kick-start his luck again, but the atmosphere there was cloying and he had quickly moved back to watch the ball spinning in the wheel, transfixed by the odds.

At four a.m. Mister Chu appeared by his side, clapping politely whenever Jack won, smiling discretely when he didn't. The pile of chips was running down. Predictably Jack had turned to him with a proposition.

"One last line of credit before I'm done?" Jack turned his smile onto full beam and gave it everything he had.

"Of course, Jack." Mr Chu had said, obligingly.

"One last twenty? For the road?"

Mr Chu barely missed a beat. "There is a small hole in the road, you understand Jack?"

"How small?"

"Actually, fairly large. An eighty thousand sized hole, to be precise."

"Well, that'll make a nice round hundred then, won't it? Perfect." Jack winked but Mr Chu did not reciprocate.

"I think perhaps some collateral would be in order." Quietly, discretely, Mr Chu made sure that this could not be interpreted as a question.

"Sure!" Jack shrugged, more coolly than he felt. "Like?"

"I have -" Mr Chu paused and took Jack by the elbow. "This way, Jack. I have a proposition for you."

"Hey." Jack shook Mr Chu's hand free. "Mind the cloth, Chu-ey baby. What's the proposition that you can't propose it while I reel in some moolah?"

Mr Chu showed minor irritation. "The table will wait for you, Jack. This proposition should, perhaps, be raised more privately." He looked meaningfully at Jack and then turned to walk slowly away. Jack took a regretful look at his chips and followed obediently behind.

He was led through a door marked Private just off to the right of the cashier counters and through a second door into a private gaming room, a large round table covered in blue baize sitting beneath a low-hanging light. Mr Chu invited Jack to sit and they both did so.

"What's the big secret then, Chu-Chu." Jack was more than a little tight with drink. Mr Chu ignored the over-familiarity and bent in close for emphasis.

"Two-nil. Saturday."

Jack was confused and his face showed it. "That your prediction is it? To us, yeah 'bout right I'd say."

"To them." Mr Chu said quietly.

"No way!" Jack scuffed the table with his right hand, gesturing away in disagreement. "We're five places above them. They'll be lucky to get nil."

"You get nil." Mr Chu clarified. "They get two. You get your hundred thousand credit line."

"Wait, what?" Jack sat back in his chair and looked at Mr Chu afresh.

"Two-nil." Mr Chu repeated calmly, spreading his hands as it it was all too obvious. "You make it happen. I make it happen."

"Now, hang on a minute." Jack was momentarily stunned.

"You want another twenty?"

"Well, yes." Jack shrugged. "Of course."

"Two-nil."

Jack sat in silence, mental wheels whirring. This was a whole new ball game as far as he was concerned, one he hadn't seen coming. At all. Where would this lead? And would it matter anyway - I mean, if he took the twenty, used it to get it back to a hundred, clear his credit line, there'd be no need to throw the match would there? And he'd have had a fine nights entertainment for free.

Jack looked at his watch. He needed to make a decision quickly.

Mr Chu examined his fingernails, then looked up intently at Jack.

"So. What do you say?"

"Do you have any dice handy?"

Conrad started to screech over the sound of heavy machinery whirring into action. "Look, this must be a mistake. I don't know about any grave, I'm a fashion designer! Not Burke and Hare."

Cullen stood dispassionately watching as Conrad sensed something moving above his head and looked up.

"You know me!" He jabbered to Guy. "Tell him! I didn't damage any grave."

Guy shrugged almost imperceptibly and then turned his head away, not wanting to hold his friend's gaze. Conrad rounded on Cullen.

"Look, ok? I'll fix any damage, hmm?" He bargained. "You show me a photo, hmm? Get an estimate. I'll pay for repair, hmm? How about it?"

Above him a large heavy hook loomed into sight, suspended on a chain from a track running along the length of the shed roof. Conrad realised that a number of canvas loops were starting to rise up around him and he whirled around to see he was standing in a kind of large sack, secured to the hook above him by a loop at each corner. As the hook moved, the loops started to rise and lift the sack into the air, threatening to take him with it.

"Wait! What are you doing?" Conrad panicked. "I'll fix the damage. What more do you want, hmm?"

"An apology." Cullen intoned, resonant over the humming machinery. "Acknowledgement of the damage done. Regret."

"What?" Conrad felt the canvas rising, taking him slowly clear of the floor. He was being hoisted into the air by a huge mechanical finger, like a dog turd in a carrier bag. Bewildered, he frothed at his antagonist. "Ok, I 'm sorry, ok? I'm very, very sorry. I'll never do anything like that again."

"Like what?"

"I don't know!" Conrad protested. "Whatever you want me to apologise for, ok? I didn't do it but I'm very sorry for what I did, ok? Happy now? Can I get down now, hmm?"

"That's not an apology."

"That's all you're gonna get, Mister!" Conrad shrieked, clawing at the canvas cage which was now holding him in the air like a struggling child in a bed sheet. "You're a fucking crazy man! Guy, tell him this has gone far enough, hmm? He's the madman, not me!"

"The kirkyard at Stobo, remember?" Guy prompted, looking on anxiously, urging him to remember.

"Stobo?"

"You did a photoshoot."

"Stobo? Stobo? Ah, ok, Stobo! Yes I did a photoshoot. In the cemetery. So what?" He made a face at Guy, nodding to the control panel at his fingertips. "Can you press the red button now please?"

"No, he can't." Cullen spoke to Conrad but glanced sternly at Guy who remained motionless.

"Come on! Stobo? Stobo? Was just a shoot! No big deal. Place was a dump anyway." Conrad shook his head, unable to believe his predicament was down to this completely forgettable incident. He looked over at Cullen with a sceptical grin on his face, and then felt his mouth fall as he took in the man's dead eyes and the set of his jaw. "Ok, ok. Not a dump. Not a dump." Conrad back-pedalled, but it was too late.

Cullen strode over to the leftmost tank and dragged the sack holding Conrad as he did so. Conrad started kicking and struggling but it was no use; he was held fast in the heavy canvas trap. When he was directly over the

390

tank, Cullen signalled to Guy who pressed the red button and Conrad felt himself being lowered, the whirr of the pulley motor sounding like a lift descending.

"Stop! What're you doing? What're you doing?" Conrad increased his struggle and received a hard punch in the midriff for his pains, Cullen now had hold of him and was manually guiding him downwards into the empty tank. Conrad's shouts started to echo and bounce off its circular metal walls. "Guy! Let me up! Back to green, ok? Guy?"

Conrad felt his feet hit bottom and he stood up, half-bent over from the pain in his stomach. The canvas sack pooled around him and he had barely a second to look up and see Mr. Friends stony face as he pulled down on the heavy lid. "No! Wai-"

There was a deafening clang and Conrad felt a heavy thwack as the lid swung down on his head. He crumpled to the floor and the blackness was complete.

"What now?" asked Guy, walking across the floor of the dye shed and up onto the gantry way that ran alongside the two dyeing tanks. He looked at the buttons and switches sitting there invitingly. "Do you know how to work one of these?"

"Nope." Cullen flicked two switches and spun a dial randomly. A small blue light came on and there was a sound of water flowing through a pipe, a sluice opening.

Guy turned behind him and looked at a dark blue liquid pouring down a large transparent tube about 6" in diameter. They both listened but could detect no sound coming from Conrad inside the tank. Cullen watched the gauge move as the dye poured into the tank. When it had reached 3/4 full, he shut the pipe off and listened again.

Nothing.

He looked at the large white clock up on the far wall of the shed and did a quick calculation.

"If the shift starts at 8am, I reckon he'll still have air left in there."

"Yeah." Guy added, thoughtfully. "But when they open it, it'll be blue."

Back out in the cold, Cullen stopped while they were still in shadow. Over at the main gate there was some activity and one of the security guards left the gatehouse and started walking towards the dyeing shed.

"Shit. Must have triggered some alarm or something." He puffed out his cheeks. "Which way was the fence you climbed?"

"On the other side of the quadrangle." Guy scanned the grounds. "They'll see us."

"Let's try the gift shop over there." Cullen pointed to a side door, half-glazed, sitting in the corner of the courtyard out of sight of the guardhouse. He winced in expectation of an alarm when he shattered the door glass with his elbow. When none sounded, he reached in and opened the door from the inside. "Guess they only alarm outside doors." He said.

"Yeah, well. Probably not expecting anyone to break *out*." Guy said.

They hustled through the doorway and turned sharp right into a showroom or gallery. About ten yards long, there were designs and photos in display cases along both walls and thick sets of material swatches hanging from pegs above them.

Guy reached out and brushed one yearningly with his fingers. "Ooh, I like this one." He lifted the swatch book off its peg, taking it with him. Cullen shook his head wearily as he kicked the central safety bar from the fire exit and the double doors flung open. The air was filled with sirens and a blue light started flashing in the ceiling behind them, casting their shadows onto the empty street in front of them. They raced along the pavement towards the adjoining woodland and plunged straight in. Brushing through between the trees, they ploughed towards the river, where they emerged under a streetlight on the tow path. Cullen stood and tried to make himself look undishevelled, scanning left and right for anyone who might be around at this time of night. When he turned back Guy was fondling the swatches in the book, examining the rear of each one and cooing quietly.

"Come on!" Cullen urged. "The car's this way."

Guy protested and waived one of the swatches in his face as they lurched along the tow path. "What about this one, hmm? Do you like this one?"

Cullen winced. "A bit too modern for my tastes."

"Oh, traditionalist huh?"

"Aye." Said Cullen, looking back as the sound of the sirens faded and the path behind them remained empty. "Dyed in the wool, you might say."

"I said rub *him* out, not rub *one* out, cumshot."

Such was Toenail's gift for language, as spoken to a new recruit to his unit. Toenail spat in the muddy ground and looked on as the newbie pulled himself up from out of the rutted caterpillar tracks left by one the armoured vehicles and stood apologetically to attention in front of his unit leader.

"Sorry, Corporal." The unfortunate reserve muttered, looking down in dismay at his new uniform- which he'd had to pay for himself - covered in mud.

"Don't fucking sorry me, arsewipe." Toenail strode through the ankle-deep mud and thrust his nose right into the poor boy's face. "The goal here is to crush the other team, right? Boogie Night's team, right?"

"Yes, Corporal."

"And, in the process, impart maximum pain and humiliation on Boogie Night himself, yes?" Impart was a new verb Toenail had overheard his Sergeant use earlier that morning and had been keen to introduce it into his own vocabulary. The unit Sergeant had divided them into two groups, one to be headed up by Toenail - natch - the other he had called for a volunteer to lead. The group had taken a collective intake of breath when none other than Boogie Night had stepped forward and saluted. From that moment on, Toenail had decided that the only satisfactory way to end this day was going to involve a stretcher with Boogie Night on it and a celebratory pint and a fag in The Eagle afterwards.

"Yes, Corporal. Sorry, Corporal."

"So, pull your finger out of your arse!" Toenail poked an index finger into the boy's cheek, leaving a vivid white smear on his mud-soaked face. He looked down at the ground in disgust, thinking. "Can you drive one of these things?" he pointed to the RV standing over by the trees.

"Don't know, Corporal." He was startled at the prospect and blinked furiously. "I've got an HGV license so there's no reason-"

"Right, get your arse in the driver's seat. Scabby!" Toenail addressed this last shout over to the remainder of his group, standing under a shaky tarp shelter smoking and chatting, their kit on the ground. Private Scarborough looked across in surprise and threw his cigarette butt on the ground as he was addressed.

"Yes, Corporal?"

"Scabby. Get over and ride shotgun with young bollock-breath here. The rest of you, look sharp. We're going to tramp alongside the RV and make our way to the copse over there for some cover." Toenail pointed downhill towards a dip in the valley where a small clump of trees provided the only notable feature on the landscape amidst the grey, green and yellow scrub of this spartan section of the Borders countryside. "There's a burn down there, we can refill our water bottles while we're at it." He manhandled a map he'd been referring to into a roughly folded rectangle and shoved it in the pocket of his tunic. "Face up!" He commanded and the members of the unit scrambled over and formed a loose line in front of him.

Hiding in this same copse, watching through binoculars, Dougie's brain was ticking over quietly. The goal of the exercise was to capture the flag - a tired-looking red pennant which Dougie's unit had found an hour ago tied to a tree in this small clump of woodland - and get back to base without any casualties being inflicted by Toenail's defence unit. Dougie's team had been ecstatic on finding their target and had started to look at Boogie Night in a different light - almost something approaching respect at the intelligent but hands-off way he had led them so painlessly to the half-way point in their mission. All they had to do now was get back to base as quickly as possible. Boogie- as Dougie's team were now referring to him - had other plans, though.

Toenail was unknowingly coming down to meet them and Dougie had no intention of letting this gift of an opportunity go to waste. He lowered his binoculars, wincing with the pain from his armpit injuries. He sat in the turret of his own RV, while his driver, Max, was sitting hidden beneath him in the belly of this tank-cum-lorry, thinking. "Shut the engine off" he said to Max and then sat in the enveloping silence, listening to the slow grumble of Toenail's unit approaching.

Up on a neighbouring hill, lying prostrate amidst some gorse, Platoon Sergeant Midhurst was observing his two teams exercise through binoculars. He had seen the red team reach the pennant and expected them to head for home, but now the blue team were approaching and it was clear there was going to be some sort of skirmish. Still curious about Boogie's assured manner in volunteering to lead the red team, he wondered how this would play out.

Toenail led the blue team towards the copse, his rifle strap wrapped around his forearm, safety off, scanning slowly left and right as he padded through the mud. He could feel his pulse quickening as he neared the trees, sensing Boogie's presence. The newbie watched through his tiny windscreen as Toenail came to a halt and, without looking back, waved to him to circle round the copse. He wrestled with the unfamiliar gears and crunchingly swung his RV right, following the tree line slightly uphill. His visibility was strictly limited, like a blinkered horse, unable to see pretty much anything which wasn't straight under his nose. When, within seconds of turning, he found himself facing up the backside of another RV with a red flag, he immediately panicked and ground his gears again, looking for reverse.

Dougie had been so enthralled watching Toenail padding slowly this way he had forgotten he had instructed his RV driver to kill his engine. Trance-like, his senses had focussed on the visual and he had unconsciously put the increasing trundling sound of the blue team's own RV down to a gentle backwash of sound, its rumble rising as the tension rose with Toenail's approach.

When he saw the front of the blue team's RV tentatively poke itself, as if from nowhere, round the edge of the trees and then immediately throw itself into reverse, he suddenly forgot all about Toenail and shouted heatedly down to his driver.

"Shit, they're on us. Attack!"

His driver started the engine, pushing a cloud of black smoke from the exhaust, and revved it up in first as it gave chase to the receding RV.

Sergeant Midhurst looked on first in amusement, then in despair and finally in disbelief at all of the stupidities of his teams down below squeezed into forty seconds of madness. He saw the red team's RV crept up on as if the idea of keeping a lookout for attackers was a novelty;

then he saw the attacking blue RV become the prey as it unintelligibly turned heel and immediately relinquished the advantage of surprise; finally he watched in fascinated slo-mo as the blue team leader, completely unaware of his surroundings, turn belatedly to see the back of his own RV reverse over him and crush him into the mud.

He dropped his binoculars, shut his eyes and exhaled deeply into the gorse. Another accident report to write.

When one of the blue team stormed around in front of the driver and frantically signalled for him to stop and pull forward, he did so obligingly. He had taken his teammate's gesture of a hand slitting his throat as the signal to cut his engine, which he did with relief, and then removed his earguards and climbed down into his own muddy tracks.

It was only when his team mate took his helmet off and pointed sadly behind the RV that he turned and saw the unmistakable shape of Toenail, glistening flatly face down in the tracks. All engines quieted, the only sound now was a muffled whining fizz coming from one of Toenail's earbuds lying unscathed in the mud, it's coda drifting out amongst the trees:

"Don't blame it on the sunshine, don't blame it on the moonlight, don't blame it on the good times, blame it on the boogie."

When Tuppence opened her front door to collect her things she was surprised to see Jack sitting on the sofa watching the football on TV.

"Oh." She flustered, trying to avoid his eyes. "I

thought you'd be at the game."

A trio of burly men in overalls appeared from behind her and started laying down sheeting and hauling in cardboard boxes. She waved them through to the bedroom and told them she'd be through in a minute.

"Coach says I'm not match fit." Jack pointed to his groin, wincing.

"Ah, right." She wondered whether to apologise or not and decided against it. "Just collecting my things." She nodded to the men audibly rummaging in the bedroom.

"'Course." He seemed preoccupied with the match

"Everything... ok?" She realised this was a stupid question to ask but didn't want to stand in silence while the removal men did their thing.

"Un-huh." She couldn't work out whether this was a yes or a no.

"I'll just..." She pointed to the bedroom even though Jack wasn't looking at her, and then went to give the men instructions.

When she came out five minutes later, Jack was sitting in silence with the TV off. She assumed the game had ended.

"Did you win?"

"Three-nil." Jack said hollowly.

"Right. Ok." She wrinkled her nose, assuming he'd been happier with the result if his soon-to-be ex-wife wasn't taking all her belongings from their home. She bustled off into the kitchen and busied herself in there, marking out crockery and cutlery she wanted the men to box up. When she returned, Jack was still sitting in silence, staring at the blank screen.

She fiddled with her phone until one of the men

signalled to her that they were all done.

"Well, Jack. I'm going now." Despite everything, she suddenly felt herself tearing up. "Are you going to be ok?"

Jack nodded slowly, his back to her. Tuppence pulled her house keys off a ring and laid them gently on the worktop.

"Bye, Jack." She whispered, and walked slowly out of the house, clicking the door gently closed behind her.

She took a deep breath standing on the doorstep, the sunlight peeking through the clouds, glimmering through the trees. Gathering herself, she walked down the drive one final time and got into her car, forcing herself not to look back at the house.

The hills around Stobo bucked and rolled under a bright blue sky. Clouds raced and leaves jittered as the breeze blew the cobwebs from the clear morning air.

Cullen was on his knees, head bowed, silently weeping at the sight of his wife's grave. The Celtic cross had been replaced and freshly engraved; someone had lain a bright bouquet of flowers on the marble-white gravel; new turf around the plot was still bedding in. The fresh green winking against the frost hurt his eyes.

He laid his hat down gently on the grave itself, mouthing a few words that no-one would ever hear. His salt-and-pepper hair was ruffled by the gusts which eddied around the kirk tower into this little corner of the churchyard. Cullen felt, rather than heard, the approach of someone from behind and his senses quickened, immediately on the alert. Turning to look up, he suddenly felt old and weary. For the briefest of moments he stood outside himself, looking down at a man kneeling, exhausted, done. Only the energy left to mourn what once had been.

Dick and Tuppence were standing over him, the sunlight throwing their faces in shadow, halos around their heads. They were holding hands.

"Hello again." Tuppence said brightly.

"Mister Cullen." Dick nodded his greeting.

Cullen looked from one to the other, unsure. Climbing to his feet, he knocked the soil from his knees with dirty hands. "Just Cullen, Reverend…?"

"Dick. Just Dick."

"Are you ok? You look… tired." Tuppence reached out to touch him on the arm and Cullen instinctively flinched away.

"Sorry." He blinked slowly, not meeting her eyes.

"It's ok." Dick murmured. "We have repaired and restored-" .

"I can see." Cullen's face struggled to remain stony. "Why?"

"Your wife lies here still. One of God's children. In His garden, if not His house. In His care. I asked him to provide and He has."

"Dick organised a cycle ride to London to raise money for the church." Tuppence beamed. "And it was incredibly successful."

"Quite unexpectedly so." Dick agreed, and squeezed her hand briefly.

Cullen looked from one to the other again before settling on Tuppence. "Did you…?"

"Yes, thank you. I found Jack and … came to a resolution, you might say." She glanced at Dick. "I will be spending more of my time here now."

Cullen's mouth turned up at the edges by the tiniest amount; his eyes glinted but he said nothing.

"Did you, erm, resolve your issue?" Tuppence arched her eyebrows at him.

"Hmm?" Cullen queried innocently.

"With Conrad. Did he ... what was the word you used... " Tuppence remembered. "Atone?"

"No." Cullen shook his head sadly. "No, he did not."

"Atonement?" asked Dick. "Or was it revenge you wanted?"

"Justice." Cullen replied.

"Justice? Who's? The law's? Or Our Lord's?"

"Mine. He's not *my* Lord. He was hers." Cullen nodded at the grave.

"Never take your own revenge, but leave room for the wrath of God, for it is written, "VENGEANCE IS MINE, I WILL REPAY," sayeth the Lord. Romans 12:19"

"He had his chance, long ago. He didn't take it."

"You could've given him a second chance."

"Conrad?"

"The Lord."

"They've both had all the chances they're going to get from me." Cullen bent to pick up his hat, plonked it back on his head and stood awkwardly. "Thank you. For this."

Dick smiled uncertainly. "You are welcome. And you are still welcome inside my church - if you ever wish to attend service. Maybe *she* would appreciate it?"

Cullen half-turned towards the grave again, eyes cast down,. When he raised his face back to them, his eyes had softened. "Maybe."

"It's been a long time?" Dick coaxed.

"Maybe." Unsure whether to shake hands or not, he thrust both hands into his pockets and nodded to them both.

"Take care, Cullen." Tuppence said, blinking furiously, and watched as he crunched down the gravel path around the side of the kirk. "Give my regards to Paul!" she yelled, waving at his broad back.

Cullen paused at the gate to look back at them, then turned and headed out of sight towards the main road.

POSTSCRIPT

Olivia "Liv" Nightingale reclaimed the designs she had done for Chanel and augmented them with new ones, continuing with her slashed tartan aesthetic. She signed a five-year agreement with Bankholm Mill to manufacture her garments to order with industry-beating short lead times whilst retaining the highest quality standards. Two years later, her Couture-to-Go range was launched at London Fashion Week to universal acclaim.

Conrad Ho was found unconscious from fumes in the one of the dying vats at Bankholm Mill. He was a solid shade of Prussian Blue from his nipples down. He returned to his native Hong Kong where he runs one of his father sweatshops in Tsim Sha Tsui, and insists on wearing long sleeves and gloves at all times.

Reverend Richard "Dick Dosh" Money became a local celebrity due to his charity work which raised almost £500,000 for the kirks and parishes in the Scottish Borders. He has his own weekly show on Borders Radio every Sunday morning and is now happily married.

Tuppence Lowry signed a three year modelling contract with LIV Designs to become the face of Couture-to-Go. Many of the iconic photos of her wearing LIV clothes feature her cat, Paw, who has his own Facebook page. She was married to Dick in the grounds of Stobo Kirk the following autumn after her divorce from Jack was finalised.

Jacek "Jack" Carel Imbiorkiewicz lost half his fortune in his divorce from Tuppence and spent most of the remainder on women, drugs and gambling. The rest he wasted. He was suspended indefinitely by the SFA for match-fixing and drug abuse, and retired from professional football. After several stints in rehab, he now runs *The Haunted Man* in Haddington, and plays for their Sunday pub team in front of crowds of thirty or more. He has only two fingers on his left hand.

Guy Hence runs an independent clothing store on Grassmarket in Edinburgh. He spends a lot of time hanging around the nearby Edinburgh School of Art, encouraging students to develop clothing he can sell in the shop at ludicrous prices. He is doing quite well for himself.

Dougie Knight returned to his career in IT and has worked his way up from Junior Support Analyst to Support Analyst. He earned two promotions within the Army Reserves, rising to Sergeant, and spends two weeks each year on manoeuvres trying to shoot new recruits. He was found not guilty by a military tribunal over his involvement in the death of Corporal Anthony Nail, which was ruled accidental.

Paul "Big Paul" McInnes finished his cabin in the Soonhope valley but continues to work on the snagging list. His friend, Cullen, appears from time to time to provide constructive criticism and add items to the list.

Mungo James Cullen lives alone. On the first Sunday of each month, he can be found sitting quietly at the very back of Stobo kirk, listening.

AUTHOR'S NOTE

As a middle-aged, heterosexual, white male I, of course, know nothing about fashion whatsoever. If this comes across in my writing I can only apologise. Research only gets you so far.

My thanks to everyone who read or listened to early drafts and scenes and generally made encouraging noises. For some reason the badger was universally popular and a common question was: "Why the badger?" The answer is: I honestly don't know - it seemed like a good idea at the time.

Wherever possible I have referenced actual locations and tried to render them accurately, although I have taken some liberties with Stobo Kirk. I'm sure the Church Of Scotland will forgive me. Bankholm Mill is not real — it is an amalgamation of mills I visited (in Hawick, Elgin and New Lanark). But it sure looks pretty in the sunshine.

I'd like to thank Big Paul for letting me use a completely unrepresentative depiction of him (again). He liked the first book but hasn't read this one yet (he's a slow reader). Only time will tell if he makes it into book #3.

All other characters are completely fictitious and exist only in my imagination (and hopefully, now, yours). If you've ever met me and think you can see yourself in one of the characters in the book, you're dead wrong. My lawyer says.

mjf
19.09.2017

Tell others what you thought...

If you enjoyed this book, please leave a review on Amazon or Goodreads.

You can leave a review on Amazon here and on Goodreads here.

About the Author

You can learn more about Mark Farrer at www.markfarrer.com, like him on Facebook here or follow him on Twitter @mark_farrer

Printed in Great Britain
by Amazon